# BREAKING THE LANGUAGE BARRIER

Jean Claude had come to Madeline with the highest recommendation. Astrid Zealand, the Swedish sex bomb whose love for lust was legendary, had rated this handsome young Frenchman as a perfect lover. The trouble was that Jean Claude spoke only French. And Madeline spoke only English.

Now she returned to her room to find him sitting naked on her bed. Calmly he studied her face, seeing her nervousness.

"*Cherie?*" he asked gently, patting the bed, making room for her.

He made no move to grab her when she sat down, and slowly she began to relax. She closed her eyes, breathed deeply, taking in the subtle masculinity of him.

And when he began kissing her, stopping, resuming, leading her at each stage into a deeper, fuller commitment, Madeline knew that no words would be needed in the long, long, night ahead. . . .

# A ROMAN TALE

BY

CARROLL BAKER

A SIGNET BOOK

NEW AMERICAN LIBRARY

NAL PENGUIN INC.

NAL BOOKS ARE AVAILABLE AT QUANTITY DISCOUNTS WHEN USED TO PROMOTE PRODUCTS OR SERVICES. FOR INFORMATION PLEASE WRITE TO PREMIUM MARKETING DIVISION, NEW AMERICAN LIBRARY, 1633 BROADWAY, NEW YORK, NEW YORK 10019



This is an authorized reprint of a hardcover edition published by Donald I. Fine, Inc. and published in Canada by General Publishing Company Limited.

SIGNET TRADEMARK REG. U.S. PAT. OFF. AND FOREIGN COUNTRIES
REGISTERED TRADEMARK—MARCA REGISTRADA
HECHO EN CHICAGO, U.S.A.

SIGNET, SIGNET CLASSIC, MENTOR, ONYX, PLUME, MERIDIAN and NAL BOOKS are published by NAL Penguin Inc., 1633 Broadway, New York, New York 10019

First Signet Printing, April, 1987

1 2 3 4 5 6 7 8 9

PRINTED IN THE UNITED STATES OF AMERICA

*For my husband, Donald Burton*

# *BOOK ONE*

# CHAPTER ONE

MADELINE MANDELL'S famous body—ripe and nude as the day she was born—was snuggled between smooth linen sheets and an eiderdown quilt, and surrounded by what seemed to be dozens of soft bolsters, lacy cushions and dainty satin pillows. Her head throbbed, partly from the alcohol she'd consumed, more from feelings of disorientation. Her gorgeous throat ached with dryness from the endless cigarettes she'd smoked and the liter or so of Sicilian red wine she'd drunk. There was a tumbler of water on the bedside table, but she had already drunk two full glasses of water and was conserving this third refill as long as possible. The room was pitch black and bitterly cold outside the covers, so that each trip to the bathroom faucet demanded a force of will almost beyond the urgency of her thirst.

For a world-renowned sex symbol she had remained remarkably vulnerable and even somewhat timid. To Madeline, this entire day had been like some daring improvisation. She was naked because she had never expected to spend the night in a bed other than her own. But here she was in a sumptuous villa on Rome's Appia Antica, in an unfamiliar bed and with nothing to wear because, after all, she couldn't have slept in her best afternoon dress.

She lay thinking about the twists of fortune that had led her to Rome and this strange bed. She thought about a *Variety* headline she might have written about herself: "MADELINE MANDELL . . . HOLLYWOOD'S VENUS . . . DIED ONCE AT THE BOX OFFICE. AND A SECOND—ALMOST FATAL—TIME ON THE INSIDE . . . *But found she had enough left to fight her way into Italian heaven . . .*"

When she had arrived in Rome this September Madeline had felt blessed by Saint Peter and all the angels. Then, somberly, she wondered if they were even gifting her with a second chance at life.

For twelve years she had been a slave to the studio and its system, to the studio bosses and most (worst) of all to her sex-symbol image. The image had taken shape after her first film, *Venus Awakening*—yes, that was, God help her, the title. Ever since, when she had been talked or written about, it was as Venus, not Madeline.

Madeline could not remember ever having been in charge of herself. From the beginning of her career she had relied on an army of advisers to "protect" her interests, and who mostly had colluded with the studio bosses to see that their interests were the ones served. An old story, maybe, but no less devastating when you were on the receiving end. In fact, it had taken a disaster at the box office, leading to a lawsuit with the studio and then the firing of her advisers finally to free her. But freedom also had meant that the world, as she had come to know it, had collapsed around her cosmetically perfect ears. She was to learn that her army of advisers had cross-collaterized—Hollywoodese for finagled—her considerable earnings into an array of companies, all of which had gone broke, leaving her virtually the same. Then with no work, no money and no one to fall back on for support, she had turned her anger inward on herself. For several months she had even contemplated ending it all.

Short of that, she had closed herself off from the world. Fortunately, she no longer had the money to go to a Hollywood doctor, who surely would have called her condition a nervous breakdown and put her on stupefying, addictive drugs. Instead her home-grown self-hypnosis not only provided her with some relief from those outside pressures, it also brought on a beneficial and intensive self-analysis. In common-sense language—taking stock.

It had, though, taken her nearly a year out of combat before she could begin to think about things objectively again, and to take the sensible step of changing her environment. Fortuitously, her decision to escape from a town that confronted her with nothing but a crippling rejection coincided with an invitation, plus free air fare, to the renowned Venice Film Festival. It was a new chance at a new start . . . to try for a career in the booming Italian film industry that was centered in Rome. And to escape the old suffocating hothouse that had raised her, and dropped her down.

At the same time that she accepted the invitation and air ticket, she put her house on the market and left behind all of her once so-prized possessions. No looking back, no regrets, she told herself.

Money, and therefore work, was her first priority. But she hadn't returned from the near dead to exist on bread alone. Even fancy bread. This was to be not only a brand-new day for her. The sixties had seen a new day for all women. Now she was going to experiment the way she should have done when she was a teenager and the puritanical moral restrictions of her time, of her background, had made it impossible.

Wouldn't the press, she thought with a wry smile, be in for a shock if they knew that the big deal they'd created had been among the most sexually frustrated women of her time? That Venus had spent the years of her one and only short-lived marriage in a state of frigidity? That the alleged sex symbol was longing to make some of those "hot" movie scenes come true? Madeline sometimes shook with ironic laughter when thinking that *Venus Awakening* should have more aptly been entitled, *Venus Not Yet Awakened* or *Venus Awaiting to Be Awakened.*

Well, the timing at least was right for a real-life awakening. Madeline was approaching thirty-five—heading for her sexual prime, if the books and doctors were to be believed. But she didn't realize that she was a perfect candidate for the rampant *la dolce vita* sex scene, about to be awakened far more than she had bargained for . . .

At the moment, Madeline was stretching restlessly in the strange bed. She had been the first of the guests to retire, but now she wasn't sure she could sleep . . .

The massive wooden door that led to a maze of corridors was opening slowly, throwing an ever-widening beam of light on the floor in front of Madeline's bed, and Astrid Zealand's tall, pale form appeared silhouetted in the doorway. Madeline thought of a Viking goddess as Astrid's cascading blonde hair fairly shimmered in the back-lighting of the hall lamp. Her very presence commanded all the space about her, making it her domain. Within a few hours of their first meeting Astrid had in a single afternoon seemed to take charge of Madeline, changing her, foisting on her a strange, dreamlike and uneasy new sense of herself.

Now Astrid was asking if Madeline was all right, if she needed anything, if she felt cold.

Madeline didn't answer immediately. She was still marveling at Astrid's startling appearance and at her apparent fortitude. She must be impervious to the cold, dressed lightly in a corn-colored shantung skirt and a matching transparent silk blouse that did nothing to conceal her hard, protruding maroon nipples. The thin clothing clung closely to Astrid's remarkably solid, muscular, yet highly sensuous form. A spellbinding androgynous shape that, once photographed for the cinema, had never been forgotten by either the motion picture industry or the public. Indeed, Astrid Zealand was an internationally famous beauty with such magnetism onscreen that it was easy to overlook that she wasn't really acting.

The vision of Astrid standing in the doorway sent an excited chill through Madeline, caused her to snuggle deeper into the bed. It was very much like the excitement that had surprised her earlier that day, when she'd first encountered Astrid in the Piazza del Popolo.

Madeline had settled that very morning into a modest studio in Via Cola di Rienzo. It had been past midday when she unpacked her suitcases and hung up her clothes. Rather than buying groceries and making lunch, she'd decided to put on her prettiest sheath and take a sightseeing walk across the bridge and into Rome's more glamorous shopping district. She'd been standing in the center of Piazza del Popolo observing the twin churches when she happened to glance sideways at the terrace of a restaurant.

For a moment she thought the hot September sun was playing tricks with her eyes.

It wasn't possible. You didn't take your first stroll after moving to Rome and suddenly come on three of the world's most famous (or was it notorious?) female stars breaking bread together. Not likely, but there they were, no larger than life, sitting at a table by the railing, facing the piazza in clear view of any passerby.

Madeline forgot herself and just stood staring at them.

True, she too was a celebrity, a *Hollywood* movie star, but she had never worked with or met the likes of Astrid Zealand, Helga Haufman or Cleo Monti. They were European, international. Astrid, the Scandinavian screen goddess; Helga, Germany's sex symbol; Cleo Monti, the reigning Italian movie queen. In Hollywood such notorious beauties would *never* have been seen together . . . certainly not just casually having lunch like ordinary mortals.

Astrid had then actually waved at her. Madeline reflexively waved back, and Astrid got up from the table, left the terrace and strode across the piazza to greet her. "Hello, you're Madeline Mandell, aren't you? I'm Astrid Zealand." Like just plain folks.

Astrid tossed the long golden blond hair away from her face as she reached out to shake Madeline's hand. "I've seen all your films . . . and *Venus Awakening* I've seen at least seven or eight times . . . you really deserve the Venus billing. I'm so delighted to meet you . . ."

Before Madeline could answer, Astrid added, "Are you by yourself?"

Madeline managed a nearly inaudible yes.

Astrid went on with spontaneous enthusiasm. "Well, then, please join us for lunch. Oh, please do. I know Cleo and Helga would both like to meet you. Come on. It would be an honor and a pleasure for us."

Honor and pleasure? Madeline thought. She now found herself walking self-consciously across the piazza beside this stunning, self-confident woman, and the honor and pleasure were all hers. In California they weren't even answering her phone calls.

Madeline was five foot seven in her stocking feet, above average height, but she felt uncomfortably petite walking alongside the much taller Astrid, and then all but wiped out once they entered the restaurant terrace and she came face to face with Cleo Monti.

Madeline reminded herself that in Italian Monti meant mountain, and this actress had first come to prominence on account of her extremely *large* . . . some even said outlandish . . . proportions. Yet nothing could have prepared Madeline for actually being in the presence of Cleo Monti. Everything about Cleo was as outsized as the enormous sunglasses she wore. Her black-brown hair, though neatly combed into a pageboy, was incongruously bouffant. Her glossed lips protruded like succulent pink sausages, and her breasts appeared, literally, overblown.

Cleo Monti now raised an arm as solidly round as one of Madeline's thighs, and the hand she extended was easily the largest Madeline had ever seen on any woman. But when Madeline grasped it, that hand remained limp, not only unthreatening but also unappealing. Indeed this giantess seemed to have the manner of a submissive *little* girl who wanted desperately to be thought of as small, cute, and adorably feminine. It all added up to an unharmonious, bizarre contrast to Cleo's overwhelming physical presence.

Helga Haufman's handshake proved to be strong and forceful, as did her voice, which was gravelly with a deep resonance. Her face, large and square, was accentuated by a frame of auburn hair straight down the cheeks and fringed across the forehead. There were flecks of gold in her charcoal eyes, eyes that gleamed with a more or less permanent look of defiance. Helga, like Astrid and Cleo, was broad-shouldered and large-boned. She, too, was big, well-sculpted and, of course, highly photogenic. Although Helga was perhaps closer to Madeline's height, all three women gave Madeline the impression that she had been invited to lunch with some sisterhood of Amazons.

Astrid indicated a chair for Madeline as she poured her a glass of wine from a carafe on the table.

"Helga and I have ordered the pasta mista. It's a house specialty of four varieties of pasta . . . and Cleo is having pasta fagioli . . . that's pasta with beans." Astrid's almost perfect English had only a hint of accent, which sounded more French than Scandinavian.

"The mixed pasta sounds good," Madeline said.

"Pasta fagioli is deadly," Helga volunteered in her deep voice resonant with the guttural German sounds. "But, then, Cleo's got a cast-iron gut," she added in a tone that might have seemed harsh if she hadn't been smiling. Helga's defiant eyes flashed brightly as she followed with something in German that at least *sounded* obscene to Madeline's ears.

Madeline sat for a time marveling at the language versatility of these women who conversed for a while in German and then French before sliding effortlessly back into English at Astrid's command: "We must remember to speak English for Madeline." After which she called the waiter in Italian and ordered Madeline's pasta.

Brunette Cleo Monti shifted her awesome proportions forward and in a kittenish voice, humorously incongruous, asked Madeline in heavily accented English, "How do you get your hair that wonderful silver blonde?"

"Hours of work every week"—Madeline laughed—"and days of a burning scalp, I'm afraid."

Astrid, the golden one in Madeline's mind now, asked, "Why do you do it?"

"Well, my own hair is such a dull, dishwater blond. If I had your natural blonde color, Astrid, I'd never touch it—"

"Forget the word *natural* at this table," said auburn-haired Helga with a gruff laugh. "You don't think this is the hair color or even the nose I was born with, do you? And Cleo might be a true brunette, but she never seems to get off the operating table."

"That's *not* true," Cleo said, pouting like a small child.

"She never admits to all the plastic surgery," Helga went on, "but she's had everything reduced from her lips and upper arms to her ass. However, she's still so big all over that no one really notices the difference."

Madeline was surprised that Cleo's reaction to this was just to ignore it good-naturedly and pour everyone another glass of wine. The waiter brought the pasta at that moment, and Cleo squealed with delight when hers was placed in front of her. She also made the waiter's day by bestowing on him one of her extravagantly toothy and dazzling smiles.

Astrid, cool Scandinavian, was more businesslike and ordered another carafe of wine and the second course for everyone. Since the three were all having another house specialty, bolito misto, Madeline decided to go along.

Cleo Monti looked at Madeline over a raised fork of pasta and beans, and after smacking her full lips grinned to show Madeline her teeth. "The only thing I've had done over and over are the caps on my teeth. I was a poor bambina and suffered from malnutrition, so my teeth were bad. First time I had them done I could not pay for a good dentist . . . he ruined them and now I can never get them right."

"Her teeth aren't the only thing she's had done," Helga said, breaking into laughter. "She also had a cap job on her pussy."

Astrid laughed sedately. Cleo giggled like a naughty schoolgirl. Madeline, who was shocked at the language . . . she'd never been at ease with the Hollywood ladies who talked like truck drivers . . . tried to hide her feelings by dropping her napkin, then leaning under the table to retrieve it. She also glanced around at the other diners, hoping that no one had overheard, and was relieved that people at nearby tables seemed deep in their own conversations.

Helga was in the process of elaborating on the so-called "cap" on Cleo's pussy . . . "She's put an invisible cap on her pussy by having so much plastic surgery." At which point Helga roared with throaty laughter.

Madeline, still uneasy, again glanced around at the other diners, who still weren't paying any attention.

"Shh!" Cleo giggled. "Someone at other tables might understand *Inglese.*"

The goddess Astrid, with a suitably divine smile, mouthed, "Fuck them," then began speaking French, which led Helga and Cleo to do likewise.

At that moment Madeline felt like the most provincial and ignorant ex-sex goddess on the face of the earth. Helga, noticing Madeline's unease, proceeded to translate her French: "Cleo's been cut so many times she has to sleep on specially constructed contour cushions and her husband," she sputtered into her wine with a new fit of laughter, "can't get over them to get anywhere near her pussy . . ."

Cleo raised her enormous sunglasses to dry tears of laughter and told Madeline, "And so Helga—how you say—donates *hers.*"

With that, all three went into renewed storms of laughter, and Madeline, acutely uncomfortable, stopped sipping and gulped down the rest of her wine.

Helga, who had almost recovered from the laughing jag, refilled Madeline's glass, then the others'. "The problem is," she began soberly, "my cunt is so *cavernose* . . . how do you say it in English? . . . cavernous . . . that Paolo Piccolo Monti gets lost in it." Delivered straight-faced this time, followed by more delighted laughter from the three—feeding on each other's ribald naughtiness.

The captain was approaching with the hot table, so the ladies made an effort to control themselves by changing the subject from sex to food. But while Cleo was discussing with the captain all the boiled meats available on the bolito misto hot table, Astrid leaned over and whispered into Madeline's ear, "Cleo's husband is bigger than she is, if you can believe it. I mean Paolo Monti is a true mountain of a man. But Helga claims he has no cock. So we've nicknamed him by adding the word *small* to his name: Paolo *Piccolo* Monti. Isn't that delicious?"

Madeline was not a little shaken up by these women. Anglo-Saxonisms rolled off their tongues with an air of total detachment. But it wasn't just the words—it was the attitude. She leaned over to Astrid now and whispered, "Do you mean that Helga sleeps with Cleo's husband . . . and Cleo doesn't mind?"

Astrid nodded, shrugging her shoulders, smiled beatifically at Madeline, then turned her full attention to the varieties of boiled meat.

After lunch the four walked down the Via del Corso, thereupon bringing the traffic on one of Rome's major thoroughfares to a complete standstill. The silver blonde, golden blonde, brunette and auburn-haired knockouts first succeeded in slowing the curious, gaping motorists, then once they had been recognized as Madeline Mandell, Astrid Zealand, Cleo Monti and Helga Haufman, the disbelieving spectators became near traumatized and all movement simply ground to a halt.

The ladies, on the other hand, accustomed to an admiring public, strolled the Corso hardly aware of the traffic jam they were creating. Madeline, not accustomed to drinking at lunchtime, in her alcoholic daze only vaguely noted the attention.

When they stepped into a bar for an after-lunch espresso, some of the customers froze in place while others stood aside, forming a pathway to the counter.

After coffee they left the Corso and turned into Via Condotti to inspect the boutiques. When they came to Roma Alta Moda, Helga spotted in the window an emerald-green outfit that they all agreed would be wonderful next to her auburn hair. They entered the shop and literally tore the place apart. Madeline stood openmouthed as she witnessed the insouciance with which the three tossed about the store's property as if it were somehow their inalienable right. Astrid took down, studied and tossed aside an entire rack of dresses along the righthand wall while Cleo did the same with the clothes on the left. Helga, after trying on the emerald-green, tossed it and a further rack of clothes onto the heap.

Madeline had one especially terrifying moment when Astrid insisted that a pale blue pants suit was perfect for her and that she simply *must* purchase the whole *completo,* the *completo* including a blue-dominated paisley silk blouse, a separate scarf and leather belt, the price for the complete outfit being over 300,000 lire. Which was more than enough to pay Madeline's rent for the next quarter. The very thought sobered her up, something the *ristretto,* or double-strength espresso, had not succeeded in doing. In fact, all the money she had in the worid was from the sale of her Beveriy Hills home, and after paying off the mortgage and the California sales taxes, she'd been left with only $8,000 to live on until she found work.

Fortunately, for Madeline, Cleo distracted Astrid by asking to borrow some money, giving Madeline the opportunity to hide the pale blue *completo* under a pile of equally expensive but discarded outfits that now looked like a heap of shapeless fabric.

The proprietress, who had instantly switched from Italian to English at the prospect of Madeline spending money, was busy converting the price into dollars. When the proprietress broke into English the other three automatically took her lead and also began to speak English. Cleo was saying that she wanted the red coat-dress she'd chosen to be altered and sent to her villa on the Appia but that she hadn't any money with her. The proprietress said that she would be most happy to deliver the dress C.O.D., but that if the Signora Monti wished it to be altered, then a 50 percent deposit would be necessary. At that, Helga's gold-flecked eyes flashed with anger. What an outrageous insult to ask for a *deposit* from Cleo Monti, she said. Astrid silenced her by taking a fat wad of 100,000-lire notes from her handbag and offering Cleo whatever she needed.

Madeline estimated that since one 100,000-lire note equaled approximately $160, Astrid was casually carrying as pocket money nearly $5,000. This was the good life, all right. At least the rich one. There obviously was a lot of money to be earned in European films, and Italian taxes took only 13 percent of your income . . . maybe one day she'd have such a bankroll of her own. A heady thought.

After turning a few more boutiques upside down they decided to have a real English tea at Babington's near the Spanish Steps. But when they emerged from Via Condotti into Piazza di Spagna the paparazzi, who had been lurking near the fountain, sprang at them with drawn cameras, flashbulbs blazing.

The three European women had anticipated this, making sure that Cleo's car and chauffeur were never far behind, and now the chauffeur waved from the parking space at the side of the Piazza di Spagna and all four ran to the protection of Cleo's Silver Cloud Rolls-Royce.

Some of the photographers had cars parked nearby and took off in hot pursuit of the Silver Cloud. But when Cleo's Rolls began approaching the Appia Antica they gave up. Once they had reached Cleo's villa, Madeline understood why the photographers had not persisted on their trail . . . the grounds of the villa were enclosed by a high spiked iron fence and an electrically operated iron gate—making them impenetrable.

Paolo Monti was one of Italy's leading industrialists and wealthiest men. Madeline remembered seeing pictures of the famous Villa Monti in magazines and newspapers, much publicized as Paolo Monti's multimillion-dollar present to his wife on the occasion of their tenth wedding anniversary.

It was about six o'clock when the four sat down to tea on Cleo's patio, surrounded by her parklike lawns and gardens.

Helga was saying, "You know that film Alfonso Razzi is doing would be perfect for Madeline . . ."

"Mmmm," Cleo agreed, mouth full of chocolate eclair.

"What a *good* idea," Astrid said between sips of tea, then to Madeline, "darling, would you like to stay here for a while and do an Italian film?"

"Yes, yes, I would," Madeline said, trying to sound casual. Obviously these women knew nothing about her circumstances. To them she was still a successful Hollywood star. Well, she *was* a big name and *did* receive publicity . . . photographs of her at the recent Venice Film Festival were probably printed in most of the world's newspapers, and before that there had been reams of print about her lawsuit with the studio and her messy divorce trial of six weeks. But she had carefully guarded any information about her financial situation, determined that no one would know that job offers had stopped cold. She'd made a point of telling reporters that since the two court battles she felt drained and was looking forward to a long sabbatical—enforced sabbatical, if she'd been able to afford the truth.

So this remarkable chance meeting with these European stars seemed heaven-sent. Indeed, how better to learn about the possibilities in the Italian film industry than getting it from its biggest stars?

Actually, Alfonso Razzi was a director Madeline hadn't heard of, but she listened closely as Astrid, Helga and Cleo told her what Razzi's new film was about . . . They were also describing the *protagonista,* the leading female role, but Madeline couldn't really concentrate on what was being said. She was too busy planning her story about why she was in Rome, thinking how in the world to justify that she was living in a cheap apartment on a noisy commercial street on the wrong side of the river.

No sophisticate, she at least had learned her lessons in survival. Producers and directors rarely gave a job to anyone anxious to work or needing the money. They only felt happy thinking they'd *convinced* a star after an exhausting sales pitch. Everyone had to believe you were both independently wealthy and couldn't care less about the work.

So now Madeline said, lying through her teeth, "I'm not sure I want to go back to work again so soon after all my troubles . . . but I love Rome . . . and maybe it would be fun to do a movie here." Literally crossing her fingers behind her back, she added, "I mean, at least I might consider it . . ."

Helga brushed a fly away from her auburn fringe and said with typical bluntness, "What a prick your ex-husband must be. We all read about how he behaved during the divorce trial."

Astrid and Cleo nodded in sympathy.

Astrid said, "And how do you survive those awful pressures in Hollywood? When I make a film there I can't wait to get out."

"Oh, sure," Helga said sarcastically, "wait till Madeline works for some of the crumbums here . . . she'll go flying back to Hollywood so fast—"

Cleo interrupted: "But Alfonso, he is nice to work with. I did three films with him . . . no . . . four."

"Why aren't you doing this one?" Madeline asked.

"I'm not finished with the one I make now . . . but even if I were free, I have bigger fish to stew."

"Fry," Astrid said. "All three of us have turned down Alfonso's film."

"Then it *can't* be any good," Madeline said, unable to hide her disappointment.

"Oh, yes," Cleo said. "It is *molto drammatico . . . molto interessante*."

"Yes," Astrid put in, "I would certainly have done it if I wasn't waiting for a part in *Boccaccio Volgare . . .* that *doesn't* mean vulgar." She laughed. "It means more like Boccaccio for the common man."

Madeline had read in *Variety* about *Boccaccio Volgare*. It was to be the biggest, most important film of the year with a twelve-month shooting schedule and a budget of $20 million. It was four separate Boccaccio tales directed by the four leading Italian directors: Catalano, Anastasio, Mariani and de Rossi. Italy's biggest male star, Umberto Cassini, who was perhaps also their only truly international superstar, would play the male lead in all four stories. But each of the segments would see Umberto Cassini making love to a different leading lady. All the female leads were called Fiammetta (Little Flame or Flicker), Boccaccio's one true love, who appeared in most of his early writings. The fascinating thing about Fiammetta's character was that Boccaccio had given her a different quality in each story she appeared in, so that she might be an angel in one, a devil in another, and so on. Madeline now recalled that *Variety* had reported there was fierce competition for those parts—Fiammetta One, Fiammetta Two, Fiammetta Three, Fiammetta Four. She couldn't remember if Cleo Monti, Astrid Zealand or Helga Haufman had been among the names mentioned, but she did seem to remember that one of the parts had been offered to the British actress Serena Blaire.

"I think I read in *Variety* that Serena Blaire has been offered one of the parts," Madeline said innocently.

"That bean pole could never do the part of Fiammetta . . . not Fiammetta One, Two, Three *or* Four," Helga said vehemently. "That icy bitch wants to play Fiammetta Two. Well, she's got another think coming . . . I'm the *perfect* casting for Fiammetta Two. And *nobody*, certainly not that bag of bones . . . that skeleton in designer clothes . . . is going to take it away from me."

"You must admit that Serena is a wonderful actress," Astrid said. "She's won three Academy Awards—"

"And she's got the adorable pickleish quality," Cleo said.

"Not pickleish, darling, *pixieish*," Astrid corrected.

"All right, adorable pixie quality then," Cleo said. "And I love her movies."

"Well, maybe," Helga said, relenting slightly, "but Fiammetta Two is definitely *mine*. Paolo Piccolo promised it to me."

"Madonna mia!" Cleo said, and launched into a barrage of Italian punctuated by extravagant gestures.

Madeline couldn't tell if Cleo was genuinely upset or just being very Italian. She looked to Astrid for help.

"Cleo," Astrid said, "thought her husband was putting money into the film to buy her the role of Fiammetta Four. But now it seems he's also buying

Fiammetta Two for Helga, who of course is his mistress."

"Sorry for my Italian," Cleo told Madeline. "But what a shock! Paolo seems to be financing half the film . . . that's much, much money!"

"Why doesn't he put in another quarter and buy Fiammetta Three for me?" Astrid giggled at her own wittiness, Cleo and Helga joining in.

Catching their mood, Madeline added, "And Fiammetta One for me!"

Instantly the three turned stony.

"Only joking," Madeline said quickly.

The three continued to stare at her.

"Please, I was only kidding. I didn't think for a minute that you would take me seriously . . ."

Cleo seemed to ignore her and went on with her line of thought about Astrid. "We know that you'll get Fiammetta Three, Astrid. You'll get it because Catalano is directing the third story . . . and everyone knows that Catalano is crazy in love with you."

"Certainly everyone knows that," Helga said with a note of contempt. And Madeline was astonished to see big tears well up in Astrid's ice-blue eyes. The goddess might be human, after all.

"Oh, he's such a sadist," Astrid said through her tears. "The months of my life I wasted being a slave to that man . . . he's so selfish . . . cruel . . . Angelo Catalano is . . ." And here she was overcome. When she regained her composure she went on to condemn Angelo Catalano with a sequence of French expletives whose meaning was, of course, lost on Madeline.

Cleo and Helga were making sympathetic noises but the talk was in French, which left Madeline to her own thoughts . . . She knew she would have to wait until later to bring up again the subject of the other film . . . the Alfonso Razzi film . . . the one none of these three wanted but Madeline wanted desperately. Hard to believe, but after months of depression the promise of work actually seemed a possibility. And then she allowed herself a dark, secret thought that she wouldn't dare express to this trio . . . maybe she could even compete for a role in the film of the year, just maybe she could somehow win out and be one of the highly sought after Fiammettas . . .

That evening there was more food and wine mixed in with endless cigarettes, laughter and a few more tears. Paolo Piccolo Monti was out of town on business so the ladies were free to continue with their girl talk. Madeline, though very tipsy, tried to stay alert to take in whatever scrap of information that might help her build a new career.

She had found and taken the opportunity to speak again about Alfonso Razzi and his forthcoming film, and Astrid had, to her astonishment, placed a telephone call to the director on Madeline's behalf. Alfonso had not been home, but Astrid had left a message on his answering machine, telling him that a great American film star was in Rome and that if he was *lucky* he just might persuade her to be in his film.

By nightfall it had turned very cold in the villa heated only by the odd fireplace. Madeline had felt not only chilled but, frankly, drunk, not to mention overcome by the events of this extraordinary day. Cleo had offered each of them a guest room for the night, and Madeline had been the first to accept her offer.

In her strange bed Madeline had tried to relive in detail, although a bit fuzzily, everything that had happened and been said that day. And even now, with Astrid standing in the doorway of her bedroom, she had slipped momentarily away into her thoughts.

"Are you all right?" Astrid said again. "Would you like another blanket?"

"No, no, thank you, I don't need another one—"

And it was then that Madeline shuddered, in disbelieving shock . . . Astrid, dressed in a corn-colored blouse and skirt, still golden and glowing in the back-lighting from the hall, had just said, "Would you like me to come to bed with you?"

# CHAPTER TWO

LIKE MADELINE, Umberto Cassini, the Italian screen idol, also had had a shock that night. He had to be up at seven in the morning for a difficult day's work on his latest film, *Domani e Domani e Domani,* with the actress who most tried his patience, Cleo Monti, and he'd had no business, he knew, bringing a girl home to fuck. But this aggressive little starlet, Pina, had been after him for weeks, and when he'd taken her to dinner that night she'd fondled his cock nonstop under the table.

But in spite of all that promise he should still have guessed that the night would finish the way it did. He'd met starlets like Pina before, a typical Italian career girl. He was nearly thirty-five and had been playing sex games with girls since he'd been nine. And still he knew nothing.

In the car this Pina had been all over him, panting and tearing at his clothes so that he could barely steer his Ferrari up the steep roads of Monte Mario. Then the moment he'd gotten her onto the bed she'd turned frigid; turned into an untouchable, impenetrable mannequin.

"Nooo, Umberto, nooooo!" She'd said it so loudly that Umberto was afraid she'd wake up his mother, who was just down the hall. His father could snore through a hurricane, but his mother was always wakeful. Many a night she'd thrown open the door of his bedroom when he was in the very act itself to ask him if everything was all right. She would search out every detail of his latest girl friend and then imperturbably go back to her own room. Italian mothers!

Pina had even screamed "noo" when he'd merely kissed her . . . "Noo, Umberto, don't kiss me so hard, you'll ruin my makeup . . . Noo, Umberto, don't tear at my blouse, it's a Valentino original . . . Noo, Umberto, don't nuzzle my ear, you'll mess up my hairdo . . ." Then, poutingly, she'd said, "Three hours . . . three hours I spent at Elizabeth Arden and I want my hair to be nice for tomorrow . . ."

She'd taken an interminable time to remove her clothes and place them one by one on hangers. Then she'd lowered her body on top of the covers with such exaggerated attention to her hair and legs that one would have thought she was in danger of disintegrating. In the end she'd lain there stiff as a board with her legs spread wide apart and presented him with the only part of her anatomy he might venture to disrupt—her unfeeling cunt.

Long before she was ready, Umberto's penis had gone limp. As he'd stood there observing that cold offering he'd seemed to be staring at an inanimate object—puffed pink plastic saucers leading to a dry dungeon surrounded by black bushy hair that stretched to her thighs and most of the way to her belly button.

The upsetting image had sent him racing to the bathroom for some seltzer.

Once in the bathroom he'd locked the door, then stayed there for the rest of the night. If he'd come out she might have wanted an explanation . . . He couldn't have explained. If he'd come out he might have tried to fuck her for politeness' sake, and he didn't want to fuck her. If he'd come out she would have expected him to drive her home, and he didn't want to drive her home. He just wanted her to *disappear* . . . So he'd spent the night in the bathroom.

When his mother called him at 7:00 A.M. he had to dislodge himself from the bathtub, stiff, cold and twisted up in a dozen bath towels, rugs and washcloths. And today he had one of his most difficult scenes, fourteen pages of monologue. He had studied those pages for weeks, prided himself on being a professional. Now as he looked in the bathroom mirror at the bloodshot eyes and drooping expression, he couldn't remember one single word of that fourteen-page monologue.

After a quick shave and a sponge bath (he couldn't bring himself to get back into that tub), he unlocked the door and tiptoed into the bedroom. She was gone. "Thank *you,* Jesus . . . and your father, Joseph . . . and our Holy Mother." And as an afterthought, "The Holy Ghost too."

But when he had dressed and gone downstairs for breakfast—there she was. Pina at the kitchen table sipping coffee and being solicitous to his mother. And his mother *liked* her. His mother was smiling that well-this-girl-would-make-you-a-*good*-wife smile.

Pina, perfectly made up, coiffed and outfitted, was sitting there like some high-fashion model in a TV breakfast advertisement. But Umberto, as he stared at her for a few seconds, could picture nothing but her wide-spread, cold, inanimate cunt with the bush of black. At that moment his mother was holding aloft from the frying pan a sausage speared on her cooking fork. *Basta* . . . Enough. Umberto fled the house.

He drove down Monte Mario, the Ferrari's accelerator pressed to the floorboard, and arrived at Cine Citta before even the technicians.

In his dressing room he paced the floor and said his monologue out loud as if trying to drown out the vision of Pina's cunt juxtaposed with that sausage speared on his mother's cooking fork.

He ordered coffee from the cantina and laced it with brandy, something he normally never would have done on a demanding working day. Feeling a bit soothed, he reshaved and took a shower before going to the makeup department. Once he was made up he returned to his dressing room and concentrated again on his monologue, finding to his relief that he did, in fact, know the lines.

Filming was to begin at nine, but at eight-thirty, with nothing left to do, he decided to go to the set and perhaps make some lively conversation with the director. Ralph de Rossi, after all, was a great friend of his, and they loved to argue about everything from politics to acting.

Ralph was already there, seated at his worktable to one side of the set and going over his shooting plan for the day. De Rossi was a tall, dapper man with a thin, light brown mustache to match his neatly trimmed head of light brown hair. He had a svelte figure and carried himself with a pride that tended to make the most casual of his working clothes appear elegant. He also had a keen intelligence and a fine sense of humor. His green eyes danced with a hint of mischief and his winning smile was always quick to show itself. He excelled all other Italian directors when it came to warm films with humor. Ralph de Rossi was also credited with getting the best performances from actors, possibly because he was a fine actor in his own right. He was the only director who had gotten Cleo Monti to show that she had a genuine talent and a beautiful quality inside all that mammoth flesh. Ralph had directed Cleo and Umberto Cassini in a series of box-office hits, and, inevitably, the present one, *Domani e Domani e Domani* (Tomorrow and Tomorrow and Tomorrow), was a sequel to their *Oggi É Oggi* (Today Is Today) and *Ieri Era Ieri* (Yesterday Was Yesterday).

Precisely at nine o'clock the technicians had completed lighting the set, and Ralph had sent his first assistant to the makeup department for word when Cleo Monti would be ready for a rehearsal. The assistant returned minutes later with a message from Cleo that she had run into some unexpected problems with her hair and makeup and, so sorry, she would be late arriving on the set.

Ralph took it in stride, but Umberto began to bristle . . . that giant bitch was always late, she always kept them waiting until he'd run out of creative steam. He was ready *now,* anxious to rehearse, then shoot. He knew his lines, he was feeling good, he wanted to transmit his energy onto film, an unforced, spontaneous sort of energy so essential to comedy. He was, in fact, a master of comedy, but Cleo often managed to drain him of his spontaneity because she exasperated him, made him tense, made him lose his concentration or dissipate his energy on their squabbling.

He went to his dressing room, ordered another coffee, again laced with brandy, and sat down grumpily to go over his lines. It was a few minutes before ten, and Umberto was beginning to feel sleepy. Why hadn't anyone called him to the set? Well, he'd walk back to the stage, be around some activity to make him alert again. He arrived on the set just as the assistant was delivering another dispatch from Cleo.

"Go back and ask Cleo if she can come for a rehearsal," Ralph told the assistant. "She can go back *afterward* and finish her makeup."

The assistant quickly came back to report that Cleo was sorry but she was at a crucial moment in her preparations and couldn't possibly stop in the middle of them.

Umberto, whose voice raised an octave, said, "Go back and tell her that if she comes now for rehearsal, Ralph will film my close-up first." And then, before the assistant reached the stage door, Umberto blew up. "Wait, it's my monologue . . . all she has to do is *listen.* Tell her to come and rehearse for the camera positions only. Ralph can just photograph my monologue, work around her. She can spend the rest of the day in makeup. Ralph can film her tonight at midnight, if she's finally glued, chewing-gummed and cemented together by then. Hell, she can spend the rest of the week in makeup! Ralph can film her on Sunday. She can have another face-lift and Ralph can do her close-up three months from now . . ."

Umberto had gone near purple in the face. Ralph gripped his shoulders and suggested they go out for a walk around the lot.

It did the trick. People greeted him warmly. Umberto was extremely popular; anyone who'd ever come in contact with him couldn't help but like him . . . he was a big, handsome puppy, was loving and kind and long-suffering. No one ever really took offense when he was upset. In fact, the more exercised Umberto became, the funnier he tended to be. It was one of his endearing qualities that Ralph de Rossi managed to capture on the screen.

Ralph knew he'd catch hell from the producer at the next production meeting for the delay in schedule, but right now his chief concern was for his leading man. Being an actor himself, Ralph also realized what a nerve-racking job Umberto had ahead of him with the monologue. Cleo's tardiness was damned exasperating, made things worse. To calm Umberto down further Ralph took him to the cantina for a beer and a sandwich, and it was eleven-thirty when the two once again entered the set.

Cleo was there, waiting on the set's sofa, looking, of course, gorgeous and relaxed, smiling benevolently and blowing them each a kiss.

The rehearsal began. Umberto went through his monologue without a hitch. The crew applauded, as did Cleo, who'd curled her massive weight into a kittenish position on the sofa and puckered her large lips to mime Umberto a kiss.

For a moment that puckered mouth vaguely reminded Umberto of something else, but he quickly shook the thought from his mind as Ralph asked if he was now ready to film the monologue. Umberto waved his hand, not wanting to break his concentration before the camera rolled.

"All right, silence," Ralph called. "*Roll them.*"

"Ou, ou," Cleo broke in. "Just a minute, darlings . . . I fear I need more lipstick."

Umberto reacted on cue, Cleo's cue. "But it is my close-up, she's off camera . . ." He turned to look at her. A makeup girl was standing over the sofa holding a handmirror while Cleo applied a glob of vaseline to her lips.

Something churned in Umberto's stomach, but he forced himself to turn back to the camera and try to concentrate on his first lines.

Ralph said, "All right now, quiet on the set and . . . *Roll.*"

When the cameraman said, *"Speed,"* Ralph whispered, "Umberto, take your time . . . whenever you're ready it's *Action.*"

Umberto took a deep breath to calm himself, then stepped into his key-light and faced the camera. He said his first line letter-perfect before his mind turned to blank, and he stood, helplessly, looking into space.

When Ralph ordered, *"Cut,"* Umberto, no longer able to suppress his frustration, went into another rage Italian-style, which caused them to lose the rest of the morning's shooting time.

At lunch Umberto had another brandy but never really recovered, and in the afternoon he fluffed one take after another. Finally Ralph decided to send him home early and begin the monologue the next day with a fresh start.

So it was only Cleo who had been photographed that day, unaffected by Umberto's tirade. She had been relaxed, charming, beautiful. Ralph had spent the afternoon photographing her *reactions* to the monologue that Umberto couldn't deliver. With time on his hands, he had filmed her from every angle and with a variety of lighting effects.

It was Umberto's monologue, Cleo had not one word to say, but everyone in the projection room at editing time would have to agree that Cleo had stolen the scene.

The lion had been screwed by the pussy.

* * *

Umberto had decided to go directly home after that disastrous day on the set. Driving through the midafternoon traffic he thought about having a quiet evening, certainly no more to drink. Perhaps he'd ask his father for a game of chess. His father was a professor of ancient history, taught for only a few hours and normally got home from the university about this time. After the game he'd ask his mother to give him just broth for dinner and he'd go to bed early.

After he had parked the car in the garage he took the path that crossed by the kitchen, where the light was on. He stopped to look in the window . . . Oh, no, it was distinctly not his day. Pina was *still* there. It was nearly four o'clock and for God's sake she was still there, still sitting at the kitchen table . . ..

Umberto hurried back to the garage, wondered if she'd actually been there all day. Could it be she hadn't even moved from the chair? Whatever, the girl was set on hooking him; she'd never leave the house until he promised to marry her.

Which meant he couldn't go home. He'd have to live in a hotel, and God how he hated hotels. Well, at least the Hilton was nearby. He'd check in and keep a close watch on his house until Pina got tired of waiting and left. Of course he'd have to telephone his mother and tell her not to worry . . . he'd make up some story about staying at the studio on account of work. It was no good asking his mother to get rid of Pina . . . that would only lead to endless talk about why a man of thirty-five couldn't settle down and get married and so forth.

Well, being a bachelor wasn't his fault. Women today were strange, single-minded creatures. He'd been in love three times. Three times he'd asked a woman to marry him, and all three times he'd been turned down. Each had been willing to live with him but none had wanted to be "tied down in marriage." They didn't even want children! He loved children.

Yvette had gotten pregnant, but by accident. He'd literally had to beg her to keep the baby. She was a French model and hadn't wanted to ruin her figure. Umberto remembered how he'd spent those nine months in France indulging Yvette's every wish, and some he'd thought up for her, and watching closely over his unborn child. Yvette had agreed to give him the baby to take back to Italy and raise in his parent's house. But when the baby girl was born Yvette had changed her mind, had decided she couldn't part with little Nicola. And Umberto couldn't stay forever in France. Now he only saw Nicola on certain holidays and occasionally when he could manage to get to Paris for the weekend. Women . . .

As he checked into the Hilton, Umberto was still thinking about how much he missed his little girl and wondered, as he often did, if he'd ever find the right woman, ever have other children. His two brothers were happily married—he'd recently become an uncle for the fifth time. Why couldn't he do what his brothers had done? No wonder his mother was at him continuously . . . his mother . . . he had to phone her.

Fortunately, his father answered and Umberto was able to explain his dilemma truthfully. At least his father would know how to reach him in case something urgent came up.

To hell with his diet, he thought when he hung up. He deserved a treat. He ordered a bottle of wine and a pizza, then phoned his agent. He'd been meaning to ask Luigi how things were coming along on the next film, *Boccaccio Volgare*.

Luigi told him, "It looks as if they may be able to convince Serena Blaire to play one of your Fiammettas."

"Fine, she's a good actress."

"And a big box-office name," Luigi said. His voice sounded a bit strained.

Umberto suspected more bad news was on the way. Luigi's voice always sounded that way when he was about to give Umberto bad news.

"Umberto, are you still there?"

"Yes, yes, Luigi. You have something to tell me. What is it?"

Luigi cleared his throat and hurriedly said, "Serena Blaire always insists on first billing. I'm afraid she'll want her name to appear above yours."

End of a perfect day for Umberto Cassini.

# CHAPTER THREE

FOR MOST of Serena Blaire's thirty-nine years she had been, without reservation, head over heels in love with herself—who else was so adorable, so thin, so rich and so devastatingly clever? What other actress had successfully broken the balls of every male chauvinist she had worked or dealt with in the Hollywood jungle and still walked away each time with the air of a perfect lady? Who could speak other than well of her? And what actress had reaped as much as she'd sown . . . in money, favorable attention, excellent reviews, Academy Awards? No one had ever beaten her at anything because she was as shrewd as—no, shrewder than—anyone else she knew in the business.

She had believed this also of her personal life until a year ago, when she had fallen in love with a smooth-talking Italian boy and married him almost overnight. Now the infallible Serena Blaire was obliged to concede that she had married a dud, a jerk. Also a real prick.

What had made her lose her head? Well, that whirlwind romancing on the isle of Capri had, she supposed, been partially to blame, but more than that, to be honest, it had been her age. When she'd been younger, she'd never given any serious thought to having children. But with the childbearing years rapidly coming to an end—they called it the biological time clock—suddenly she'd felt desperate to have a baby. Which meant a husband, which meant swiftly accepting the next presentable thing in trousers.

But what a disaster Primo Galiano had turned out to be . . . her so-called lawyer husband, that pompous ass of a twenty-seven-year-old, who'd stopped screwing her immediately after the honeymoon.

Each day that she was forced to endure as Primo Galiano's wife, Serena made an effort to reinflate her ego by reminding herself of all those times she *had* made the right choice. She was British, but after her first film hit she'd avoided the high British taxes by going to live in Switzerland. She had also managed to sweet-talk the mayor of her chosen canton, and with the help of a society lawyer, who hadn't charged her a fee, she'd struck a lifetime deal to pay the Swiss only $4,000 per year regardless of how much money she earned. Serena was a tough, uneducated kid from the East End of London who had been rejected by the Royal Academy of Dramatic Art as hopeless, but she had worked and worked and worked on both the King's English and a posh French accent. She had been her own Pygmalion, and so within a few years had been able to pass herself off even to the French, and of course the Americans, as a cultured English aristocrat. She would never have been able to fool her own countrymen for very long, but what the hell . . . the British could keep their welfare state, with its measly salaries and exorbitant taxes. Hollywood, lotus land, was where the money and fame were to be had. And the snobbish Swiss French had been taken in completely, thereby providing her with piss-elegant respectability that made those Southern California hotshots believe that her morning's shit was sweetly perfumed.

Screw the Royal Academy of Dramatic Art, being true to your character and the script . . . that was for self-deceived suckers . . . she'd mastered her own art of portraying cute and pixieish to the point of irresistibility. First she had made herself highly desirable to Hollywood, and then she had played hard to get by refusing to set foot out of Switzerland until producers gave her top money *and* top billing. As a result, she had starred above numerous old-time actors who had never before in their lives surrendered lead billing to a female. When one of her films was unsuccessful at the box office, she always had found a way to make the leading man take the rap through shrewdly concocted plants fed to the trade papers. So-and-so was too far over the hill, or so-and-so was hitting the bottle too hard, or you see, you can't take so-and-so out of a cowboy suit. But as for Serena . . . she was adorable, what an actress, what a true star, what a *lady*. Hollywood especially loved "ladies."

Serena, aware of her shapeless body, never failed to dress her skinny frame in the very finest designer clothes. The result, of course, was that people commented only on her sensational wardrobe. She was naturally thin, with almost no breasts or hips, but she had also deliberately starved herself until there wasn't a trace of excess fat in her face, and those already prominent cheekbones became photogenic magic.

She had gotten everything she had ever wanted, including a healthy baby girl (and just at the eleventh hour). But the one thing she had acquired that still brought her profound agitation was that washout of a husband, Primo Galiano. How to dump him? He didn't sleep in the same bed with her any more, but of course she couldn't let anyone know that because it would be bad for her image . . . so there went her most substantial grounds for a divorce. Serena also had strong suspicions that Primo was cheating on her, but Primo never permitted himself to be caught in the act. The private investigator Serena had hired had cost her a disturbing $100,000 to date.

Primo Galiano had pretended that he was an important lawyer, but he had turned out to be nothing more than an apprentice with no credentials. Primo also claimed that his family was well-to-do, but once they were married Serena discovered they had gone threadbare, had in fact lost everything during the war. So as his wife she was expected to keep not only Primo but his entire family in a style becoming her status as a superstar.

Serena had gone one whole year without work because a film script worthy of her had not been forthcoming. She had lost another year on account of having the baby. Had she remained in Switzerland she might not have worried unduly about living solely from her considerable capital, but moving to Italy had meant huge expenditures that were eating too heavily into those previously guarded assets. It had meant buying and furnishing another mansion fit for a movie queen while at the same time retaining her Swiss residence. There was the nanny she'd brought from Switzerland to care for the baby and another entire household of servants to pay, house and feed.

Her trips to Paris each season to replenish her wardrobe had always been her largest single expense, over a quarter of a million dollars annually, an expense that had seemed reasonable when she'd only dressed and catered to herself. Now Primo also demanded the finest of everything, and his tastes were alarmingly extravagant. He thought nothing, for example, of ordering fifty or sixty hand-tailored suits at any given time, and without asking her he regularly invited large parties of friends and acquaintances for a lavish supper of lobster and champagne. And more and more of the Galiano relatives kept appearing from out of the very woodwork, and each arrived with his or her hands held out, palms up.

What grated on Serena most of all was that Primo made not the slightest attempt to join her in their conjugal bed. How ironic that his surname meant rooster. Capon might have been more appropriate. Primo meant first, so his full name translated into First Rooster. What a joke. And how tacky for his mother to have named him First in the first place. Only illiterate peasants named their children First, Second, Third and so on. Primo had a brother Secondo, and Terso, and Quarto, and Quinto, and the very last baby had been called Ultimo for last. As far as Serena was concerned that huge family of roosters numbered *infinito.* Both immediate and distant, they added to an endless, greedy horde of roosters feeding off the treasure that represented her lifetime's work.

They were, cumulatively, the reason Serena felt obliged to return to the silver screen. Of course she was too great a star to take just any old film, and Hollywood had momentarily assumed that out-of-sight, out-of-mind attitude even toward her. Still, one film was about to be made in Rome that was prestigious enough for her to lend her talents to: *Boccaccio Volgare*. And so Serena was calling forth all her well-honed and well-tested tricks not only to appear as one of the Fiammettas but in the process grab off the lion's share of both the money and the billing. The male star, Umberto Cassini, could go screw himself. Of course Umberto Cassini was also very yummy . . . maybe, just maybe she'd have him screw her before proceeding to snip away at his balls.

Serena, like the self-made thoroughbred she was, sniffed the air and found it invigorating.

In another part of Rome, Serena's husband, Primo Galiano, was in the sauna of the exclusive men's club he had recently joined. The law firm could do without him this morning. At any rate they only used him to sort the mail or as a runner to deliver packages or to go for coffee. Naturally, they wouldn't fire him. He brought them prestige, he was married to the world-famous Serena Blaire. No, this morning he planned to treat himself to the works—sauna, massage, shampoo, trim, shave, manicure and pedicure.

As Primo lay on the deliciously hot boards of the sauna with the perspiration oozing, he could not help but reflect on his unbelievably good fortune. The one and only Serena Blaire loved him. It seemed to be too good to be true, but she loved him. All his life he'd been a loser, then suddenly at twenty-seven he had caught the elusive golden ring, actually married the wealthy, famous, beautiful Serena.

And she was so sweet, he nearly said out loud before catching himself and then rolling over onto his soft, rounded belly. And she loved him, he thought, barely able to contain his joy. She really did. She adored him. She enjoyed buying him the best of everything. Why, it gave her the greatest of all pleasure to spoil him, to indulge him, to make countless exceedingly generous offerings toward his family and friends.

He, Primo, was still like her adored little boy. Their baby daughter had not stolen Serena's affection as he had feared throughout Serena's pregnancy. He remembered how he had hated sharing his mother with Secondo . . . and then there had been Terso, Quarto, Quinto and Ultimo. But unlike his mother, Serena had never made Primo aware that he was sharing with the baby. Serena's feelings for him were different, separate from whatever she reserved for their daughter. And here he scratched his oily blond head because he was unclear just what it was that Serena did reserve for the baby.

Never mind. What a joy to have married an older woman who so tenderly looked after and cared for him. Secretly he'd actually begun to think of Serena as his true mama . . . His own mother, after all, had made him feel like a failure. All his life he'd been nothing more than a gross disappointment to her, bungling the things she had set her heart on his achieving. The only thing he'd been able to do for his mother that genuinely pleased her was to clean up his plate and ask for seconds. The more refills he requested, the more his mother loved him. Which was why he'd developed such a big appetite and why he tended to be pudgy. Well, he no longer needed to clean off his plate and request seconds. Serena's love didn't depend on his liking her cooking. In fact, Serena never cooked, and she herself ate like a bird.

He would slim down for Serena . . . beginning today he would take saunas and massages and start a diet.

Primo had done poorly in school, been hopeless at sports, never really had friends. But everyone was proud of him now, looked up to him, wanted to be his friend. He would strive for a trim new look to match his new successful image, the image of the desirable young man that Serena Blaire had chosen.

But he had wanted to do more for his *tesora* . . . that's what he always called her, his treasure, his sweet, adorable treasure. Oh, yes, he knew she wanted nothing more than to make him happy. For an English girl she was surprisingly like the typical Italian wife. If only he could think of something truly special he could do for her. Something wonderful and unexpected, a glorious surprise.

Certainly he made every effort to be considerate toward her. For example, out of respect he didn't go anywhere near her bed. Well, she was a lady. And his mother had told him time and time again, "Real ladies don't like that dirty stuff. Only your whores enjoy sex. A nice girl, a wife, only submits to that filth on account of her duty toward the church and her husband." So he had forced himself to keep away from Serena's body. He would not invade her purity unless it was to give her a baby. The church allowed him to do it for the sake of having children. But Serena didn't want any more babies, so that part of their duty was completed.

Sometimes, though, he wanted her so badly that his groin went into a painful cramp. Sometimes he wanted a woman . . . any woman . . . so much that he could not keep his mind from straying to sinful thoughts about doing it to someone. Sometimes he relieved himself. His Saturday confessions were always about these disgusting thoughts and actions.

He might kneel and say the act of contrition every day of his life, but he would never cheat on his beloved. He would rather be castrated.

The struggle to keep away from Serena was the saintlike cross he bore. And no doubt, he told himself, that was one of the reasons Serena loved him so dearly. Obviously she was touched by his physical suffering. Without doubt she admired his subjugation of the flesh on her account. They were blessed by a spiritual, an altogether ideal, marriage that truly had been made in heaven.

In her appreciation, his *tesora* Serena gave him everything else his heart desired. Money was no object to her where his wishes were concerned. If only he could do something else for her, something out of the ordinary. She wanted to go back to work . . . he, of course, wanted her to remain a star . . . she had talked about playing one of the Fiammettas in *Boccaccio Volgare* . . . that was it! He, Primo, would find a way of getting her that movie. From now on he would think about nothing else. And he would find the way. For once he would not bungle his goal. After all, he was no longer a loser. Virtually overnight he had become a lucky man, a grand-prize winner. Now he might be capable of any achievement.

Even of presenting his *tesora* with one of the treasured Fiammettas!

# CHAPTER FOUR

MADELINE HAD been truly shocked when Astrid asked her, "Would you like me to come to bed with you?" In all her thirty-four years no female had ever openly propositioned her, though there had been some supposedly inadvertent touchings that she had carefully ignored. At first she had been lost for words. Then she made what in retrospect was a scared "no thank-you," followed by, "I'm sorry, Astrid, that's not my scene." She hoped that made her sound less dopey. Astrid had smiled at her awkwardness and then blown a kiss before leaving the room. A real kiss-off.

Later that night, when Madeline was able to doze, she had had erotic dreams and *some* of them had included Astrid.

Abruptly awake, she'd been drenched in perspiration. The truth was she'd been having sexual fantasies for some time. And, trying to be honest with herself, she faced the reason—she'd never really had an orgasm. Was something wrong with her? Maybe. Had she been with the wrong men? For sure. What she needed was the right man . . . some great Latin lover. She had to smile at the cliché, but not at the need, nor the fear that she'd freeze up again as she had so many times before. Well, damn it, not *this* time . . . she'd relax, let him lead her step by step . . . she was aching to play pupil to some man who didn't expect her to play goddess and would just let her be herself. All right, so who would she choose, assuming she could have her choice? Obviously it would have to be someone experienced and . . . during the evening, she remembered, Umberto Cassini's name had come up more than once. And his name alone sent the juices flowing. She adored him on the screen . . . his warmth, humor, even his world-weary air turned her on. He had those enormous brown eyes that glowed with intelligence *and* sensuality. She acknowledged that she'd wanted to make love to him for a very long time. And from all she'd heard, Umberto Cassini was an experienced lover. Yes, Umberto was a definite possibility . . . She had curled herself around a bolster then, pressing it tight between her thighs. A poor substitute, a cold comfort.

But first, how was she to handle Astrid . . . She had little doubt that Astrid hadn't accepted the rejection, that the proposition was still there between them. If she didn't find a way to make her feelings, or lack of them, clearly understood, there would be a lingering strain and tension in the future. She couldn't afford that. Regardless of Astrid's unwanted interest in her, she must not, she decided, lose her as a friend. She badly needed friends, especially someone like Astrid, who could help introduce her to the film community—an introduction she desperately needed if she was to survive and put her career . . . her life . . . back together.

Madeline had not misjudged Astrid's ability, or willingness, to help her. The next morning at breakfast Astrid told her, "This Friday they're holding a banquet for Paolo Piccolo Monti. Everyone who's anyone in films will be there and I've gotten you an invitation. Not only that, I suggested to Cleo that you sit on the dais as a guest of honor and Cleo jumped at the idea. Of course she likes you—but her main reason for having you there is to take some of the loving attention away from Serena Blaire. Serena was supposed to be the only foreign guest star honored."

Madeline, of course, was delighted. All that week she prepared for her debut at the banquet. She tried on every gown in her wardrobe, over and over, before deciding on a flowing white chiffon. She had been compared to Botticelli's *Birth of Venus* while wearing a similar gown. Clearly this was no time to shy away from her famous image—not when she was being put up against Serena Blaire.

The banquet was to be held in the large ballroom at the Hilton Hotel. Madeline, not wanting to risk a blind date on such a crucial occasion, and also reluctant to stand the cost of a limousine for the whole evening, found a service that agreed to take her home at the end of the evening. But that meant arriving at the hotel in a taxi, so she had to get to the hotel well in advance of the banquet so the other guests wouldn't see Venus arriving in a cab.

When Madeline entered the Hilton the doors to the grand ballroom were still closed. She decided to sit for a while at the far end of the lobby, and then wait out the rest of the time in the powder room. She would then make her entrance at the appointed hour.

She walked the length of the building to a remote corner where only one chair was occupied, by a man who seemed engrossed in his newspaper; but as she approached him he looked up.

It was Umberto Cassini in the flesh! Umberto, in hiding from the relentless Pina, was still living at the Hilton. No matter how much he suffered, he would not go home—not go anywhere *near* his home until Pina gave up her hot pursuit. He did, though, so hate being alone in his hotel room that he spent hours in the lobby reading newspapers and even a book now and then. He'd read this day's paper cover to cover and was glancing aimlessly through them once more when he caught a glimpse of white chiffon floating toward him. He looked up to be stunned by the vision of an angelic face with a halo of platinum hair—the most beautiful creature he had ever seen—a painting come to life. Yes, a painting, a familiar one, but which one? *Venus.* No question. Idyllic beauty, symbol of ultimate femininity—goddess of love come to earth, to this damned hotel, to rescue him.

"Hello," she said, and smiled at him as if they already knew each other. Hello?—hello in English—with an American accent? An American Venus?

No matter. Umberto could not take his eyes off her, but felt incapable of speech.

As for Madeline, unaware of her celestial impact she had gone weak at the knees on seeing the ruggedly handsome Umberto Cassini. His enormous brown eyes seemed to glow—and his manly appearance, including those strong arms that she'd fantasized holding her . . . they'd all stopped her cold in her tracks when she saw the package in the flesh.

She had said hello but he hadn't answered her. Damn, didn't he even recognize her? Had she slipped that far back? He kept staring at her but made no attempt at conversation, like one did with someone who seemed sort of familiar but whose name didn't come to mind. She noted his tuxedo, which suggested he was here for the banquet in honor of Paolo Monti. Well, damn you, just say hello or *something* . . . he was making her squirm in her chair. Finally, she looked down, to escape, and for something to do with her hands began fumbling around with the contents of her evening bag.

When she glanced up again he was gone—just like that. Disappeared.

Odd behavior, or had she driven him away? Her answer, which she of course couldn't be aware of at the time, came in the form of an olive-skinned girl with an abundance of bushy black hair who now came rushing around the corner, then full-stopped in front of Madeline.

Pina, out of breath and not to be denied. "Where did Umberto disappear to? *Tell* me."

Madeline was, naturally, taken off-guard. "I—I don't know . . . he just disappeared."

"Then you are not with him?" Pina sighed in relief.

"No, why would you think that?"

"Well, you are Madeline Mandell, a famous actress. I thought maybe you were Umberto's date."

Pina flopped into the chair next to Madeline's and smiled brightly at her. "I'm a big fan of yours. Of course I haven't seen all of your films—I'm too young." Followed by another bright, not so innocent smile.

Madeline decided to ignore the dig about comparative ages.

"My name is Pina," Pina chirped on. "I'm an actress too—well, I'm really a language student. I do modeling and I've had a walk-on in a film. But I hope to be an actress someday."

Madeline wished this Pina would go away, but smiled and said, "I'm sure you'll make a very good actress someday."

After absorbing, or ignoring, that—difficult to tell which—Pina looked anxiously into Madeline's eyes and asked, "Is Umberto going to the banquet alone?"

"I've no idea."

Pina sighed again, so loudly that it made Madeline jump. "I'm in love with him, you know. But we had a quarrel."

What else to say except, "I'm sorry."

Pina spotted the invitation in Madeline's open evening bag. "Who are you with?"

Madeline resented the question but nonetheless answered. "I decided to come alone."

Pina shrieked, startling Madeline. She took hold of Madeline's hands and said in an imploring voice, "But your invitation is for *two*. Oh, *please*, would you let me come to the banquet with you?"

"Well—"

"I won't bother you once we're inside. I promise. Please, I must be near Umberto this evening. It's important for our future together. His mother and I have nearly planned the wedding. But Umberto is being so stubborn, he's so—" And Pina burst into tears and began to make loud sobbing noises.

Under the circumstances Madeline felt she had no alternative but to give in to Pina. Still, it was sort of disillusioning to learn that Umberto Cassini was in real life a cad, a lech, it seemed, who made advances to teen-age girls, then once he'd had his way with them took off—as he'd just done from this lobby. Apparently he'd even held out the promise of marriage to this child. It was a bitter disappointment for Madeline to discover that her idol was a bust in the simple decency department.

Once inside the lavish ballroom, Pina, true to her promise, stayed well behind. In fact, she seemed to be lurking in the doorway as if waiting to pounce on Umberto the moment he came in.

The organizers greeted Madeline with enthusiasm and promptly took her in hand. An hour later, after several glasses of champagne and what seemed like a thousand handshakes, she was shown to the dais, at the center of which Cleo and Paolo Monti, a couple of towers, were already standing in place, holding hands and smiling broadly at each other—actually, at the photographers and the large assembly of well-wishers.

As Madeline approached the steps leading onto the dais she noted Cleo switching two of the place cards so that Madeline was seated at the place of honor on Paolo Monti's right—the position originally reserved for Serena Blaire.

The Minister of Culture was on Madeline's other side, Umberto was to the left of center beside Cleo. And next to Umberto was the empty chair originally meant for Madeline. Now it was being held for the tardy Miss Serena Blaire. The rest of the places had been assigned to officials of the National Film Board.

During the introductions Madeline was impressed by the charm of both her dinner partners, the Minister of Culture Signor Salvatori Anzio, and the famous industrialist Paolo Monti, and after a few words with the giant Paolo she saw him as considerably more than the derisive "Piccolo" the girls had put on him. But it was when she was finally introduced to Umberto Cassini that her heart started pounding. In spite of herself, she again was thinking of him as the man of her fantasies . . . he had seemed so genuinely delighted to meet her, so kind and, yes, so sensitive, too. When he'd bent to kiss her hand she'd promptly wanted to run her fingers through his lush brown hair. When she'd felt the pressure of his warm lips she'd had an urge to take that face in her hands and bring those lips up to her own.

The man was, as the saying went, something else. Of course, she had to remember that he was a fourteen-carat heel, a notorious Don Juan . . . that weird girl lurking to the side of the dais couldn't take her eyes off him. Oh, come on, Madeline, let's not lose our head . . . but the head was not functioning so well . . . all thoughts seemed centered in the region between her legs.

And then he abruptly put her off with that nonsense about her being Hollywood's Venus, and so forth. She hated that . . . not taking her for what she was. He was being like the others who wanted the image . . . not the woman. She turned away abruptly . . .

Umberto was startled. At first this lovely woman had seemed so receptive to him. What had he done? He, the great Latin lover. The lover, he thought wryly, had always been at a loss approaching women. Why? Probably, to be honest, because he was lazy. Women seemed to chase him . . . like the one who had driven him out of his house. He could have women without making an effort . . . because, he was quick to remind himself, he was an actor in films. If he hadn't become famous he at least might have been forced to think up something better than clichés and easy openings. He did tend to pay the price, though . . . ending up with dumb or conniving little bitches who only wanted to use him to get ahead in their careers. When he met a real woman like this Madeline, he instantly turned her off. He should have cut out the cheap flattery and said something like, "Look, I am capable of talking sensibly. And I do want to know you. But I've also got a room upstairs . . . afterward we'll talk. First, I've got to fuck you or I can't think straight . . ." He liked that last in particular—not as a line but as the truth. Fucking cleared up more than the sinuses.

Serena Blaire, poised for a grand late arrival, finally showed up and a hush fell over the room. Wearing a white ball gown glittering with tiny jewels and a huge diamond tiara, Serena swept into the banquet like royalty, paused briefly to survey her subjects, then gifted all present with her inimitable Serena Blaire smile. Spontaneous applause awarded her, and she acknowledged it with a modest curtsy and a regal wave.

On her way to the dais she greeted each and every person along her path. Once on the dais she held forth her hand to each and every male, as though his acceptance of her gesture would bring her not only pleasure but great honor as well. Although she had never met either Madeline Mandell or Cleo Monti, she greeted each with exuberance and bestowed lingering ceremonial kisses on both cheeks.

Momentarily Serena's expression turned hard as she spied her secondary position on the dais, but she swiftly recovered and accepted her seat as if it were the place of honor.

Even those deadly jealous of Serena had to admit she projected a gracious, vibrant aura. Yes, no question . . . tall, bony, pixie-faced Serena had instantly stolen the evening's thunder right out from under all those other far more beautiful, more truly feminine women.

Her pudgy young husband, Primo Galiano, had entered three paces behind Serena and had gone unnoticed. Following Serena as far as the steps of the dais, he turned to find his assigned seat at one of the tables on the ballroom floor, and was delighted to find himself heading in the direction of table 12—the very same table assigned to the famous German actress, Helga Haufman.

Primo, of course, had no idea how Helga Haufman felt about his wife—how she spent sleepless nights thinking of ways to keep Serena from appearing in *Boccaccio Volgare.* Nor could he imagine how far she would go to destroy him, simply because he was Serena's husband.

As Helga spotted Primo Galiano heading for her table, her charcoal eyes lit up with malicious pleasure as she instantly began to concoct ways to use this fat boy to get at Serena. First off, she would invite him to sit beside her, spider to fly. She felt warm all over in anticipation of what was to come.

Astrid Zealand was at one of the most prominent tables, just below the dais and in the center, where she had an excellent view of the principals. She and Cleo had winked at one another when Cleo had altered the seating arrangements on the dais. This evening was turning out just the way Astrid had planned. She intended to do everything in her power to help Madeline. Although she had never mentioned it, she knew full well that Madeline's career was in deep trouble. She would offer Madeline the gift of a new career, and surely seduce her at the same time. But of course she would also protect

Madeline as she loved her in those tender ways no man was capable of.

Astrid had arrived with two men—a beautiful French boy, for show, and the director Alfonso Razzi, so that she might talk him into using Madeline for his forthcoming film.

Madeline, beside herself, periodically glanced down at Astrid with gratitude. The waiters had by now begun serving courses of pasta, but Madeline was far too excited to try any of them. She glanced over at Serena. She wasn't eating either. She was in deep conversation with Umberto, who had moved his chair next to her. Well, who cared? She'd been right to turn him off. If now he was paying more attention to Serena, no doubt it was just because he considered her a bigger name. To hell with both of them . . . except that even as she thought it she knew she didn't entirely mean it. The man had gotten to her, no question . . .

Paolo Monti had begun showing Madeline a great deal of attention, expert as he was at polite conversation and apparently intent on making this American girl feel welcome at his banquet. The orchestra was now playing soft music, and couples had begun drifting to the circle in the center of the ballroom set aside for dancing. After the fourth pasta course Paolo asked Madeline if she would care to dance. When they excused themselves, the Minister of Culture also got up and invited Cleo to dance. Seeing this, Serena took the fork out of Umberto's hand and coaxed him to his feet.

As Madeline and Paolo Monti arrived on the dance floor, there was a bustle of photographers pushing past them to record for posterity Serena holding Umberto's hand and gaily leading him onto the floor. In a blaze of flashbulbs Madeline witnessed Serena moving into Umberto's arms while smiling for the cameras. Madeline, awash in envy, had her view abruptly cut off by the gigantic Paolo Monti, who had taken her into his arms, burying her face in his mammoth chest.

Umberto took little pleasure in the attention. He'd never cared for the gossip and scandal associated with show business. He didn't even like being photographed, especially with an actress like Serena Blaire, who he understood only wanted to use him for her own publicity purposes. Still, he was a gentleman, and so tried at least to erase the scowl on his face as the paparazzi clicked away.

Helga, who had been firmly guiding Primo Galiano around the dance floor, tensed when she saw Serena getting attention and implying an impending romance with Umberto Cassini. Quickly as possible, she moved the dumpy Primo over to his wife, which at least put a full stop to the photographing—Helga's introduction of Serena's *husband* into the picture frame blighted the hint of promised romance and thereby turned off the photographers.

Helga had positioned herself and Primo directly between Serena and Umberto, angling Primo to face his wife, and then had liberated Umberto by asking him to dance with her. As soon as they were a safe distance away, Helga kissed her dear pal Umberto on the cheek and left him to fend for himself.

Which for Umberto was a short-lived blessing. On his own and unguarded for scarcely a moment, he was promptly assaulted from behind by the irrepressible Pina, who swung herself around his body, digging the nails of her left hand into his shoulder and of her right hand into his lower back.

Involuntarily moving his feet, he found himself

dancing with her, an interminable dance that seemed likely to go on forever without a break . . .

Of all the men at the party Primo Galiano considered himself to be the luckiest. He was dancing with his beloved Serena. She was smiling. She was smiling at everyone, of course, but she had to. She was the princess. But secretly he knew that her smile was for him alone. And he felt so handsome that night. His salmon-colored tuxedo had cost the earth but it had been well worth the price. There wasn't another like it in that whole room. True, his ruffled shirt front had popped open to expose his belly button, but he preferred not to interrupt the dance. Serena's ball gown was swishing about nicely as they moved and her diamond tiara flashed brilliantly as it caught the beams from the overhead spotlights, crowning her short black hair and highlighting her adorable pixie face . . . Indeed, sometimes he wondered what this wonderful woman ever saw in him, but then again it occurred to him that he was being perhaps too modest and underrating his own appearance and attractiveness for women. The sultry Helga Haufman, for example, had turned her full attention on him, ignoring everyone else at their table. She'd insisted on dancing with him the moment the orchestra first struck up and had held him close against her and whispered titillating things in his ear . . .

Serena, for her part, wanted to murder both Primo, in his ridiculous salmon tuxedo, and that pushy bitch, Helga Haufman. She well knew that the producers and directors of *Boccaccio Volgare* must be here at this tribute to Paolo Monti. She wanted above all to plant in their small minds the magic chemistry of Serena Blaire and Umberto Cassini. And she wanted those photos of herself with Umberto in every newspaper and photo magazine in the world as a backup reminder. She could only hope the photographers had gotten enough pictures of her and Umberto before the interruption. And certainly her entrance had been a smash . . . she'd wiped out the competition. And no matter what came up to block her path, she'd always be smart enough to overcome it. She was, after all, the one and only Serena Blaire . . .

Paolo Monti had in effect stopped dancing and was simply swaying to the music with Madeline Mandell clamped in his arms. She was, no question, a delicious little piece, and he had an erection. Closing his eyes, he tried to imagine her under him. She probably had a tight little cunt, but he'd like to fuck her just for a change of pace. Helga had a cavernous cunt, she was a wild woman—exciting but also exhausting. Cleo he loved, she fitted him in every way. She was his precious dumpling—his great huge baby whose masses of delectable flesh were beyond compare. Indeed, he only wished she'd stop having it cut away. He loved every ounce and inch of her, loved her just as much today as when they'd married twelve years earlier. If he could just cure her of her damnable obsession with plastic surgery, which left too few times a year when he could make love to her . . . recovering as she was from an operation, covered with bruises and stitches that made her too tender to touch, let alone make love to. And then there were those goddamn contour pillows she was forced to sleep on that got in his way . . . the very thought of them made his penis shrivel.

As for Madeline, she devoutly wished to escape Paolo's grip. She had felt his hard little penis stabbing into her stomach, had felt him rubbing it up against her. Then abruptly he was soft, and she wondered in alarm if he'd ejaculated—wondered if when he released her there would be a telltale yellow stain on her dress. As the music finally ended and the lights went up, Paolo let go of her, and she stepped back and glanced down at the front of her white chiffon. Thank God, it was still spotless, no thanks to Paolo Piccolo Monti.

Once back on the dais, Madeline turned her attentions to the Minister of Culture and did her best to ignore Paolo. During the meat course, when the minister became more interested in eating than in talking to her, she excused herself and went to the powder room, closely observe by Astrid, who proceeded to follow her.

Madeline, relieved to see Astrid, told her how Paolo Monti had behaved, and Astrid, all sympathy and concern, suggested that they leave immediately after the speeches and go to a disco. She would bring her date *and* Alfonso Razzi, who she said was now anxious to talk to Madeline about his new movie. Madeline, grateful and relieved, hugged Astrid, and Astrid carefully returned the embrace, a bright smile on her face.

# CHAPTER FIVE

THE REST of the evening had turned out well for Madeline. After the disco, Astrid had gone home with the French boy, Jean somebody, and so that confrontation had been postponed. It appeared that Alfonso Razzi really did want her for his film. Anyway, she was to meet him at Cine Citta in the morning for further talks.

In her apartment now, Madeline didn't feel sleepy, was too keyed up by all the new currents and cross-currents in her life. She curled herself up in an easy chair, let her thoughts drift and, as they often did, call up images of her family, her mother in particular. Which evoked the old impossible-to-answer question, asked as a little girl and even often by the girl in the adult—why had God chosen to take Maria Yalsekovitch Mandell at such an early age? Madeline had lashed out at God then, and even said she hated him. Now she was ever so much more sophisticated . . . so she did it on the inside, where it hurt even more.

Right or not, she felt she remembered everything about her mother, even though she'd only been four and a half at the time of the accident, and sometimes wondered if she had confused some of herself with an image of mother. Anyway . . . she recalled her mother as shy and modest, a lovely, round, rosy-cheeked Polish girl, who'd never acknowledged her own beauty. Her face was always free of makeup, freshly scrubbed and shiny. Her waist-length blonde hair was hidden away in a network of braids she pinned close to her head. Evenings they often took a bath together to save hot water, then mother would allow her to brush her hair, allow her to create lopsided hairdos that mother always said were pretty. They must have been laughable to anyone but a child. Afterward mother would set Madeline's blonde hair in rags so that she could make Shirley Temple curls the next morning by brushing the locks of hair around a broom handle. There was very little money, but mother saved pennies here and there from the household money so that she could take her to the movies on special Saturday afternoons. Shirley Temple movies were a must, the stuff of a little girl's dreams, and not that far from mother's own . . . she was barely twenty.

She saw again the time her mother had tripped carrying bags of groceries home. She remembered how she'd felt seeing her mother on her knees in the street . . . wanting to come to her mother's rescue, knowing she was too little to help. Ever after that, she'd never been able to see an orange without remembering the three oranges that had rolled into the gutter, eluding her mother's grasp.

It was always that small part of the event that came flooding back to remind her—almost never the big one. It was the torn stockings and the scraped knees she remembered—battered knees showing naked from gaping stocking holes. Knees that formed scabs and, of course, one day got better. A happy ending to blot out the terrible part. To blot out the truck that appeared from nowhere and struck down her mother, then sped away without stopping. One moment she was looking at her mother lying there all broken, the next someone was carrying Madeline away from the scene. It was only a moment, but it happened, and in an instant it was over—only the loneliness lingered on. And there was not a single detail of the accident to hold on to, except those three oranges rolling toward the gutter.

The lens shifted to her father, a distant, silent figure covered in coal dust from the mine. When he had taken a bath and put on clean clothes he'd somehow become even more of a stranger. Josip Mandell almost never spoke. He still didn't. It was impossible to have a conversation with him, which was why she had stopped calling him, sending short letters and postcards instead. He sent greeting cards with canned rhymes. She would never forget, nor forgive, his crying over the dead, unborn baby, but not her mother.

She knew her mother must have had a big belly at the time of the accident because she'd been five months pregnant, but she couldn't remember a big belly. Once in a while she thought about what if it had been born and was a baby boy . . . how, then, she wouldn't have grown up an only child. Would her father have cried if he knew the other child had been a daughter rather than a son? Would he have farmed out a son from one relative to another as he had done with her? Still, if she'd been a boy, she might still be living in West Virginia, going down into the pits every day—encased in coal dust, stoic, defeated.

For her, going into show business was an escape—from houses that weren't home, from a mining town whose hills shut out the future.

A pretty teen-age girl with no money and only a high school diploma had no currency but her prettiness, which won her a beauty contest, whose prize was a weekend in Wheeling. It was the first time she'd been in a city, and it made her want to go farther, to see more. The man who accommodated her and took her to New York was reimbursed . . . she saw it that way, was made to *feel* it that way . . . by claiming her virginity. He wasn't so bad really—dull, maybe, and clumsy. Definitely clumsy. He had paid to send her to modeling school, then actually cried when her photograph first appeared on a magazine cover. He had also known she would leave him . . . before she herself had known it. He once told her that one day he'd be putting her on a plane for Los Angeles. She hadn't believed it, but it had happened, and sooner than he had predicted.

At the airport he said he'd lost her and would never see her again. She promised to write. He seemed to know that she wouldn't.

She had meant to keep in contact with him, but things happened so fast that she allowed too much time to pass. And then it seemed futile to get in touch. At any rate, what would she have said?—"Call me if you're ever out this way"? She wasn't mature enough to keep him as a friend or to admit to the new people around her that she'd been a traveling salesman's mistress. Looking back, it was more honest work than a lot that followed.

In Hollywood they carried on her training in seduction . . . She learned how to round her vowels and lower her voice an octave. They taught her to emote without facial distortion by taping her face so that it appeared to remain serene. She wasn't really any better than the others in the studio classroom—but of all the young hopefuls under contract it was she who had the automatic love affair with the movie camera. The instant the camera turned—something happened inside Madeline, and she gave herself over to it without effort or struggle, as if she'd come home, finally, to the place where she was meant to live. She allowed—welcomed—the camera to possess her so completely that when the images it captured were projected on the screen a spectator had the sensation of being intimate with the woman pictured up there. And not with just a woman but with a goddess of love—because the public's first exposure to her was when she played Venus. The publicity, the columnists, the audiences took it up together—Venus, the ultimate seduction, because it could never be consummated.

The image took over her life. Offscreen she was unable to contradict the view that the movie camera presented. *It* held the magical truth that no amount of denial could wipe out. She *was* Venus. She was love. She belonged to *them,* so long as they stayed their distance. And looking back now, it also became clear that, like magicians who succumb to their own illusion, the men responsible for bringing her to the screen, the men who controlled the studio, were also taken in, blinded by the image. They held her like an ornament that only required its glamorous setting. They saw her as a marvelous specimen, a creation devised for their profit, and so to be worked without concern for the needs of a flesh-and-blood woman.

For twelve years she was like an indentured servant. The money spent on advisers who were supposed to protect her, to work for her, was wasted. They took from her, and when confronted by the studio's power got down on their knees. And they did it with a clear conscience—she was not, after all, real. How could you hurt a goddess?

She began, seriously, to lose whatever was left of her hold on reality. She could no longer perceive and react to people or situations. Only the still powerful need to find the daughter of Maria Mandell kept her from going under. She thought maybe a home and family would be the answer, but the husband she chose turned out to be no different from the others . . . he too saw her as an ornament, to be put on display, to be used. She thought she was a woman who had married a man. He never saw it—or her—that way. She wanted to be loved like a woman. He would lie back, submissively, feeling cheated when the love goddess didn't perform miracles.

The divorce was bitter and, of course, played to the gallery. There had been little intimacy in their marital relationship, and then no privacy in their failure. Feeling humiliated, it seemed, by the failure of his marriage to Venus, his masculinity under attack, her husband chose to strike first, informing the world about her cold, unwomanly performance in bed. He became a man aggrieved, an injured party, and in compensation demanded for life a six-figure alimony settlement.

In a sense, she thought, she should be grateful to him . . . the goddess woke up. Venus came down to earth and turned back into Madeline. And Madeline went to war, against him, and then the studio. She appeared in an independent film without their approval . . . high treason . . . which brought on another lawsuit. Her advisers fled the scene of the battle, so she fired them after the fact and went it alone. By now she would settle for nothing less than complete freedom. Being Venus was sheer slavery. So in the independent film she played the part of a very ordinary woman, all the old illusion stripped away. It was too much for the public. They felt cheated, betrayed. And in a way they were right. But the vengeance was swift and devastating . . . they killed her at the box office. And of course no producer wanted a box-office failure who was in a contract dispute with a major studio. Her career seemed over. Her money ran out. She had no one. Before they thought she was above need, now she was beneath their giving a damn. She felt trapped, no way out. Except suicide . . .

But suicide would have meant not carrying on for Maria, not giving her grandchildren. At least Maria had given life before her own was taken away. Maria, Polish Catholic, would have been horrified at the thought of her child committing such a mortal sin.

Maria, the mother, was now with her. Her mother would know what it had taken to go on. Her mother, at least, would be proud of a daughter who stood up and fought to survive. Her mother, watching over her, gave her the strength of two. They would go on together.

And they had, all the way to Italy, and this second chance . . . it was a good thought to fall asleep on.

# CHAPTER SIX

ON THE morning after the banquet for Paolo Monti a storm from Siberia was, uncharacteristically, heading southwest, reaching all the way into southern Italy. Autumn normally meant fine weather in Rome. This was only the first of October, but by 5:00 A.M. there was a decided chill in the air and an icy rain had begun to fall. Most of the populace were still tucked in their beds at that hour, but two of the city's most glamorous visitors, Madeline Mandell and Serena Blaire, had both been awake for some time.

Serena was sitting up in her plushly padded velvet bed, wearing a quilted designer bed jacket and watching the steam rising from the tea on her breakfast tray. Three servants were bustling about the room:

the butler was putting more wood on the already blazing fire in the fireplace; the maid was connecting yet another electric heater as companion to the two already blowing warm air toward Serena's bed; and because it was an emergency the cook herself had been called into service and had entered the bedroom to exchange Serena's still steaming teapot for one that had only moments before come off the boil.

Serena never minded how early she rose—especially not on a morning when she was taking a flight to Switzerland. Switzerland meant civilization and civility, which she'd be enjoying by lunchtime. The weather report on the radio was predicting a colder day in Geneva than in Moscow, but at least she would be in a country where everything worked. After nearly fourteen months of struggling with the day-to-day screw-ups in the Eternal City of Rome, Serena was convinced that it was a place where no amount of money could buy comfort, that it was a country where nothing could be counted on to work—least of all the Italians themselves, who always seemed to be on strike. The ancient Roman aqueducts, which were still in use, frequently crumbled and for days at a time there was no running water, not to mention that electricity and gas were problematic, the postal service was a joke and an Italian bank wasn't to be trusted with anything more than a modest household account. Matter of fact, today's trip to Geneva was mostly to visit her money. Her so-called husband was still asleep in his own bedroom, and with luck she would be on her way to the airport before Primo opened his eyes . . .

Madeline's digs were in a commercial neighborhood where even at this early hour she could hear the clanging of gates and shutters and the whining of engines starting up. Her studio apartment, with its drapeless windows and bare floor, was bitterly cold. She had slipped on her fur coat over her dressing gown and wrapped a woolen scarf around her neck. Her hands were like ice, but she couldn't recall having seen any gloves and wondered if she'd forgotten to pack them. She had lit the small gas fire in the fireplace, but as yet it had had little effect on the room temperature, and she was struggling with the gas cooking stove in the dim hope of making herself a hot drink. Since there was no direct supply of fuel, each utility had its own *bomba,* and she put a match to these cylinders of gas only after much careful deliberation. The connotation of the word *bomba* was enough in itself to make her leery.

On the other hand, her spirits this morning were altogether sunny. Why not? Last night director Alfonso Razzi had told her that the part in his new film was hers. She was meeting him today at Cine Citta Studios to be presented with her copy of the script. And after lunch she was being introduced to the film's makeup man, hairdresser and costume designer, and Astrid was sending her own agent, Luigi Luna, to the studio to discuss Madeline's contract. Astrid had also assured her that she needn't sign with Luigi unless she was satisfied with him. Otherwise another agent could easily be summoned. Madeline could not remember ever having a friend like Astrid . . . although she was also aware that mixed in with her help was a motive she had no intention of indulging.

Astrid, meanwhile, was curled up in bed with the young French boy who had accompanied her to the previous night's banquet. He had shivered in his sleep, wrapped the covers closely around his derrière and clung to Astrid in an effort to keep the front of his body warm. Astrid had sensed that the room was unusually cold, but hadn't bothered to get out of bed and close the windows. At any rate, the Nordic goddess was stoic about winter.

Last night she had been delightfully surprised to find that the young man who shared her bed was an inventive as well as a considerate lover. Earlier in the evening she had had difficulty remembering his name—it was Jean Paul or Jean Claude? Nor had she expected to use him as anything other than just a good-looking boy to be seen with and to drive her to and from the banquet. But he had kissed her in the car and she had enjoyed his touch, so she'd invited him in for an encore.

Astrid had known more and more varied lovers than she could remember. A fan magazine had once asked her how many lovers she'd had and her answer had been widely quoted: "What? But who has got such a good memory?" However, she could remember the men who had stayed the night—since they could be counted on the fingers of one hand. With women it was different, but men she was impatient to have leave the minute the lovemaking was finished. This French boy, though, had turned out to be an extraordinary lover, and she'd wanted him to stay until morning in order to further explore his potential.

A gust of Siberian wind swept through the room and Astrid opened her eyes, turned in the bed and took the French boy in her strong arms, vigorously rubbing his back to wake him.

Cleo Monti was also awakened by the wind. Her nipples, aching from her most recent operation, had made her sleep a fitful one in any case. The surgeon had felt it prudent not to remove more than an inch from her breasts this time, but even for so small a reduction it had been necessary to detach and reattach the nipples. Cleo now began urgentiy ringing the bell at her bedside. She wanted her hot water with lemon before taking any more pain killers, and she wanted someone to light the fire in the fireplace. Her nipples might be burning, but the rest of her body was freezing.

She looked over at the jeweled Cartier clock on her bedside table—5:35. In his own bedroom Paolo would soon be stirring and would then order the servants into action. He always got out of bed just before 6:00 A.M., even on weekends and holidays. He would shower, dress, and have his breakfast downstairs in his study, then join her in her bedroom for his second cup of coffee while she had her breakfast on a tray.

Last night after the banquet Paolo had been exceptionally amorous. He'd even pushed his way in between her contour surgical pillow and insisted on licking her all over before wedging his tiny penis between her aching breasts and shooting his sperm onto her upper chest and neck.

She needed Paolo to command the household into action, but she hesitated to call him on the intercom for fear of a repeat of last night's performance. If she woke him now he'd likely come straight from his bed to hers, all hot and eager. If she waited until he'd dressed the danger would be over. So she reached for the telephone and dialed her mother's number. She would tell mama how her nipples pained and how cold her bedroom felt. Mama would warm her with her sympathetic clucking, then would phone the butler and reprimand him for not rousing the household into action on such a wintry morning—

and give him proper hell for not making her little girl more comfortable.

Although a Saturday, it was nonetheless a working day at Cine Citta, where Sunday was the only day off. Today Umberto had a scene that was supposed to take place in a shoe factory and did not include Cleo. Ralph de Rossi had asked Umberto to be ready on the set by 8:30 A.M. instead of 9:00 so that they could finish with the extras by lunchtime. Umberto, however, couldn't get his car started. He was cursing himself for having left the Ferrari on the street instead of parking it in the Hilton garage, but who could know that a Siberian wind would reach Rome on the first of October? Some years he didn't even bother about antifreeze, and when he did it was certainly never before the end of December.

Never mind not putting the car in the garage, Umberto felt that last night he'd not done *anything* he should have—above all, he should have danced with that delicious-looking Madeline Mandell, but had been trapped first by Serena Blaire and then by Pina. In fact, his whole evening had been ruined by Pina, who'd kept circling the dais, keeping him under surveillance. After the speeches he had planned to move his chair over to Madeline's side of the dais and get acquainted with her but she'd left the banquet before he'd had the chance. How would he locate his platinum-haired Venus again? Oh, yes, Cleo seemed to know her . . . he'd ask Cleo . . .

It was too early to phone his mechanic, so Umberto went back to the front of the hotel to hail a taxi from the rank. Damn, the wind was tearing at him, and he again cursed Pina for making it impossible for him to be at his home where he at least could have changed into a warmer jacket.

* * *

Helga Haufman also fretted about a warm jacket this frosty morning. Her furs were still in summer storage and she had had to settle for a lightweight woolen jacket with a hood. Never mind, the bar where she always had breakfast was just around the corner from her apartment. After breakfast she would telephone her friendly furrier at his home and ask him to have her furs delivered the minute his salon opened. She needed them in any case by noon to look stunning at her lunch with director Mariani, whom she hoped to convince she would be perfect for Fiammetta Two. The fact that her paramour, Paolo Piccolo Monti, was financing part of the movie would certainly be a big plus, but Mariani also had to give his approval. As the director of that segment Mariani at least had to agree that Helga was someone he would consider for the role.

Mariani was known as a first-rate director and a serious man. He was also a partial recluse with a home somewhere in the Italian Alps and only came back to Rome for his film work. Being a private person, there had never been any gossip connected with his name, so Helga hadn't been able to find out anything about his sexual preferences. Somehow she would have to try to develop that during their lunch. If he liked women she figured she had a better than even chance of seducing him. If he was a queer, she might be able to interest him in her expertise with the dildo. Even a straight guy like Paolo Piccolo enjoyed it when she straddled his hindquarters, gripped him tightly between her thighs and worked a well-lubricated dildo in and out of his ass. Of course, if Mariani was asexual or sexually neutral she would be in trouble. An asexual was bound to adore that sexless, ethereal bag of bones—Serena Blaire.

Wimps, sissies and asexual men were, Helga was convinced, Serena Blaire's greatest fans. What if she couldn't get Mariani into the sack? Well, that chubby little nerd Primo Galiano was just about under her thumb. Through Primo she would find a way to demolish her rival.

One thing was certain in Helga's mind—only over her dead body would Serena Blaire play the part of Fiammetta Two.

By 11:00 A.M., relaxing in her dressing room at Cine Citta, which was delightfully warm and glamorous with its rosy walls and gilt furnishings, Madeline Mandell once again felt like a movie queen. It was so good to be back on a movie lot where she belonged. Alfonso Razzi had presented her with the script, but it was in Italian and she couldn't read it. She had, though, flipped through the pages and seen the name of her character on every single one of them—so hers was definitely the leading part. Alfonso had then spent an hour or so explaining the script to her in his broken English, but except that it was a mystery entitled *Paranoia,* she hadn't a clue to what the story was about. She wouldn't let that put her off, though. . . . She needed the work and the money, and she needed the joy of expressing herself in her craft, not to mention that glorious feeling of being wanted again as an actress.

Astrid's agent, Luigi Luna, had telephoned Madeline's dressing room three times while Alfonso was still there, but she didn't feel she could talk to the agent while her director was in the room. Anyway, the agent was coming to take her to lunch at the studio restaurant and they could discuss her contract then. The producers had agreed to give her exclusive star billing above the title but the money had sounded low. Luigi had mentioned two contracts: a white one and a black one. Madeline hadn't known what he was talking about. At any rate, she had in mind to tell him just to make the best deal he could. Whatever, she definitely was going to do the film, and it was scheduled to go before the cameras in a few days.

At the moment she was alone, waiting until 1:00, when Luigi would come to collect her for lunch. Meanwhile she was content to lounge on the sofa, sip the coffee and smell the roses provided by her director and daydream about the wonderful new life that she'd thought was no longer possible for her.

Umberto was on stage 4 working on the shoe factory set. Both he and Ralph were pleased with the way the morning's filming had been going. Umberto liked this particular scene—it was lighthearted and there had been a lot of jovial good spirits on the set. The technicians had been in a good mood, the setups had been swift and Ralph de Rossi was only one take away from sending the extras home.

And then the lights went out, leaving them on stage 4 in total blackout. Ralph promptly ordered everyone to stand still until the battery-powered emergency lantern came on. Ten minutes later, after checking the switches and the fuse box, the head electrician notified Ralph that the problem was somewhere in the main cabling, which could mean opening all the trunking.

It was too early to call lunch, so Ralph gave the extras a coffee break with instructions to stand by in the cantina for word from the first assistant. Umberto was given permission to go to stage 12, where Angelo Catalano was doing screen tests for his segment of *Boccaccio Volgare.* Catalano had asked Ralph de

Rossi to free Umberto sometime during the day for a brief test, and Ralph had agreed out of professional courtesy. Ralph had hoped to be finished with the wide shots of the shoe factory scene and send the extras home, thereby keeping such a large number of people on salary for only half rather than a full day, but with the delay he released Umberto until the lighting snag could be sorted out.

Umberto was not unhappy about doing some preliminary work for the *Boccaccio* film. It was going to be a huge undertaking and one of his most demanding roles. The film was in four parts with four different directors, and Umberto's was the main character running through all four segments. He needed to find those links between the four stories and the four different styles of direction that would give his portrayal some consistency.

Angelo Catalano, Astrid's one-time Svengali, was a tall, blond northern Italian with the bearing of a Teutonic knight. He had a long face accentuated by a pointed chin and a thin straight nose. His almond-shaped eyes, although an almost colorless blue-gray, were nonetheless piercing. He often wore a pinched expression, his tight, thin lips reflecting an inner coldness. His posture was rigidly correct, and as he strode forward to acknowledge Umberto's entrance onto the stage, Umberto somehow felt it would be more fitting to salute Catalano than to shake his hand. With his closely cropped blond hair and relentlessly neat appearance, Catalano struck Umberto more as a submarine captain than as a motion picture director.

"Thank you for coming, Umberto. I'm testing a new young girl and I want to see how the two of you look together on film." Catalano paused as if searching for just the right words. "This girl may seem somehow unappealing—she's stiff, a bit of mannequin perhaps. But I'm looking for an unusual type for Fiammetta Three. Before her feelings are revealed I'd like the audience to believe she has none. She'll be seen as a sort of science fiction creature—a female android, if you will."

Umberto could make her out at a distance—brightly lit as she stood in front of the camera. A wardrobe woman was attending to the folds of sheer netting draped over her otherwise naked body. And she did indeed give the impression of being made of some sort of plaster rather than flesh. On top of her skinny frame her neck and face seemed overwhelmed by an enormous bush of black hair, and her pubic hair was similarly full—

Umberto stopped dead in his tracks and forgot to breathe for a few seconds, nearly choking himself. He had not yet clearly seen the android's face, but he knew in the pit of his stomach, and below, that it was Pina . . .

# CHAPTER SEVEN

HELGA WOULD have preferred that her lunch with the director be at a fine restaurant in town, but since his return from the mountains Mariani had been spending long hours in his office at Cine Citta planning the storyboard for the filming of Fiammetta Two, and so had asked Helga if she would meet him at the studio for lunch. She'd hardly felt in a position to say no.

Helga now arrived at the Cine Citta restaurant a vision in reddish-brown—her tight woolen dress exactly matching the auburn of her straight, severely cut hair; her shoes and handbag glowing with highlights of red within the brown of the patent leather and a fingertip-length red fox jacket.

She headed for a secluded table at the far corner of the as yet unoccupied restaurant, placed her chair at an angle and sat sideways, crossing those gorgeous legs so as to present the most provocative view of them to Mariani on his arrival.

From her handbag she took a square silver compact studded with emeralds, a present from Paolo Piccolo, and checked in its mirror her full, sensuous mouth.

She was just reaching for her cigarettes when Umberto entered the restaurant, saw Helga and headed directly for her table.

Umberto was in a terrible state. The frown on his handsome face seemed permanently etched into his forehead, and his hands trembled slightly as he reached for a match to light her cigarette. He made a move to kiss her on the cheek, couldn't get around her crossed legs, decided to kiss her hand, took hold of the wrong one and burned himself on her newly lit Camel.

Helga had to laugh. After all, Umberto in distress was always charmingly funny, had amused millions of filmgoers with just such fumbling antics. And Helga adored this big puppydog whose offscreen life was as farcical as his movie scenarios. Five years ago she had dated Umberto when they had been making a movie together, but she had gone home with him only once, and during their attempted lovemaking he'd made her laugh so hard that the deed was impossible. She had been in a kneeling position on top of the sheets, literally holding her stomach with laughter, when the door swung open and Umberto's mother came in to find out what all the merriment was about. After that Helga had slipped on Umberto's robe and the three of them had drunk cocoa in the kitchen before she had dressed and Umberto had driven her home.

"Hey, pal, what's the trouble this time?" Helga said.

"Oh, Helgalina, Helgalina . . ." He took her left hand, the one without the cigarette, and buried his face in its palm.

Helga put her Camel into the ashtray, freeing her right hand, and stroked his curly brown head. Smiling down at his head, she reminded herself that he was the only man who'd ever endearingly added the Italian diminutive, *lina,* to her name. She might be tough and self-sufficient, but she was also, she privately admitted, a sucker for a show of genuine affection. Why hadn't any of the others ever called her Helgalina? Why hadn't any of them been attracted to anything but her hardest edges? She had a softer side, after all, and one sure way to bring it out was for a lover to call her Helgalina, little Helga, and really mean it.

"Helgalina . . ." Umberto said, sighing and moving a chair close to her. He paused, taking in her beauty, and momentarily forgot his troubles. "You look more beautiful than ever, Helgalina. You look positively *eatable*. Why am I not fortunate enough to be your lover?"

"Because you are my best pal, Umberto. My dear, dear friend. And sometimes that's more important," Helga said, playfully pulling at his ear. "Now then, pal, tell Helgalina what's troubling you."

Umberto's face clouded, he shook his curly brown head back and forth, and when he spoke he ran all the thoughts in his mind together, giving Helga a most confusing account.

"I've lost a Venus and my life is being ruined by a female android who won't give up her pursuit of me.

I can't go home. I hate living in a hotel. And Catalano is a mad director who may ruin his section of *Boccaccio Volgare*—"

"Whoa," Helga said. "Take one at a time. First tell me about the . . . what did you say? . . . female android."

And for the next ten minutes Umberto did just that . . . pouring out his woes about Pina. And as he did, some interesting plots to divert Pina from Umberto began to form in Helga's mind—interrupted when Helga spotted Mariani in the entranceway. First things first. She reminded herself that she was, after all, here to seduce Mariani and thereby secure for herself the part of Fiammetta Two. She quickly asked Umberto to leave her alone with the director, which he did after shaking hands with Mariani.

As Umberto walked off he saw his agent, Luigi Luna, at the pay phones—typical of Luigi, he was always on the telephone. Ralph de Rossi and the cameraman were at a table for four, so he walked over and asked if he could join them. Ralph smiled, pointed to a chair and poured Umberto a glass of wine.

By now there was a long line of people at the cold buffet table, and Mariani was one of those in line, Helga staying behind at the table distractedly consuming wine and debating whether or not she should order anything at all to eat. Mariani had quickiy taken her appetite away. They had briefly met once before at some function or other and she hadn't really observed him in any detail. Today her impression was close and overwhelming. He might be one of the better directors, but as a man—ugh. He was dirty and smelly, which disgusted her. When he had bent over to kiss her hand she'd been revolted by his greasy black hair, long, straggly and peppered with wafersized dandruff.

She watched now as he moved along in the line at the buffet. He had on threadbare woolen trousers that seemed to droop from his thin, hipless body and a faded plaid flannel shirt that was wrinkled as if he'd been sleeping in it for weeks. How could she possibly bring herself to be intimate with such a man? Maybe she'd have another look at the script of *Boccaccio Volgare*, see about playing one of the other Fiammettas.

She put her wine glass down, lit a cigarette and began to think of which of the other Fiammettas might be possible. Fiammetta One was under Ralph de Rossi's control. Ralph never screwed his leading ladies, probably never screwed anyone but his wife. He had very set ideas about casting, and anyway, she felt rather sure that Ralph didn't particularly like her as an actress. Fiammetta Two was actually the story she had wanted most to be in, but now she couldn't imagine being on the same set with loutish Franco Mariani. Fiammetta Three? Well, Fiammetta Three was being directed by that quick-tempered, cruel bastard Angelo Catalano, who would cast Astrid if she would agree to work with him again. And even if Astrid wouldn't, hadn't Umberto just told her that Catalano had a new girl in mind—some weird type with a single name . . . what was it—? Oh, yes, Pina. It seemed Fiammetta Three posed altogether too many obstacles. . . . As for Fiammetta Four, it was penciled in for Cleo. Its director, Vittorio Anastasio, had wanted Cleo Monti from the film's conception, and although Paolo Piccolo would give Helga anything, help her with anything, he would never do so if that something hurt his wife, Cleo . . .

Helga understood she could not have become Paolo's full-time mistress without Cleo's blessing.

So all in all, Helga decided, the odds seemed to be against her playing any of the other Fiammettas. Besides, she was convinced that she was perfect casting for the role of Fiammetta Two—and then an idea lit a wicked glow in her charcoal eyes. She threw her napkin on the table, got to her feet and headed for the pay phones to call her lover, her benefactor, Paolo Piccolo Monti. She would invite him this evening for his favorite sexual recreation, only she would not allow him to come until he had promised to have Mariani fired.

On her way to the phones she bumped into Mariani, hurriedly told him, terribly sorry, she couldn't stay for lunch. She'd completely forgotten—but she had to visit a sick friend.

Madeline, who was entering the restaurant at that moment, saw Helga rushing past. She wondered what was the matter, then turned again on her way to find Luigi Luna, who hadn't collected her at the dressing room but instead had telephoned and asked her to meet him at the restaurant. As she stood there she saw that all eyes were on her and once again felt selfconscious. She hoped one day these people would just accept her not as a foreigner but as one of their own.

Madeline was, in fact, misreading the attention focused on her. She had, quite simply, taken their breath away; her gently waved platinum hair falling softly on peach-tinted cheeks; her sweetly rounded breasts showing just enough in the V-neck of her ivory-colored, snugly form-fitting jersey dress; her white Russian lynx fur resting lightly on her shoulders . . . all framing a modern-day picture of a woman who lived up to her Venus billing.

Suddenly Ralph de Rossi came to her rescue, bowed, took her arm and led her to the table where the cameraman had already finished his lunch and gone back to the set, and where the smitten Umberto Cassini was rising to greet her.

"Miss Mandell . . ." Umberto kissed her hand, awkwardly, tried at the same time to pull out the chair for her and promptly lost his balance.

"Please, the name is Madeline," she said, smiling at his awkwardness and pleased that she had actually flustered him.

"We're delighted Hollywood's treasured Venus is in our humble midst, but may I ask why?" de Rossi said.

Venus again . . . she reined in her irritation. "I'm here to talk about Alfonso Razzi's new film," Madeline said, wondering what such a great director would think about her working for a mediocre one like Alfonso Razzi.

"Lucky man," Ralph said. "He always beats the rest of us to the most beautiful and talented actresses."

Madeline smiled prettily, at the same time wondering if de Rossi had really meant that or was he just being Italian-gallant? Or, worst of all, making fun of her?

Umberto, of course, couldn't seem to manage anything, except to admire and envy Ralph de Rossi's way with words. And then Luigi Luna arrived at the table, relieving the pressure. "*Ciao,* bella," he said, kissing Madeline's hand. "*Ciao,* Ralph. *Ciao,* Umberto."

The agent, always quick off the mark, before Ralph had a chance even to return the *ciao,* said to de Rossi, "Well, Ralph, here is your Fiammetta One. Is Madeline not *perfect* for the role?"

"Madeline is perfection itself, no question," de Rossi said, smiling at Madeline. "But perhaps the role is imperfect by comparison." And so he'd managed to be complimentary and noncommittal all at the same time. Then he quickly got up. "Please forgive us, but Umberto and I are due back on the set."

Umberto kissed Madeline's hand and said quickly before losing his nerve, "If you're still here when we've finished work, may I drive you home?"

"Yes," Madeline said without hesitation. Followed instantly by the realization of both Madeline and Umberto that they couldn't . . .

"I can't," they blurted out in near unison.

They laughed at the overlap, paused and looked regretfully at each other. Madeline had remembered her so plain apartment in the wrong part of town, Umberto that he hadn't come by car today.

Now trying to exclude Luigi, who had seated himself in Ralph's place, Umberto moved his chair closer to Madeline. "I was sorry you left the banquet early. I was hoping to have an opportunity to talk to you, dance with you . . . I would like to see you sometime—"

"You'll be seeing her every day," Luigi said. "I'm finishing off a deal and she'll be working here at Cine Citta."

Madeline could have strangled Luigi—either he was obtuse or thinking so much of his deal he couldn't see what was happening or trying to happen, in front of his nose.

"My car wouldn't start this morning, I need to take care of it right after work," Umberto was saying, "but may I get your number from Luigi and call you?"

"Yes . . . please do," Madeline said with ladylike reserve, at the same time visualizing him in her bed.

"Wonderful. This evening?"

"Yes . . ."

"Around seven?"

"Fine."

She seems reserved, Umberto thought. Still playing Venus? He hoped not. Feeling he had an edge and not wanting to lose it, as he got up he said, "I realize it's short notice but if you haven't already made plans for Saturday night, perhaps we could have a drink, or dinner?"

"Call me," she said quietly, and as she watched him walk off badly wished she'd been more positive. She should have shaken off her old defensiveness and told him straight out she was free and wanted to have dinner with him. Damn, now all she could do was hope he wasn't so put off he wouldn't call her. She turned to Luigi. "Please be *sure* and give him my number."

Luigi, finally aware, told her she "couldn't find a nicer fellow, Umberto is the salt of the earth."

"What about his reputation as a Don Juan?" Did she really care?

Luigi laughed. "It's a misreading of Umberto. His only real fault is that he's lazy, passive . . . so he seems to get himself trapped by starlets and the like when what he's really aching for is a wife and family."

Luigi then spent most of the lunch telling Madeline about Umberto, about his unfortunate but not serious romances, and Madeline began to get a picture of the man that altogether pleased her. He even, it seemed, could be funny, and basically was a modest fellow. When Luigi began to discuss the film contract, she told him not, under any circumstances, to lose the film on account of money. Much more, she had decided, could be at stake.

* * *

Acting on Madeline's instructions, Luigi concluded her modest, $15,000 deal shortly after lunch. With so little guaranteed, Luigi wanted the producers to draw up two contracts—one official, the other a private document. That way only half the money would be white, or taxable; the other half would be black, given under the table and free from deductions. But Madeline was uncomfortable about cheating and told Luigi she would have none of it. Fifteen thousand taxable dollars, or the equivalent in lira, would have to do.

Luigi knew Madeline deserved a much larger salary, but this was her first Italian film—a way to get her started, to let it be known that she was willing to work in European films. Eventually she might be a gold mine for him. When he had seen her with Ralph de Rossi he had suggested her for Fiammetta One—just off the top of his head, but it was a terrific idea. She would be perfect casting and he intended to pursue de Rossi about it.

It was 4:00 P.M. when Madeline knew for certain that she had been chosen for Alfonso Razzi's *Paranoia*. The makeup, hair and wardrobe discussions had gone to her satisfaction, and there was nothing more to do until Monday morning, when the official preproduction began. But it was too early for her to go home, and besides, she felt far too happy to shut herself away in her cramped, cold, lonely apartment—especially on a Saturday evening. So she telephoned Astrid, telling her that she had all kinds of exciting news and was bursting to talk to someone.

"Well, my French boy is here," Astrid said. "But that's all right. Please come and join us. He's sweet and beautiful to look at, and you can say anything you want in front of him because he doesn't speak a word of anything but French . . . Oh, please do something for me. I'll teach you the French for 'What is your name?' and you must then find out for me if my beautiful boy is called Jean Paul or Jean Claude. But come, please do come and join us . . ."

Jean Paul or Jean Claude? Madeline had to smile at the subterfuge for what seemed so simple a matter. But when she joined them the smile left her face. She wanted to faint on the spot. Astrid opened the door stark naked, gripped Madeline's arm and guided her two paces into the next room, where the French boy, also totally nude, was sitting up in bed. His eyes shone with a new excitement when he saw Madeline. As he said, *"Bon soir,* Madeline," he patted the bed for her to sit down beside him.

And Astrid was saying matter-of-factly, "Make yourself comfortable, darling Madeline. I'll pop some champagne for you and I and, uh . . . Jean will have a nice long chat and afterward a nice long, leisurely *ménage à trois.*"

# CHAPTER EIGHT

NOT JEAN, not Jacques, not any of them . . . there was only one man that Astrid had ever loved—the brilliant, volatile Angelo Catalano, the only person who could control her or force her to keep her mind on her career. Possibly because Astrid was exceptionally tall and gave an initial impression of maturity, people thought of her as older than her twenty-four years. The truth of it was that she was not only young but reckless, often out of control . . . which at times frightened even her, her lust threatening to overwhelm everything, including her ambition.

At age ten Astrid, already tall and with a natural ability for athletics, had been offered a contract to train for the Norwegian National Athletic Team and her parents had insisted that she accept the offer. Astrid had cried at the thought of leaving home but her parents had gone ahead and signed the papers committing her to the care of the state. The regimented atmosphere of the training camp changed sports from fun to a drudgery she only tolerated, looking forward to the day when she was old enough to break away. During training her supervisors had kept her a shut-in, so although she had sexually experimented in a childish fashion with some of the other young girls, she had never known a man intimately . . . not, that is, until Angelo Catalano came along.

It was Catalano who had been responsible for bringing her to Rome and introducing her to films. During the mid-fifties he had seen her at the Winter Olympics, where the then seventeen-year-old Astrid, though not winning any medals, had displayed an all-around athletic ability in the ice-skating competition. He had noted her remarkable body and had felt that she would be perfect for his latest adventure film. He needed a female who could perform masculine stunts while at the same time looking highly desirable in a bikini. Astrid, he was convinced, filled the bill, embodying as she did the best of both sexes. The public had confirmed his judgment, going mad for that image, and Astrid had become a box-office sensation.

Catalano did not become her lover until he had directed her in that first highly successful film, jealously guarding his discovery from the competition. Once he did become her lover he wanted to possess her, body and soul. Compulsively jealous, he kept young Astrid a virtual prisoner in his home, not allowing her to see any strangers, and never took her out. He hired a cleaning woman to come in once a week, but mostly Astrid was expected to do the housework, the cooking and even iron his shirts, all the while working long hours as the star of his films. Too tired even to think about affairs with other men, she was dependent on him for everything, materially and emotionally. She thought she loved him . . . she had no experience to measure him against . . . and he used her dependent love as a weapon against her. With a schizophrenic's typically extreme mood swings, Catalano kept her in a state of constant confusion and subservience. When she complained too much, he beat her, creating a perverse circle of "crime" and punishment. Her one release was in acting, which was also her escape. Astrid's later turn to women was for a human kindness and warmth she never got from perverse Angelo Catalano.

Since she had, presumably, managed to break away from Catalano . . . it had been two years now . . . she had abandoned herself to sensuality, devoured almost anyone and everyone who crossed her path, including, in spite of the brutal experience with Catalano, the opposite sex. Yes, she still had the desire to be with a man, and sometimes she wondered if every new man wasn't a substitute for Angelo Catalano who, it seemed, still had some hypnotic hold over her. Deny it as she might, she still thought of him, sometimes physically ached for him. She wished it were otherwise, and if she sought for Angelo in other males, her promiscuous devouring of them, as well as women, one after another, was also an effort to break Angelo's lingering hold over her. No wonder she worried he would get her back as before if she dared work with him again by appearing in his segment of *Boccaccio Volgare.* And yet she just had to be in that film . . .

* * *

By the end of work that Saturday, Angelo Catalano had closely observed Pina's every attitude, voice change, movement and facial expression to discover every nuance possible about this girl for the benefit of his film.

In such line of duty, he also needed to explore her sexually. He had no personal interest in this mannequin. To him she was like an animal in a laboratory experiment. But he considered directing a precise, calculated art form, and to master it one needed to be master not only of the script and photography but also of the actors. He must know his subjects totally, and most important, he must be certain of their obedience. For this, in Pina's case, it was necessary that she be further tested in the seclusion of his villa.

It had been too early for dinner but no matter, cooking was only a test. The meal she had prepared was inedible, and so he had rubbed her nose in it, as one might in training an incontinent pet dog. She hadn't cried out, which was good, but she had presumed to worry about her makeup. He had promptly smeared her face in the butter mound.

She had also objected to doing the dishes—intolerable and willful insubordination, based, so she said, on her concern for the preservation of her lovely long fingernails. He had pinned her to the floor, sat on her chest and snipped off those painted talons with the kitchen shears.

When she had undressed too slowly in an effort to care for her clothing, he had thrown her on the bed and literally ripped her clothes from her body, then had dragged her into the bathroom and held her under the shower.

Once she had emerged, wrapped in a towel, he

had directed her to go back and lie on the tiles of the bathroom floor with her legs spread wide. He would, he explained, enter her, come speedily. Under no circumstances was she to cry out or make the slightest movement in an effort to evade him.

On finding her too dry for penetration, he had slapped her face and ordered her to do something to make his entering more agreeable. She had said she had no idea how to solve the problem. He had then told her to raise her parted legs high in the air, support herself by placing her fists under her buttocks. He had thought of easing the passageway with shaving foam, which now led to another idea . . . she had too much pubic hair for the nude scenes in the film, so he spurted the foam over her stomach and thighs and with the straight-edged razor shaved her, then stood back and observed her. Shivering there on the bathroom floor, she looked like a naked, hairless rat. He would not demean himself by fucking her. And after some further consideration, he extended that rejection to her appearing in his film.

She was to be out of the villa by the time he counted to ten, slowly . . . he was not, after all, an unreasonable man. He went into his study to reconsider the casting, but already knew who he must have for Fiammetta Three. He had, he decided, known all along. He picked up the phone and dialed the number for Astrid Zealand . . .

Astrid heard the phone ringing but could not possibly answer it. She felt as though she were standing on her head, or hanging upside down from the ceiling. She could not hear or see Jean Paul or Jean Claude or whatever his name was . . . Her head was on the floor and she was gripping the legs of a nearby chair for support. Her stomach overlapped the edge of the bed, her knees slightly bent and digging into the mattress, and her rear end was feeling chilly, somehow more exposed to the draft than the rest of her naked body. Nothing, though, was happening, and there were no sounds except now from the telephone. Could her French boy be out of the room or sleeping above her on the bed? Had he finally given out? She was too exhausted to look, answer the phone or even move to a more comfortable position.

How many hours had they been making love? She was too tired to count. They had only taken three real breaks—or was it four? Well, there was a break while they had toast and tea for breakfast. They'd also eaten lunch . . . Jean had whipped up a delicious omelet with a salad. Afterward they had taken a shower together but that didn't count because he had mounted her from behind when she'd bent over to retrieve the soap. Around four they'd had a cup of tea, then had taken another shower, but he had entered her from the front while she shampooed her hair. He had dried her hair for her and combed it expertly, but she had simultaneously given him her famed blow job. An hour later she had gotten out of bed to answer Madeline's knock. Too bad Madeline hadn't been willing to play. It would have been lovely with three, and not nearly so exhausting if another partner had been there for Jean to have a go at.

He was, indeed, formidable. The more time that passed, the more energetic he seemed to become. Since Madeline left he had been positively acrobatic. She didn't for a moment think she could ever repeat all the routines or recall all the positions. At least she'd discovered that she was still agile, although it had been over seven years since her days as an athlete.

Perhaps she should make the effort to get her

head and shoulders off the floor and answer the telephone, then get into bed properly and cover herself. He was no doubt at last sleeping, and she should also get some rest . . . Suddenly she felt her rump being hoisted, a cold lubricant injected into her anus, his penis following. He took hold of her shoulders and raised her in a viselike grip, using the length of her body as a lever to press himself in and out.

Astrid drew a deep breath and thought about the telephone, which had not stopped ringing. There could only be one person with that kind of persistence. She would have to answer sooner or later, but the thought of speaking to Catalano was altogether terrifying. He knew her well, too damn well, knew how desperately she wanted to be in the *Boccaccio* film. He might, just might, be calling to offer her the part, knowing well that she would not have the strength to turn it down.

# CHAPTER NINE

AS DARKNESS descended on Rome that first day of the Siberian wind, the temperature dropped still further and the rain turned to sleet. Because of a lack of heating in the buildings, few inhabitants of the city were willing to take off their outer clothing or even their overcoats.

Helga Haufman, however, was nude and feeling quite comfortable. She had run extension cords from all the other rooms in her apartment and concentrated most of the available current into the bedroom for the purpose of operating a dozen electric heaters.

Paolo Piccolo was also nude but feeling uncomfortably hot. He was lying on his back, spread-eagled on Helga's mattress, which was exposed here and there where the black satin sheet had rumpled under his weight. His hands were tied by ropes to her Gothic headboard, his feet were belted to either side of the thick foot posts. He was twitching, further wrinkling the damp black sheet, but was unable to move about much because of his bondage.

Paolo was biting his lips as Helga knelt over his massive body, holding the telephone receiver in one hand and in the other the feather duster with which she was mercilessly tickling him. The feather duster was Paolo's, kept for him as one of Helga's instruments. As for the receiver in her other hand, well, Helga was one of those people whose lives revolved around the telephone. At the moment she was talking to Madeline, who had just called and seemed very much in need of advice and consolation. "Look, Madeline," Helga was saying, "it sounds as if you should not be alone. Come here for the evening. Just ring and my maid Giuseppina will let you in . . . just wait for a while in the kitchen where it's warm and I'll join you as soon as Paolo leaves."

Helga, looking between her spread knees, noted that Paolo's unattended little pickle had lost its erection. So while Madeline spoke she brought her head down, ear still to the receiver, and nibbled on its weeny knob until it once again swelled to capacity. Then, before answering Madeline's last question, for good measure she flicked it with the feather duster.

"No, no, it's fine," Helga told Madeline. "Cleo is expecting Paolo home for dinner."

At which point Paolo cried out, "Please, Helga, let me come . . ."

"Never!" she answered sharply.

"What?" Madeline asked.

"Nothing," Helga said into the mouthpiece. "I'll expect you soon. *Ciao*, Madeline."

The instant Helga hung up the telephone it rang again.

"Please, don't answer it. Please, Helga, let me come . . ."

Responding at the same time to both Paolo and the telephone, Helga inadvertently said into the mouthpiece, "Shut *up*, you naughty, naughty boy . . ."

An agitated male voice on the other end of the line said, "Oh, what have I done Miss Haufman?"

"Who is this?"

"It is Primo Galiano. Do you remember me—from the banquet last night?" And then, out of his insecurity, hurriedly added, "I'm Serena Blaire's husband."

Helga's voice turned seductive. "Of *course*, you are. How could I possibly forget you?"

Just those guttural sounds of hers made Primo's cock rise to attention. He reached for it and promptly felt guilty. He was standing in a phone box across the street from the Immaculate Heart with a clear view of the church. He had just finished his longer than usual penitence after his usual Saturday visit to confession.

This week, Primo's confession centered around the bad thoughts brought on by the sultry German actress. He had not been able to get her out of his mind since she had danced so closely with him and whispered these titillating things in his ear. He had slept late that day because of the cold and because Serena was going to be away in Geneva. And he had felt so sexy and cozy in the bed that he'd masturbated twice before ringing for his breakfast tray. He had masturbated once again in the warm soapy suds of his bath, but nothing had seemed to quench his thirst for those juicy parts of the female body. Indeed, as contrite as he had felt for his sins, even when recounting his forbidden thoughts about Helga to the priest, he had not been able to control getting an erection right there in the confessional.

After kneeling so long reciting his rosary and his acts of contrition, his body was painfully stiff and his knees all but numb. Still, when he had seen the phone box outside the church he had been unable to overcome the temptation just to hear Helga's voice one more time . . .

Now that voice was saying to him, "I want to see you. Tonight. Come here at ten o'clock sharp. Don't be a minute late—or a minute early either." Helga hung up with out a good-bye.

"Who was that on the phone?" Paolo wanted to know. "Who were you flirting with? Who's coming here at ten tonight—?"

"You have no reason to be jealous, you great mountain of a man. Now will you or won't you do what I asked of you?"

"I can't, Helga. I'm only a financier. I can't interfere with the artistic side of the film—"

He gasped as she squeezed his balls. "Wait, *wait* . . . all right, I can make it known that it would please me to see you cast in the part, a certain pressure can be put on the director but I can't—"

The phone again.

"Please don't answer it, Helga, please let me come, then untie me so I can go home . . ."

"Hello," Helga said into the phone, ignoring him.

"*Ciao,* Helga, it's me, Cleo. Has Paolo come yet?"

"No."

"You must please make him come many, many times," Cleo said. "My poor breasts are packed in ice. I want no more sex with Paolo until I've recovered. Please, please Helga," Cleo went on, "I want you to make my Paolo very happy—and for me you must make him very, very tired . . ."

When she was finished with Cleo, Helga left the receiver off the hook, twisted the telephone cord around Paolo's penis, and began tugging it up and down. "You see, my phone is off the hook and I am going to concentrate on doing unspeakable things to you."

"Ohoooh . . . yes, just like that, just like that, don't stop, I'm coming—"

"No you are *not.*" And she abruptly stopped the action, unwound the telephone cord from his penis and put the receiver back on the hook. "You are *first* going to make me a promise. I want Mariani fired. I want him replaced by another director."

"Helga, be reasonable, I can't do it. Please, darling, please let me come—"

She squatted on top of his miniature erection, then refused to move a muscle.

The telephone again.

*"Don't answer it,"* Paolo screamed out. "No more, for God's sake—"

*"You* don't tell *me* what to do," Helga said. "*I* am in charge now."

Paolo began to make pitiful sounds, which Helga interrupted by moving herself forward and settling down on his face, thereby covering his mouth.

The telephone ringing . . . Helga, looking over her shoulder, reached around and picked up the receiver. But now it was her turn to be abruptly diverted . . . just as she was about to say hello, Paolo began energetically to suck at her, and the "hello" came out part meow—"Helleow," she purred, eyes closed, breathing deeply.

"Is that you, Helgalina?" Umberto was saying. "Am I . . . interrupting anything?"

"Well, yes . . . but tell me why you're calling."

Followed by a short tap at the door, then Giuseppina opening it a crack and sticking her head in. "A Madeline Mandell is outside," Giuseppina said, observing but indifferent to the scene on the bed, which she had witnessed countless times during her years with Helga.

"Well let her in," Helga ordered.

"What?" Umberto asked.

"Nothing," Helga said. "What can I do for you, you lovely man?"

"Can you give me Madeline Mandell's phone number?"

"I—but here she is!" Helga said in surprise. "She just walked in."

Giuseppina had ushered Madeline directly into the bedroom.

Madeline stood there in shock—staring at a naked Paolo tied to the bed, a naked Helga squatting on his face, Helga holding the phone out to her and saying, "It's for you. It's Umberto."

A moment of silence. Then: "She's there?" Umberto was asking. And when he heard nothing in reply he hurried on . . . "Hello, hello, *hello,* Helga? Did you say Madeline is there?"

When Helga's voice at last came through to him, it sounded strained and distant. "Well, she was here, a moment ago . . ."

"Did you say *was*? Did you tell her I wanted to talk to her?"

"Yes, Umberto . . ."

Actually, Helga was sorry that Madeline had witnessed such a scene, then realized it was all Giuseppina's fault. "Giuseppina," she shouted, all but breaking Umberto's eardrum.

*"Ouch!"*

"I am sorry, Umberto, but that stupid—"

Giuseppina stuck her head in the doorway, looking sheepish.

"Hold on a minute, Umberto." Helga placed a pillow over the telephone to safeguard Umberto's eardrum, then screamed, "Giuseppina, you *idiot.* When I said to let her in I meant let her in the house. I did *not* mean bring her into the bedroom. Now get out—no, wait—where is she now?"

"She left," Giuseppina said, shrugging her shoulders. "She was in a very big hurry to get out the front door . . ." Giuseppina then hesitated, trying to think if there was something else she should say, a hesitation that seemed to reignite Helga.

"Get out, get out, and go home, damn you. I am sick of looking at you . . ."

Following which Giuseppina withdrew her head and shut the door.

Helga took a deep breath. "Now let me see, where were we?" she asked huskily, leaning down and gently stroking Paolo's half-hidden face.

She raised herself off his mouth, turned completely around, wiggled her bottom and adjusted herself again so that she and Paolo formed the figure 69, oblivious to the telephone voice that was smothered under a forgotten pillow.

Umberto, whose repeated hellos received no response, eventually hung up, troubled by what might have been going on at Helga's apartment. Why had Madeline refused to speak to him? It had all sounded peculiar . . . like an orgy? Could the divine Madeline be involved in such a thing? The very notion had a shattering effect.

Shattering was also the effect on Madeline of what she had seen and her presumption that Umberto was involved. Huddled by the fire in her tiny apartment, she was thinking the worst of Umberto, and all the rest of *them* . . . This Italian movie world was apparently full of nothing but degenerates. At the drop of a hat they all stripped and went at it. Astrid had been casual as you please about inviting her to make love in a threesome. Helga had told her maid to bring her right into the bedroom so she could witness Paolo in bondage—with Helga actually squatting there on his face. What was she expected to do—watch? Is that what Cleo did? Or did they all do it together?

And what about Umberto? Why had he been on the telephone at that moment, asking to speak to her? And if she had taken the call what would he have said to her? "Take your clothes off and I'll be right over . . ." Had her invitation to Helga's apartment been a set-up for a *ménage à quatre?* Complete with *bondage?*

What she craved right now was some old-fashioned sex, which seemed in short supply in this city. Failing that, she could at least use some warmth and comfort, a strong shoulder to lean on, at least a *normal* human being to talk to. Her only prospect, though, at 7:00 P.M. on this bitterly cold evening, was a long, lonely Saturday night. *Arrivederci, Roma* . . .

# CHAPTER TEN

SERENA'S MISSION in Geneva was to conclude a secret deal she had been working on for months, ever since she had decided that *Boccaccio* was the film for her. Today, with all negotiations completed, she had flown in to witness the signing.

It had been her brainchild and she had hired top legal advisers to come up with the structure for a film investment company, then had personally gone to the banks and gotten their commitments. The newly formed company's first maneuver was a take-over bid for the investors' share of *Boccaccio Volgare*. She would be a silent member of the company's board of directors. Her name, of course, would never surface, but she would have effective control. Secrecy meant vital documents never leaving Switzerland, never discussing confidential business over the phone. She might need to fly to Geneva often, perhaps every week in the early stages, but today she was anxious to get back to Rome.

Concocting, and especially finishing off, wicked schemes had a special, delicious effect on Serena . . . it made her sexy. And this had been such a great day in that department that she had spent it all but possessed by erotic thoughts . . . which centered around Umberto. She wanted him, she had decided, wanted him before the filming began. Because once the cameras rolled, she would, of course, have to dump him. She never mixed business and pleasure, never gave the man an upper hand, a chance to use or threaten sexual blackmail. Since above all she wanted Umberto as her leading man, she could hardly keep him as her lover when the time came to screw him out of first position on *Boccaccio.*

For now, though, all her thoughts were on a much more basic kind of pleasuring herself with Umberto. Even the thrill of viewing her gold bullion faded with the closing of the vault, but thinking about Umberto produced a longing that refused to go away. He was, no question, a very appealing man . . . gentle and sexy all at once. There was also that reputation of his, which acted as a sort of aphrodisiac. And, above all, she was just badly in need of a good solid fucking . . . like the acton she at one time had gotten from Primo. Why the hell had he stopped screwing her? She never knew, he never said. Too bad, because what else was he good for?

She had telephoned Umberto twice that day on the set at Cine Citta, and he had let her know that he had no plans for the evening. Both times, though, he had seemed a bit reluctant to commit himself. She had told him she would call again when she got to the Geneva airport, and she felt hopeful when he said that he would be in his hotel room at seven to take her call.

It was seven now. She could be in Rome before ten, in time for dinner. Swiss Air was always punctual so there was no worry about leaving Geneva on schedule. There was no worry about Primo either. She hadn't given any indication about when she planned to return to Rome so he wouldn't know if she slipped into the city tonight.

Umberto was staying at the Hilton. Perfect. A hotel room already reserved, with no need for that awkward moment at the registration desk. She could go directly to his room without anyone knowing. They could order room service, then spend the night in bed—or on the couch—or on the floor. Who cared where? She hadn't had a man since Primo stopped coming to her bed over a year ago. If her desire had cooled after the baby, it was back now, full force, stronger than she'd ever known. She felt herself become flushed in anticipation as she asked the operator to place the call, felt deep down inside her a delicious ache of anticipation . . .

When the telephone rang, Umberto was in his bathrobe, sitting on the sofa, staring into space. He'd taken a shower but had not gotten around to dressing because he had no special place to go. He'd been wondering what to do that evening. If he went out on the town drinking he knew he'd end up with some easy-target starlet just to get his rocks off. And after his experience with Pina he had made a resolution not to get involved with unpredictable young girls. They also, like Pina, scared the hell out of him . . .

Until he heard her voice he had completely forgotten that Serena Blaire had told him she would call at seven. And no wonder. He'd had Madeline on his mind—had hoped at least to take her to dinner, maybe manage to make love to her afterward. Well, his illusions about this Venus from America had turned to disillusion when he'd accidentally found out her real penchants . . . it seemed he was far too square to satisfy the tastes of the lady from Hollywood. She hadn't even wanted to take time out from the noisy orgy to talk to him on the telephone. One more disillusionment for the Latin lover . . . He had better look elsewhere for some satisfaction, and be careful not to get involved.

Serena Blaire seemed to fit the bill on both counts. Here she was inviting herself to dinner in his hotel room. An unexpected piece of good luck to divert him from his disillusion over Madeline Mandell. She was delivering her body right to his door, he didn't even need to step foot outside in the cold wind and take her to some damn restaurant before getting the relief he was after. No courting Serena . . . she'd be only steps away from his bed. No dissembling necessary . . . she must know very well what to expect—and she must even want it.

True, Serena wasn't exactly his type . . . too thin, for one thing, but never mind, she was a gift on a platter when his table had been bare. And, in fairness, she *was* vivacious, and cute, even pretty. All in all, under the present circumstances, she was the perfect unencumbered gift for a cold Saturday night.

Although he may have at first sounded a bit remote, he now warmed up and told Serena Blaire to hurry over, that he'd be delighted to see her.

A few minutes before ten, there was a tapping on his door. Serena to the rescue. After her phone call he had dressed in gray trousers and a smoking jacket, ordered dinner, now delivered: cold lobster and champagne. He had even remembered to tell the switchboard operator to hold all his calls. He intended to get the famed British star out of her panties without interruption.

He opened the door, which framed a smiling Serena in a white woolen suit with a large fur hat setting off her adorable pixie face—just the way she looked in her movies. Well, play it like a movie, he told himself. Lights, camera, action. He shut the door behind her, promptly took her in his arms and kissed her full on the lips. Ralph de Rossi couldn't have directed it better.

He proceeded to uncork the champagne as the imaginary cameras rolled. Serena removed her jacket and hat, deftly arranged the ringlets of her short dark hair. When he handed her a glass she smiled her radiant smile and brushed his outstretched arm with her fingertips. The cameras continued to roll. The scene was working to perfection. Umberto felt like a tiger—sure, smug, altogether in control.

Now Serena held her glass up to his, they clinked and toasted one another while looking directly into each other's eyes. At dinner, which both understood without so saying was a brief preface to the main event, she spoke gaily, amusingly, telling him piquant if somewhat spicy stories about this one and that. Never one for gossip, he was nonetheless grateful to have the burden of conversation taken over by Serena. And through it all, Serena Blaire was somehow the lady. Yes, thank heavens there were still *some* of them left, he thought, thinking briefly and ruefully about his disenchantment with the once and no longer so divine Madeline.

He found he enjoyed listening to Serena's cultured voice, her witty turns of phrase, her use of the French language. He spoke some French but his was the crude argot of the streets. He'd never studied the language, had simply willy-nilly picked it up over the years thanks to its similarity to Italian.

Umberto's obvious fondness for lobster clued Serena to insist he take most of hers, without making him feel that he was being greedy. When they had finished the meal she stood up, still gaily laughing and talking, came over to his side of the table and slid it away. Finishing her last amusing anecdote, she kicked off her shoes, sat down in his lap to remove her stockings, all accomplished naturally and casually, as though they had been intimate for years.

Umberto, at once grateful and excited, commenced nuzzling her neck as he unbuttoned her blouse. She smiled, waited, stopped her chatter. He moved his hand down the front of her slip—she wore no bra, had no need for one with her diminutive breasts, and began rubbing one of her nipples. Instantly she put back her head, closed her eyes, opened her mouth and quickened her breathing. He quickly pulled her head forward and covered her open mouth with his own, sucking on her tongue, then moved his hand up her skirt, pulled the crotch of her panties aside. She was ready and wet.

He stood up and carried her over to the bed. He eased her skirt up to her waist, again pulled the crotch of her panties aside, bent down and slowly, very slowly, began licking at her, and at the same time entering her with his thumb, gently moving it back and forth. It took only a few moments for her body to go rigid, then into the relieving spasms of orgasm.

While she rested, smiling up at him, he stood up and quickly got out of his clothes. He again knelt over her, raised her to a half-sitting position. He coaxed her slip straps down around her shoulders, exposing her breasts. He lifted her up until her back rested against the headboard, then took her nipples between thumb and forefinger of both hands, massaging them with firmness until they were hard, red and distended. He lowered his head, alternated sucking one and then the other nipple while continuing to manipulate the unattended one.

He still hadn't taken off her clothes, he'd been too mesmerized watching, feeling her reactions. This lady was hungry, starved. He could tell by her startled cries, quick breathing . . . very different from the phony moans and groans some women gave out with to impress without really feeling. Serena Blaire was a neglected female. She seemed *grateful* to him, so appreciative, he could hardly not treat her to the works. He'd show this proper little English lady how a real Italian lover could take her out of this world, out of herself. They had the whole night in front of them, there would be plenty of time later for him to think about his own needs.

And so he spent who knew how long stroking and licking and sucking her—in all directions, in all ways, until she had come so many times that at last she was limp as a ragdoll. At which point, with her clothes still on, he pulled off her soaking French panties, entered her and began fucking her as she lay back, happily unresisting, opening herself wider and wider for him.

Primo Galiano was also a participant in the erotica of this Saturday night. At precisely ten o'clock Helga had opened the door to find a love-sick puppy on her doorstep. Over a drink she'd tried to plant a number of self-serving ideas into Primo's thick skull, but he had seemed unable to concentrate. So Helga had decided there was nothing for it but to let him do her . . . and get it over with. And so at the same time Umberto was banging Serena, an overjoyed Primo was banging the girl of his fantasies, the wondrously sultry Helga Haufman.

Helga was taking his blows courageously, but was getting impatient with the buffeting. Primo had been hammering at her for what must hold the record, she thought, as the longest single fuck in history. And with his large, hard cock she was feeling a decided irritation with each consecutive thrust. Who would have thought that this little puppy could be such a stud? If she had known she might have insisted on some foreplay, but it had started without her feeling any excitement. Then she'd been startled to realize it was a cock of such extraordinary proportions that it traveled to regions within her where no man had ever gone before. If this was supposed to be a way of getting a hold over him and, through him, Serena . . . Helga now had to ask herself, who's fucking whom?

She had tried every trick in her considerable repertoire but she could not get him to come. She was worn out, almost desperate to get him off her, so finally she decided to ask the man himself what the liberating secret might be.

"Tell me, Primo, what would excite you enough to make you shoot off?"

"I don't know, I don't know," he said, straining even more.

Helga winced with the pain. "There must be *something* you like, something that makes it happen . . ."

"Your voice, your voice—"

"What about my voice?"

"Say something to me . . . something dirty, the worst things you can think of . . ."

Helga was lost. Dirty words? It seemed ridiculous. Earthy language was her everyday vernacular. Did he mean like bodily functions, parts of the human body? What was dirty about natural life functions?

"Like *what,* Primo?" she coaxed him. "Give me some help . . ."

He blushed as he thought of some of those forbidden dirty words, the ones his mother had washed his mouth out with soap for saying when he was a child. But when he tried to whisper them he couldn't bring himself to say anything but childish substitutes.

After he'd come, Umberto picked up the phone and asked for room service. He would order a big rare steak, some French fries, a liter of beer. Screwing always made him hungry and thirsty, especially a screwing like he'd just given the not-so-ladylike Serena Blaire. He had also offered to order something for her, but Serena had merely flopped over on her side and waved him away in a small gesture of delicious helplessness . . .

Helga too was feeling helpless. She'd been repeating every scatalogical word, phrase, joke she'd ever heard, but it seemed useless. She was lost, beginning to parrot herself. But Primo's cock was still hard as a rock with no sign of an approaching ejaculation. It seemed he might go on hammering into her cavernous cunt forever.

Desperation became the mother of inspiration . . . Try some terrible image. Primo seemed burdened down with guilt. Many Italian men, she knew, were—it came from their mothers and the church. Yes, she would try an image, even act it out. What the hell, she was a good actress. She'd better be, or risk literally getting fucked to death . . . She managed to raise herself up on her elbows, looked fixedly at an imaginary person in the doorway, pointed and shouted at Primo, "Look, you dirty, dirty boy. It's your *mother.* Look, she's standing right there in the doorway watching you, Primo. Every move you make. Your mother is shocked, your own mother is actually watching you—"

Primo yowled and shot off.

Helga lay back, saved by her art.

# CHAPTER ELEVEN

THE SUNDAY newspapers carried the story of the movie world's new illicit romance accompanied by blowups of Serena Blaire in the arms of Umberto Cassini. Even the sober *Il Messaggero,* which condemned such liaisons, prominently displayed the couple on its front page, and *Il Tempo* devoted a centerfold to them, including a photograph of Primo wedged between the alleged lovers with the caption "DIVORZIO?"

Primo was among the first to see the headlines. He hadn't been home since Helga ordered him out of her apartment around midnight. He had too much on his mind, his adultery . . . not with a whore, a *putana,* but with a famous movie star like Helga. If

Serena found out . . . Not to mention the terrible guilt he felt over the scene Helga had concocted just before he came—too terrible even to think about . . .

Helga lived on Via Calabria, which merged with Via Veneto at the site of the American embassy. Primo had turned right and walked up the Veneto to Harry's Bar, where he'd forgotten his pledge to diet and ordered a plate of the late-night drinking person's spaghetti, which had no real sauce but an olive oil spiced with garlic and hot peppers. Then, as the respectable places closed down around 2:00 A.M., he had gone to the coffee shop at the Stazione Termini and sat there among the other lost souls. It was at the train station that he'd been on hand to get the first editions of the Sunday papers as they were distributed.

After his Saturday confession, he'd sinned even more. He was no longer cleansed and so could not accept the sacrament. But he still would go to mass and afterward in one of the small chapels pray for understanding of the weakness of his miserable flesh. Until he had done at least that, he didn't have the courage to face the family over the traditional Sunday lunch . . . He always drove twenty miles out of Rome to Zagarolo to spend the day with his mother and various members of the Galiano family. Even after the longest contrition he didn't know how he was going to look his mother in the eye . . . that image Helga had called up for him of his mother standing in the doorway . . . somehow his mother would know what he had done, she always had when he was little. She would only need to look at him and see adultery written all over his face. Adultery *and* betrayal of his *tesora,* his Serena. Should he confess and ask them both for forgiveness? And if he did, would he lose the two most important women in his life? Perhaps later in church he would ask the Virgin Mary for a sign . . .

But the sign presented itself before the asking, in the Sunday papers. It was Serena in a supposed scandal, and in view of the attention it would get, his own transgression might best be forgotten, never mentioned. Except once again he felt the sting of guilt. It was he who was the adulterer, they were just slandering his *tesora.* He knew it wasn't true what they said. He'd been there at the time and she'd only danced with Umberto. Serena would be terribly upset by the headlines. Thank God she was out of town. He would suggest that until the gossip died down she stay in Switzerland . . .

Serena was not, of course, in Switzerland but a few miles away at the Hilton, and not in the least bit troubled by the headlines. At 8:00 A.M., dressed only in one of Umberto's shirts, she was sitting up in his hotel bed surrounded by Sunday's papers. Umberto was asleep beside her. Serena smiled, first at him, then at the papers. Exactly as she'd planned it. The more the two of them were linked, the better her chances of being the major force among the Fiammettas. Whoever had Umberto had the female side of the picture.

There was a knock at the door and Umberto stirred in his sleep. Serena had sent her clothes to be pressed and the valet was now returning them. She gave him some coins, closed the door and went into the bathroom to dress. She must get home and telephone her agent in Hollywood. She could do it in peace because Primo always spent Sundays in Zagarolo with the rest of the roosters. Before tiptoeing out of the hotel room, Serena carefully folded the Sunday papers and took them with her. What Umberto didn't know wouldn't hurt him.

Cleo Monti was sitting up in her bed crumpling the Sunday newspapers and throwing them to the floor. She had expected to find a picture or two of herself with Paolo as he was presented with his award from the motion picture industry. Instead there were all these damned photographs of Serena and Umberto, the captions speculating about a budding romance. And not a single mention of Paolo's award! It was enough to make her cancel her subcriptions.

She picked up the phone to complain to her mother, then changed her mind and dialed the Hilton. She would talk first to Umberto, give him a piece of her mind. He couldn't *seriously* be thinking of having an affair with Serena Blaire. The switchboard operator kept her waiting, then came back on the line to inform Cleo that, since early last evening and until further notice, a hold had been placed on all calls to Signor Cassini's room.

Vittorio Anastasio, one of the directors of *Boccaccio Volgare,* got a busy signal when he tried to reach Cleo. Well, he thought, at least it gave him an excuse to put off telling her the bad news. Vittorio had promised the part of Fiammetta Four to Cleo. In fact, he had considered her his first and only choice to play that role, but when he had seen the day's newspapers, seen the photographs of Serena Blaire with Umberto, seen how well they looked together . . . well, he also realized that Serena Blaire would make for much better chemistry with Umberto. He regretted hurting Cleo, but still . . .

Vittorio Anastasio was a nobleman, the aristocrat of directors, although at first glance he looked less like a White Russian count than he did a robust country peasant. To the discerning eye, his well-worn, expensive tweeds were a sign of that status, where old money had no need of exhibitionism. He lived well off the interest from the family wealth, which had been smuggled out of Russia just before the Revolution and was still hidden safely in a bank in Zurich. When Italy's Communists had become a political force the vast estates he had inherited from the Italian side of his family had been placed in trust, so now he didn't need to be concerned about looking after their management. While he spent most of his time with his dogs and horses or with his friends at the country club, directing motion pictures was the outlet he had chosen for his somewhat limited artistic energy. As films were a sort of hobby, he need not get involved in any but the biggest, most important productions, and then perhaps no more often than once every four or five years.

Vittorio Anastasio's films tended to ramble at the same leisurely, undirected pace as his life. Pretension aside, they should have been called boring. But the vast sums he spent, his apparent unconcern for commercialism and his absence of story line, all taken for profundity, contributed to his reputation as some sort of cinematic *auteur*. The *Boccaccio* project had been much to his liking from the start. It was to be a prestigious film and he had neither a long work schedule nor full responsibility for the film.

This Sunday morning at the country club his friends had been speaking of nothing but Serena Blaire and her apparent involvement with Umberto Cassini. They might become the screen couple of the century . . . surely Vittorio was going to cast Serena Blaire in his segment of *Boccaccio*?

Yes, he would, but he knew it would be difficult to

announce a change of plans to Cleo. He would prepare the way, suggest to Cleo that his concept had been altered. At the same time he needed to make sure of Serena Blaire's interest in the project. He also had to discuss his intention with the producers. Paolo Monti, as he understood it, was investing heavily in *Boccaccio Volgare,* and they couldn't afford to have the film's financing endangered. There was no question that Cleo Monti would have to play one of the Fiammettas, but instead of his segment why not one of the others . . . why not, say, Fiammetta Two? Franco Mariani, director of that segment of the film, at one time had expressed interest in Cleo for the Fiammetta in his section. He would talk it over with Mariani. But not, God forbid, in person. The man's aroma was scarcely tolerable. Perhaps he should first discuss the casting with Ralph de Rossi. Although there were four directors directing the four different segments, it was Ralph who was chosen to edit the film, and had been assigned overall artistic control. Also Ralph had the patience and energy for this sort of thing. Yes, why not leave the whole distasteful, time-consuming business in the capable hands of Ralph de Rossi, and spare his own?

Ralph de Rossi was alone this Sunday. His son and daughter were both in college, living on campus, and his wife was visiting her family in Ancona. It was too cold and windy for his usual Sunday morning golf game, so he was in his study trying to catch up on some work. While directing the present *Domani e Domani e Domani* it had been difficult for him to find time for planning the forthcoming *Boccaccio Volgare,* and yet the latter was by far the more important of the projects. He did, though, have the general concept of his own segment, which was the first. He had insisted on directing that first segment, inasmuch as it would set the tone for the rest of the film, establish the humor of the story. And to manage that his greatest asset was his leading man. Umberto had the perfect comic talent needed for the leading character, who, once the humor had been established, would need to carry the comic overtones into the other three segments.

Basically the story was a simple one and depended heavily on characterization. Umberto was playing the writer Boccaccio, who, as he created a poem about the love of his life, Fiammetta, began visualizing her as four different women. So obviously the casting of the women was also of vital importance. Ralph would not cast the first segment until the other imaginary Fiammettas had been decided on . . . he saw his Fiammetta as the genuine woman subsequently defamed by Boccaccio's fantasies, jealousy and doubt . . . because, truth to tell, none of the actresses he knew had the quality necessary for the real Fiammetta—until he had seen Madeline Mandell standing there in the middle of the studio restaurant. A vision in white, soft silver hair, subtle lines . . . an embodiment of sweet vulnerability to be crushed by a jealous lover. Ralph had not needed that vulgar agent Luigi Luna to point out the value of casting Madeline in the role of the real Fiammetta, but he still felt obliged to hold off until the three other directors had made up their minds, worked out their own concepts. If, for example, one of them should decide on a virginal Fiammetta, then he might be forced to change his own concept. It would be a pity and he would try not to let that happen, but as overall artistic director he first had to allow his colleagues to have their individual say.

Thinking about the other three segments, Ralph

knew he had the most faith in Mariani's ability. Mariani might be personally hard to take, but he was a genuinely dedicated artist with, ironically, the most immaculate taste. Just the previous evening the powerful financier Paolo Monti had telephoned Ralph intimating that he might suggest to the producers a replacement for Mariani, and Ralph had interrupted him, saying he would fight to keep Mariani, whose work he considered vital to the project.

Ralph was not as certain about Angelo Catalano. He had originally agreed to Catalano because he was taken with the idea of one of the segments being rather detached and dreamlike. But Catalano was unpredictable, a bit of a madman. He produced either startling, bizarre work that was unique, or hopeless rubbish. There seemed to be no middle way in that schizy brain of his. And Catalano also needed to be closely watched to make certain he didn't turn his part of the essentially humorous tale into something inappropriately dark and sinister.

As for Vittorio Anastasio, Ralph felt he was a little lazy and vague. However, Anastasio brought, deserved or not, prestige and a reputation for class to the film. Also, Anastasio was entirely predictable, sure to provide something beautiful if undefined. Ralph knew he would easily cut into the long, slow-panning shots of the scenery and be able to retrieve the story line. He was also sure that Umberto's performance would be there for the finding, but he had serious doubts about Cleo's performance. Cleo, left to her own devices, tended to play the grand lady that she longed to be. Which was why she had only been successful in his films. He took advantage of her true character, an honest-to-God earth mother—vulgar, uneducated and as real as the hard streets of Palermo, where she'd been an impoverished bastard child. But Vittorio Anastasio would allow Cleo to do her grand-lady impersonation because his eye would be forever straying past her in search of an unusual sunset or an arresting color composite in the town square.

So it was with relief that Ralph listened to Anastasio's phone call proposing Serena Blaire as Fiammetta Four. Suddenly he saw the chance to salvage that last segment. Serena Blaire didn't need a strong director to give a charming, sophisticated and witty performance. As yet Ralph had not seen the Sunday papers, but they wouldn't have swayed him if he hadn't believed Serena ideal for Fiammetta Four. Anastasio had only to find out if she was interested in playing the part; Ralph would handle the consequences, spelled Cleo. Perhaps he would ask Umberto to help. True, Umberto disliked giving his opinion when it came to such delicate casting matters, but as the main star Umberto's word could carry the final weight. Ralph had looked at the papers after Anastasio's call. And if he truly was involved with the Blaire girl, perhaps he would change his mind this once and recommend her . . .

Umberto had no idea that Ralph de Rossi was trying to reach him because Umberto had completely forgotten about having the "do not disturb" instruction removed at the switchboard, nor did he know about Serena's extending it. He also had no idea of the barrage of other messages waiting for him. As the papers had been delivered to his room once that morning, the hotel would not deliver them again except at Umberto's request. And since Umberto had decided to take a shower before ordering breakfast and reading the papers, he was one of the few people in the city of Rome unaware of the headlines.

Rubbing himself briskly with the bar of soap while letting the hot-water jets massage his body, Umberto was thinking of the advantages Serena Blaire brought, in addition to the obvious ones . . . no risk of emotional scenes or a lengthy involvement. Serena was, after all, a married woman. She'd even had the good taste to leave quietly this morning without waking him . . . Of course, carrying on with a married woman wasn't an ideal situation, but neither was hanging around bars picking up starlets. Especially at his age. As his mother would energetically agree, he should be married, living in a house of his own, raising children while he was still young enough to play rough games and be a pal to them. Which made him think of his little daughter, Nicola. Maybe he'd ask Ralph for Saturday off and fly over to Paris next weekend to be with her . . .

As he stepped out of the shower and began drying himself, his thoughts went, unwillingly, to Madeline. Damn, he must be infatuated with the woman, couldn't get her off his mind . . . Was it possible he'd been wrong about her, been mistaken about what he *thought* he'd overheard? Maybe his feelings for her had made him so jealous he'd jumped to conclusions. Maybe he'd been unfair to her . . . Besides, who was he to judge? She was, after all, a free agent, divorced from a rat, so far as he could make out from what he'd heard . . . yes, she was free—and available. Available, but not for long. What a fool he was . . . Some damn smooth-talking character was bound to capture her, and it should be *him*. If it wasn't already too late. Yes, she had refused to talk to him, but maybe there was a good reason she couldn't talk to him while she was at Helga's apartment. Don't be an idiot, admit how you feel, think only the best of her, stop rushing to believe the worst. He would ask their mutual agent for her unlisted number, call and invite her for Sunday brunch. For anything she'd agree to . . .

Madeline had gone to sleep very early Saturday night and although she had been awake by first light, she'd put a pillow over her head and stayed in bed until nearly ten, daydreaming, damn him, about Umberto Cassini. She couldn't help it. Her flat-out desire for him drowned her misgivings. Besides, she could have been mistaken—jumped to all the wrong conclusions. After all, Umberto hadn't been in Helga's bedroom, he'd been on the other end of the telephone. Maybe he had no more to do with the acrobatics in Helga's bedroom than she did. The least she could do for him, *and* herself, was not to assume the worst. Give the man the benefit of the doubt, Madeline. You aren't, after all, Venus immaculate. That's the image you've been trying to shake. Stop acting it out . . .

Feeling much better, she'd gotten out of bed, made a rude gesture toward that *la bomba a gas,* put on her coat and gone to a Tavola Calda for breakfast. Just as she was finishing her hot chocolate a man had sat down across from her and opened the pages of *Il Messaggero,* displaying the front page so that Madeline had to see the photograph of Serena in Umberto's arms. The end of a beautiful morning, not to say romance . . .

Back home, Madeline was still feeling shaken when Umberto's call came. In spite of her reborn doubts, even anger, she felt a shiver at the sound of his voice, inviting her to brunch. She knew she shouldn't act petulant but that was the way it came out . . . "And what will Serena be doing? How many women can you make love to at one time?"

Umberto was speechless. How was it possible? How did she know? Good lord, Rome was the most incredible city for gossip. Serena had left his room only a short time ago and already it seemed the whole city knew what they'd been doing the night before.

"I see," Madeline said, feeling miserable that her worst thoughts were apparently true, "that you are not denying it."

Still no answer. Her heart sank. She bit her lip, forced herself to press him. "Well . . . do you deny you're lovers?"

Umberto was still speechless. How could he deny what had happened, now that people knew?

"Aren't you going to lie and tell me you are not?"

"Yes . . ."

"Yes, you are going to lie—no, you are not going to lie?" She knew she should stop, went on anyway.

"I don't want to lie to you," Umberto said miserably.

Tears were in her eyes but she at least controlled her voice. Damn it, Umberto. "Yes or no?" she said. "Even you should be able to manage that."

"Yes."

Click. Madeline had hung up on him.

# BOOK TWO

# CHAPTER TWELVE

MADELINE SET out on Monday morning for Cine Citta to begin her preproduction work convinced that the weather in Rome was as capricious as the people whose lives it affected. The Siberian wind had disappeared sometime during Sunday and had now been replaced by what the Italians called Il Sirocco—a hot and dry dust-laden wind from northern Africa. Those prevailing southeast currents, it was said, caused people to feel nervous and irritable, and their subtle, abrasive force was responsible for exacerbating the not uncommon Monday morning blues.

Madeline, of course, had her share of those, thanks to Umberto's confession about Serena, but it could have been worse . . . she had only a few hours of work scheduled—a wardrobe fitting and some preliminary tests for makeup and hairstyles—and then Helga was joining her at the studio for lunch and after lunch had offered to drive her while she went to look at apartments in some of the better neighborhoods. More important, though, was the conversation she'd had with Helga Sunday afternoon. Helga had telephoned to explain how she never intended for Madeline to witness that *vivid* bedroom scene. It was all the fault of her idiotic maid, Giuseppina. Helga felt absolutely *dreadful* about the whole unfortunate incident and had insisted on apologizing in person. Even better, Helga said she was going to explain more about Umberto and his feelings for Madeline. Plead his case for him. It seemed that after Madeline had hung up on Umberto he had telephoned Helga all upset and had kept her on the phone for an hour telling her about his "predicament," asking for her advice.

Madeline had already heard that Serena Blaire had invited herself to Umberto's room on Saturday, that Umberto had really been hoping to date her that night. Whatever it was with Serena had been a sort of accidental meeting. *And* Umberto had sworn up and down that he wasn't in any way in love with Serena or even serious about her—it was just an encounter, not even an affair, never mind what the papers said. Madeline badly wanted to believe it . . . and as she thought about Serena inviting herself, Madeline wished *she* had that kind of confidence or nerve or whatever it was. No wonder Serena was a more successful actress; she took the bull by the horns, or was it the balls?

Madeline looked forward to hearing in detail *everything* that Umberto had said. It did seem that the picture Helga had painted of him fitted with what Luigi Luna had told her. Now she thought about maybe running into him in the restaurant at lunchtime . . . if she did, she at least would go out of her way to say hello, let him know that she was no longer angry. Well, not *so* angry . . . Once all the misunderstandings were behind them, maybe they could begin again, and *this* time when Umberto asked to see her she wouldn't be so damn silly, she would accept his invitation.

With a new movie to begin work on, she thought, soon I'll have money, a cozy apartment to move to, and on top of all that a possible romance . . . as the Italians would say, *Che dolce vita, che c'e.* Yes, what a sweet life there is . . . Madeline was rarely without the Italian phrase book and dictionary she had brought with her from Los Angeles.

*"Buon giorno,"* Madeline said as she opened the heavy double doors and entered the makeup department. Instantly her face fell and she was jolted into her mother tongue. "What do you call *this?*"

Six young girls were lined up all in a row. They were holding their skirts up to their chins. All were stark naked from the waist down.

*"Buon giorno,* Madeline," responded her director, Alfonso Razzi. "And for to say 'what you call this,' you say *come si chiama questo.*"

"Well, *come si chiama questo,* and in spades," Madeline said.

The half-naked girls began bending backward, unashamedly thrusting forward their exposed pubic areas. Several makeup men knelt in front of the girls, holding brushes and pots of tint. They were about to dye the pubic hair of the starlets . . . With the exception, that is, of one rather plastic-looking girl. Her pubic area had recently been shaved and she was being fitted there with a toupee, now hanging precariously between her legs. She looked vaguely familiar . . .

"*Ciao*, Madeline," Pina said, grinning broadly, wanting to ingratiate herself with the star. "Remember me? Pina? We went to the banquet together on Friday night—"

"*Si, si,* you know Pina," Alfonso said with some pride at having cast a girl who was a friend of Madeline's.

"We've met . . ."

"Too bad Pina is *senza* hair there," Alfonso said, pointing to the toupee, "but she gived a *buono* reading from the *battuti.*"

"*Battuti* is slang for the lines of a film script," Pina, the ever-real translator, translated.

"*Si,*" Alfonso said. "Pina, she talks the very good English. She is a *studentessa* of the *lingua.* She does a small *personaggio* in the film and I pay her some *soldi* to be *traduttrice* for you on the set."

Pina to the rescue: "Alfonso says that as I'm a student of languages he has hired me to play a small part in the film and also to be your personal translator on the film set."

Madeline nodded, turned to Alfonso. "Why are they having their pubic hair dyed?"

"*Perchè? Perchè* I like to see all the hairs is the same in the scenes *nuda.*"

"He wants all the hair to match the hair on our heads for the nude scenes," Pina said.

"*What* nude scenes? Alfonso, I have no intention of doing any nude scenes—"

"*Ma, certo,*" Alfonso said, kissing Madeline's hand. "You are not *nuda* in the film, only your *schiave* girls are to be *nuda.* You," he said, kissing her hand again, "you . . . *tu sei la strega.*"

"Only your slave girls will be nude in the film, you will never be nude, you are the witch," Pina told her.

"The witch?"

"Oh," Pina said hurriedly, "it has a very good meaning in Italian to be a witch. A *strega* can be a woman who is dazzling and bewitches everyone."

Well, at least Alfonso didn't expect her to appear nude. She hadn't been able to read the Italian script and now it sounded pretty awful. Tacky, in fact, but what could she do? She'd decided to accept the film no matter what; she had to have the work, and the money . . . how else could she hope to make a deposit this afternoon on a new apartment? Without a salary, that would cut much too deeply into the small reserve of cash she had left from the sale of her Beverly Hills home.

Pina now was asking with exaggerated sweetness, "Madeline, would you like me to translate a copy of the script into English for you?"

"Yes, please," Madeline said, forgetting for the moment that this girl had had any connection with Umberto. She'd just started to get over the new threat of Serena. How many hot-panted ladies could she keep track of?

It was then that the hairdresser called Madeline over to the makeup table to show her, with pride, the long gray wig interlaced with black crusted cobwebs for the dream sequence in which Madeline was to be the thousand-year-old witch. For the same sequence the makeup man, by using hand-dried liquid rubber, proceeded to make Madeline's face into a mask of grotesque, cracked wrinkles. When the three hours of makeup were finished, Madeline took one look at herself in the mirror and screamed in terror. She had scared the hell out of herself.

It was decided that a test of the glamorous makeup

was unnecessary, and the wardrobe mistress was not yet ready for a costume fitting, so Madeline was released for the day. She removed the hideous rubber makeup, but it took her a long while before she could reapply her own street makeup.

When Helga arrived Madeline decided she would not bring up her misgivings about the film. First of all, she needed to keep up a front, and second, since it was her film she should be the last person to start bad rumors about it. But Madeline also realized that to offset the predictable effect of this bad film she needed quickly to secure a part in a good one before *Paranoia*'s release. Its filming schedule wouldn't prevent her from appearing in *Boccaccio Volgare;* she'd be free just before *Boccaccio* was due to go before the cameras.

She must talk to her agent, Luigi Luna, about his idea that she'd be a possibility for Fiammetta One, the Ralph de Rossi segment. Somehow she must try to get a look at the script.

Luigi, also Umberto's agent, might be able to get one for her. She dared not ask Helga or Cleo or Astrid if she could borrow one of their copies . . . the *Boccaccio* casting had already stirred up far too much bitterness and jealousy. These were her friends. She couldn't risk it.

At the restaurant, Helga and Madeline took their seats at a back table that had a view of the whole restaurant. Madeline took advantage by looking about at the other diners—and promptly lost her appetite. Umberto was at a table by the windows, having lunch with Ralph de Rossi *and* Serena Blaire.

And if Madeline's stomach had suddenly gone to her shoes, Helga's reaction was a sympathetic "shit,

shit, shit" between clenched teeth as she blew out the match after lighting her cigarette.

"Umberto lied to me about his feelings for Serena—"

"No, no, no," Helga said impatiently. "That's not a social get-together, it's obviously a business meeting, and the *only* business those three could have would be about *Boccaccio Volgare* . . ."

*"What do you think it means?"*

*"It means,* my lovesick friend," Helga said, tugging at a lock of her auburn fringe, "that that skinny bitch must be in the film—"

"You think Serena definitely has the part of Fiammetta Two—the part you wanted?" Madeline had lowered her voice because the waiter was putting a carafe of wine and a plate of appetizers on their table.

"No. Something much bigger is happening," Helga said. Her charcoal eyes were staring into space and she was squinting in concentration.

"You mean Ralph de Rossi is going to cast Serena as Fiammetta One?" Madeline said, panic-stricken.

"Maybe . . ."

And Madeline's heart sank.

Helga began tapping the salt shaker with one of her long, russet-painted fingernails. "Maybe . . . but I don't think so."

Madeline sighed in relief.

"No," Helga said, "no, it's something more complicated."

"*Please* tell me what you're thinking," Madeline said.

"Well, Ralph could cast his segment without complications . . . I mean, Umberto wouldn't need to be there. But if Ralph has had to get Umberto involved, get Umberto's support"—Helga dragged deep on her cigarette—"it means Ralph has *some* fight on his hands with the producers or with one of the other directors . . . it wouldn't be with Mariani—I already know from Paolo Piccolo that Ralph is in complete agreement with Mariani. So if Mariani wanted Serena, again that wouldn't be a problem . . ."

"Lord, Helga, spell it out. *Please* . . . how *would* Ralph need Umberto's help?"

"Pour us some wine." She did. "You know, I presume, that Ralph is overall artistic director on the film. But even so, art follows money . . . I mean, he has to be careful not to step on *certain* toes. He might not always be able to get what he wants on his own. That's where Umberto comes in—if *both* Ralph and Umberto agree . . . well, that carries a lot of weight."

"Then, in whose segment would casting Serena cause a problem?"

"For example, suppose Ralph felt Serena would make the difference between the success or failure of Fiammetta Three, Angelo Catalano's segment. Catalano, of course, wants Astrid, and if Astrid agrees to play the part Catalano would never trade Astrid for Serena Blaire."

"But," said Madeline, beginning to penetrate the Byzantine haze, "if both Ralph and Umberto *insisted* on Serena for that segment, then Catalano would have great difficulty in resisting."

"Exactly."

Madeline sipped her wine, let her attention wander to Umberto's table, where it seemed he was being very cozy with Serena Blaire. Umberto must think a great deal of her to fight to have her cast next to him in *Boccaccio Volgare*. But that, she tried to remind herself, didn't mean he was in love with her . . . or was it possible he was so devious he'd make a play for Madeline to use her as a smokescreen while carrying on his affair with Serena? Serena *was* a married woman and—

Helga broke into Madeline's contorted thoughts with, "If Serena was signed for Fiammetta Three, well, in a way there's even a sunny side to that. At least Astrid maybe wouldn't let herself get involved again with that sadist Catalano . . ."

Except she had no sooner said the words than Astrid walked into the restaurant on Catalano's arm.

"Who's the tall blond man Astrid is with?" Madeline asked.

The gold flecks in Helga's eyes were sparking among the charcoal. "*That* is none other than Angelo Catalano. Oh, brother . . ." Helga began to whistle softly. "If Astrid can bring herself to have lunch with him this way—she's no doubt already made up her mind to work for him again."

"Look how friendly they are being at Ralph's table," Madeline pointed out. "It hardly seems that there could be a rift. Look—Catalano has just shaken Umberto's hand, and Ralph is kissing Astrid on the cheek."

"You're absolutely right," Helga said. "The big meeting is not about Catalano's segment." Then she chewed on a carrot stick and grinned maliciously. "Just watch when Astrid and Catalano sit down at their own table. Time it! I'll bet that within five minutes from now, Astrid will be crying."

They sipped their wine. Suddenly Helga slammed her glass down, spilling wine on the tablecloth.

"That's it!" she exclaimed. "I've got it!"

"What is it?" Madeline asked in alarm.

"I know which part Serena Blaire is going to play!"

At that moment Helga stopped what she was saying because Umberto was approaching their table.

"How is it that I am not the lucky man to be sitting

at this table with the two most beautiful women in Rome?" Umberto seemed pleased with his entrance . . . for once he had managed to say something appropriate in front of the divine Madeline.

Madeline, in spite of herself, actually blushed. She felt it when he kissed her hand, tried to recoup as he leaned over and kissed Helga on both cheeks, calling her, of course, Helgalina.

"May I sit down for a minute?"

"Please do," Madeline said, and quickly added what she'd been wanting, planning to say, "I'm sorry, Umberto, that I hung up on you. I didn't really understand . . ." At least she hoped she didn't, wanted very badly to convince herself she didn't . . .

Umberto looked at her. "That doesn't matter. Not any more. What matters now is that you agree to see me—"

Helga said impatiently, "Of course she will," then went on to the subject she felt more importantly at hand. Business over romance for Helga . . . "So, tell us, Umberto, what's going on with Serena Blaire? Why is she here? Which Fiammetta is she going to play?" Although she believed she had already figured it out.

Umberto threw his head back and laughed. "Oh, Helgalina, you are a devil. Why can't you wait to hear it officially?"

And then Helga came out with it, startling Madeline. "Cleo is being replaced, isn't she?"

"Helgalina, Helgalina," Umberto said shaking his head slowly. "It's better not to speak of these things now. Nothing has been exactly set and we don't want to hurt Cleo unnecessarily—"

"Then I'm right."

"I'm not able to say anything more," Umberto said, getting up from his chair. "Now, if you lovely ladies will excuse me, I must return to my own table."

Damn it, Madeline thought as she watched him walk off, if Helga hadn't driven him away with all her casting talk he might have stayed long enough to have asked her for a definite date. It seemed Il Sirocco could be an ill wind after all . . .

# CHAPTER THIRTEEN

MADELINE DID manage to find two apartments she liked very much, nearly the same price and both well furnished. The one on Via Panama was larger and more modern and near the big park, Villa Ada. But Via Panama was a main road with shops and a great deal of traffic. The other was on a small side street, Viccolo della Cancelleria, in the old part of the city, in an ancient building crowded against other ancient structures, and the living space was rather cramped. Still, it had a charming little balcony that afforded a spectacular view of the Piazza Navona. Being in the neighborhood would give her much more of a feeling of what ancient Rome might have been like.

Helga agreed about the one facing Piazza Navona and so Madeline put down a three-month deposit for immediate occupancy. She didn't even mind losing the money she'd already paid in advance for her studio in Via Cola di Rienzo, wanting the pleasure of moving that very same day, even though there was no telephone and wouldn't be, as Helga pointed out, for several weeks.

After the papers were signed Madeline walked Helga back to where they'd left the car. Helga showed her the taxi rank just across the street on the left, kissed Madeline on both cheeks, wishing her the best of luck in the new apartment, and drove off for an "appointment." Madeline didn't press her about what kind of an appointment. She was, she thought, smiling to herself, getting to be a real sophisticate.

Madeline took a taxi to Via Cola di Rienzo, told the driver to wait while she rushed upstairs, left a note for the landlady and threw her clothes into the suitcases. The driver then took her back to the old part of the city, helped her up the three flights of stairs with her suitcases and put them down inside her front door. She tipped him and closed the door, relishing her first moments alone in her new home. She unpacked her cases but draped her clothes over every available piece of furniture rather than taking time to put them away. In the morning she had an early fitting and since it was already late afternoon she decided her first priority was to buy bread and coffee for morning plus a few things for the evening's meal.

She found the neighborhood enchanting, lingering over her purchases, going from one shop to the next, comparing the range of goods and taking in the ambience. At one *alimentario* she saw a display of wines in the window that included Pinot Grigio, which

Helga had told her was Umberto's favorite white wine. The two heavy bottles were a lot to lug to her new home, but just buying them made her feel she and Umberto were somehow more possible . . . they'd be waiting to be shared with him when he came. If he came . . .

As she started back home the sky was black and the street lights were on. Her small Viccolo, however, was lit only by the uneven illumination coming from lights inside the buildings, which made it difficult negotiating the rough cobblestones . . . or, as she approached her building, making out just who was the man sitting in the doorway. Should she be afraid in this neighborhood? She really could only see his faint outline, but he did appear to be well dressed. No tramp . . .

Just as she was about to brush by him to enter the narrow hallway he suddenly was on his feet and taking the bags of groceries from her arms and, scaring her to death, saying "*Buona sera,* Madeline."

*Umberto.*

"Helga told me where you live now. Since you have no telephone I decided to come by. I hope it's not inconvenient for you." He paused, pulling himself together. Such frontal efforts weren't exactly his style. His mother would have been proud of him. "I hope that you will have dinner with me."

Madeline managed a quick, "Oh, yes," then led him up the three flights of stairs, he enjoying the sight immediately in front of him. On the landing he stopped and peered into the heavy bags of groceries. "I see you look first to your wine supply. *Buono.*" He continued climbing to catch up with her. "That is more Italian than American, I think," he called up.

On the last stairs before her floor Madeline glanced over her shoulder to make sure he was really there, and also to call back, "It's Pinot Grigio," pleased with herself for having hoped enough to buy it. The Sirocco had blown in Umberto, proving once again that it was an ill wind that blew no good. She giggled to herself at the thought, at the same time saying a silent obeisance to it.

"I can see that," Umberto said as Madeline opened the door and turned on a lamp. "It's one of my favorites, too."

"Oh . . . well, then perhaps you'd like to open a bottle." She moved back, watching him enter her apartment.

He put the packages down on the table by the doorway and walked toward her. She could definitely hear her heart pounding, imagined that he could too. God, get ahold of yourself, she instructed, you're acting, or about to act, like a silly schoolgirl.

He took her hands in his, comparing this lovely creature to Serena, who was uncomplicated, straight sex. With Serena it was like taking a train—nothing happened until you got on, and nothing after you got off.

"We must certainly have some wine," he said, "but for our first time, I recommend a restaurant I know. It's modest and informal but it's near a very special place. A place I hope I'm the first to show you." He was proud of himself for taking it slow.

"Of course." Umberto was on her mind at the moment, not food, but she was enjoying his romantic approach, and fantasizing about what she hoped would be dessert.

He let go of her hands. She wished he hadn't. "There's a breeze tonight but the Sirocco is mild. We could walk from here," he said, then quickly added, "but, of course, we could also go by car. I'm parked just near the piazza."

"No, no, I'd love to walk."

Before leaving she went into the bedroom to get a sweater, but also hurriedly threw the clothes she'd left on the bed into the closet and checked to see that the bed was made. It looked clean, and inviting.

Moments later as they came out of the building she wondered if he had any idea how being near him affected her, even if, despite her desire, she still had a bit of reservation because of his encounter . . . she could handle it better, thinking of it that way, with Serena Blaire . . . He was taking her hand now, tucking her arm under his, and with the possessive gesture driving the last thoughts of Serena from her head.

Once they entered the smooth paving of the Piazza Navona he held her hand by his side while they walked the width of the piazza and out the opposite side. When they stopped at a traffic light on the Corso Rinascimento he put his arm around her waist, leading her across the busy road. And he kept it there as they strolled the dozen or so blocks toward the restaurant: crossing in front of the Pantheon, through Piazza Colonna, across Via del Corso, which he explained became Via dei Fori Imperiali and led to the Colosseum, then into a maze of narrow streets.

"The restaurant is called Dal Moro, Of the Moor. As many times as I've been there I'm still never quite sure which of these side streets it's on."

As he talked and they walked he kept squeezing her waist in a delicious fashion. If they were lost, she thought, she didn't care, in fact was glad . . . it kept them together this way a little longer, until he could hold all of her . . .

Once he located the crowded restaurant and they entered it, most of the people ogled them and some were calling to Umberto, who was, after all, a screen idol. Well, she wouldn't have to share him for long, she thought, hoped . . .

Dal Moro was, as promised, informal, with its plank tables, straight-backed chairs and sawdust on the floor. The owner hustled over to greet Umberto and escorted them to the prize table next to the one authentic Roman pillar the restaurant claimed.

"They have the finest spaghetti alla carbonara del mondo," Umberto said for the benefit of both Madeline and the owner, then asked her, "Do you like carbonara?"

"Very much," she said, smiling at them, wondering if she'd ever had it. Who cared?

"For after," the owner was saying, "I recommend the scampi alla griglia."

Umberto approved, turned to her and asked if she'd like the grilled scampi. He also called her "darling," unless her ears were making up their own dialogue.

"That would be wonderful," she said, trying to sound nonchalant.

Umberto added, "And we will have a bottle of Pinot Grigio. The *signora*'s favorite."

They lingered over the meal for almost two and a half hours, finishing that bottle of wine and the better part of a second one. Sometimes they held hands, most times they looked directly at each other. After a while she thought she was seeing two of him, and reasoned the more the merrier. Umberto was refreshingly open. He even talked about his child, all of which made it easy for her to tell him about her own past . . . the years in Hollywood, her short-lived marriage.

After dinner, as they moved outside, a breeze sprang up, swirling under Madeline's full-skirted dress, and they laughed at the suddenness of it.

Madeline caught her skirt, looking down to see how much of her was exposed. At this point she really didn't much care.

She felt Umberto's hands on her shoulders now, and raised her head expectantly, thinking he was about to kiss her. No luck. He was smiling down at her and asking her, "Which of Rome's landmarks have you seen?"

Landmarks? Oh, God, forget about landmarks, she wanted to tell him. "Oh, well, let's see, I haven't even been to the Colosseum, or Saint Peter's . . ." She caressed his arm. "My first look at the Pantheon was when you took me by it on our way here—"

"Marvelous." And suddenly he had put his hands under her arms, was lifting her straight up in the air. Now, she thought, when he brings me down he'll kiss me . . . except at that moment another breeze came up between them, billowing her skirt until it completely covered Umberto's face.

Laughing, he lowered her back to the pavement, helped her hold down her dress. "Come on, then," he said, putting his arm around her shoulder, "there's something I want to be the first to show you." After a few steps, he said, "It's very near. Do you hear anything?"

She stopped. "Yes, sounds like a waterfall."

He moved her forward in long strides. "Have you ever seen the film *Three Coins in the fountain?*"

"Yes, sure. It's the wishing fountain, that's where you're taking me." She knew what her wish would be.

As they approached the end of the narrow dimly lit street she saw brilliant light streaming on the dark walls where they met at right angles to the piazza beyond. Umberto moved in front of her, turned so that the lights were behind him and on her, took her hand and led her into the piazza, where she saw for the first time the famed Fontana di Trevi.

For a moment she was stunned by the beauty of it, gripping his hand and then doing a little dance step forward. "It's incredible. It's huge. It's truly one of the most beautiful things I've ever seen . . ."

"Yes," he said, watching her face, thinking that there was nothing man-made to compare with her exquisite features, wanting to say it in English, but then stopping himself. He was afraid she might find the speech extravagant, operatic. Instead he said it softly in Italian.

"What are you saying?"

"Nothing, really. We're . . . we're fortunate it's not the tourist season, we would never have the Fontana all to ourselves like this." He turned and they walked arm-in-arm down the steps to the pool's marble edge.

"Now, you must make a wish." He took some coins from his pocket, offering them to her. "And you may make as many wishes as there are coins. But your first wish must be the one that only this fountain can make come true."

"And what's that?"

"You must wish from the Fontana that you shall always be able to return to Rome."

"How do I say it?"

"Well," he said, turning her around with her back to the edge, "you throw the coin over your shoulder without looking, and if you simply say '*a Roma,*' the fountain will know that the city has become part of your heart."

She whispered the words as she threw the coin over her shoulder. Then she threw another, this time making a silent wish. Umberto now made his own silent wish, and she asked him what it was, tugging at his lapels, teasing him.

But Umberto's expression was serious. He lifted a strand of windblown hair from her forehead, then reversing the motion of his hand brought it down to caress her cheek, leaned to brush his lips across hers—

Madeline threw her arms around his neck, and he instantly took her in his arms, moving his hands over her back, waist and hips, then kissed her passionately, but with a controlled strength that startled and delighted her.

She wanted to stay that way forever, but ever so slowly he released her, then led her to the steps where he sat down, easing her onto his lap so they faced the sparkling pool together.

He held her close, tight against him as they sat without speaking, watching the jets of fountains and the rush of waterfalls, slowly recovering some semblance of balance before attempting the walk home.

It was almost midnight when they arrived at her apartment door, but before she could put the key in the lock he had taken her hand in both of his, bringing it to his lips, kissing each finger separately. The sensation was incredible, she could feel it all over her body . . .

"Madeline, darling, don't ask me in . . . once I come in—I could never leave again."

What? She thought she would die. The wetness in her panties and the ache would not go away. She had to have him . . . now.

He paused, forced himself to let go of her hand and took a step backward. "I know myself, darling. I couldn't possibly leave you after only a few hours."

She couldn't hold back the trembling in her voice. "Do you have to get up early for the filming?"

"Yes, I do. And so do you, I assume."

"Yes . . ."

"Madeline, I am not playing games with you. I want to be with you entire nights, *and* days. Let's wait until the weekend, with no obligations, no interruptions. Please now, go in quickly before I lose control and—"

For a moment she was too stunned to move, then turned quickly and entered. As she shut the door she forced herself to try to see the wisdom in all this restraint and denial. Her back against the door, squeezing her legs tight to control the ache, she wished for something to stop the throbbing. If only she weren't so damned Catholic, she could masturbate. But the nuns had forever conditioned her against that . . .. So instead she flopped across the bed, shut her eyes tight and tried to fantasize what it would be like on the weekend when they would finally be really together. She did not sleep that night, her head filled with visions of Umberto Cassini making wild love to her in a fashion she had never known or even thought she could imagine. And, at last, she did find a blessed, if guilty, relief.

# CHAPTER FOURTEEN

ON HIS way back to the Hilton that night Umberto worried that he'd been too restrained with Madeline, had perhaps even offended her. He hated having to be practical when he was, finally, in love, but he also knew himself. If he'd gone to her apartment he'd have made love to her all night, been incapable of getting up for work in the morning. Now, though, he wondered if he hadn't lost the battle with himself anyway. His balls were tight and ached badly. His cock was still hard as a rock. It was late, and he probably wouldn't be able to get any sleep. Well, he'd take a freezing cold shower, try to get her off his mind long enough for an hour or two's rest.

With that intention he began tossing off his clothes. When he got down to his socks and undershorts he paused and picked up the telephone to ask the operator for a 6:00 A.M. wake-up call. No sooner had he put down the receiver and begun removing his socks than he heard a tapping near the bed. He stood up and walked toward the sound that was coming from the connecting door between the rooms . . .

He got closer and put his ear to the door. The tapping became more persistent, followed by a female voice saying his name. "Umberto, Umberto, Umberto . . ."

The voice sounded familiar, all right, but he was exhausted, tense, couldn't quite place it . . .

"Umberto, I know you're in there, I just heard you on the telephone. Open the door, silly. It's me, your darling Serena."

He didn't want to, he wanted to . . . he unlocked the adjoining door. Darling Serena stood there in a filmy pink nightgown that, as intended, left nothing to the imagination, and without permission Umberto's cock leaped in his undershorts and saluted her. He quickly put his hands over it and stood in that absurd position wondering what he could say to her. What popped into his head was, "Why are you speaking English?"

"Because I am English, silly boy." She then took his hands away from his cock and led him into her bedroom. "Would you prefer we spoke French?"

"No, my English is better than my French." And it occurred to him that this dialogue was completely irrelevant.

Now he was standing rigidly, in all respects, in the middle of her room. "I can tell you're happy to see me," Serena said as she lowered his undershorts, touching his cock only lightly as she went, but the desire pent up for hours over Madeline swelled, broke loose. Self-control was gone as he pulled her nightgown up over her head, flipped her over and onto the bed, where she lay twisting, squirming, moaning in anticipation.

Umberto paused for only a moment, looking down at her bony frame, thinking, *The hell with her. She no doubt arranged matters figuring she would have me to provide her with countless orgasms like the last time. Well, not this time. All she's going to get for her trouble is fucked.* At which point he clambered over her legs to straddle her narrow pelvis and, once positioned, without preamble, made one thrust, entered her, came, and rolled off onto his back. His sexual tension relieved, he felt spent, but Serena wouldn't let him catch his breath, commenced tickling him all over.

"Where were you all evening, you bad boy?"

He yawned and turned on his side to escape.

But Serena climbed over him and began tweaking his nose. "You were with Madeline Mandell, right?"

"Yes," he groaned, trying to brush her hand from his nose.

"Where did you take her?" she asked, now pinching his stomach.

"Serena, enough, it's late and I've got to get some sleep—"

"Did you fuck her, too? Was the little American darling as good as I am?" She reached for his balls, gave them a squeeze.

He groaned, took her hands away and turned onto his stomach. "No, *no,* I've got to get some sleep, my wake-up call is for six—"

But Serena had climbed onto his back and was pulling at his hair. "Where did you take her?"

"Fontana di Trevi," he muttered, his face buried in the pillow.

"Where *else?*" And she pulled his hair until he was obliged to lift his head.

"For Christ's *sake,* Serena, stop it. I'm going to my room to get some sleep. Good *night.*"

"Okay, okay," and she jumped up, rushing over to block the doorway. "Just answer my questions and I'll let you go."

Umberto sat up wearily on the edge of the bed. "What? *What* do you want to know?"

"Did you fuck her?"

He got slowly to his feet, stumbled toward the doorway. "I took her to Dal Moro, the Fontana, walked her home. Now please get out of the way."

Serena smiled and moved toward him, kissed him almost maternally on the cheek. "Sleep well, Romeo. I'll see you tomorrow."

Eyes half closed, Umberto stumbled into his own room and closed the adjoining door, remembering to lock it. He heard but tried to ignore Serena's ongoing chatter from behind the closed door as he sank onto the bed.

Serena's mission was to plant in his mind the notion of her playing *all* the female roles. She planned to capture them one by one, but was far too cunning to force herself on the production all in one go. Little by little, though, she intended to divide and conquer. She could afford to wait, the big investment guns were on her side. After all, she was a member of the board. She called out loudly, "By the way, Umberto, I intend to be the only actress in the film. I'd really *love* to play all the Fiammettas. Please keep that in mind, my love. I'll be *good* for the production. And for you."

"I tell you, she wants to play all the Fiammettas," Primo was saying to Helga, who kept pushing him for information in spite of the blasting sounds of the discothèque.

"How do you know?"

"I heard her talking to her agent in Hollywood . . ."

Strange things were happening to him under the table. When he first had sat down, a girl named Pina had picked him up. Shortly afterward Helga had come in, left her party of friends, joined him and Pina and stayed at their table. Now both were doing things to him . . . Pina moving her fingers up and down his right leg, Helga squeezing his left, forcing him to answer her questions.

Helga glanced over now at the party of friends she was supposed to be with, a group three tables away that included Paolo Piccolo with his Cleo, and Angelo Catalano with Astrid. Helga's date was also still at that table . . . the French boy Astrid had passed on, calling him in turn either Jean Paul or Jean Claude but in any case definitively recommending him as a remarkable lover. Astrid no longer dated the boy, having gone back into the clutches of the outrageously possessive Angelo Catalano . . .

Catalano was leaning close to Astrid, telling her, "You see how nice I can be. You see that I'm willing to change to make you happy. You see how when you wish to be taken to one of these loud, tasteless entertainments for idiots I am only too willing to oblige." As he spoke he slid his hand under the table until he found the crotch of her thin slacks, then squeezed hard at her tender pubic area.

Astrid, still unable to fight back, bit her lower lip, tears suddenly appearing in her eyes.

Catalano, a specialist in his sadistic craft, studied her, then whispered excitedly, "Wonderful, I can never make you cry out." Satisfied that she had passed the test, he released his grip. "You are really a splendid specimen of your race, hard and stoic." Continuing with his peculiar concept of loving talk, Catalano told her, "You haven't those pitiful feminine traits found in most of your sex, and in my Fiammetta Three I intend to show you in all your glory." He took a deep breath and sat up straighter, apparently carried away by the inspiration of the moment. "I shall have a martial theme song written as background for your character—a character of genuine strength that embodies the beauty of an *unbreakable* spirit . . ."

Cleo was holding Paolo's hand as she leaned over to ask the French boy if he would please pour her a little more champagne from the bucket alongside him, the waiter having apparently deserted them. When Jean Claude had poured the wine Paolo said, "Cleo, my precious, don't you think I should take you home? You do have work in the morning."

"Oh, just one more little glass of champagne," she said, puckering her lips, "and one more for Daddy Bear."

Daddy Bear took the glass but merely toyed with it. He had something distinctly unamusing on his mind, wondered how, or when, he would break the news to Cleo and, of course, Helga as well . . .

He was, to put it bluntly, being pushed out of the *Boccaccio* film. It seemed a consortium of Swiss banks were making a bid to take over his share of the financing, were about to beat him out of the project because their offer was just too good for the producers to turn down. The newly formed Swiss company was willing to risk money with a ridiculously low guaranteed return on investment. By his lights it was a bad deal, the sort he himself would never make. In fact, nobody could afford to make such a deal, except such a consortium of banks, ten in all here, sharing the burden. And they weren't interested in the normal facts of motion picture financing, weren't competing with the Italian banks, lending half the money at a high percentage. They were only after his share, the investors' share, where any return came strictly from the film's profit . . . if it made a profit. These Swiss seemed willing to gamble that their investment might be a write-off. Making, as it did, so little sense in normal business terms, logic told him that someone with a personal motive must be behind the move. He also was quite certain that with the Swiss banking community's reputation for secrecy, it was most unlikely he would ever know the source.

It was a puzzler, all right, and he hated like hell even to think about breaking the bad news to his ladies.

# CHAPTER FIFTEEN

CONSIDERABLY BEFORE her alarm clock sounded, Madeline woke up feeling happy if not altogether fulfilled. Well, she was in love and this weekend Umberto would be with her to savor, make love to and be made love to without interruption. She lit *la bomba a gas* in her new kitchen, put the kettle on to boil, then crossed into the sitting room, from which she swung open the glass doors of her balcony. Once she'd made her instant coffee she carried her cup out onto the balcony and sat on one of the two small iron filigree chairs to watch the day break in the still pale morning sky.

Some birds egan to wake up too, their warbling seeming to signal the church bells that now began ringing all around her. An especially loud set of bells sounded nearby, and looking to the roof of the building next door she saw a group of monks emerge to line up on its flat surface, all the while chanting prayers.

Across Piazza Navona the Bernini church was catching the early rays of the sun. Before it, in silhouette, the Michelangelo fountain was pointing one of its sculptured fingers out of the shadows, as if indicating what some critics considered an inferior creation . . . Neighborhood children now appeared in the huge piazza and began to use it as an open playground. Madeline, looking down on them, tried to imagine what it must have been like in Roman times when they flooded Piazza Navona to use it to race boats . . .

Lord, lord, she thought, what a glorious scene to wake up to. Then, just beneath her balcony, she spotted a young boy setting up tables for a sidewalk café. *"Buon giorno,"* she called down to him.

The boy looked up, smiled at the beautiful woman greeting him from her balcony. *"Buon giorno, signora. Desidera qual cosa?"*

Did she desire anything? She thought how lovely it would be to have a cup of real coffee but wasn't too sure what the various types of coffee were called in Italian.

The boy, still looking up at her and still smiling, seemed to read her mind . . . and why not? Wasn't this a magical morning in the most magical of cities? *"Caffè latte? Espresso? Cappucino?"* he asked.

*"Cappucino, si,"* Madeline called to him. *"Per favore."*

*"Subito, signora,"* and the boy disappeared inside for her order.

Within moments, the boy was knocking on her door, handing her the cappucino, followed by a single white carnation, which he ceremoniously presented to her.

"Oh, *grazie,*" Madeline said, touched by the gesture. "*Mille grazie.*"

"*Grazie a lei, signora,*" he said before turning and racing down the stairs without giving her a chance to pay him, then called over his shoulder, "*A domani.*"

Until tomorrow, she silently translated, but right now last night was on her mind, last night when, among a lot of other wonderful firsts, Umberto had taught her to say "*a Roma*" at the Fontana di Trevi —"to Rome." Oh yes, absolutely, to Rome . . .

As she sipped the cappucino with its foam of milk sprinkled with chocolate, watching the splendid beauty of Piazza Navona coming to life, she wondered if any woman alive could possibly be as happy as she was . . .

Umberto's morning began quite differently, his mood one of gloom and irritation at the loss of his hard-won privacy now that Serena had moved herself in next door. "*Porca miseria, porca miseria,*" he mumbled sleepily. Yes, very apt, a pig's misery, no question about it.

The moment he'd received his wake-up call there had been an insistent tapping at the adjoining door. When he'd finally forced himself to throw off the covers and pull himself out of bed to answer it, Serena had been standing there in a full-skirted dressing gown that enveloped her thin figure in yards of yellow ruffled taffeta. She had been holding a tray full of breakfast things, smiling brightly, too damn brightly, and ever since he had been grumbling "*porca miseria*" to himself.

He scratched his head and rubbed his eyes and hoped that somehow she and her yards of taffeta and her breakfast tray would all just magically disappear.

"What's that you're mumbling?" Serena said, as she swept her masses of yellow taffeta, and her large breakfast tray, past him and into his room.

*"Porca miseria . . ."*

"Now, now, we mustn't be so grumpy, especially on such a beautiful morning."

"Pig's misery," he said in English, hoping that if he used her language she would maybe take the hint.

No such luck. She began to put the dishes from her tray onto his table, humming as she worked.

Umberto sank onto the bed, holding his head in his hands, but it was no use, she would not be discouraged. Strange, these English women. Looked so fragile, seemed to have wills of iron. He sighed, sat resignedly watching her flit about the room, understanding the advantages of living in a monastery—except that would mean no Madeline. Somehow he must find a less drastic solution to the Serena problem.

After struggling to get through the unwanted breakfast, he stumbled into the bathroom to take a shower.

There was no water. More *porca miseria.*

Serena then went into her own bathroom to shower, still humming merrily, turned on the taps. No water. Oh, shit, she thought, the fucking Roman aqueducts have done it again. In disgust she returned to her bedroom to dress, and Umberto, for the moment, was rescued from his *porca miseria* by the periodic perverseness of Rome's temperamental water system.

*"Porca miseria,"* a far-ranging term this morning. Helga was muttering it now as she closed the front door behind the French boy—Jean Paul or Jean Claude or whatever his name was. By *any* name he was, no question, a *stud.* He had kept her up all night

with one sexual feat after another. For the first hour or so it had been great, but then she had wanted to rest and he wouldn't let go of her. Finally, at 6:00 A.M., she had handed him his clothes, told him to leave, figuring that since she couldn't take another night of his lovemaking, there was no reason to be tactful about it.

Now she was exhausted, and on a day when she had something so important to attend to . . . Primo had told her about Serena's plan to campaign to play *all* the Fiammettas. She had to think how to begin the counter-campaign, but her head wasn't clear enough. What she needed was a strong coffee and a long hot bath. She picked up the kettle and held it up to the kitchen faucet. Oh, God, no water. She couldn't possibly go without washing, she must smell like a brothel after all that sex. She had to phone someone who had water.

But neither Paolo nor Cleo were able to take Helga's phone call when it came, Paolo being in his shower and Cleo in her sunken Roman tub. Both were unaware of the water emergency since, in building the Villa Monti, Paolo had seen to it that they had their own deep well and electric pumps. Such problems, as in ancient Rome, were, after all, for plebians only.

At his villa Catalano had an old-fashioned standing pump in the garden that needed to be cranked by hand, but at least was insurance against the vagaries of water failure plaguing certain of his colleagues this morning. He had promised, in a burst of newborn generosity, to allow Astrid to sleep in on the mornings when she was not making a film. This morning, however, was an emergency. No water for his habitual 6:00 A.M. bathing. Expressing his regrets, he had gotten Astrid out of bed to work the pump . . . as a Roman gentleman he could hardly be expected to perform such a chore himself. Astrid was so occupied when the phone rang. It was Helga urgently requesting to speak to Astrid, but Catalano said that she could not be disturbed until she'd finished an important project she had undertaken for him. Helga, projecting, assumed it had to do with servicing the bastard's sadistic demands, and, in a sense, she was right.

As for Madeline, she discovered the water affair after stripping down and getting into the tub, only to be greeted by the rattle of pipes, a few impotent splutters and then nothing. No matter . . . nothing could diminish this glorious morning. She would go to Cine Città early and take a shower in her dressing room before going for her costume fitting. She must remember, though, from now on to keep a supply of bottled water.

When she arrived at Cine Citta she hurried into her dressing room to answer the ringing phone.

It was Helga, with what seemed all Rome's preoccupation this morning, though in Helga's case phrasing it more colorfully than most.

"I've just got to wash my pussy. Do you have any water, my pet?" Madeline checked, found that she did and so informed Helga.

"Thank *God* . . . listen, darling, would you mind terribly if I came over to use your facilities? I smell like a two-lire whore."

Madeline blanched slightly, told her to come right on over . . .

After her costume fitting Madeline returned to her dressing room to find that Helga had arrived, had already taken her desperately needed shower and was dying for a coffee, so Madeline walked over to the cantina with her.

On their way Madeline told Helga about Dal Moro and the Trevi Fountain, about how she thought she was getting to know Umberto better. How even, she believed, she was falling in love with him and after only one evening . . .

"Ah, darling, love can easily happen in an evening, with a great lover like Umberto—"

"But we didn't—"

"Oh, yes, he's never fooled Helga with that innocent little boy act . . . he's a lover all right, that one."

"*Helga,* please, we did not make love . . . although I admit it wasn't my idea not to, not at all."

"Ah, more's the pity, but Umberto must be truly in love with you to have played the role of protecting your sainted innocent crotch from his depredations. Umberto, the sly one . . ."

Helga would have gone on about her favorite subject, the varieties of sex and its practitioners, if they had not been suddenly confronted by Serena Blaire, who turned out to be the only person waiting at the counter. "Hello, Madeline," she said cheerily, obviously ignoring Helga, then promptly got off her stool and hurried over to buss Madeline European-fashion on both cheeks. Helga, observing, smelled trouble.

"Hello, Serena," Madeline said, taken aback somewhat by the show of friendliness. They had, she and Serena, only met for the first time at the banquet for Paolo Monti and hadn't exchanged more than a few words even then. "I'm sure you know Helga Haufman."

"*Hello,* Helga," Serena said, smiling brightly and shaking her hand. "Of course we know each other."

Helga looked at her a moment, then: "I know your husband *well,*" her smile even broader than Serena's.

Serena appeared oblivious to the dig. "Yes, Primo has many friends. He's adorable, how could one not like him?" She then invited them to sit with her at the counter, saying the coffees were her treat.

Still smiling, Serena said to Madeline, "I understand you're about to begin a new film. I think that's wonderful. Congratulations."

"Thank you . . ." Madeline felt self-conscious about the quality of *Paranoia*—she hated that title—especially in front of an actress of Serena's acknowledged stature, and did something she ordinarily never would have done—she apologized for it.

But Serena was unassailably gracious, and in a tone that sounded altogether sincere said, "If you are in the film, Madeline, I am sure it can't help but be wonderful. Your reputation has, you see, preceded you."

A doubled-edged, lefthanded compliment if Helga had ever heard one, but she did have to admit that cunty Serena was capable of quite a performance—onscreen and off. She still was holding her breath, waiting for the knives to show . . .

As the coffee appeared on the counter Serena said with seemingly guileless enthusiasm, "It must feel great, Madeline, to be going back to work. You must have hated being off the screen for such a long time—"

Helga snorted. "And for you *too,* Serena."

Serena would not be goaded. "Helga, you are quite right, it has been some time for me as well. Of course, lucky me, I do have the most beautiful baby daughter to show for my time off," still said with a smile.

"*Sugar?*" Helga said, plopping the bowl in front of Serena.

Serena shook her head, kept her eyes on Madeline. "Don't you love Rome, Madeline?"

"Oh, yes, I do," thinking of the previous night she'd spent being romantically introduced to it by Umberto.

"Especially Dal Moro and the Fontana di Trevi?" Serena was saying, almost so casually that at first Madeline wasn't sure she had heard the words, doing a silent double-take in her shock.

Helga instantly recognized the knife, and where it was going. She took hold of Madeline's arm, tried to pull her up and away from what she knew must be coming. Madeline shook her off, looked directly at Serena. "What are you saying, Miss Blaire?"

"What? Oh, dear, did I say something to upset? I'm sorry, Madeline, truly I am. Why, I was merely pleased that Umberto had taken time off from, well, from me, to show a foreigner some of Rome's sights. Didn't you know . . . Umberto and I are, as they quaintly put it, living together at the Hilton." Her pixie smile in her pixie face was never more dazzling—Helga wanted to smash it with her fist but at the moment could do little more than watch her new friend suffer.

Madeline froze. Not able even to speak.

Helga tried to take up the slack. "What are you doing here at Cine Citta, Serena? This isn't your set or your film."

Serena said, large eyes even larger, "I've been sort of looking things over, Helga, trying to decide which dressing room I would like to have. Cleo Monti was generous enough to show me hers this morning . . ."

Helga's mouth dropped open; for a moment she

too was speechless. "You've been talking to Cleo this morning?"

"Yes, we had a lovely long chat. But I'm afraid I upset her too. It seems to be my day for that . . . You see, I thought by now she would have known, been told, that I'm taking over her part of Fiammetta Four."

Helga hit the counter with her fist. "Come on, Madeline, let's get out of here. I think the atmosphere is poisoned." This time she did pull Madeline off the stool, leaving in their wake a Serena Blaire with a smile to rival the Cheshire cat's.

They found Cleo hysterical in her dressing room. Furniture was upside down, every object at hand was smashed. Now she was at her dressing table, her recently applied eye makeup running in black streams down her cheeks.

"Well," Helga said, "the English cunt has struck again."

Meanwhile on the set of *Domani e Domani e Domani* no work had been done that morning. The set was lit only by a work light, and Ralph de Rossi had sent the technicians off on an extended break. Umberto was straddling a chair on the dimly lit stage and wringing his hands. Ralph was pacing back and forth.

"Who told her?" Ralph was saying. "Who the hell would be so crude to tell Cleo that she was being replaced before she could be prepared for it?"

Umberto shrugged his shoulders, went on ringing his hands.

"*Damn* it," Ralph said. "Cleo should never have been hurt this way. It's cruel and unnecessary. Mariani might have accepted her for his segment, still might. At least that could have been held out to her."

"I know, I know," Umberto said. "Poor Cleo, her husband out, now her too. What can we do now to help her?"

Ralph lowered his voice. "I was going to find her another part in the film first, make an even exchange."

"Yes, yes, it was merely going to be a matter of choosing one of the other Fiammettas for her—"

"Look, Umberto," Ralph said, putting his hand on Umberto's shoulder, "please, you go and talk to Cleo. She is refusing to see me."

"Yes, I'll try," Umberto said, getting up. "I'll try to explain to her, to make her believe what we had intended to do."

Umberto had almost gotten to Cleo's dressing room door when he saw Madeline leaving and rushed up to her, calling her name, reaching out to kiss her—and finding himself nearly straight-armed by his new love.

"Madeline . . . darling . . . what's wrong?"

She looked at him for a moment, fighting back the tears that she felt coming on, wanting partly to kill him, partly to pull him into her arms and wipe out the memory of Serena Blaire, and feeling altogether miserable. She started to speak, shook her head, turned and ran off, knowing she must look the fool, and resenting him for that too.

Umberto was about to go after her when Helga came out of Cleo's dressing room just in time to see Madeline's backside disappearing and Umberto's face all grief-stricken and confused.

"Helgalina," he said, taking hold of her hands, "what's wrong with Madeline?"

Helga pulled her hands out of his grasp, shaking her head. "Come on, Umberto, you have been a bad boy, a very very bad boy. And with such a bag of bones. Really, Umberto, have you no taste at all?"

"But Helgalina, it's not as it seems. I didn't intend or want—"

Helga felt like ruffling his curly brown hair as she would a naughty child, which was the tone she used on him now. "Umberto, stop it, this is Helgalina you're talking to. You knew damn well what you were doing, and now you're paying for it. Good, maybe you'll learn that—"

"I swear to you, Helgalina, whatever you may have heard has nothing to do with what I feel for Madeline. You are a woman of the world, you understand—"

"I *understand* that you left Madeline at her door, then went home to fuck her royal highness Serena Blaire. Ugh. I repeat, what a shocking lack of *taste* . . ."

Umberto could only slam the palm of his hand to his forehead and mutter the words he had used from the start of this day. "Oh, *porca miseria* . . . I tell you, I am innocent—"

Helga looked at him a moment, half smiled in spite of herself. "You may be, Umberto. But your cock is guilty as hell."

# CHAPTER SIXTEEN

SIGNOR ROMOLO Volpe of the Romulus and Remus Detective Agency was sitting with his feet propped up on his desk looking out of his office window in the EUR: the Universal Exhibition District, which Mussolini had commissioned. His office faced a broad avenue studded with pine trees and was across the wide intersection from the large building that was headquarters for the Federal Agricultural Organization. He did most of his work at night, sometimes having to stay up the whole night trailing suspects, but this morning his wife had rousted him out of bed and the house since it was the maid's day to clean the floors.

And so here he was at the office, with nothing to

do and not even able to have a decent cup of coffee, his secretary, Luciana, not yet having come in to make it for him. When he made it, it was mud. He would have to check up on Luciana's hours. He was seldom in the office before eleven or eleven-thirty, but Luciana was supposed to be there every morning at nine to answer the telephone—which just now rang, jolting him out of his thoughts. He swung his legs off the desk as he lifted the receiver.

"*Pronto, Romulus e Remus.*"

"I want to speak to Mr. Romolo Volpe," said the English-accented voice. This is Mrs. Serena Blaire Galiano."

"Oh, *Signora,*" Volpe said, commencing to gush. The lady was, after all, his highest-paying, not to mention most celebrated, client. "Volpe, here. How may I serve you, *signora?*"

"Listen, Volpe, cut the lasagna." She had to smile at her witticism. "You've been of fuck-all service to me so far. I'm about to fire you."

"Please, *Signora,* not now when we at last have a breakthrough—"

"What do you mean?"

Serena had, indeed, begun looking for another detective agency. Volpe had been on the case for months with no results. Serena had to have the evidence to sue Primo for a divorce on the grounds of adultery, and she couldn't wait much longer. Not with her own infidelity in danger of being discovered. After all, she now was practically living in the same hotel room with Umberto, even though he did show a certain foolish resistance out of some misguided loyalty to that nothing American . . .

"*What* breakthrough are you talking about?"

"Last week your husband visited several bars and discothèques—"

"I *know* that."

"But, *Signora,* he was alone and he picked up a girl and went home with her, and he's been going to her address every night since."

"A *week* ago. Why haven't you told me? I knew Primo must be screwing around, but why has it taken you all these months to discover it? Why do I have to fire you to get the information that I've been paying you a fortune for? *Well?*"

"But *Signora,* it has just happened. I swear to you that Signor Primo has never before gone with a woman."

For the previous months Volpe had not been following the chubby young man on a regular basis, but he had followed him enough to feel that the guy was dull, apparently seldom went anywhere or did anything of interest. (He had underestimated him enough to miss his involvement with Helga.) He had been surprised when his assistant, who had been following someone else, had called him the previous week to say that Primo Galiano was at last on the move. It was then that Volpe had told his assistant to drop the other subject and stay glued to the Blaire woman's husband. When his assistant called back to say that Galiano had gone home with a girl two hours before and had not left her apartment building as yet, Volpe felt they might finally get the goods on the little creep. Since that first break, Volpe had been spending every night in his car outside the girl's apartment. But his big mistake, Volpe realized, had been in not notifying Serena Blaire immediately. He should have called her with the information, not waited for her to call him.

"I'm sure we'll catch him in the act, *Signora—*"

"Who is the girl?" Serena asked, only mildly curious.

"Her name is Pina, *Signora.*"

"Pina *what?* Don't you even have a last name for her?"

"I think she uses only the one name, *Signora.*" Then trying to sound confident, he hurriedly added, "I'm sure that we will have the photographs and recordings as evidence of adultery in a matter of days now."

"One week," Serena said. "I'll give you one week, then I'll either double your fee or fire you." And she hung up . . .

Umberto, the dear boy, didn't like to talk at breakfast time, she had quickly learned . . . she always was a quick study . . . so she had soon taken to leaving the Hilton every morning and spending her days either at home or in Geneva. No matter, it was the nights with Umberto she cared about, the nights when she had the matinée idol cocksman at her mercy . . . which was where she needed and wanted him. Making Primo, thereby, excess baggage. Poor Primo, he simply couldn't be of service in her great career renaissance, whereas Umberto was the key player just now. Not to mention a considerable stud on his own. That might not be her prime interest but it was a nice fringe benefit. True, some nights he behaved like a selfish bore, fucked her without benefit of even foreplay, but on other occasions he did indeed give her a terrific workout. And now that she had contrived to put Madeline Mandell out of the picture, those terrific workouts were happening with increasing frequency . . . even if, afterward, he always seemed to be in mourning. Silly damn Italian. But useful.

In a sense the awfulness of *Paranoia*, which had begun filming, was a blessing for Madeline, diverting her as it did from thinking *all* the time of Umberto and his deception. The director, Alfonso Razzi, was a disaster, a man whose tastes gave prurience a bad name. The script was unbelievable, incoherent. Madeline had listened to Pina's translation, not believing it, but it was even worse on the stage than on the page.

*Paranoia* was supposed to be a mystery, but the only mystery was why it was being produced. There were frames of the film showing a hand opening a drawer to reveal a gun but it was never clear whose hand it was and what part the gun played in the business, never mind the story. There were enormous cobwebs draped on the movie's set, creating the unintended mystery of why Madeline's character, a wealthy woman, hadn't ordered her housekeeper to take up a broom and clear them away. Silliest of all was the way Madeline's character chased around the villa turning *off* the water. Madeline could not bring herself to look scared in scenes merely because the faucets were running. (A little while ago, she recalled, Rome's problem was just the opposite.) She suspected that once the film got into the theater the audience would talk back to the screen, yelling, "Lady, get a *plumber.*" Worst of all, she felt, was the way Razzi imposed a sexual connotation on even the most ordinary occurrences: the postman put his hand inside his fly as he delivered a letter; the old housekeeper fondled her sagging breasts as she poured coffee; the grocery boy leered, for God's sake, at a *salami.*

Madeline didn't have any nude scenes, but she was always surrounded by a harem of nude slave girls, their pubic hair dyed to match the thatch on top. They were to have appeared once in a dream sequence, but Razzi obviously found photographing the nude young girls so exciting that the dream sequence kept spilling over into the rest of the film.

When Ralph de Rossi, artistic director of *Boccaccio Volgare,* had asked to meet with Madeline, she was almost afraid to show her face but had agreed to come to his office after work that day. The mere fact that he was interested and wanted to talk to her about Fiammetta One was, she hoped, a good sign . . .

De Rossi had gone to his office an hour before Madeline was expected. *Domani e Domani e Domani* was winding up its last week, and with the relaxation in pressure he had asked Umberto to come to his office so they could talk in private about the *Boccaccio Volgare* casting.

"Look, Umberto," Ralph said, perching on the desktop to face Umberto, who had stretched out on the leather couch. "What I wanted to pose to you was the . . . the possibility of Serena Blaire playing all the female parts. I know, I know, it would break some hearts, but for some reason the producers are making a real move toward this, and, frankly, I too can see some merit in it. I think we all agree she's perfect for Fiammetta Four, and Franco Mariani and I do believe that she could bring a different and interesting quality to his sequence. As far as my own sequence is concerned, I think I could get out of Serena a certain amount of the purity the character calls for. So that would take care of episodes one, two and four—"

"But Cleo?" Umberto said. "That confuses me still. Paolo pulls out his investment if she's out, and yet . . ."

"Yes, the producers don't seem to care about Paolo pulling his financing. Obviously they must have another investor offering better terms than Paolo."

"What about Fiammetta Three?" Umberto asked, lacing his hands behind his head. "Catalano would never agree to give up Astrid Zealand, would he?"

"That's right, he wouldn't," Ralph agreed. "But he plans on a science-fiction feel in his episode. There's a metamorphosis where Fiammetta changes into a Viking goddess. All we'd need for continuity would be a brief openng scene using Serena Blaire, then Astrid Zealand could take over and play the bulk of the scenes."

"Yes, I see your point," Umberto said. "I guess it could work that way."

"Yes, it could be good," Ralph said. "But what I wanted to ask you, Umberto, is how would you feel about Serena Blaire taking all the parts? She's a ballsy lady, and in some of the episodes—not mine or Catalano's but perhaps in the other two—you might find yourself in a little trouble keeping in first position."

Umberto shrugged, stared at the ceiling, seeing not Serena but Madeline.

"I think it deserves some careful thought," Ralph prodded him. "You *are* the film's main asset. Yours is the performance I'm counting on to tie it all together, with humor and talent. I don't want you under any unnecessary strain—"

Umberto kept looking at the ceiling.

"Forgive me," Ralph went on, "but I understand that you have a sort of personal involvement with Serena. Do you feel that her being an equal costar would adversely affect either your relationship or your performance?"

"It won't make any difference." His voice was flat, weary.

"It's a decision with consequences," Ralph pressed

him. "The producers can only push the artistic side so far; we have a say. It's just that if Serena Blaire would make everyone happy, well, then I'd say we have no problem."

Umberto sat up. "Look, Ralph, it's your film. I think I better stay out of the casting decisions . . ." He got up from the couch and walked over to look out the window, then began speaking quietly, almost as if he were talking to himself. "I've really made a mess of things . . . Cleo doesn't speak to me any longer, she knows I was in on the decision about Anastasio's segment. Obviously her husband, Paolo, is cool toward me, never mind about other pressures behind the decision to replace Cleo. The lady who used to be my greatest friend, Helga Haufman, is disgusted with me because of what I did to Cleo—and because of another more personal matter where I behaved with my usual unthinking stupidity. And if Serena thought I was lying when I said that I am no longer taking an active part in the casting, I would have no peace from her."

"Are you in love with Serena?"

"*No, no.* Not in the least. Ralph, if I never saw her again it would be a relief. I didn't invite her into my bed, I assure you. The trouble is, I didn't kick her out either."

"What about Madeline Mandell?"

Umberto turned from the window. "What about her?"

"How would you feel about working with her?"

"Are you still considering her for Fiammetta One?" Umberto asked, trying to keep his feelings out of his voice.

"Yes, I am. Matter of fact, she's coming to see me in a little while. I still consider her the perfect image of the pure Fiammetta," Ralph said, then paused, rubbing his chin. "It's a damn difficult decision. I'm torn between that casting and the pressure I'm under to give all the characters to Serena. All right, I'll respect your wish and try not to get you directly involved in the casting, but I still would like to ask you for some helpful reaction from time to time. This is going to be a rough period for me."

"What is it you're really asking me about Madeline Mandell?"

"Well," Ralph said almost apologetically, "again, you'll have to forgive me, but I have noticed the way you behave whenever we happen to run into her, or her name is mentioned. Sometimes you're not such a good actor, at least not in real life. So as your director I feel I must ask you if playing scenes alongside Madeline would be too . . . distracting for you."

"No, not at all," Umberto said briskly, but feeling excited for the first time in this discussion. "I mean, if she's the best actress for the part, then by all means cast her . . ." He glanced at his watch. "If that's all, Ralph, I'd like to go."

"That's all, my friend," Ralph said, patting him on the back. "I'm glad we had this talk. I think I understand a good deal more than before. You surely do know how to make a drama out of your life . . . well, try to save a little for my picture."

Umberto, appreciating Ralph's attempt to relieve his gloom with a bit of humor, smiled and gave a half salute. "I shall do my best, director," and exited with a mock flourish.

In an office down the hall from de Rossi's, a happier man, Franco Mariani, was waiting for the young girl who had changed his life. He had just taken what had recently become his daily shower, washed his hair and changed clothes. But she had changed more than his customary aversion to soap and water. She had affected the way he felt about *Boccaccio* as well.

Mariani, for all his unlovely personal habits, was a serious director with artistic credits to his name. In the past he had always worked on a project alone, being independent. He had only agreed to direct a segment of *Boccaccio* because he also realized it was time he got involved with a *hit* movie . . . Knowing the industry as he did, he realized if he didn't have a commercial success soon the money boys might well cut off his funding, and that would be a disaster. Films were his life, he was too old to change professions.

These past weeks had been driving him crazy, what with the indecision over the casting of his *Boccaccio* segment. Paolo Monti originally wanted Helga Haufman in the part, then began pushing for his wife, Cleo. And when she lost Fiammetta Four, the artistic coordinator, Ralph de Rossi, also suggested Cleo, *then* changed his mind in favor of Serena, who had become *numero uno* with the producers. He *should* have gone along with Helga Haufman, she'd been his first choice, but he'd hesitated about casting producer Paolo Monti's mistress, worried that she'd have too much power on the set. If only he had cast Helga the matter would have been settled and he wouldn't have come under such damnable pressures.

Actually, Mariani realized, he had been close to quitting the whole business, had locked himself in his office to make a decision that could have had him walking away from the project. As he waited now for

Pina, he realized he probably would have done just that if it hadn't been for her. At first he hadn't quite been able to believe that so young and attractive a girl could possibly be interested in him. Or if she were, he assumed it was the usual would-be starlet's pitch with a director, a pitch that in his case, as it always had before, would surely stop short of the bedroom. So he sent her away from his outer office those first few times, but she persisted, refused to be insulted or discouraged, and was there, every afternoon at five, waiting for him, asking only to see him, to talk to him. And when he agreed, still telling himself there was no fool like an old fool, she quickly changed things around by practically seducing him on his office couch, a delicious nineteen-year-old sexual athlete who made him feel neither old nor foolish, but alive again, ready and able to take on the world, including the annoyances of the *Boccaccio* casting business. Did she want something in exchange? Who knew? Who cared? And at the moment her only demand—more a suggestion, really—was that he reacquaint himself with the benefits of the shower and clean clothing, a small enough price to pay for the pleasure and release she brought him . . .

As for Pina, now making her way to Mariani's office for their afternoon session, she had no regrets, none at all. At first Umberto Cassini had seemed the best prospect, at least professionally, in view of his star position in the industry. But he had proved altogether impossible, even when his mother was on her side in her campaign to hook him. Then when she'd switched off to Primo Galiano, husband of the famous and influential Serena Blaire, she decided that even if her relationship with puppyish Primo didn't yield immediate benefits it was at least more promising than the nonexistent one with Umberto, who had only run from her, and the sex with him was just about the straightest and most uncomplicated she'd known in her already extensive experience, spiced by his touching sense of guilt each time they did it. Ordinarily sex had been just a means to an end, but in Primo's case there was at least this other added attraction.

Still, for all his qualities and important marital connection, when Primo hadn't yet been able to do anything for her professionally, which, after all, was the primary objective, she had sat herself down one night and evaluated the directors of the hot new film *Boccaccio Volgare* for their possible availability. She had quickly settled on Franco Mariani, the man everybody sneered and sniffed at, a man getting on in age who would surely welcome the attentions of a girl like her. And, of course, she had been right, although it had taken her longer than she'd thought. He simply couldn't believe she could really care about him, at least enough to go to bed with him. Of course that to her was the least of sacrifices, but, as the saying went, what he didn't know wouldn't hurt him. Meanwhile, he was so appreciative, so grateful, that she felt for the first time in her life she was actually doing something for somebody besides herself, which, to her surprise, made her feel good. And none of that stuff about Mariani's odor really bothered her. To the contrary, she even rather liked it . . . it was different, and sort of exciting, and better than all those phony smells most of the men she'd knew doused themselves with before going to bed. She had only urged him to bathe more often and wear clean clothes for his own sake, not hers, telling him what was clearly the truth . . . that he was offending people and making his life needlessly difficult.

After a while she began genuinely to *like* Franco, seeing the proud and vulnerable man beneath the less than lovely surface, the man few had ever seen or taken the trouble to look for. As a matter of fact, she decided that she probably would have to break off her times with Primo, not only because it was yielding few dividends, but because she found it increasingly a chore to screw him when she was beginning, for the first time in her life, actually to care about a man for himself instead of for what she could get out of him. Life, she decided, was certainly getting interesting. . . .

Closing the door to Ralph's office and going down the stairs and out of the building, Umberto was thinking very much about the last question Ralph had asked him—would playing scenes alongside Madeline be distracting for him? Oh, *yes,* and how he would welcome such a distraction. Especially the love scenes, which out of stupidity he'd forfeited in real life. Maybe he could begin to recoup in the make-believe medium what he seemed to do best in. Of course, he had voiced none of this in answer to Ralph's question. Instead, he had pretended a sort of generous indifference to personal considerations, telling Ralph to cast whomever he thought best for the part . . . Still a phony, he thought ruefully, but at least this time perhaps his pretense would help Madeline, who, if word at Cine Citta was to be believed, was involved in a bad film and would need an important one like *Boccaccio* if she was going to revive her career.

Without thinking where he was going, he found

himself walking by the stage where he knew her filming took place. Realizing where he was, and that the time of her appointment with Ralph was no doubt approaching, he accelerated his pace so he wouldn't run into her. He didn't want another unpleasant confrontation to make things even chillier between them. As he turned to walk off he spotted the sign on the stage door—PARANOIA. He could only hope that the memory of it would soon be only a bad dream for Madeline. It certainly would if he had anything to do about it . . .

It was a week after Serena had given Volpe her ultimatum. She was in the customized gym of her villa doing dance exercises when Primo opened the door and came in quietly, trying his best not to upset her routine. But he did. Serena stopped, turned off the tape recorder and gave him one of her rehearsed smiles. She would be, she had decided, particularly nice to Primo until Volpe had the evidence and was ready to strike. "What is it, dearest?"

"I'm sorry to disturb you, *tesora,* but something strange is happening."

"Well, what in the world could that be, love?" she said, dabbing at her neck with a towel.

"I think I'm being followed, I *know* I'm being followed . . . I'm afraid someone is going to kidnap me!"

Serena buried her face in the towel to keep from laughing. "Now who would want to kidnap you, my dearest?"

"Well, Sicilian bandits . . . because I'm your husband."

Serena bit her lip to stop the giggle she felt coming on. Of course it was Volpe, she thought, but if it *were* bandits, what a favor they'd be doing her . . . they could bloody well wait till hell froze over before she'd ransom Primo, whose presence was continuing to complicate her plans for herself and Umberto.

"What makes you think you're being followed?" she asked now, hoping she sounded reasonably concerned, taking a deep breath to help her play the scene straight.

Primo couldn't understand her attitude. "*Tesora*, I'm serious. I see the same men everywhere I go, they follow me everywhere—"

"What nonsense, love. You're being paranoid. Now just relax, dearest, nothing terrible is going to happen to you." Then with a kiss on the cheek she dismissed him and turned the music back on.

Primo accepted her dismissal from the room, but not her dismissal of what he believed was happening to him. He was not imagining things. He did always see those same men everywhere he went. The same car was always parked outside Pina's apartment building. And why? A kidnap plot was certainly the most logical explanation . . . no doubt they would torture, maybe kill him, which he gloomily concluded would be his punishment for all his sinful fornication. He'd even given up trying to repent or asking for forgiveness, the sin was too great. He'd become a lost soul, hopelessly compromised by his gratification of the flesh. And the odd thing was that he didn't even like the girl . . . there was something increasingly cold and indifferent about Pina. But she did still spread her legs for him, and he kept going back for more, like an addict . . .

Trying not to upset his *tesora* too much, he had not even told her about the most alarming incident. It had happened a couple of nights ago. One or both of those men following him had been on Pina's bedroom balcony. They had been bold enough to flash a light on him and Pina, had even taken pictures during the act of fornication . . . they were perverts as well as kidnappers. And they were definitely after him. He was *not* just being paranoid. His *tesora* would be sorry . . .

# CHAPTER SEVENTEEN

PAOLO HAD come to see Helga at breakfast, something he had not done since the early days of their affair. With the trace of a reflective smile she remembered those early days: getting to know him had been better than becoming his mistress, a crazy klnd of mistress who had the wife's consent. But now she was devoted to Cleo as well as to Paolo, who, it seemed, had an urgent matter to discuss with her. How many years had it been since they'd talked, really talked?

Paolo was obviously troubled, refusing coffee and asking for a scotch.

"Paolo, darling, you look tired."

"I have a lot on my mind."

"Is there anything I can do?"

"Yes, you can help me by explaining to Cleo what I'm about to tell you . . . The thing is, Helga, it appears almost certain that I won't be able to keep my financial interest in the *Boccaccio* film."

"You mean the Swiss consortium is actually pushing you out?"

"It looks that way."

"What about the Italian banks who are putting up the other half of the money?"

"What about them?"

"Well, couldn't you exert some pressure on them to keep the consortium out? Maybe offer to switch some of your accounts if they help you stay in the film."

Paolo smiled, reached over to stroke her auburn fringe. "You're a clever woman." He took a sip of his drink. "I might have been able to do something like that a few weeks ago but I've got a cash-flow crisis at the moment. I'm just not free to wheel and deal."

"The strikes?"

"Yes."

"But there must be something you can do."

"Helga, as I've told you, my money doesn't come from film investments. I consider them a pleasurable gamble, or used to. I haven't time to spend worrying about a movie when two of my factories are on strike. I have to lobby the damn government. The lousy Communist ministers are even talking about expropriating one of my biggest land developments."

"But the Communists are a minority in government."

"Yes, and I have lots of friends among the Christian Democrats. But to keep peace they sometimes trade off things . . . throw the Commies a bone to keep them in line."

"And this time you think the bone might be your lands?"

"My beach properties, which they want to expropriate for a park, or so they say."

"Darling, I'm sorry, you must be under a terrible strain."

"I am, and that's why I don't want to have a scene with Cleo. Not now. Please, just explain to her that I'm in a bad bind. Try to make her understand I did all I could to have some control over the movie, but it's turned out to be one battle I seem to have lost."

He didn't mention, he didn't have to, whom the consortium favored: the darling snow-white pure—ha!—Serena. What she would really have liked to do was arrange some fatal accident for the bitch, thereby taking care of all their problems . . .

She sighed, said she'd take care of it, reminding herself that once he also would have been concerned about losing on her account. Hey, if she didn't watch it she'd become everybody's maiden aunt. Like the whore with the heart of gold . . . oh, she wasn't a street whore, of course, but she respected them. What the hell, they were in honest work, not like the hypocrites who spouted morality . . .

Helga's mother had raised her backstage, so that being in a cabaret was not only her mother's life but hers, too. As for papas, she had had plenty of them, including the owners who found little Helga irresistible, brassy and sexy even at six, when she first began to sing risqué songs to the foot-stomping delight of the customers. When her mother's tuberculosis got bad Helga took over, and even though Berlin had been devastated by the war there always seemed some back street cabaret open for business. Her mother passed away just as the postwar boom was beginning, and Helga, now of Amazon-like proportions, brassy and professional, was snapped up by the new film industry. Mostly she'd made out fine, so long as she didn't make the mistake of remembering too much, and lived for the present, without illusions, understanding that without the kindness of men she had no life at all . . .

Of course she would help Paolo. In her fashion she still loved him, and to be practical, if Paolo was losing *Boccaccio,* she might be losing it too. No time for tears . . . there never had been. Tears only got people in trouble. She only hoped Cleo wouldn't make too much of a scene. She'd ask Astrid and Madeline to go with her. No sense facing Cleo's impending tantrum all on her own. She wasn't, after all, a masochist.

Before he left, Paolo looked so distraught, even assured as he now was that she would help him out with Cleo, that Helga did what she had done so many times before for him. Only this time there were no rude jokes about the size of his penis, which, as a matter of fact, did very well for itself, and for her too . . .

Primo was at the wheel of the long black Mercedes, Serena by his side. He was driving her only a short distance from their villa on the Cassia, along the same road to the country club at Olgetta, but Primo always felt on top of the world whenever Serena asked him to drive her. She didn't often permit him that pleasure, but it was a Sunday and she'd given the chauffeur the day off.

Vittorio Anastasio, director of Fiammetta Four, had invited Serena to be his guest, but not Primo, who tried to tell himself that no doubt it was a way for the director to get to know Serena before they worked together; but since it was for lunch and others would no doubt be there with *their* spouses, he couldn't help but feel a bit slighted. Never mind, *he* was married to her. Remember *that* . . .

After dropping her off he would have the interminable drive to Zagarolo for the routine family gathering at the house that Serena had built for them. Not that it was so far to Zagarolo, but against his advice Serena had chosen to buy a villa on the Cassia, which without a doubt was Rome's most traffic-congested road, a main artery that extended for miles without side roads and was too narrow for passing. On Sundays like this the traffic crawled bumper-to-bumper, and he knew he would be stuck in the line for at least an hour.

Still, when Primo glanced over at Serena he thought how beautiful she looked and how well dressed in casual elegance—yellow cashmere sweater adding a touch of color beneath her beige sports suit, beige felt hat tipped at a pert angle and setting off her short dark curls and enormous doe eyes. She truly was a picture, just as the fashion magazines had described her, and he told her so. "You're a picture of casual elegance today, *tesora*." And reached over to touch her kid-gloved hand.

She allowed the touch, patted his hand in return, even forced a smile of sorts.

Momentarily encouraged, he said, "I'd love it if you'd agree to come with me some Sunday to Zagarolo . . ."

She reverted to her prevailing mood. "I've seen it."

Well, he had to admit that Zagarolo was not too pretty. It might be someday when the newly planted saplings grew, but for the time being the countryside did look barren . . . There had been a construction boom in the area and developers had cut down the trees to make room for rows of houses, close to one another. And in the rainy season the once beautiful hills looked like mud slides. His mother had wanted one of those modern wooden houses because many of her friends were moving to the area. It might not have been fashionable, but the houses had been going for a reasonable price, a price he had felt Serena would agree to pay. Serena had been to his mother's new house only once, and refused to go with him on Sundays or to be with his family on any occasions except the most important ones, like birthdays or weddings. Still, how could he complain when she was so generous to all of them? Which was what he tried to tell his mother, who in colorful language disagreed, punctuated by a gesture that spoke the feelings of a good many about his darling *tesora* . . .

They were driving now alongside the white wooden railings that enclosed the country club. "Do you want me to pick you up after lunch?"

"No," she said checking herself in the mirror on the sun visor. "I'll call a taxi. I may want to leave early."

As they turned into the gateway and stopped, the guard wrote down only Serena's name, then saluted Primo, thinking that the young man in the dark suit was her chauffeur.

Serena paused before leaving him. "I'll need to talk to you later this afternoon, Primo. It's rather important, so please be home at a reasonable hour—before dinner time, at any rate . . ." She did not smile when she said it.

Primo was worried. Important, she'd said. What could be so important that she needed to talk to him this afternoon? Unless . . . unless she had somehow found out about his indiscretions. "Oh, *mea culpa* . . ." he intoned as he drove off, scarcely able to grip the wheel.

Serena walked briskly into the clubhouse, paused, stood posing in the columned hallway. People from adjoining rooms stopped and stared . . . she'd have died if they hadn't. Now a heavy-set fellow in tweeds fitting the description of Vittorio Anastasio was coming toward her. She had heard that Anastasio was pleasant but dull, hoped that spending time with him and his friends wouldn't be too excruciatingly boring. Actually she had planned to spend the day with Umberto but he had decided to fly to Paris to spend some time with his daughter. No matter, it was just as well. She needed today to present her wayward husband . . . who hadn't touched *her* in months . . . with the investigator's evidence . . .

"Umberto has gone to Paris for the weekend," Helga was telling Madeline as they drove toward Cleo's house.

Madeline was pretending interest in the catacombs as they sped by, but a chill had run up her spine at the thought of Umberto on a romantic weekend in Paris with Serena.

"Don't worry, pet, Serena isn't with him. He went to see Nicola. Did you know he had a six-year-old daughter by a French model?"

"Yes, he told me . . ." Madeline looked at her and began to laugh quietly. "I shouldn't even try to hide my feelings from you, I really can't hide *anything* from you, can I?"

"I'm nosy, that's the truth, my dear. I'm probably the nosiest friend you'll ever have."

"And how do you know where Umberto went for the weekend?"

"The telephone. It's like an extension of my head. I do some of my best work on the telephone. And I can tell you I let him know I'm pissed off at him for having anything to do with Serena. Actually, though, this latest tidbit comes from Umberto's dresser. I pump him every day for the latest gossip. Some of it is a lot less fun than you'd think."

Madeline nodded. "Too bad we couldn't use your favorite instrument to give Cleo the bad news you've just gotten."

Helga looked at her, said straight-faced, "Not my *favorite* instrument, Madeline. If I could use that, well, I could take on a whole consortium of bankers . . . providing they were horny enough. Which most of them aren't. They'd rather make money than love. *Merde.*"

Cleo was waiting for them in her glass-enclosed patio, which faced the rose garden.

"I'm happy you're here," Cleo said, kissing Helga and Madeline on the cheek. "We have fresh vongole. They been soaking all night and cook is making for us spaghetti alla vongole." She smacked her full lips.

"Did Astrid phone you? Is she coming?" Helga asked.

"Perhaps yes, perhaps no. It depends if that terrible Angelo will allow her. So I told her to come if he allows. But we won't wait to start our spaghetti."

The butler had entered with the wine, and began pouring. When the towel around the bottle slipped, revealing the label, Madeline saw it was Pinot Grigio. "My favorite wine," she said automatically.

"Imagine," Helga said, "it's Umberto's favorite too."

Cleo pouted. "Please do not mention the name in my house."

"Oh, stop it, Cleo," Helga said sharply. She parted the auburn bangs in the center of her forehead to see better, then raise her glass to the others. *"Chin, chin,"* and after a sip added, "I think we've all—me included—come down hard enough on Umberto.

Even if he's been thinking of staying away from Serena, we've certainly done our best to drive him straight back into her bony arms."

Madeline, snuggling into an easy chair, wanted to change the subject. "Oh, the sun feels so warm through the glass. I'm glad to have a day off. My work has been tough this week . . ."

"We eat in here too," Cleo said, looking about with satisfaction at the flowered mats and napkins on the glass-topped dining table, then pulled out one of the white wrought-iron chairs and straightened its cushion.

Helga took a deep breath for courage. "Please sit down for a minute, Cleo. Before we eat I have something to tell you." Then looking at Madeline, "Forgive me, but I think it will be easier for Cleo if I speak Italian. Anyway, you know what I have to tell her."

As she began talking to Cleo in a low, confidential tone Madeline looked out at the rose garden, not even trying to follow Helga's Italian, bracing herself for the emotional scene sure to follow.

But Cleo's voice remained calm. There was a sudden outburst but it came from Helga. "Jesus Christ, I don't believe it . . . Madeline, can you believe that this hugeness is actually a shrewd cookie? Maybe we don't need Paolo. Cleo's been to see the Minister of Culture, talked to him about threatening the producers with the loss of their government subsidy if they take money from a Swiss consortium!"

"That's great. Do you think it can work?"

"It might, but I don't know the figures involved. We just have to keep our fingers crossed."

"And now," Cleo said, raising her glass, "I think there is another good reason to celebrate."

"Tell us." Said in unison.

"Well, Catalano says no to his *episodio.*"

"Christ, your English, I can't believe that you've worked in English-speaking films," Helga said, refilling her glass from the bottle on the table. "You really are Italian right down to your pussy, especially when you get excited." Helga waved her off before she could protest. "Okay, okay, now let's see what the situation is . . . we've been eating our hearts out because it looks as if Serena might be getting to play all the parts—"

"All except in Catalano's segment," Madeline corrected.

"Yes, but even in his episode there's talk of Serena making an appearance as the real Fiammetta before the metamorphosis takes place and the part gets taken over by Astrid—"

"But," Cleo put in, "Catalano says no to that. He will not to have Serena in the same *episodio* with Astrid."

"Well, at least that means she can't play all the Fiammettas," Madeline said, but without much enthusiasm.

"Yes, thank God for that difficult bastard, Catalano," Helga said. "So now what have we got . . . at the moment Serena has Fiammetta Four, but she's out of Catalano's segment. And if this thing with the Culture Minister works out, she won't get the other two . . ." Whereupon she sagged into a chair, taking a gulp of her wine. "Fuck, ladies, I don't see what *I* have to celebrate, I'll be left out in the cold no matter what. Cleo, you'll no doubt do Fiammetta Two, and Madeline is Ralph's first choice for One."

"I don't know which I'll play," Cleo said.

"Are you sure I'm Ralph's first choice?" Madeline asked.

"Yes, yes." Helga was impatient. "Ralph's secretary

is a friend of mine, he tells me everything that goes on in his office."

Cleo turned up her nose. "Mariani is dirty person. How can I do Fiammetta Two with that smelling man?"

"Never mind, you'll work with him just the same. Besides, I hear he's had a change of heart in that department. It must be a woman. Anyway, it's the only part for you if you want to be in *Boccaccio Volgare.*" Helga downed the rest of her wine, shrugging her shoulders. "Believe me, if I had the chance now I'd work with him. I'd even lick his sweaty balls for him."

Helga's dramatic pantomime broke the tension, with laughter all around, Madeline's included.

They had already finished their spaghetti alla vongole when the maid announced that Astrid Zealand had arrived. Astrid, tall, straight and golden, wearing a yellow satin jumpsuit, strode—she never just walked—into the sun-filled room, radiating her own sound and light. Add a shield and helmet, and she could have stepped straight from the pages of a Nordic myth, Madeline thought. Without greeting the others, she sat abruptly in the vacant chair at the opposite end of the table from Cleo, looked at them stonily, then gave up the front, putting her head between her arms on the place mat and sobbing heavily.

The girls immediately ran to comfort her, but it took several moments before she could collect herself, dry her eyes and accept the glass of wine Cleo handed her.

After taking a long steadying drink she said, "He gives me no freedom. He didn't even want to let me come here today. He treats me like his slave. I just can't be kept like a prisoner anymore. I was stupid to go back to him . . . I'm going to have to leave Angelo Catalano for good—"

"Oh, *no,*" they all said more or less at once. If she quit Catalano, they reminded her, she quit the film and left the way open for Serena to take her place. She could fight for more freedom but she couldn't *leave* him, they told her. At least not until after the film. And once Astrid, finally, gave in, they even escorted her back to him, threatening her with a fate worse than Angelo Catalano if she didn't play along for at least a while . . .

Primo had had too much wine at his mother's house and was worried that Serena might notice he was a bit tipsy. He also felt nervous because Serena had closed the door so that the servants would not overhear or disturb them. In spite of the fact that she had something serious to say to him, and that it might be very unpleasant, Primo had an erection as he watched her sit at her vanity table brushing her lovely dark curls.

He was sitting on the edge of her bed—what should have been their bed—though it was clear she hadn't invited him into the bedroom to be intimate with him. He could see her expression in the mirror, sterner than he ever remembered. Still, despite her mood (or because of it), he squirmed with an overwhelming urge to take her in his arms, carry her to the bed and . . .

They had, he remembered, made such beautiful love once upon a time. Before the baby. To make a baby. But he had never stopped wanting her. He had only thought that out of decent respect he shouldn't behave like an animal. True, she had never said she didn't want sex anymore, but it had been his assumption, the way he was raised. A respectful husband didn't violate the mother of his child. The Madonna . . .

Right now, though, he was feeling bolder than usual, thanks to the wine. He was, by God, an Italian man, boss of the family. She better not challenge him too much, his *tesora,* or he'd—

"I'm going to divorce you," she said to his reflection in her mirror.

Primo didn't respond, he couldn't.

She turned to face him now. "I have all the photographs and recordings. *You,* Primo, have been *fucking around.* Naturally, I can't allow that." She restrained the impulse to smile at her last words.

When he still did not answer, she pressed on . . . "You haven't been anywhere near my pussy in *twelve months,*" her delicate voice rising, "but you stick that big cock in any other pussy that comes along . . ."

Primo could not believe it. Serena, his *tesora,* talking dirty. His pure Serena, whom he'd refused to defile all this time, sacrificing himself, bringing down God's wrath, drowning him in guilt, was talking dirty, like a street woman. And, of course, nothing excited him more than to have a woman talk dirty, as Helga had discovered. He no longer heard the word *divorce,* only those other terrifying, exciting words coming out of his pure *tesora*'s mouth. He became so excited he got a ringing in his head, saw her under him, taking him inside her.

Now, propelled by a force beyond his control, he was at the dressing table, tackling his slutty beloved's legs, throwing her on the carpet, forcing her skirt up, her panties off, her legs apart, extracting his cock without lowering his trousers, and began to fuck her with a whole year's quota of frustration behind each thrust.

Serena, startled, did not move. Nor did she complain. She felt his enormous member pounding at her, taking her breath away. She stared wide-eyed at the young man on top of her. What he was doing to her she had missed with Umberto . . . The memory of the love they'd once made together every night came flooding back. Now his cock began filling her with wondrous sensations, the kind only he had ever been able to give her. He was, as she'd almost forgotten, a sensational stud once he got down to it—

She screamed with excruciating pleasure. No other cock had ever performed as Primo's. She had known what she was doing when she'd married him. Digging her nails into his back, she realized how foolish she had almost been, and murmured her gratitude into his ear. "Primo . . . thank you . . ."

Neither Primo, nor anyone else, had ever before heard those last two words from Serena Blaire.

# CHAPTER EIGHTEEN

"THANK YOU . . ." Never one to persist in a wash of gratitude, Serena was a realist, able to sort out the odds and to calculate her particular self-interest. The long-missing pleasure that Primo had provided definitely settled into the plus side of the sexual ledger, leaving Umberto in its wake. But, having many of the instincts of an accountant, Serena did not immediately decide on moving out of the Hilton and away from Umberto until she had also added the professional pluses and minuses—and come up with a bottom line that put her, at least so far as she could tell at the moment, in a strong position, thanks to her role in the consortium, in securing the Fiammetta roles she wanted in *Boccaccio*

*Volgare.* And so, all things considered, it was *caio,* Umberto, as lover; welcome home, Primo, premier husband as stud.

When Serena gave up her room at the Hilton, Umberto was not aware of it, having decided to spend the rest of the week in Paris to be near Nicola, take her to and from her *école* and stay for a short time each evening to play with her and help with her homework.

Yvette, it seemed, had matured. She had always been a good mother, recently cutting down on her modeling hours to look after Nicola. Now she was even thinking about getting married. Her fiancé was an engineer, mature, serious, and with a far steadier existence than Umberto's. Yvette had introduced her engineer to Umberto, who had to concede that Yvette was making a good decision for herself and their daughter. And so, during these days in Paris, Umberto couldn't escape the thought that the best thing he could do for his daughter was distance himself from her, at least for a while, to give her time to adjust to a new home and a new father. Having decided this, it wasn't surprising that he kept postponing his departure. After all, these would be the last days he would spend with his daughter for a very long time. Something like this helped a person put his life more in perspective, he thought. *Boccaccio* and all the conspiring and infighting for its choice roles tended to pale in importance compared to a father's feeling for his little girl, who inevitably was moving farther and farther away from him. Even Madeline, for the moment, was pushed to the back of his thoughts . . .

Madeline, too, had come to some decisions. Her life had been an emotional roller-coaster almost since she had first come to Rome, and certainly since she had met Umberto Cassini. She was going to have to ride with the punches better or she'd end up punch drunk. She remembered an old saying of her mother's . . . when things seem worst, look on your glass as half full instead of half empty. And, God knew, her glass, compared to her mother's, was considerably more than half full. The Italians had a knack, she was beginning to realize, for taking one day at a time, blowing up fast, perhaps, but then cooling off just as quickly and going on as though nothing much had happened. It was a way to survive and they'd been doing it for a long time. So take stock, Madeline . . . you have some money coming in from *Paranoia,* never mind whether it's Academy Award quality. You have a charming place to live, in one of the most beautiful cities in the world. You know damn well you're crazy about Umberto, but you're driving yourself up the wall over what female he sees or doesn't see. Well, it's the way you were raised, you've been possessive and a one-man woman all your life, never slept around like those other Hollywood women. You were, probably still are, a square. But you have to live on. You still have your needs as a woman. So keep your promise to yourself, break out of your shell. If not, Umberto, well . . . And as for the *Boccaccio* film, it looks like Serena Blaire has probably eliminated you, maybe not but likely yes. So what are you going to do, fold your tent and crawl away and give up your career? Come *on,* Madeline, let's not let it all beat you this soon. You're from good solid American stock. Fighting stock . . . She had to smile to herself at the conclusion of her self-addressed pep talk. She only hoped her resolutions would stick—not, like the ones for New Years, be honored in the breach . . .

* * *

Even Helga seemed reconciled to playing the waiting game about *Boccaccio,* recognizing that the worst might happen. Astrid, at least, was secure in her role and even a little better off with Catalano, who was actually giving her some freedom. Now she, Helga and Madeline had become a trio of striking beauties nightly out on the town, going to fine restaurants, hugely enjoying one another's company. Madeline had to be up early for the shooting of *Paranoia,* but she had no dialogue to learn at night, the sound would be dubbed in at completion time. So even if she went to bed after midnight her night's sleep was a reasonably sound one. On the upcoming Saturday they were all invited to Cleo's villa for her birthday party, and Madeline, in accordance with her new resolutions, had agreed to accept a blind date with the French boy, whose name finally had been established as Jean Claude . . .

Primo Galiano decided that he was the luckiest of men. Since that Sunday afternoon when he had once again been accepted by his *tesora,* turning aside the thought of divorce, Serena had been treating him the way she had at the time of their wedding—even better, because now they not only slept in the same bed and made love, but spent time actually *talking* to each other about her career, his family, the weather, it didn't matter, he was delighted and Serena seemed content. She had even suggested they take Baby Debbie to Zagarolo some Sunday to visit Grandmother Galiano. Heaven . . .

Unknown of course to Primo, Serena had seen to it that all evidence of his indiscretions had been destroyed and had paid off and dismissed Romolo

Volpe along with the services of the Romulus and Remus Detective Agency.

For his part, Primo had intended to notify Pina that their relationship was over, but when he got around to it, it seemed she had already left him for one of the *Boccaccio* directors, Franco Mariani. He had made one last confession about his adulterous behavior, but now going to confession seemed unnecessary. After all, he was no longer a sinner. He was a man devoted to his wife and child, adored his baby daughter and lusted after his wife—and on both counts the church blessed him . . .

Cleo, still far from happy over her Paolo's inability to secure her a role in *Boccaccio Volgare*, was also taking stock and beginning to work on what she told herself was a far more important project.

On Saturday she would celebrate a birthday, announced as her twenty-fifth but in fact her thirtieth. Time, Cleo decided, to begin a family. She had stardom, a beautiful villa, a wealthy husband, though with a diminutive cock . . . well, nobody was perfect . . . a woman needed a baby to be complete . . . she'd always intended to have children, it had only been a question of when. Before she turned forty she hoped to have three or four babies, so it was time to begin. There was another advantage—she could stop sinning by throwing away the pill. She had never felt good about using contraception forbidden by the church, but she also knew she wasn't clever enough, or patient enough, to follow the sanctioned rhythm method. So in her thirtieth year she would have the double blessing of a baby and freedom from sin. Surely such prospects compensated for losing a mere movie role she wanted so badly she could taste it . . .

* * *

Pregnancy was a prospect decidedly not on Serena's agenda. Having tried the pill and been put off by its side effects, she had long ago switched to a diaphragm plus spermicide, and had rarely been caught unprepared. That terrific Sunday when Primo overwhelmed her was one of the exceptions. She thought briefly about the possibility of pregnancy, then dismissed the idea as highly unlikely. After all, it was not wanted, did not fit into her plans.

And Serena reassured herself with the reminder that she was a woman who got what she wanted. She was close to getting three out of the four female leads in *Boccaccio Volgare*, a film that would confirm her star status. Primo was the young stud and willing pupil she had been right to marry. Giving up Umberto had bothered her only briefly. Besides, she'd always planned to break it off with him when the filming began. Yes, things were coming together nicely indeed . . .

Madeline, as an early test of her recent resolutions, told herself early on during the evening of Cleo's birthday party that she might find it . . . rewarding to let the French boy, Jean Claude, make love to her. He was easy to be with, not a bit pushy, and somehow very seductive. The rave notices both Astrid and Helga had given him, plus the champagne, all helped to bolster her courage.

Jean Claude was, in fact, a beautiful boy. Perhaps twenty-seven, he had honey-colored hair, large blue eyes and amazingly long eyelashes. Altogether appealing without being threatening, he was well built but not overly muscular. His skin had a smoothness, a glow of health, and he smelled delicious, like orange blossoms. His dancing was expert, he held her so as to let her know he wanted her yet without being openly aggressive. Even though she couldn't understand a word of his French, it sounded appropriately romantic, enhancing her mood.

But by the time Jean Claude had escorted her home she felt panicky. The unaccustomed daring she had managed in a crowded party had vanished.

The moment the door closed behind them and Jean Claude had put his hands on her shoulders she moved away from him, went to turn on a lamp. Meanwhile he lit a candle and carried it into the bedroom. When she diffidently followed, he had already begun to undress.

She ran like a schoolgirl into the bathroom, furious with herself, but she just couldn't go through with it . . . Now how could she possibly explain to him that she'd changed her mind, that it had nothing to do with him, that the truth was she was worried about herself . . . she'd never been able to relax enough to reach an orgasm, didn't feel she could face another such frustration to herself and disappointment for him . . .

He had found some music on the radio, and she could hear it playing through the closed door. When she finally opened the bathroom door and entered the bedroom still fully dressed, she felt completely ridiculous that at her age she was still behaving like some nervous virgin.

But Jean Claude wasn't looking at her. He was sitting up in bed, naked but with the covers up to his waist, leafing through one of her art books. When he did glance up, he merely smiled, accepting that she hadn't undressed, as though it was a perfectly reasonable thing, which, of course, it wasn't.

She sat down stiffly in the chair next to the bed. Not being able to speak the same language would make it even more difficult to let him know she had changed her mind.

Jean Claude studied her face. His own, lit by candlelight, wore a sweet acceptance. He studied her innocently, without seeming to be aware of her nervousness.

*"Chérie?"* he asked gently, moving over and patting the bed next to him. She at least found the courage to walk over and sit on the bed beside him, resting against the headboard and stretching her legs out on top of the covers.

She thought, he's going to grab me, but what he did was point out some of the pictures he'd been admiring in the book. After a while he began to hum along with the tune coming from the radio.

Still humming, eyes closed, he put his arm over the cushions behind her, not touching her shoulder.

She began to relax.

Several minutes went by this way, listening to the radio, leaning back against the headboard. Madeline closed her eyes too, felt his lips brush against hers. He still did not put his hands on her. She opened her eyes and he pulled back to look at her. He was smiling, inviting her to rest against his shoulder.

She inched over, noted that his eyes were closed again, put her head on his shoulder. When he now put his hand on her shoulder he did so with a light, unobtrusive touch.

She relaxed a bit more, being quiet with him, close to him, and began to sense the lovely smoothness of his skin, to smell its fragrance. She closed her eyes, breathed deeply, taking in the subtle masculinity of him.

With a movement she'd hardly been aware of, he had brought his head toward hers, had begun kissing her, stopping, resuming, leading her at each stage into a fuller, deeper commitment. When he pulled back, still holding her in his arms, his good-humored pout clearly indicated she now ought to take off her clothes. Without a word she got off the bed and went into the bathroom, feeling like she was in some sort of trance.

Which abruptly left her once she was inside the bathroom and undressed.

She didn't want to go back into the bedroom . . . flushed with excitement . . . since she was terrified she would lose that feeling once he began making love to her. Just as she had so often before . . .

He opened the bathroom door without knocking, smiled at her with the same expression as when she'd been dressed. He held out his hand, she took it. He did not lead her into the bedroom, he waited so they entered it together, holding hands.

She saw now that Jean Claude had taken the large piece of plastic covering her evening gowns and, after having folded the blankets to one side, had spread the plastic over the sheets. Madeline stood staring uneasily at the plastic, not knowing what to make of it, but also not having time to go tense, not with Jean Claude behind her, beginning to massage her neck with long gentle strokes. Then he had taken the baby oil from her dressing table and began rubbing it on her back and shoulders. Madeline went weak at the knees, Jean Claude helped her onto the bed, indicating that she should lie on her stomach on the plastic sheeting. And then he was kneeling over the back of her legs, giving her a complete massage.

Madeline began to feel any resistance melting away under the warmth of his hands on her back and neck and legs and arms, a slippery, sensual warmth that brought an unintended moan from her.

Now he was turning her onto her side so smoothly

that until she rested on her arm so as not to slip, she'd hardly realized she had changed positions. She was fully aware, though, when Jean Claude slid the front of his body along the length of her back, his hot body pressing against hers, his hard penis against her buttocks.

She felt no panic, rather a kind of gratitude along with unspeakable pleasure as his oil-covered fingers began massaging her nipples, followed by an ache of desire deep inside her vagina.

And yet with her arousal, signaling that she was ready to begin the climb to orgasm, Madeline was still afraid she might not be able to climax. And again Jean Claude put aside her inhibiting fears as his hands slid swiftly down, one past her belly, one past her buttocks, and in an instant he was simultaneously rubbing her clitoris and anus with generous measures of oil, and Madeline felt two hot surges as his fingers probed her in front and from behind. Swiftly now he teased her clitoris as he pushed his penis up her anus—

Madeline was shocked into orgasm, an orgasm that was prolonged as he switched into low gear, teasing every bit of tension into spasmodic contractions . . .

And that was only the beginning of their lovemaking, which continued all during that night and well into the following day. Her inhibitions now totally driven out of her, Madeline soared with him, not only keeping pace with Jean Claude but at times her energy and enthusiasm even surpassing his. Eventually he was the one who decided he could no longer go on, and Madeline giggled with delight and amusement that she had outlasted the supposed master at his own game.

One thing was for certain—whatever private fears she'd had about being frigid were forever exorcised.

As for Umberto, well, too bad for him . . . he didn't know what he was missing. Of course, if he played his cards right . . .

No question, she thought with a deep satisfaction, smiling to herself, a new Madeline had been revealed this night.

# CHAPTER NINETEEN

MADELINE, HELGA and Astrid were dining at Il Passetto, near the Piazza Navona and Madeline's apartment. Il Passetto was one of the finest restaurants in Rome, its pure white linen tablecloths and plain wood paneling going with its reputation as a serious eating establishment. Madeline had chosen the restaurant, and dinner was to be her treat. She had ordered a bottle of Santa Christina instead of an ordinary house red, and all three had decided on carciofo di Giudea, Jewish-style fried artichoke, as an appetizer. To follow, Madeline had suggested that they order the large Florentine steaks.

They were seated in the main dining room by a large wood-burning fireplace, and their conversation centered on the invitation each had received to the wedding of Giuseppina Eleanora Bozzetti and Francese Agostino Mariani.

Astrid was saying, "Imagine Franco Mariani getting married. They say he hardly ever washes."

Helga laughed. "Love isn't only blind, maybe it can't smell either."

The girls smiled at that one, followed by Madeline saying she'd never met the man but knew he was an important director and intended to be there. "Besides," she said, "I've never been inside any of those Capitol buildings. You don't think of Italians getting married by a justice of the peace; I always thought Italian weddings were in a church."

"Not if they're in a big hurry," Helga said, laughing.

"Or if they've been divorced," Astrid put in.

"Well," Helga said, raising her glass, "here's to Mariani, another bachelor down the drain."

"Maybe he wants to get the wedding out of the way before he begins filming his segment of *Boccaccio Volgare,*" Astrid said.

"Or maybe he's gotten the lady pregnant. Who is she anyway?" Helga asked.

"Giuseppina Eleanora Bozzetti . . . I've never heard of her," Astrid said, brushing her long golden hair behind her ears before commencing to cut into her artichoke. "What an ugly name."

"Which one?" Madeline said.

"Bozzetti, but actually all three together don't exactly sing."

"Any Giuseppina always reminds me of a maid," Helga said.

"I wonder why Mr. Mariani invited me," Madeline said before cutting her carciofo. "I mean, it's flattering that he did, but I wonder how my name got on the guest list."

"Well, usually the girl makes out the guest list," Astrid reminded her. "Think hard, are you sure none of us knows the bride . . . ?"

"Pina is getting married," Umberto's mother told him the moment he entered the house. "You see? She wouldn't wait for you—"

Umberto put down his suitcases and swooped his mother up in his arms. "It's good to be home again, mama."

"Put me down, you silly boy, and for heaven's sake close the front door."

While he closed the door she straightened her hair and apron. "Look here," she said, producing the wedding invitation from the pocket of her apron, "Giuseppina is marrying an important director, Franco Mariani, and we're all invited to the wedding. You, me and papá."

Umberto bent to kiss her forehead, then picked up his suitcases. "I don't know if I want to go, mama. She's really your friend, after all, not mine," he said, and started toward the stairs.

"You could have married that nice girl," she said, shaking her head.

As he began climbing the stairs his mother called after him, "I'm going to get papa to give you a talking to about coming to the wedding." And when that had no effect on her errant son she added, "You shouldn't be such a bad loser."

Umberto paused on the landing, wrinkling his nose at her. Mama was being mama, but maybe he'd attend the wedding to please her, and besides, Franco Mariani was an important director and would be involved with one of the segments of *Boccaccio.*

As he put the cases down he could still hear his mother talking more to herself than to him, asking herself her perennial question about why of all her sons only Umberto had no wife . . . Umberto smiled, looked around his room, relieved and happy to be home. He should have moved out of the Hilton before going to Paris, except he had only planned to be away for the weekend and Serena still had been living next door. He had returned to find a short note from her signed only with a scrawling *S*:

> Dear Umberto,
> It was quite fun, but I do love my husband.
>
> Affectionately,
> S

Good, he thought, packed up and headed for home base.

"Who is this girl Franco Mariani is marrying?" Cleo was stretched out on the bed, doing her nails.

Paolo was getting undressed. "I don't know and I don't care," he said, struggling with his suspenders. Suspenders might be out of style, but a huge man like Paolo needed them to hold up the bulk of his trousers.

"Daddy Bear, you seem in a very bad mood." She was lying naked on top of the sheets, her contour pillows scattered on the carpet beside the bed. She had planned for them to make love by the light of the fire, but while Paolo undressed she had put on the pink nightlamp, and now her considerable expanse of flesh was bathed in a pinkish glow.

"It is not," Paolo grumbled, "the time I would prefer to make love, Cleo. I've just finished a difficult day at my office. I would like to have a drink and my dinner and relax for a while before—"

"But, Daddy Bear," Cleo said, affecting her incongruously babyish voice, "the doctor said I should have intercourse early in the evenings. Before I get too tired."

Paolo sat down on the bed next to her. "Look, my dumpling, I know how hard you're willing to try for a baby. So am I. But I've also got to be in the mood. Why don't we make love after dinner? Then tomorrow I'll come home for lunch and we'll spend the whole afternoon in bed."

Cleo slowly raised herself onto her elbows to look more closely at Paolo, her mounds of pinkish flesh shifting position with her. She could see by Paolo's expression that he had already made up his mind. "All right then, Daddy Bear, but tonight and tomorrow afternoon, *both.* We want to make a sweet little baby bear. Otherwise, this dumpling is going to be *very* unhappy, and Daddy Bear knows how *unpleasant* that can be . . ."

When Madeline, feeling increasingly festive, was about to order a third bottle of Santa Christina, Astrid and Helga told her enough, the main course was over and they'd had enough wine. Now the ladies were considering the tempting sweet things on the dessert trolley the waiter had just wheeled to their table.

"I think I'll settle for a fresh peach," Astrid told Madeline. *"Pesce per la Signora,"* Madeline said, smiling broadly at the waiter.

"You've just ordered me a *fish.*" Astrid laughed. "*Pesce* is fish, *pesca* is peach."

Madeline giggled at the mistake. The red wine made the distinction too much for her. With a slight slur in her speech she turned to the waiter again. *"Fica per me. Per favore."*

The waiter looked embarrassed, then pretended to busy himself with rearranging the plates on the trolley.

"Whoops," Madeline giggled, "now what did I say?"

"You asked for a cunt," Helga said delightedly.

Madeline shook her head, flushed from the wine and embarrassment. "I couldn't possibly have, I said *fica* for fig . . ."

"*Fico* with an *o* is fig," Astrid told her. "*Fica* with an *a* is cunt."

"It's clear my Italian studies have taken a giant step backward," Madeline said, not really at all upset.

"Actually you've been doing very well," Helga told her. "Maybe, though, you shouldn't try speaking it when you're tipsy."

Astrid, watching the waiter's expertise in peeling her peach, nodded. "Perhaps you spend too much of the day relying on your translator—"

"That could be *it,*" Helga said, slamming down her wine glass. "I think maybe Giusep*pina* is your translator . . . *Pina.* Don't you have anything with her name on it?"

Madeline began searching through her handbag, managed to extract several slips of paper, one of which was a receipt for a money conversion order that Pina had signed: "Bozzetti."

Helga took the bank receipt from Madeline and looked at the signature. "My God, it *is* her. Now how the hell does she get around so far, so fast?"

The waiter now served Astrid's peach and a plate of fresh figs for Madeline. "*Signora?*" he asked Helga.

"*Solamente caffè per me,*" she told him, to Astrid and Madeline: "This Pina truly is Parmegiano."

"Parmegiano?" Madeline was cutting open one of the soft moist figs, looking secretly for the resemblance between the fruit's red flesh and that part of the female anatomy called in Italian by the same name.

Astrid, sprinkling sugar over her peach, explained. "The Italians sprinkle Parmegiano cheese on everything—so when a girl gets around everywhere, they say she's like Parmegiano."

Helga put in, "The last I heard, she was seeing Primo Galiano every night." Astrid remembered that Catalano had tested Pina for his Fiammetta Three . . . "And she's my translator," Madeline said, "and one of the slave girls in my film." She grew suddenly quiet then, mumbling that Pina had had an affair with Umberto, had told her they'd been practically engaged.

"Don't believe it," Helga said. "That was all in little Pina's overactive imagination. She spent one night at Umberto's house, but he told me he never even touched her and I believe him. Umberto doesn't know how to lie to me, or to you, for that matter."

Astrid, thinking Madeline looked doubtful and was in need of a change of subject, asked her if she was seeing any more of Jean Claude.

Madeline nodded, allowed herself a smile. "Yes, but only on weekends."

"Isn't he a great stud?" Helga said.

"I suppose so . . ." she looked serious again. "But after a while even great sex on its own gets to be, well, sort of meaningless . . . I mean, without love. It's great but it's like a Chinese meal, you feel empty the minute it's over."

"Well, well, our Madeline has become a philosopher," Helga said. "Good for you, darling, but don't overdo it . . . you badly needed to get laid. You're what, thirty-four, thirty-five? And you've probably had about one man per decade."

Madeline laughed. "I think that's just about right."

"There's nothing like making love to a woman," Astrid said, since they seemed to be on the subject of sex. "You really must have the experience sometime—"

"Oh, shut up, Astrid," Helga cut her off. "That's not for Madeline. No offense, darling," she said to Madeline, "but if you ever did it with a woman you'd probably think you were a dyke forever and feel so guilty you'd never be able to function again with a man."

Madeline smiled, nodded and agreed that Helga was probably right. "Once a square, always a square," she said, and then suddenly, in spite of herself, had unwanted tears in her eyes. "I guess I wish I was the one getting married. Sorry . . ."

"You wish you were marrying grubby old Mariani?" Helga, of course knew perfectly well whom she meant. "Well, darling, to tell you the truth, I'd marry Umberto myself if he asked me, which he won't. We're more like brother and sister."

Astrid then surprised them both, and perhaps herself, by saying, "I know he's a bastard and often makes my life hell, but I don't think I'd say no if Angelo Catalano asked me to marry him . . ."

"Well, come *on* ladies," Helga said. "We're supposed to be famous and happy. Let's stop lousing up our image. Movie stars don't cry, remember that, goddamn it."

"Why did you ask me to marry you?" Pina said as Mariani rolled off her.

Franco caught his breath and covered his sweaty body with the sheet, then told her, "I didn't, you asked me."

"I guess I did," Pina giggled as she jumped off the bed to check her hair and makeup in the standing mirror.

"Well, I'm glad you did." He rested on an elbow and watched her smooth young body. "I also got tired of living alone. I'll be sixty soon, who wants to be an old bachelor?" He smiled then. "Besides, no teen-age girl has ever offered me her body *and* her hand in marriage. That's some combination . . . I want to thank you for it." And he was no longer smiling, was dead serious, still amazed at how he was able to show feelings he'd always before hidden.

Now he caught sight of himself in the long standing mirror, his thin wrinkled body a poor background for her lush firm one. But he knew Pina was genuinely pleased to be marrying him. He could believe it. She had made him believe it. As far as she was concerned his advanced years were of no importance. He was a man, and a successful one at that. She liked *that* combination and was frank enough to tell him so. Like him, when they were together she could say things she had not been able to admit before. She might be young but she was smart, at least street-smart. She'd had to be, growing up with a mother who had gotten pregnant with her out of wedlock and had run away from Naples to Rome, working long hours as a seamstress with nothing to hold onto except dreams of her daughter becoming a star. She'd even raised Pina in the area around the movie studios, spending every hard-earned lire to educate her daughter, prepare her for marriage to a successful man in films who could help her have a career . . . Pina had told Franco all this, and he had promised her, and himself, that if he was what she had been raised to get, he at least would do his best not to disappoint her.

When he seemed to be getting too sober and solemn, she told him, "No girl has ever proposed before only because you never used to take a bath. You see, I've made you a new man," and completed twisting one loose curl back into place.

"Actually," he said with a straight face, "washing is a waste of time for the truly intellectual man." And still admiring her image in the mirror added, "My fear is that you may have scrubbed away my intelligence." He had to duck quickly to avoid the hairbrush that went whistling past his ear.

# CHAPTER TWENTY

SALVATORI ANZIO had been content with his appointment as Minister of Culture and so a bit regretful about the Cabinet reshuffle. Being the Minister of Culture was a glamorous life—first nights at the opera, contact with the stars of stage and screen. However, crime was on the upsurge and a man of his convictions was needed to combat it, so he could hardly deny the President's wisdom in appointing him the new Home Secretary. Anzio had been elected on the moderate Christian Democrat ticket, but his sentiments were farther to the right. In a coalition government the pie had to be divided; the moderates and right wing agreeing that the Communists could do less harm if allocated responsibility for things such as art, recreation and public parks. One of Anzio's last duties in his present post, if it could be called a duty, was an appointment later that afternoon with the remarkably proportioned Cleo Monti.

This morning he had been briefed on some of the more annoying of recent crimes. One priority of his new office would be to get the whores off the Aurelia. They sat at bonfires alongside the busy highway, a bypass for long-haul trucking, causing pile-ups as they waved at truck drivers and, when in close view, spread their legs, revealing private parts without underpants. Yesterday's collision had held up traffic for hours . . . It wasn't safe for a woman to walk wearing a fur coat. The latest scam involved the use of an egg, the thieves working in pairs. One came from behind, cracking the egg on the lady's head but looking accusingly to the windows above before solicitously helping her out of the fouled fur as the partner ran up to snatch it . . . Kidnapping had reached the point of absurdity. All this week an impoverished cleaning woman had been on the television news appealing for donations to meet the ransom demand for the return of her *parrot* . . . Criminals were becoming bolder. A tiny Fiat recently had blocked a city bus and, reminiscent of the old stagecoach holdups, the crooks ordered the passengers off the bus, then relieved them of their valuables . . . Perhaps the most scandalous incident was the one that took place at the Quirinale Palace, the very headquarters of the national government, and in clear view of the sentries. A moving van, parked across from the palace at the home of the President of the Republic, presented the guards with a falsified renovation order and, without interference, removed the furniture, carpets and art treasures.

It was, indeed, awesome to contemplate the grave responsibilities the new Home Secretary would be assuming, but at least this afternoon he would have the pleasure of an interview with Cleo Monti. He had promised her that he would explore the possibility of refusing the government subsidy to *Boccaccio Volgare* if they brought in foreign investors. In actual fact it couldn't be done. So long as the investment did not exceed one half of the budget, the producers would be entitled to the subsidy. The movie industry relied heavily on coproductions and he couldn't cancel *Boccaccio's* subsidy without canceling those of almost every other film. However, he wasn't going to pass up the opportunity of having Cleo Monti in his office. He would simply stall her, using the occasion to be close to her, perhaps even . . . well, in any case, he need not be the one to give her the bad news. By tomorrow the appointments would be announced, and he'd tell her in confidence of the impending Cabinet reshuffle, promising personally to hand the matter over to his colleague, making it a commission for the new Minister of Culture. Let the Commie take the blame for disappointing her, and keep alive the possibility of some future relationship with her. After all, what was she really? An actress, and were not all actresses only a step up, if that, from those women on the Aurelia?

With nothing standing in the way of the Swiss consortium taking over the investors' share of the production, by the end of the week the deal had been concluded, and Ralph de Rossi, having been of two minds, was now swayed by the producers to use Serena in his segment.

Ralph met promptly with Franco Mariani, explaining to him that since Serena was now going to play both Fiammettas One and Four, it made little sense for Franco's Fiammetta Two to be played by a different actress. Franco saw the logic and agreed, thinking to himself that in future he must keep away from this type of big commercial project where the political pressures forced a man to give up control.

Only Catalano was holding out. He did not want Serena to have even a small scene in his segment. To hell with consistency or showing the audience that Serena's character was the true Fiammetta. He was going to film only his concept, no one else's, and his heroine was going to be embodied by Astrid and *only* Astrid.

Step by step, Serena was informed of the progress. She was, after all, a member of the board of directors of the company representing the consortium of Swiss banks, although a silent member. No one would ever be able to connect her to the newly formed company (Prometheus Productions), although she held substantial control. And those investing the capital, knowing little about the motion picture industry, looked to her for advice and counsel.

Serena had spent $10,000 on the formation of Prometheus Productions and assigned her services for *Boccaccio* plus two other future films. She felt it was a good deal, and good for her career . . . she would have control over *Boccaccio* plus two film projects to come, and of course she would be the one to find those projects for the company.

Her only regret was not being able openly to gloat. Hers was a great personal victory, but she didn't dare share it with anyone, not even the Swiss, who looked on Prometheus Productions as a profit-making enterprise, and on her as both a valuable asset and a level-headed businesswoman, which, of course, she was. But how she would have loved to throw it in those ladies' faces, especially that bitch Helga Haufman, who Primo, in his confession to her, had admitted fucking.

As for Catalano, let him think he was keeping her out of Fiammetta Three. Once he'd finished directing his segment, his participation in *Boccaccio* would be over. When it came time to edit the film Prometheus Productions would again exert its influence and it would be a simple matter to film scenes of her as the true Fiammetta to intercut in the final version in place of that dyke Astrid.

When he heard that Serena had won three of the four female roles, Umberto was unhappy that Helga, Cleo and, in particular, Madeline, had been shut out. He also felt partly to blame because Ralph had given him the opportunity to veto Serena and he'd refused to get involved. He also figured—wrongly—that he'd had some influence on Serena during their brief affair, which had apparently cost him what he really wanted—Madeline. Of course he had no notion that it was Serena who was consolidating her position in the film by being with him . . . Astrid, having no idea what lay ahead for her, was saddened to learn that her friends had been passed up in favor of Serena . . . Madeline, according to her new philosophy, tried to accept it but nonetheless was heartsick over Umberto still, as well as losing the part . . . Helga was furious, consigning Serena to more hells than Dante ever dreamed of . . . and Cleo threw her long overdue tantrum, feeling she'd been let down by her husband and led down the garden path by the Home Secretary. As for her husband, Paolo felt humiliated at being pushed out as an investor, worse at seeming to be inadequate in the eyes of his ladies.

No longer a big man with a small cock. Now just a *piccolo* . . .

Fortunately, in a few weeks Franco and Pina were to marry, and winners and losers alike in the *Boccaccio* sweepstakes all planned to attend. A wedding, after all, was a wedding, a day to celebrate, to put one's sorrows and differences aside. They all needed it.

# CHAPTER TWENTY-ONE

FOR HELGA, the prospect of a wedding was hardly sufficient diversion from the fury consuming her. Reasonably quiescent so long as she thought there was still a chance for herself and her friends on *Boccaccio,* she felt her blood boiling at the excessively fortunate turn of events for "that skinny little English bitch," whom she had to admit was a lot shrewder than she'd given her credit for. Now that Serena had effectively demolished all of their hopes, Helga craved blood. And, as usual, she and her friends had depended too much on the resourcefulness of men, with the usual disastrous results. Paolo, despite all his money, hadn't been able to maintain his control over the production, even had asked her for her help in breaking his bad news to Cleo. Umberto, when he should have been especially strong on behalf of them all, had simply not gotten involved. That idiot government official that poor Cleo had thought was going to save the day had turned out to be nothing more than an ineffectual lech. Well, she might be losing out to Serena, but by God, she'd decided, at least she would have the satisfaction of baring her claws and, if not fatally wounding the bitch, at least leaving a few scars.

But where to find her? Of course, Primo, the dear boy who performed best when she invoked his sainted mother in distinctly unsainted terms. Primo had once given her a private number when they were seeing each other. When she now tried it she was informed it was no longer in service, *terminato.* Dead end. All right, hell hath no fury like a star screwed . . . fury enough to play the waiting game, to wait about the movie lot until Serena showed up for a conference with Ralph about the forthcoming Fiammetta roles.

It happened one day after Helga had had a few too many drinks at the commissary. Serena rewarded Helga's waiting game with an appearance, and even better, she had Primo in tow. They were in the dining room, where Helga had gone for a bite and spotted the twosome in a far corner, just finishing. Helga took a deep breath and approached their table.

"My dear Serena," she said, not waiting for an invitation to sit down and join them. "May I join you? How delightful to see you. And Primo, how is *it,* darling? So good to see you again, this is a treat for me." She waited for the explosion.

Instead, Serena, living up to her name, merely turned her large doe eyes on her, opened them even wider than usual and smiled innocently. She not only invited Helga to join them, which, of course Helga had already done, but even leaned over to buss her briefly on the cheek. Helga, rarely outdone in such matters of oneupmanship, was momentarily stunned, then fought back an urge to wipe the smile off her face not with a kiss but with a well-planted punch in the face.

As for Primo, he was distinctly uneasy. True, he had told his *tesora* about his brief time with Helga, and she had forgiven him. But there were still the old guilts from adultery that only the church could forgive. And Helga's sudden appearance had awakened some of those, so that the palms of his hands became sweaty and he tried to look away, at the same time answering her with, "How are you, I am fine," and some other casual to inane words he fumbled to get out.

Serena, sensing why Helga was there, proceeded, as she usually did, to put herself in a role—this one being the superior, gracious lady, who thereby countered fire with smothering sweetness. "I'm so *pleased* to see you, Helga. You're looking very well indeed, and I do hope there's a wonderful film in your future, one that is up to your talents. It's a pity the way so much real talent goes to waste these days on inferior projects. I understand your friend . . . oh, yes, Madeline . . . Madeline Mandell, the lovely American actress, is just wasting herself in that awful thing about slave girls and lord knows what else. *Paranoia* they call it, right? Too bad. But never mind, darling, she too will get her proper reward—"

"Serena, can we cut the shit?" Helga said with a broad smile to accompany the expletive, taking in Serena, Primo and the entire restaurant, which was nearly empty, it being after 3:00 P.M. "I understand you, you understand me. I don't know exactly how you did it, but I know this much . . . before this is over you'll regret what you did, and even if you keep all those Fiammetta parts you stole, you'll damn well wish you hadn't. Don't bother to get up, Primo, after all, you never could when it counted . . . But I trust Umberto didn't have that problem with you, did he, Serena?"

And she was on her feet, back turned to them, sailing away from the table, feeling that cat's eyes burning holes between her shoulders as she moved out the door.

All right, she had had her confrontation, and maybe she hadn't accomplished so much, but at least she'd shaken up the little bitch, she was sure of that. Primo obviously hadn't known about Umberto. Not that it would make a hell of a lot of difference . . . but at least she had some satisfaction from seeing Serena tense up, especially after enduring all those goddamn Cheshire cat smiles. Maybe it would take more than threats. Maybe it would take an act of God . . . Right now, she thought, the heady flush of the confrontation fading some, it sure as hell looked like it . . .

# CHAPTER TWENTY-TWO

THE SUNDAY of Franco and Pina's wedding broke warm and bright. The civil ceremony was to take place at 11:00 A.M., but Madeline would arrive early, walking alongside the Capitoline Hill, past the remains of the Roman insula and just across the street from the Forum. The Hill's buildings had changed from the Sabine huts to the Golden Age edifices to the Middle Age structures, lasting until Michelangelo's buildings, which stand today. Since the early tribes chose it over 750 years before Christ it had never ceased being the site of Rome's city government. When she reached the foot of the stone stairway leading to the square above she turned to look once again at the Forum. It was all right here

. . . the sites of Rome's earliest glories. She turned back and paused a moment before climbing. To either side of the top of the broad stone stairway were the magnificent Dioscures—the statues of Castor and Pollux alongside their horses.

When she got to the top to enter the square, there was only one other person enjoying the sights, a gray-haired, distinguished-looking gentleman, standing there admiring the equestrian statue of Marcus Aurelius. He seemed dressed too formally to be a tourist and Madeline wondered if he was a government official. Minus her guidebook on this wedding day, she decided to approach him: "Excuse me, do you speak English?"

"Indeed I do, Miss Mandell," he said, smiling and taking off his hat.

"Oh . . . I'm sorry, have we met?"

"I know you from the cinema. One of my sons is also in that profession. I'm Professor Cassini of Rome University."

"Oh . . . you're Umberto's father." Madeline blurted it out, knowing her face must be flushed.

The elder Cassini ignored it, took her attention back to Rome and away from his son. "This wonderful bronze might not have been preserved if there had not been a false assumption that it represented the Emperor Constantine."

"Oh, you know, I wish I could spend some time with you learning more"—about your son as well as the glories of Rome, she added silently—"but I'm on my to a wedding—"

"Miss Bozzetti's?"

"Yes . . ."

"Then we are here for the same reason. And I too have arrived early to enjoy the sights of the Capitol.

I spend far too much of my time reading instead of looking."

"Is your wife coming too?"

"Yes indeed, but it will take her considerable time to get ready for such an occasion. My wife loves weddings. I've entrusted Umberto to drive her here at the appointed hour. Now, what questions do you have, Miss Mandell? We professors thrive on questions, you know."

Madeline could see the resemblance in the professor's ruggedly handsome face and his broad-shouldered build. She wondered if she could be natural with him, knowing who he was.

The professor was saying, "We have no history, you know, only legends about the first Roman kingdom. Surely you know the one about Romulus and Remus?"

"Yes . . . sort of."

He took her arm and led her toward the shade of the adjoining gardens. When they found a bench under a tree they sat down and he gave her the *full* story, with rather obvious professorial relish . . . "Among the tribe known as the Latins there were two young men, twins—Romulus and Remus. On their mother's side they were descendants of Aeneas, the Trojan hero who fled to Italy when the Greeks sacked his city. Some said he brought with him some of the most sacred things of Troy—things with great magical powers. And on their father's side they were from the gods. Their mother, Ilia, had been condemned by her uncle to be a Vestal Virgin and so they were fathered by the god of war, Mars. Ilia's uncle, a cruel man, ordered them thrown into the Tiber, but the basket containing the babies came to rest beneath the sacred fig tree—more magic, you see. They were discovered there by Mars' favored bird, the woodpecker, and suckled by his favored animal, a wolf, who raised them. Of the two boys, most of the magic rubbed off on Romulus, so that when as young men the twins decided to found a new city on the left bank of the Tiber, on the very border of Etruria, and when they could not agree on the exact site, Romulus' powers won out. His superior magic was enhanced by the fact that he slew his brother, Remus, and on the very spot where Romulus foresaw that the gates of Rome would be built. Such a rare family sacrifice to the gods convinced the Latins that the city founded in such a way would become a mighty one, which indeed it did, and Romulus became the first king of Rome."

"*And* the city was named after him."

"Some say that," he paused, smiling at her, "but we have no way of knowing. There's another theory about the city's name, one I happen to prefer . . ."

"And that is . . . ?"

He laughed. "For the most beautiful of all women." By the way he was looking at her he might have been referring to Madeline. "The city's Italian name is Roma, feminine, and earlier than Romulus and Remus, Roma was personified and worshiped as a goddess. Her head is symbolic of the Roman state and appears on our coins. On Velia, one of the other seven hills, there's even a temple to Venus and Roma."

Madeline suspected, hoped, that just maybe the professor had said this last with a little foreknowledge, that she had been likened to Venus, and this time she didn't mind the association at all.

Madeline stood up, looking about for a moment, then turned to him. "I'm really glad to have met you, professor, you've made legend come alive for me."

"For that I'm grateful, but you should have a young man's arm to take," he said, patting her hand. "A young man who is capable of *showing* you Rome . . . My son Umberto may be an actor, but he too has learned his history. Perhaps if you were planning to go unaccompanied to the reception Umberto might drive you. There are, after all, many historical sights on the way to the restaurant." The professor, like his wife, was always hoping that his famous son would settle down. This lovely American seemed an excellent prospect. "Well," he said, looking at his watch, "we still have time, shall we have a look inside the museum?"

Madeline and Professor Cassini spent nearly an hour viewing and discussing the treasures of the Capitoline Museum. Meanwhile, the other wedding guests began arriving, and since it was such a fine day everyone congregated in the square.

The bridegroom, Franco Mariani, had come with Ralph de Rossi and his wife, and as each guest walked into the square their first comment was inevitably about the bridegroom's appearance. Franco had had his dark, gray-streaked hair cut short and neat. His navy blue suit looked new and was well pressed, his stiff white shirt was spotless. He was an event on his own. Ralph de Rossi was to be the best man, and he and his wife, Christina, were in a festive mood. Mariani had been a close family friend for more than twenty-five years and this was just about the first time they'd known him to be so outgoing and happy. When Christina had first heard of Franco's intention to marry a nineteen-year-old girl she had been disapproving, but as soon as she had seen his new attitude toward life she'd had to admit that the girl, *whoever* she was, had worked absolute miracles. Christina, slim, chic and in her early fifties, was wearing a blue chiffon print under a plain blue woolen coat and carrying a matching felt hat. The sunlight picked out the streaks of gray in her blond hair, which was drawn back in a classic chignon. Christina, known for her beautiful smile and infectious laugh, was now holding onto Mariani's arm and teasing him about wedding nerves.

They were joined by the director Vittorio Anastasio, who had brought his ex-wife, the Countess of Rimini. Belonging to the same horsey set, they had stayed the best of friends and many wondered why they had bothered to divorce. Anastasio and the countess were, not surprisingly, dressed in sports clothes, a step up from the well-worn expensive tweeds they wore for everyday. Whatever Vittorio wore tended to twist out of shape around his stocky peasant build, whereas the countess was a trim, athletic-looking woman. Both were in their mid-forties. He was vague and lackadaisical, she lively and full of good cheer. Without her coaxing Vittorio might not have given up his Sunday at the club even to attend the wedding of his fellow director.

Now the countess spotted Serena Blaire, whom she had met at the club the day of Vittorio's luncheon party. The countess promptly left Vittorio with the first group and went over to join Serena, who had arrived on Primo's arm. Primo was looking less pudgy and almost handsome. His thick blond hair and freshly scrubbed face made him appear even younger than his twenty-seven years. Perhaps most noticeable was his newly acquired self-confidence. He was wearing a light gray suit with a white shirt and a gray-and-white striped tie that Serena had picked out for him. His gray, as intended, complemented her pale lavender suit and hat. While Serena smiled and nodded as usual, on closer observation one could detect her exuberance springing from some deeper than usual self-satisfaction.

Astrid and Helga had come together, wearing identical suits they had purchased the day before, identical except that Astrid's was lime green and Helga's was salmon pink. Angelo Catalano was taking large strides to catch up with them, looking tall and even rather handsome in his formal morning suit and carrying his silver-tipped walking stick. Helga made a point of looking straight at Serena, trying to make some points by direct eye contact. No luck. Serena, if she was aware, was having none of it. No confrontations today. All right, Helga thought, not today, but there's always tomorrow . . .

Amid such display of finery on the square, reminding Madeline of a fashionable Easter parade, appeared a dark, faintly sinister-looking group mostly wearing somber black. Pina's relatives from Naples. Two of her mother's brothers were experienced criminals and three others had been convicted of petty theft. Of the males, these five seemed to swagger with exaggerated confidence, while the rest of Pina's family appeared ill at ease in the presence of a glittery movie crowd.

Madeline was still holding Professor Cassini's arm as they came out of the museum doorway. When they emerged into the sunlight Madeline's eggshell-colored suit seemed almost to match the color of her platinum hair as they paused on the museum steps to watch the arrival of the bride.

Pina was in bridal white, her long gown adorned by yards of tulle veiling. She was surrounded by the five young girls who played slaves in Madeline's film *Paranoia,* holding her skirts and veiling off the paving.

Pina's mother, who had raised her daughter for this moment, was a wizened little figure in black, her black shawl having slipped off her head to rest on her stooped shoulders.

Umberto and his mother were now talking with the other late arrivals, Cleo and Paolo. When Umberto's mother left her group to greet the bride and the bride's mother, Cleo and Paolo decided to join Astrid, Helga and Catalano, but then Umberto spotted Madeline with his father and quickly went over to them, taking advantage of the unexpected opportunity.

"Papa, leave it to you to find the most beautiful girl at the wedding." He looked seriously at Madeline as he spoke, then kissed her hand. "It's wonderful to see you again, Madeline."

The professor, no slouch himself in the female-appreciation department, patted Madeline's hand resting on his arm. "Miss Mandell is not only a beautiful woman, but intelligent and most sensitive to our works of art and history. I think she would have made one of my better students. It's a pity she hasn't had more of an opportunity to see our monuments, but perhaps she'll catch a glimpse of some of them when we pass by on the way to the restaurant . . ." He looked meaningfully at his son as he spoke, hoping he would take the hint.

Umberto did. "If you would allow me to drive you to the restaurant I would be more than happy to be your guide. How would you rate me on history, Papa?"

"Rather poor for a professor's son, good enough for a thespian."

They laughed and Madeline laughed with them, although she was feeling distinctly nervous about later being alone with Umberto. She didn't know how she would handle it. After all, she should still have some mixed feeling about him. Should . . .

Umberto then tried to sound casual as he said,

"Madeline, we'll have plenty of time to get out of the car and look about—"

"Indeed," the professor put in, "Roman wedding feasts never start on time and it will be hours before we sit down to eat. We Latins, just like our forefathers, will use any excuse for *endless* conversation."

Umberto then saw his mother approaching them. "Doesn't Mama look well today, Papa?"

"She does, yes. She's still a wonderful-looking woman," and then smiled broadly. "I see she couldn't resist dressing to look more like the mother of the bride than the real mother of the bride." He turned to Madeline, who had released his arm. "Miss Mandell . . . Madeline? . . . you mustn't mind my wife if she gushes over you. We've had three sons and Maria has always missed not having a daughter. Even our five grandchildren are all boys—well, with the exception of little Nicola, whom we never see. I fear our daughters-in-law find themselves smothered in affection."

Mrs. Cassini in her pearl-gray dress and coat, gray hair neatly done in a bun beneath her large-brimmed hat, the orchid that Pina had sent pinned to her lapel, did indeed look as if she were the mother of the bride. But the moment she spied Madeline between her husband and her son, her thoughts turned away from her disappointment at losing Pina for a daughter-in-law and took up the idea that this darling Madeline Mandell might be the perfect one for her Umberto. She then, as predicted by her husband, proceeded to gush over Madeline, making Umberto feel acutely uncomfortable. Not so Madeline. She felt a rush of affection for this older woman who seemed anxious to mother her, something that hadn't happened since her own mother had died.

Now she and Mrs. Cassini walked together into the

government building housing the office of the justice of the peace, Umberto and his father walking behind them. Maria Cassini had taken Madeline's arm and was talking quietly but rapidly to her, attempting to communicate in a very nearly incomprehensible mixture of Italian, French and broken English. For Madeline, the words didn't matter. This woman made her *feel* that she cared about her. And to hell with mixed feelings, this woman was also Umberto's mother. The professor was Umberto's father. Umberto's family. It was a lovely thought to go into a wedding with . . .

# CHAPTER
# TWENTY-THREE

THE CHAMBER designated for the wedding had a somber atmosphere. Its windows, heavily draped in maroon velvet, shut out the sun, and the modest light from the brass chandeliers and wall appliqués was absorbed by the dark rococo paneling of the walls. Medieval armchairs, their hardness padded by cushions of maroon velvet to match the draperies and carpeting, had been set out in rows.

At the head was a large carved desk where the justice of the peace stood in a black suit and elbow-length black cape with a red sash looped over one shoulder. His assistants began ushering people to their seats—the chairs to the right of the aisle were for the bride's family, friends to the left.

Pina's maternal grandparents, confused at the mention of a wedding (they thought they were attending someone's funeral, which they more regularly did), took forever to get to their seats, and Pina's mother had to be coaxed to accept one in the front row. With one unsteady hand she clutched the black shawl and with the other toyed with the orchid pinned to her dress as if it were some suspect foreign object.

It took considerably less time for the left side to begin filling up, but nonetheless the guests in the hallway were disgruntled by the wait. Mrs. Cassini had already accepted the seat on the aisle directly across from Pina's mother, sitting straight, adjusting her skirt to fall smoothly over her knees, checking that her orchid was prominently displayed. Next to her sat the professor, and to his left, Christina de Rossi. But before one of the ushers could call the names for the second row Serena had stepped in front of everyone and moved smartly up the aisle to take the seat directly behind Mrs. Cassini. She was closely shadowed by the countess, who had no intention of relinquishing her visible connection with the famous actress, quickly taking the seat beside Serena. To the usher's chagrin, she placed her handbag on one chair, her scarf on another, a way of saving them for Primo and Anastasio, who had been left behind.

Angelo Catalano, also impatient, had stridden by everyone to the third row, where he turned and motioned for Astrid to join him. When the slave girls from Madeline's film tried to enter the row to secure themselves a good view, Catalano shook his walking stick at them and they moved off.

Helga had been whispering less than endearments into Umberto's ear while Madeline stood beside them, looking and feeling a bit left out, so Astrid took hold of Madeline's arm and they went together to the already active third row to join Catalano.

By now the Bozzetti family was just about seated, and Madeline turned her attention to them—deep olive-skinned people with abundant black hair and large dark eyes. The women were mostly round and large-breasted with set expressions, while the men were lean and hard-looking, their faces seemingly trained to mask their feelings.

An usher checked his list and noted that Umberto Cassini was supposed to have been seated in the second row. Hearing this, Helga took hold of Umberto and went up the aisle, where she demanded that Serena and the doting countess move over. Umberto, not realizing what Helga was up to, tried to duck out, but Helga held him firmly. Serena, playing lady bountiful, smiled sweetly, stood, and not wanting to sit next to Helga, deftly changed places with the countess. Helga decided that this small encounter was at least a draw. Not too bad with Serena as the antagonist . . .

Now Pina's gangster uncles shuffled into their chairs in the last row on the bride's side of the room. The three younger ones looked peaceful enough at the moment in their dark suits and white shirts, but the two older ones had a distinctly arrogant manner. The older ones had been given heroic names: the eldest was Espartaco after the gladiator Spartacus, and the next in line was named Cesari after Caesar. Perhaps their mother had run out of ideas after the first two were born, because the three younger boys were named Terzo, Quarto, and Quinto, the same as Primo Galiano's brothers.

Cleo and Paolo, chatting with the bridegroom, walked with him to the front of the room, Franco seeming grateful not to be left on his own before the ceremony began. Pina waited in the hallway with Ralph de Rossi, who had promised to tell her when to enter—Ralph ever the director.

There was to be no music or bridesmaids or set march to a church altar. Pina had forsaken the pomp and circumstance in favor of a quick bond, and Franco, grateful and pleased to be marrying this lovely child who actually *liked* him, had quickly gone along. Pina did, however, insist on a long white gown, which her mother had hand-sewn, plus veil and a bridal bouquet of white roses, baby's-breath and miniature orchids. Some unkind remarks were made sotto voce that the bride was overdressed for a civil ceremony, which were overheard by Pina and troubled her not at all. Screw you, she said happily in her own sotto voce.

Even without music, Ralph decided to help Pina make a grand entrance by giving her the benefit of his experience as a director, instructing her to count to twenty and then to walk slowly with a measured gait until she reached the bridegroom's left. He came ceremoniously to the center of the entranceway and stood looking toward the justice of the peace, waiting until there was silence in the room, then proceeded up the aisle as if an organ were sounding. When he arrived halfway, all heads turned toward the doorway as the bride paused there, taking her time, entering slowly and solemnly as she moved toward her future husband.

Mariani watched and admired his young bride-to-be as she paced her way alone up the aisle with no paternal arm for support. She had not wanted a friend or relative to act as substitute. She was going to face this the way she'd faced everything else in her young life, without the help of a father. As she took the last few steps toward him, Franco smiled, holding out his hand to reassure her. Just a few more paces and she would never need to feel alone again, he thought.

The justice of the peace now leaned over to Ralph to tell him the second witness was needed, which Ralph relayed to Pina. Pina said that her mother had arranged for the second witness but she didn't know which of her relatives it was to be. Ralph suggested that the justice simply ask out loud that the other witness join them.

"Will the second witness please step forward," he said.

Abrupt silence while people looked around the room to see who the second witness was, but no one came forward. Then, glancing at the instructions before him, the justice read the name: "Will Espartaco Bozzetti please come forward."

A shuffling at the back of the room as the eldest of Pina's gangster uncles rose, tugged at his black suit jacket, straightened the white necktie over his black shirt and stroked the sides of his slicked down hair. Two of his younger brothers stood and patted him on the back, as if Espartaco were about to enter some competition or perhaps face another tribunal. His hands in his pockets, Espartaco walked up the aisle with an air of defiance, and when he reached the desk he stood beside Pina, legs spread, hands clasped behind his back.

Some tittering, some black looks in return.

Each time before the justice finished his obligatory question, Pina cut off the last words with a "yes." Mariani thought her spontaneity delightful and had some difficulty to keep from chuckling. Ralph looked at him and winked. This young lady was clearly in a hurry to get where she was going.

The justice now was asking for the ring or rings to

be presented, and Ralph was just reaching for his vest pocket when Pina's Uncle Espartaco produced from behind his back two large wedding bands studded with sapphires, which he proudly held out in front of Pina. She was clearly thrilled, though the bridegroom and best man looked surprised. Mariani quickiy whispered to Ralph that they had better accept the gift and not bring forward the preset plain bands.

Various members of the Bozzetti family were standing to get a better view of the jeweled rings, giving forth a chorus of oohs and aahs from their side of the room, and in the last row of the bride's side the gangster brothers elbowed one another happily.

By the time the justice pronounced Pina and Franco man and wife, women on both sides of the room were drying their eyes. Maria Cassini crying openly, as much for her unmarried Umberto as for Pina, while Pina's mother attempted to stifle sobs of pleasure beneath her black shawl.

Mariani took Pina in his arms but gave her only a perfunctory kiss so as not to disturb her makeup, and also so as not to offend certain of those present, by displaying an older man's passion for his young bride. Pina pulled back momentarily to smile at him, then threw her arms around his neck and kissed him full and hard on the mouth. With that, her side of the aisle got to their feet cheering and applauding. They crowded forward to congratulate the newly wedded couple. It was clearly Pina's and her family's day, and to hell with the stuffed shirts who didn't like it.

# CHAPTER TWENTY-FOUR

ALONG WITH customary congratulations, male guests got to kiss the bride, which provided the five criminal brothers an excuse to fondle the beautiful women present. Madeline, Helga and Astrid had been mauled at least twice by each of the five, and the brothers would have gone on getting in line to feel up the actresses if the justice hadn't raised his voice, insisting the present wedding leave the chamber in order to make way for the next.

Serena and the countess had come directly onto the square to wait for the bridal party, and when the five spotted Serena Blaire *herself*, they proceeded to circle her, cut her off and then all lay on hands like some human octupus. Serena smiled and kicked one high and hard, which at least temporarily made him and them back off, though without them being further diverted she was in danger of heating their blood to an intolerable boil. Fortunately her experience with Italian men, including her husband, made her wary of this and she tried not to overly provoke and stimulate them. The countess waited expectantly for the raffish men from Naples to have a go at her, but after Serena they spotted and made a beeline straight for the wonderfully endowed Cleo Monti, one of their own they figured.

When the wedding photographer got everyone to pose on the steps of the Capitol the enterprising brothers seized the opportunity to slip behind the actresses and give each a proper goosing. Though their outcries went unnoticed in the general commotion, Madeline, Astrid, Cleo and Serena took to placing their handbags behind them to protect the tender regions from further assault.

After the photographs the plan was for all to reassemble at the restaurant for the reception. Madeline, finding herself alone, began looking for Umberto, who had been missing from the group photograph. At that moment someone came from behind and grabbed her waist. Looking over her shoulder, she saw Espartaco. Then Terzo, Quarto and Quinto on the steps beside her, making puckering sounds with their mouths. As Espartaco began squeezing her waist until she thought her eyes would pop, the one called Cesari appeared on the step directly in front of her, and putting his nose directly to hers, said, "How would Venus like to ride to the restaurant with me and my brothers? With *real* men, not these movie fops."

Astrid spotted the scene, took it in quickly and rushed forward, pulling Espartaco's hands away and shoving Cesari down a step. Which, of course, only encouraged Espartaco and Cesari, not to mention the three young thugs who began whistling derisively.

They were regrouping for another try when Catalano's silver-tipped walking stick glittered as he poised it on the step beside Astrid. "Sorry, *gentlemen*, the ladies have already promised to ride with me."

As Madeline and Astrid took Catalano's arms and proceeded down the steps the Neapolitans called after them:

"See you at the reception, baby."

"Venus is going to heaven with me, aren't you, honey?"

Catalano stiffened, but Astrid clung tightly to his arm. "Angelo, please don't answer them, don't say anything or there's liable to be a fight."

Angelo nodded, gritted his teeth and proceeded down the steps with the ladies on his arms, his walking stick striking the steps ahead, but he said in a loud voice full of disgust. "What kind of *scum* has Mariani married into—?"

Helga and Umberto ran in just then, turning aside the Neapolitan lover boys.

"I'm sorry, Madeline, but Helga and I stopped to talk to some people we knew in the other wedding party," Umberto said.

"Yes," Helga certified, "it was my fault for keeping Umberto so long."

Umberto held out his arm for Madeline, who promptly linked hers in his. Remember your resolution, she told herself as they started down the hill. This is better than you'd hoped for a week ago. Take it and stop hedging your bets with mixed feelings . . .

The street angled sharply down, and Madeline gripped Umberto's arm tighter. He noticed the height of her heels and paused. "I had to park my car at the bottom of the hill in the piazza. Would you like to wait here while I go and get it?"

"No, it's my own silly fault for wearing these shoes. But I'd really like to walk."

"How have you been, Madelina?"

She stopped short and looked at him. "Did you say Made*lina?*"

"Yes, I'm sorry, you may feel I've no right to be so familiar with you."

She looked straight ahead and began walking, momentarily letting go of his arm. All right, she thought, maybe he had no right to call her Madelina; he'd led her on, or seemed to, at the same time as he'd been practically living at the Hilton with Serena. It still makes you angry, she thought, but don't overdo it. Speak up, but remember you're with the man you still want. "I see that Serena Blaire has jilted you." She tried to smile when she said it.

He threw his head back and laughed. "Yes, she certainly has. And I couldn't be more pleased about it. I know I've disappointed you more than once, but please try to believe that. It's the truth."

He stopped and pointed out the Teatro Marcello, then took her hand and brought it to his lips. "Madelina?"

In spite of herself she turned away, examining an imaginary run in her stocking. When she'd got her bearings back she looked up but not directly at him. She began walking ahead of him, telling herself to take it easy . . . not too fast, not too slow . . .

He caught up, offering his arm, which she took in an almost casual manner. She wanted, for now at least, to lighten the mood. His car was parked below in the Piazza Bocca della Verità, the Mouth of Truth. On their side of the street, before reaching the piazza, was the enclosure for the stone face with the open mouth. Umberto, opening the gate, suggested she have a look, and they walked down the steps to where she could stand directly in front of the face.

"What you're supposed to do," he said, "is put your right hand inside the mouth and answer any question truthfully. Ready?" he said with a steady smile.

"Yes . . ."

"All right, then, put your right hand into the Mouth of Truth."

Madeline put her fingers tentatively inside the rim of the stone lips.

"No, not partway—all the way inside."

Slowly her hand moved into the mouth until only her wrist was visible.

Umberto took hold of her wrist, holding her hand in place. He was no longer smiling.

"Now answer my question," he said. "You know what it means when I call you Madelina, that it is a term of affection. Do you agree that I call you that? Do you want me to?"

Madeline shot him a look, refusing to answer, although it hardly seemed a major commitment.

"If you lie," he said in a deep stagey voice, "the Mouth will bite off your hand—"

"Yes," she answered quietly, in an echoing sepulchral voice, as she pulled out her hand and they both laughed delightedly.

"You're a good honest lady. I may always have to bring you to the Bocca della Verità," he said, then led her up the steps and over to his car.

Umberto circled the Ferrari back around the Capitoline Hill, and onto the wide Via dei Fori Imperiali, where he'd been her cicerone to Rome on their only date, with the abortive ending that he'd sworn wouldn't happen again. Now he slowed the car. "This is the Trajan Forum, and that marvelous column is the Trajan Column. If you look to the lower level and just beyond you'll see the Forum Julium."

Since the Forum was closest to the driver's side Madeline leaned to look over Umberto's shoulder as he went on about the monuments, about which she really didn't give a damn at the moment . . . her concentration shifting from past antiquities to such immediacies as the smell of his hair and his skin, to the feel of his breath. She moved away before she did something that would keep them from ever getting to the wedding feast.

They were driving again, slowly around a magnificent arch. "I'm sure you've passed by the Arch of Constantine before. Too bad the scaffolding is up, but the traffic and fumes seemed to be taking their toll."

He looked over at her.

Again she hadn't been listening, and tried to pretend she had. With all the time that had passed since she'd last seen him, she hadn't gotten over him. Not at all. She couldn't take her eyes off his lips, stop wanting to trace her fingers over them.

They drove on for a few minutes and then parked. Walking around to an iron railing, they stopped to look down into the large oblong race track of the Circus Maximus. "They say in its days of glory it could hold a hundred thousand spectators." He put his arm around her shoulder. "I bet you know this place from the chariot race in the film *Ben Hur.*"

He hesitated, apparently unsure if he should keep his arm around her shoulder.

Madeline quickly put her arm around his waist, *she* reassuring *him.*

He squeezed her to him, then pointed to the Palatine Hill. "It overlooks the Circus Maximus; you can see traces of pillars where the hill was reinforced. It was the site of many palaces—"

"Including Nero's." As she said it, she tightened her arm around his waist.

He laughed and bent to kiss the tip of her nose. Which act ignited her desire for him, which was right at the tip of every part of her.

Back in the car, both going through the motions, they passed by the enormous outer walls of the Caracalla.

"Terme di Caracalla, it means baths," he was saying. "Emperor Caracalla didn't much like to bathe alone, apparently preferred to bathe with all the noble families of Rome filling up the bathing rooms." He pulled the car to the curb. "They hold the opera here in the ruins during the summer."

"Oh, I'd love to see *Aida.* I've heard they ride live horses and elephants onstage."

"*Aida* it shall be," he said. "But I'll bring you every night if you'll allow it."

If she would *állow* it! Lord, she had to do something to move this along. On the spot she invented a party. "I'm having a few friends in for a party next Saturday night. I hope you'll be able to come . . ."

"Oh? Damn, we have some location shots to pick up on *Domani e Domani e Domani.* I'll have to be in the north of Italy fur the next two weeks—Turin."

She tried not to show her disappointment. "Well, you'll be back. Two weeks isn't so long." Except right now it sounded like two years.

"Damn," he said, hitting the steering wheel with his fist. "All of a sudden Ralph decided that the film lacked in atmosphere and these locations were added. He says he wants to get them over with before the

*Boccaccio* begins. Once we get into that film it's going to be a year's work at least."

"And you'll be working the whole year with Serena Blaire—" The thought, meant to be unspoken, just popped out, startling and embarrassing her.

He took her hands in his. "I'm sorry about *Boccaccio,* sorry it was decided to give all the Fiammettas to Serena. You would have been the ideal choice for the first one, the pure Fiammetta."

Her sudden blush was not from his praise but from her thought of how pure she was, now that she'd been having sex nearly every weekend with Jean Claude. True, sex just for the sake of sex, but it hardly qualified her for Miss Pure.

"I've made you blush," he said, stroking her flushed cheek. "You're very beautiful when you blush."

He removed his hand from her cheek, looking straight ahead. After a moment he said brightly, "I tell you what, why don't we leave right after the wedding banquet, go somewhere for a quiet nightcap, just the two of us?"

Madeline, relieved, quickly accepted, and he roared away from the curb, headed down the Via Cristoforo Colombo, drove her through the E.U.R. so she could see the Universal Exhibition District with its wide tree-lined avenues and modern buildings. Not far from the ocean now, he made a detour onto the Via Ostiense to show her the beaches. "This is the Lido di Roma and we're coming to Ostia. You'll be able to see Ostia Antica to your right. It's near the mouth of the Tiber. Once it was Rome's principal seaport, centuries before Christ . . ."

"But you said to look to my right and the sea is on my left."

He signaled and pulled off the road. "There are the ruins," he said, putting his arm around her while pointing to them. "The sea was much farther inland way back then." He looked at her for a long moment, then laughed. "I'm afraid I've run out of excuses to keep you with me. Unless you can think of something else I guess I'll be forced to take you to the restaurant."

Before driving off, eyes straight ahead, he said, "If I kept straight on this road we'd come to the airport and . . ."

And if you did, she thought, I'd get right on a plane with you. She supposed she should be grateful he didn't act on his impulse. Instead she could only smile at the thought of being "kidnapped" by Umberto.

# CHAPTER TWENTY-FIVE

MADELINE AND Umberto drove onto the shoulder of the country road, Via Pratica di Mare (Almost to the Sea), to allow an oncoming truck to pass, and Madeline, looking out her window to see how close to the ditch they had come, saw in it a twisting mass of thin, greenish-brown serpents.

"My God, Umberto, you've stopped at a *snake* pit."

Umberto stretched to look out her window. "The sun must have brought them out. They're vipers."

She shuddered as he pulled out again onto the road. "Vipers? So close to the city?"

"Deserted farms mean mice and that brings the snakes. Vipers have gotten to be a plague in Rome. They've even been spotted on terraces in the city."

Madeline shivered again and Umberto reached over and drew her against him. She could almost be grateful for the vipers. Moments later they had come to a one-story red-brick building, turned in and skidded to a halt on its circular gravel driveway.

Il Mulino Restaurant was long and low and looked nothing like its namesake: the Windmill. It stood in isolation and seemed deserted. However, as soon as Umberto had turned off the engine, the screams of children and the drone of adult conversation filled the air, and as Umberto came around to help her out they heard the wail of a siren in the distance.

Approaching the entranceway, they heard sounds of scuffling and hoarse angry voices. Umberto put his arm around Madeline and lifted her bodily, swung her away from the door as a group came stumbling out: men in tuxedos, arms flailing, being restrained by a small army of waiters.

"What's *happening?*" Madeline said, still in Umberto's arms, feet barely touching the ground.

"Nothing much, just another wedding reception that's ended in a brawl," Umberto said, moving to put her down. Just then one of the men fell, not from a punch but slipping, full of vino, on the gravel.

"That's the groom," Umberto told her.

"What's the other one saying, the one standing over him?"

"He's calling the bridegroom *cornuto,* that he has horns. It's the worst insult to tell a husband he's a cuckold."

"Somebody's a fast worker," Madeline said. "They're only just married. Or is it a prediction?"

Umberto, getting hot under the collar and inching forward, didn't respond to her try at humor.

"Look at the bastard making the horn sign over the poor guy. I've a mind to put a stop to him—"

"Umberto, *please,*" Madeline said, realizing he was serious. "It's not your fight."

But it took two waiters to hold off Umberto. Italian blood rose quickly to the boiling point.

Just then the Neapolitan hoods' car skidded to a halt and the five brothers scrambled out, delighted at the prospect of a fight. The three younger ones came on the scene first and began shoving anyone at hand. And then an ambulance screeched into the driveway—an official signal, it seemed, for hostilities to stop. Both warring factions became subdued, the waiters released their hold on them, and Espartaco whistled his boys to come to heel. The wedding guests, in disarray, were herded into the back of the ambulance by the attendants; the waiters, straightening their uniforms, went back to the restaurant; and all was once again tranquil, until the next time.

Umberto, Madeline noted, seemed as disappointed as the Neapolitan hoods that it was all over.

"Really, Umberto," Madeline said, walking up to him, "why get in a fight with people you don't even know?"

Espartaco, overhearing her, called over his shoulder as he and his brothers entered Il Mulino: "It's part of the wedding, *Americana.* You've got a lot to learn . . ."

"He's right," Umberto said, smiling. "No good wedding is complete without a fight. It's our way of blowing off steam, I guess. Marriages seem to bring it out in us. I'm not exactly sure why."

"The women ought to put a stop to it—"

"Nonsense," he said, kissing the tip of her nose. "The women have a wonderful time screaming, which excites us even more."

"Why the ambulance? No one was hurt."

"Normally no one hardly ever gets hurt. We Italians

like to make a good show of combat. Instead of the police, an ambulance is *always* called. It's traditional. The arrival of the ambulance signals the end of the fight, not the result of it."

Madeline shook her head, laughing. "I guess I've got a way to go before I stop being *Americana.*"

Inside, the restaurant consisted of glass-enclosed reception rooms leading off a large courtyard at the center. Not only Pina and Franco's wedding party but two others were occupying separate sections of the open space, while the children from both had mingled into one group inside a playground area.

Madeline and Umberto joined Christina and Ralph de Rossi, who were standing with the bridegroom, and were promptly served sweet aperitifs, small glasses filled with syrups in pink and reds and greens.

"What are they?" Madeline asked.

"Sweet but utterly undrinkable poisons," Christina said, then turning to Franco added, "Really, Franco, with all the money you've saved by being a bachelor all your life, one would have thought you'd break out the champagne when your wedding day finally arrived."

Franco smiled. "You're absolutely right, Christina darling, but it's a bit of a delicate situation," and then he whispered so that only their group could hear, "Mrs. Bozzetti made all the arrangements and refuses to allow me to help with the cost. I feel terrible, knowing that the poor woman probably will be sewing into the nights to pay for this reception. But it's a matter of her pride, and I must respect it. I might add Pina has inherited some of her strength, for which I am grateful."

"Still," Ralph said, "as your best man there's no reason why I can't offer the champagne."

"A splendid idea," Christina said. "I'll go over to

Mrs. Bozzetti and tell her it's our present. Ralph, order the bottles."

"Where is your bride?" Umberto asked Mariani.

"She and her friends are taking photographs of one another—over there by the swings," Franco said, and added wryly, "with the rest of the children."

Professor and Mrs. Cassini came up to them. "I trust Umberto was a good guide, Madeline," the professor said, while his wife nodded hopefully.

Mrs. Cassini fussed at Umberto's tie, straightening it as if he were still a small boy, then turned all her attention on Madeline.

Eventually the guests were shown to the dining room reserved for "Bozzetti," the bride and groom seated center at a horseshoe-shaped table and surrounded on all sides by Pina's relatives. Tables in the middle of the room were for the guests, but no place cards had been provided. Madeline found herself being guided to a table by Mrs. Cassini, where she sat between her and the professor, with Umberto sitting directly across from her, and next to him were Christina and Ralph de Rossi.

Serena Blaire took the next table and sat facing Umberto. When their eyes met she merely nodded to him. She and Primo had obviously become allies again, with Primo opting to believe that his *tesora* was the innocent victim of Helga's malicious gossip. Now he was regulated to the chair across from his wife since the countess had slipped hurriedly into the seat beside Serena. Vittorio Anastasio, with typical vagueness, hadn't yet found his way to the dining room.

When Madeline looked past Umberto she met the steady gaze of Espartaco and the brothers, who sat at the end of the horseshoe table facing her, making suggestive signs. She thought of saying something to Umberto, but didn't. They'd all been geared up for a fight that didn't happen and she didn't want to be the cause of a renewed round of macho posturing.

Once everyone's glass was filled, the guests' with champagne, the Neapolitans' with home brew, the toasts to the bride and groom began. Madeline had some trouble with the Neapolitan accent, but *A gli sposi* was clear enough.

Madeline was about to dig into the first pasta, her favorite spaghetti alla primavera, when Umberto cautioned, "Madelina, I suggest you eat only a small amount of each dish, there will be dozens of courses to come—" and his mother promptly scolded him, "*Stai zitto. La ragazza è troppa megra. Lasçiata mangiare.*" He laughed and told Madeline that his mother had just told him to shut up—"Not shuta up," Mrs. Cassini broke in. "What I said was to be quiet, *era più raffinato.*" Umberto nodded. "Mama means to say I should let you eat because you are too thin. Of course I think you are *perfetto*—"

"*Talco,*" the countess was calling out, and a large container of talcum powder, always at the ready in the establishment, was dispatched to their table. Vittorio Anastasio and Primo had both splashed the oil from the primavera sauce on their jacket fronts, and Serena was not amused when the countess covered the lapels of Primo's new gray suit with talcum to soak up the oil. Umberto's mother, taking due notice of the spillage, motioned for Umberto to use his napkin like a bib. He was about to protest until Madeline winked at him and tucked her napkin in the neckline of her suit, after which Umberto grinned and dutifully made himself a bib.

After the spaghetti alla primavera there was tagliatelle with cream and peas, penne with cheese and asparagus, ravioli with cognac and truffles and then the antipasto assortment. The main course was roast pork with kidneys, sausages, roast potatoes, and spinach puffs. As the cheese and fruit were being served the musicians arrived—an accordionist, a violinist and two guitarists—a space was cleared for dancing and the bride and groom had the floor to themselves for the first dance.

The combination of the music and seeing her daughter waltzing in the arms of a famous movie-director husband, moved Mrs. Bozzetti to tears, thinking as she was about her long-ago lover, Pina's father, who had not married her, as well as this fulfillment of her ambitions for her daughter.

As other couples took the floor the bridegroom headed for his mother-in-law and asked her for a dance. Mrs. Bozzetti hid her blushes beneath the hood of her black shawl, and it took two of her female relatives to drag her to her feet and onto the dance floor. As Franco Mariani took Mrs. Bozzetti in his arms, the musicians struck up a bawdy Neapolitan song, in response to which her family stood and cheered, clapping in time to the music, singing the risqué words.

And suddenly Mrs. Bozzetti was standing tall, her black hood fallen to reveal a smooth girlish face framed by prematurely gray hair. She threw back her head, laughed, stamped her feet like a young woman who had just been liberated from some ancient malaise, and as Pina watched her mother having the courage to dance for the first time in some twenty years, it was her turn to cry . . .

Now Madeline spotted Espartaco coming toward her, and before she could get Umberto on his feet . . . he being in deep conversation with Christina de Rossi . . . Espartaco had pulled her onto the dance floor, where he proceeded to push her through huge exhausting steps while squeezing her and nuzzling his nose and mouth into her cheek, hair and ear, all the while muttering in licentious tones Italian phrases whose intent was all too clear.

Christina de Rossi, noting the look on Madeline's face, called it to Umberto's attention. Instantly he was on his feet, cutting in on them, elbowing Espartaco, who released Madeline with a muttered challenge to Umberto and a clear-cut suggestion to Madeline about trying a real man and not some movie star.

Umberto, about to answer back, was grateful that Madeline had pulled him away. Espartaco was no joke. "Did that bastard make a pass at you?" he asked Madeline.

"No, no, it's just all the food and wine and the heat in here. I'll feel better if we step outside." Umberto might not want a confrontation, but he could be pushed too far, she realized, and quickly took his arm as he guided her out the doorway to the courtyard and to a bench in the shade. He put his arm around her, lifted a damp curl from her forehead. "Madeline, I know I've disappointed you, more than once. And maybe I have no right to ask you for another chance but I'm going to anyhow . . . Just now when I saw you dancing with another man I went crazy with jealousy. I am not exactly a natural-born warrior, but—don't laugh—I have this urge to protect you. I can't stand it if another man even touches you, let alone molests you." He grinned sheepishly. "I guess I want to molest you myself."

Madeline fought mightily to suppress a show of her pleasure at his declarations. After all, she had some of her own games to play, was entitled to them. "What about leaving me at my door and going back to the Hilton and Serena Blaire—?"

"I did *not* go back to be with Serena—she was just

*there.* Madelina, believe me, it was not something I planned. She checked into the room next to mine and there was a connecting door . . . ah, how can I explain to you what a fool I am?"

He wrinkled his brow and scratched his head, reminding her of his movies when he had gotten into one or another romantic dilemma, and it was all she could do not to grab him and shut him up with a barrage of kisses.

And now he was saying, "What will I do if I've made you so angry that you never forgive me? And how can I blame you if you don't?"

He had that look again, and she couldn't bear it, or bear keeping him in misery, so she kissed him lightly on the cheek and said, "Of course I'm angry! I'm mad as hell that you didn't molest me that night—"

He grabbed her instantly, hugging her to his chest and burying his face in her hair. "Let's leave right now, I have plans that can't wait, I've got to get you off somewhere alone—"

"Um-ber-to," his mother interrupted from the doorway. "They're ready to cut the wedding cake."

Umberto could not believe it—his mother's timing was, as always, precisely inopportune. How many times had she walked into his bedroom just at the crucial moment? And *she* was the one so eager to see him married. Well, no matter, the moment the cake was cut he would do his best to talk Madelina into leaving with him.

Just as Madeline and Umberto were about to enter the dining room they heard a scuffling sound behind them in the courtyard and turned around to see a man being hotly pursued by two others, all in tuxedos and obviously from still another wedding party. The man being chased squeezed by Madeline and Umberto and ran for safety into the dining room, where Pina and Franco were poised to cut the first slice of wedding cake. He joined the circle of guests and family in hopes of melting into the crowd. At first his pursuers stopped in the doorway, unable to see him, then one of them spotted him and they both came in after him. As he emerged from the circle of people around the wedding cake he yelled at his pursuers what had not doubt started the fight in the first place—"*Putana.*"

Instantly the Neapolitan women screamed and Pina's mother fell in a heap on the floor. Pina's uncles knocked over the wedding cake in their haste to get their hands on the man who apparently had just called their niece a *whore.* The word went around the room like wildfire that someone had accused the bride of being a prostitute. More female screams and more men running into the courtyard ready to come to Pina's defense.

Madeline assumed Umberto was still beside her, until she heard his mother trilling, "Um-ber-to, *no,*" and Madeline looked around only to see Umberto's back disappearing out the doorway, his hot Italian blood now overcoming whatever good sense he might have about not playing warrior and losing his chance to spend the rest of the evening with Madeline. She was about to follow him, but Professor Cassini took her by the arm and led her away to the table.

Mrs. Cassini was wringing her hands and muttering words Madeline couldn't translate. The professor helped her out: "When Umberto gets into a fight he always seems to end up with a bloody nose. His mother can't stand the sight of her son's nose bleeding."

Screams, moans, assorted imprecations were coming from outside and the waiters began a rerun to the courtyard to break up the fight. As they did, Helga managed to grab hold of one of them by his coattails and pull him to the table. "Oh, no you don't, buster, you stay right here; if there's going to be bloodshed I'll need more champagne. I'll need it anyway." Angelo Catalano, ignoring all, rose from the table, lifting his silver-tipped cane in military salute, and marched outside.

Primo Galiano stripped off his new gray jacket and headed for the doorway. When Serena saw him heading for certain trouble she abandoned her usual English aplomb, threw down her napkin and went after him. The countess went after Serena, and Vittorio Anastasio followed the countess. A glittering procession indeed.

To Primo's momentary humiliation, it was not the perceived enemy but a group of children running to safety that unceremoniously flattened him as he stepped into the courtyard. Serena, emerging from the doorway, saw Primo stretched out on the ground and Umberto leaning over him. Assuming, or wanting to believe, that Umberto, consumed with jealousy, had taken this opportunity to punch out her husband, Serena took pleasure in striking her future leading man in the face with her handbag. His ample nose, taking the brunt, immediately began spurting blood, at the sight of which the countess screamed and Vittorio Anastasio went so weak in the knees that the countess was obliged to recover sufficiently to help him to a bench.

Madeline, who by now had left her table to observe, feeling mildly titillated and even amused, noted the distinguished director Ralph de Rossi at the center of the courtyard doing some expert footwork and shadowboxing. His wife, Christina, came to the doorway and called out to him to stop making a damn fool of himself and come back inside. Her good sense turned out to be bad luck, since when he turned to her someone's roundhouse punch hit him flush on the side of the head. He sank to his knees, bringing Christina to his side to attempt to revive her fallen warrior.

The man from the other wedding party who had yelled "whore" being now nowhere in sight, the three hoods—Terzo, Quarto and Quinto—had no good focus for their anger and so had resorted to slapping at one another.

A more significant struggle, however, was taking place between Catalano and Espartaco. The waiters were in a respectful circle, as spectators, being careful to stand well back. Catalano had already demolished Pina's Uncle Cesari who, unable to admit defeat by a superior male force also could not bring himself to stand up and take more punishment, and so was sitting in the gravel, faking an ankle injury. Now and again he moaned—an Academy Award performance, Madeline thought. Cesari, however, was not yet out of danger. His attention was riveted on the contest between Catalano and Espartaco. He had no warning of the small poodle that pranced over to him and, after sniffing at his crotch, became aroused and commenced riding up and down on his leg. Forgetting that he was supposed to have an injured ankle, Cesari kicked out at the little animal, causing it to squeal. A fat matron turned on the bully Cesari and began pulling his ears until, under her instructions, he apologized to the dog.

By now the reception room was empty and everyone was crowded into the courtyard. Helga, with her waiter in tow, had set up a ringside table for herself, Astrid, Cleo, Paolo and their bottle of champagne. Umberto was stretched out under a tree, where his mother was applying cold compresses to his forehead while he tilted his head back. Madeline had gone to join the professor, who was watching his wife attend to his son. The professor had his arm around Madeline, reassuring her. Mrs. Bozzetti's sisters had carried her into the courtyard for some air, and Franco was consoling his bride, her gown smeared with frosting, who was sobbing over her ruined wedding cake. Under another tree Serena was fanning a supine Primo, and the countess was rubbing ice cubes on Vittorio's temples. A few yards away, Christina de Rossi was administering to Ralph's bruised knees.

These, however, were bit players in varying stages hors de combat. In the main ring Catalano was doing brilliant footwork, dodging Esartaco's punches as he drove his own jabs home. Espartaco was increasingly like an angry bull, charging wildly, while Catalano operated with cold precision, scarcely a hair out of place. It appeared that Catalano was on his way to a gladiator's execution of Espartaco when Astrid, both annoyed and bored at the performance, got up and walked out to the parking lot. Catalano, his concentration momentarily lost as he watched her go, left himself open to Espartaco's charge, ending in a bear hug that brought them both down, hitting the ground and rolling over and over. In the distance a siren wailed, announcing the arrival of the next ambulance.

Pina, seeing Catalano stripped of his arrogant elegance down in the dirt, had not forgotten the humiliation he had put her through during the so-called screen test at his villa. She left Franco and went over to her Uncle Cesari, still sitting in the gravel, demanding that he further the humiliation of Catalano. Cesari promptly scurried on all fours over to the wrestling match and managed to rip away Catalano's shirt front. The director, stripped as he now was of his pride and his dress, seemed stunned, unable to comprehend this outrage against his person and his dignity. An altogether pleasing result to Pina, and a shocking one for those who had never suspected Angelo Catalano could look ridiculous, just like any other mortal man . . .

Meanwhile, Paolo, hearing how close the ambulance siren now was, decided it was perfect timing to join the fray and avoid the humiliation of not having been bloodied. Seeing Catalano being attacked by both brothers, he lumbered to his feet, stalked to the center ring and launched his enormous weight on all three wrestlers, knocking the wind not only out of them but also himself.

Fortunately the ambulance arrived then, and all the principal men were helped into it, it requiring six waiters to hoist and carry Paolo.

Christina de Rossi shook her head as she watched Ralph clambering aboard, Franco Mariani following closely behind his best man to lend appropriate aid and comfort . . . Catalano, with Espartaco and Cesari, their arms actually around each other's shoulders, climbed on together. Terzo, Quarto and Quinto crowded in beside them, unscathed but not to be left behind, wanting to be a part of the warrior contingent . . . Primo and Vittorio Anastasio held onto one another for support as they went up the steps of the ambulance. The countess tried to cling to Serena for moral support, but Serena, fed up with her attentions, gave her an unladylike shove.

Then a few men nobody knew were helped into the back.

Among the chorus of women surrounding the ambulance were Pina and her mother, Pina's grandparents left alone and still apparently uncertain which family member's funeral they had been attending.

Umberto was the last one to be helped into the ambulance. He sat on a stool by the doors, and with large sad eyes looked out at Madeline over the icepack clamped to his nose. Madeline stood disbelieving, watching as the ambulance doors shut and it drove away. Apparently she and Umberto couldn't even plan a nightcap together without something coming between them. But who could have predicted *this?* They ought to book it into the Caracalla as an opera, she thought.

She declined Professor and Mrs. Cassini's offer to come to their house for a calming drink, but did accept a ride home. It was nearly eight o'clock when they dropped her off in front of her building. When she got to her apartment she threw off her clothes and took a long hot bath. Then, wearing her bathrobe, she sat on the balcony to watch the lights come on in Piazza Navona, and began to think about her mother. If her mother were alive she would invite her to Rome, introduce her to Mrs. Cassini and, of course, to the professor, and yes, Umberto, who surely could play the fool. Most of all Madeline felt that her mother and Mrs. Cassini would get along . . . both were simple women, loving, devoted in their fashion to their families. They even had the same Christian name. One was Italian, the other an American of Polish descent, but Madeline believed that the two Marias might have been kindred souls: Maria Cassini and Maria Yalsekovitch Mandell—

The house phone buzzed, startling Madeline out of her reverie. She pressed the button to release the lock on the street door and ran into the bedroom to put on some clothes. Whoever it was had to climb four flights of stairs. When the knock came she ran to the door, hoping it was Umberto. Instead it was a bouquet so large that the boy delivering it was almost completely hidden. She thanked him, shut the door and quickly read the attached note:

> My darling,
>
> I must catch the six A.M. flight to Turin. My nose still bleeds now and then, but they have packed my nostrils with gauze and are sending me home. I look very silly, but as you know, I am indeed a silly man. I have again behaved like a fool and missed out of my nightcap with you. And just when I felt you might allow me more than a nightcap. If you can (once again) forgive a fool, I shall be a lucky man who has a rendezvous with you in two weeks' time.
>
> I embrace you,
> Umberto

*Rendezvous?* . . . Two weeks? . . . oh, no. Madeline still had no telephone, so decided to call him from the phone box at the corner. She put on her shoes and coat and on the way down the stairs rehearsed what she might say, but by the time she was inside the phone box she had made up her mind not to make the call. He wasn't expecting to hear from her, might even have gone to bed early. His note had really said it all, for now. She would leave it at that. Except who was she kidding? She didn't want to leave it at that. She wanted him. Yes, he'd acted the fool but what a lovable one. Face it, it was simple . . . she totally *adored* the fool.

# CHAPTER TWENTY-SIX

AND SO at approximately nine-thirty on the evening of Pina's tumultuous wedding, Madeline found herself in the phone box at the corner of her street, holding between her fingers a *gettone* she had decided not to use to call Umberto. Perhaps if she had had to walk to the coffee bar to buy a *gettone*, she might not have made the call she did make—to Helga, and so might never have been exposed to the uniquely Italian party game waiting for her.

It was Helga's rather dim-witted domestic, Giuseppina, who answered her call and told her that Helga was unavailable at the moment and asked if she could relay a message. Madeline, capable now of a simple conversation in Italian, said she had been thinking of dropping over for a nightcap and a chat. She needed to come down after the wedding spectacle and the disappointment at not seeing Umberto. "Come, come, *Signorina,*" Giuseppina told her, "the Signorina Astrid is also here, and you know Signorina Helga is always pleased to see you."

Twenty minutes later Giuseppina was opening the front door for Madeline. "Come in, *Signorina.* Give me your coat. The Signorina Helga is no doubt out of the shower now. You may go straight into the bedroom."

The phone rang. Before hanging up Madeline's coat Giuseppina stopped to answer it. As Madeline walked toward the bedroom, she could hear Giuseppina inviting someone else to come over and wondered briefly at Giuseppina inviting guests without consulting Helga.

Madeline opened the bedroom door a crack and was about to call out—when she froze at the scene in front of her. Helga and Astrid were naked, lying in opposite directions on the bed. She had *heard* about oral sex between women, never liked the image it conjured up, and *never* thought she'd be witnessing it. After the initial shock, though, she became mesmerized, wanting simultaneously to shut the door and to observe them. She was surprised to find that she wasn't really revolted, as she would have expected. Maybe it was because Helga and Astrid were so extraordinarily beautiful. Their actions at least looked to be loving, tender, and, of course, highly sensual. So much so that in spite of herself Madeline felt some arousal . . . she quickly shut it off and closed the door, realizing that she was being a voyeur.

There was a knock at the front door and she quickly stepped back into the hallway, to see Angelo Catalano handing Giuseppina his coat. He had a slight limp from the wedding wars and was leaning on his silver-tipped walking stick.

Two thoughts, one of which was perhaps stimulated by her frustration over not having the anticipated evening with Umberto, tumbled over in Madeline's head: one was how surprisingly attractive she found Catalano; the other, how threatening.

When Giuseppina returned to the kitchen, leaving Madeline alone with him, she felt distinctly ill at ease, with an urge to get away at the same time that she felt held by his eyes . . . And with that feeling she began to understand better his hold on Astrid.

He was standing still, continuing to watch her.

And she felt herself responding. Were her senses heightened—or lowered?—by the scene she'd witnessed in the bedroom. She wasn't sure which.

She had little doubt he sensed her reaction, maybe even her willingness, surely her vulnerability. She tried to bring things back to the ordinary and forced herself to speak. "Hello, Angelo." He didn't answer. "Did you hurt your leg?" Her voice sounded thin, hollow in her own ears.

A smile formed at the corners of his mouth and he began speaking to her, and in English. "Have you just come from the direction of the bedroom? Why are you so flushed? Did you see something exciting?"

She tried to sound casual. "I'm not sure I know what you mean."

"I think you do, Madeline. You're red as a virgin's cherry. It's really quite refreshing."

His tone was at once suggestive and angry. Was he suspicious of Astrid? Jealous? Angelo Catalano was someone to be careful of even at the best of times. She was terrified of him, what he might do. If he discovered what was going on in the bedroom, what would he do to Astrid and Helga?

He raised his cane and pointed it at her. "What have you just seen, Madeline? *Tell* me."

She stared at the cane, didn't answer. She couldn't.

"Giuseppina told me our friends were in the shower. I know my Astrid. A bitch in heat."

Catalano made a move toward the bedroom, looked at Madeline, stopped, clamped his hand on the back of her head, drew her face to his and kissed her.

In spite of—because of?—her fear, she felt herself go weak at the knees.

He darted his tongue between her teeth, raised his walking stick and laid it across her body. She shivered as he pressed the stick into her breasts, rubbing it up and down over her nipples. She felt a heat radiating through her. Her nipples swelled, became hard, and the wetness from her vagina dampened her panties. He took a handful of her hair and pulled her head back until she was forced to look at him over the tip of her nose and felt too weak to struggle, even to resist. It was an incredible feeling. Was this really happening to *her?*

He leaned over her. "Are you ready to take a penis? Mine? Or would anyone's do? You got hot watching the lesbians licking each other, didn't you? Perhaps one of them was teasing cunt with a dildo?"

She gasped for breath as he let go of her hair and pressed his hand on her shoulder. "Get on the floor, Venus, and I'll make you come, put you out of your misery. I said get on the floor."

She made an attempt to push him away but her arms had gone as limp as her knees. He took hold of one of her wrists, gripping it hard, and with his other hand turned his walking stick, tracing its tip down her belly until it slid between her legs, then lifted it until it pressed snugly and began rubbing it back and forth over her clitoris as she began sagging toward the floor—

It was not her good sense or sudden resolve that stopped him but a very fortuitous knock at the front door, and Giuseppina showing up to answer it. He abruptly released her, and she scrambled to her feet and ran into the guest toilet. As she closed and locked the door she could hear a man's voice—Paolo's.

Madeline splashed cold water on her face and the back of her neck, held her hands under the faucet, allowing the ice-cold water to run over her wrists. She massaged her scalp where Angelo had pulled her hair, smoked a cigarette and stayed closeted until she'd regained something of her composure. The trembling inside, however, did not stop, no longer from sexual arousal but from astonishment at her own behavior. If it hadn't been for Paolo's arrival, Angelo could have fucked her on the spot. The innocent abroad was not so innocent . . .

When she came out of the toilet she saw that Jean Claude had also arrived. When he came forward to kiss her she turned aside and walked hurriedly into the living room, where Paolo and Angelo were having a drink and watching the sports news on television. It looked like a reunion. Paolo greeted her casually. Angelo, absorbed with the scores, behaved as if nothing had happened between them, ignoring her just as he usually did.

Jean Claude followed close behind her and after shaking hands with Paolo and Angelo came to sit beside her at the opposite end of the room. He looked puzzled at her brush-off, and she realized he must be wondering what was wrong. He would, she hoped, never know. It occured to her that she must stop seeing Jean Claude now that there was the possibility of a romance with Umberto. Her French still too rudimentary for such delicate communication, she would have to get someone to explain to him why she no longer could see him . . . Helga would do it for her, and as she thought of Helga the picture of her and Astrid making love came back vividly and she squirmed slightly in her chair.

Now she heard the bedroom door opening, and seconds later Astrid and Helga came strolling into the living room, arm in arm, barefoot, and each wearing a filmy dressing gown. Their hair was tousled, their cheeks glowing and they carried with them not only the ambience but the aroma of sex.

Helga stopped abruptly in the archway. Her charcoal eyes flashed as she tossed her auburn hair back, let go of Astrid and put her hands on her hips. "Well, well, I didn't know I was throwing a party. Where did you all come from?"

After each explained that it was Giuseppina who had invited them, Helga laughed her deep guttural laugh, clutched the near-transparent gown around her and assured everyone that they were welcome to stay. She then excused herself and headed for the kitchen, from which, moments later, one could hear muffled cursing as well as a few short, sharp cracks. Later, as was their fashion, they would make up and Helga would buy Giuseppina an extravagant present.

In the living room, Astrid was turning down the bright lights, and at the same time Paolo and Angelo moved to turn off the television. As Astrid went from lamp to lamp her odors circulated, and with each lamp she lowered her tall androgenous shape came into view beneath its filmy covering. When she bent over the cassette machine to put on some romantic music, Paolo audibly sucked in his breath.

With the lights low, the music playing, Jean Claude

began nuzzling Madeline's neck and ear, and she thought to herself that a girl could only be expected to endure so much. She would finish her drink and take him home with her, for one last time.

Helga had come back now into the dimly lit room and Paolo, over the strains of soft guitar music, was telling her that Cleo was going to Turin early in the morning, would be gone for two weeks, and that she and Umberto had some added scenes for *Domani e Domani e Domani.* Lately, he said, Cleo had been draining him, she wanted to make love day and night to get pregnant. He cherished her, of course, but it would be nice not to have to be a stud twenty-four hours a day. Still, Paolo was saying, he felt rather sexy even if tired, and he went on to make a suggestion that Madeline thought she could not possibly have translated correctly . . . her knowledge of Italian was, after all, still limited. Then Paolo repeated what he'd said and she thought maybe his words had some sort of a double meaning. He *couldn't* be saying what she *thought* he was saying. *Could he?*

But now Paolo made the same suggestion in French, and Jean Claude agreed with an enthusiasm that surprised and disappointed her. He was also the first one to stretch out on the carpet. Paolo and Angelo moved the coffee table. Helga lay down in the center of the room. Astrid turned the lights down even lower, then found a place for herself on the floor near Helga. Paolo took off his huge shoes and lay back on the couch.

Angelo came over to Madeline. "Aren't you going to join us?" he said in English. "No one will touch you. This is merely a party game . . . group masturbation. We all played it when we were young and the girls wouldn't let us touch them. Surely you Americans must have done the same."

He was smiling when he said it, and she suddenly felt naked, as though he were about to repeat the earlier scene.

"It's very nice," Paolo called to her. "All you do is lie down and listen to the music. When you feel like it you masturbate or watch others masturbate."

Madeline got unsteadily to her feet. "Start without me," she said, heading toward the hall.

She went to the closet, collected her coat, and quietly let herself out the front door.

# CHAPTER TWENTY-SEVEN

MONDAY, THE day after Pina's wedding, marked the beginning of Madeline's last week of filming on *Paranoia*. She arrived at Cine Citta late and had to rush through makeup. Not being able to sleep the night before, she felt as if gremlins had invaded her head.

She couldn't banish the replay of yesterday's events. First the reconciliation with Umberto, followed by the ludicrous brawl after the wedding that had ruined the chance for a nightcap and more, then finding herself a voyeur at the scene of Helga and Astrid making love, Angelo Catalano turning her to jelly and nearly seducing her on Helga's floor, Paolo beginning a game of group masturbation and Jean Claude apparently preferring it to her.

It was a night she wished she could forget but doubted she ever would.

Last week she had arranged a luncheon for today with Helga, and was sorry that it had to be right after the craziness of last night. Today was surely too soon to come face to face with Angelo Catalano, but chances were she would run into him somewhere on the lot. No day would be ideal for coping with Alfonso Razzi and his ridiculous film, but if she could get through today and the rest of the work week, at least by Friday night *Paranoia* would be finished.

Pina, not surprisingly, was also late, and Madeline couldn't find a copy of the day's scenes or shooting schedule. Maybe now that Pina was married to an important director she had decided she no longer wanted to be a translator and secretary. Or maybe she was having a one-day honeymoon; she and Franco had not planned a trip because his preproduction work for *Boccaccio* was beginning so soon. She thought of Serena Blaire having three of the four roles, but then reminded herself that Serena's career had been full of great roles. It seemed Serena always managed to capture first prize. Her *reputation* was one of ladylike refinement, sweetness. Actually she must have an outstanding ability for manipulation. Not only was she the top lady in the *Boccaccio* film, but she'd managed a fling with Umberto before leaving him for her husband, Primo. Well, at least she had a husband—*and* a baby. All you have, she told herself, is an army of gremlins marching through your head.

Think of the devil . . . As Madeline left her dressing room she saw Serena up ahead with, of all people, Catalano. They were facing away from her, walking in the direction of the cantina. Madeline hurriedly turned the corner to avoid catching up with them. Serena and Catalano . . . something must be brewing . . .

At lunch the first thing Helga said was, "So you ran out on the party game." Madeline shrugged, not wanting to discuss the previous evening.

Helga laughed. "Never mind, darling, I understand, it's a stupid Italian invention. Personally I'd had enough sex for one day."

"It looked like it could turn into an orgy."

"Jean Claude was the only one who wanted an orgy. Jean Claude wants everything all the time. Paolo was too tired, and Catalano wouldn't have tolerated it. As long as he's there to prevent it, no one else fucks Astrid."

"But you and Astrid . . ."

Helga laughed again. "He permits Astrid to have female lovers. What he won't stand for is her fucking another man."

Madeline could only shake her head, and Helga, warming to her subject, went on, without encouragement, to say that Astrid had seduced her while they'd been taking a shower together. It had always seemed a possibility, but she'd avoided that kind of involvement with Astrid, avoided it because she never wanted a threesome with Catalano. He frightened her. And where Astrid was, Catalano was sure to be lurking somewhere in the background. "Maybe you're not aware of it," Helga said, "but I've been acting as a sort of buffer between you and Astrid."

"Yes, as a matter of fact I have noticed, and I thank you for it. You're a friend, Helga."

"That's me—everybody's friend, nobody's true love." There was an edge of bitterness to her words. Could she be referring to Umberto? Madeline wondered.

"Anyway," Helga went on, "Astrid has had her eye

on you from the first day—that day in Piazza del Popolo when she brought you over to our table. And it's not just because you turn her on, she's a big fan, has seen all your films. It was you she wanted the affair with, it was just me who was handy on the spot when the fancy struck her. She is a bitch, no question. Of course we were both feeling sort of weepy after the wedding. I was probably in the mood to be taken . . . needed some tenderness. Yes, even tough, independent Helga. Anyway, I have to tell you, it was pretty great. You know, if I'm not careful I could get myself hooked on Astrid. But I don't want to know about Catalano, I won't even go to his villa for dinner when Astrid invites me. I don't trust him. I've no idea what he might do, except I'm sure it would be something nasty."

Remembering Catalano and his silver-tipped cane between her legs, Madeline could only nod vigorously.

Helga pushed her plate away and lit a cigarette, and Madeline took the opportunity to change the subject: "I saw Catalano with Serena this morning . . ."

Helga shrugged. "Haven't you heard? It's all over the lot. Catalano finally gave in to the pressure. Apparently he asked for a hand in the editing of his segment, was told he couldn't have it unless he agreed to use Serena at the beginning to link all the characters. So now the little bitch has the whole thing sewn up . . . all four episodes."

"Serena getting Fiammetta One is still a big disappointment to me, I have to admit," Madeline said.

"You're not alone. I'd give my left tit for one of the Fiammettas. Maybe my right one too . . . Oh, by the way, I'll probably be leaving soon, I've got an offer to do a film in Germany."

"Is it a good one?"

"It's not bad." Helga grinned. "I'd been holding

off, not taking any jobs—hoping that someone might push Serena under a steam shovel."

Madeline, too, found herself having wicked thoughts, or could it just be the gremlins in her head wishing something terrible would happen to Serena? It really would have been terrific if the female leads were herself, Astrid, Helga and Cleo . . . Thinking of Cleo reminded her that she was in Turin with Umberto. She wished she could be in Cleo's place, might even have been willing to make Helga's proposed sacrifice to be there. At least the thought made her smile, which she'd done precious little of lately.

On a back street in Turin, Cleo, so envied by Madeline, was delaying the shooting. The scene was one in which she was to deliver her husband's lunch basket. The scenic department had dressed the outside of a deserted warehouse to represent the exterior of a shoe factory. The lights were set and the camera ready. Umberto was stationed one flight up on the other side of the door. He had been there in the dark, dank warehouse for twenty minutes waiting to make his entrance.

Cleo was supposed to come down the street swinging her hips, the lunch basket on her head, and climb the fire escape to the door, from which Umberto would then emerge. Three times she had rehearsed sashaying down the street. Three times she had stopped at the bottom of the fire escape without climbing the stairs.

"What is it, darling?" Ralph said in his measured, patient way. "Would you rather not rehearse climbing the stairs? Shall we just go for a take?"

Cleo removed the basket from her head. First she pouted and then she sighed. "Why don't I call to my husband? And Umberto will come down the steps to get his lunch from me?"

Ralph put his arm around her waist. "I have the camera set at an angle to see your pretty legs as you climb. And you know perfectly well an Italian husband would not come down to collect his own lunch."

Cleo shrugged her broad shoulders, causing her mammoth breasts to rise and fall. "Could Umberto not lower a rope—I tie the basket to it—"

She was interrupted by Umberto, who stuck his head out of the door on the landing. "Why not rewrite the scene while I wait in the dark. Why not rewrite the entire script while I play with the spiders and rats. I can just stand on the damp concrete until the writer makes the trip from Rome."

Ralph promptly called for a ten-minute break, then tried to coax Umberto to come down into the fresh air and sunlight. But Umberto was well into his rage, Italian-style: "I could just lean against the slimy walls and recite my catechism . . ."

Ralph went up the stairs, took Umberto by the arm and began leading him down as he raved on: "I could sit among the trash, chewing my finger and toenails."

When Ralph finally got Umberto to the bottom of the fire escape, Cleo began: "You are both cruel, stupid men. Your mothers would be ashamed of you. I don't want to climb stairs. I must think about my future baby."

At the mention of a baby Umberto forgot his ranting, and both he and Ralph helped Cleo over to one of the folding chairs. Ralph then hurried off for a cup of water while Umberto fanned her, Cleo now smiling and nodding and purring at the attention.

Actually, of course, Cleo was not yet pregnant and eventually had to admit it. She was being careful, though, because she hoped and expected to get pregnant soon. Soon . . .

Which revelation sent Umberto into renewed rage, and by the time Ralph had gotten him calmed down the daylight was gone and shooting had to be called off for the day.

Eventually the scene was cut from the script. No one on earth could convince Cleo that climbing stairs was not a threat to her impending pregnancy.

As it turned out, a great many other scenes were cut as well. Ralph pared the shooting schedule from twelve days to nine—but not because of Cleo. He left Turin at the end of the first week, entrusting the last few days to a second unit director. Ralph, a new crisis on his hands, had to return to Rome as quickly as possible.

# CHAPTER TWENTY-EIGHT

SERENA WAS pregnant. Which was a breach of her contract and grounds for automatic cancellation. Better than a steam shovel, Helga said. It was the insurance doctor who discovered the condition during the routine medical examination for the film, the pregnancy test coming back positive.

Serena had read the contract and approved every clause. Enraged, she went to her own doctor for verification, and again the result was positive. It was an early stage but there was no mistake. The rabbit had died, and its demise killed Serena's coup with *Boccaccio*. She, member of the consortium, manipulator par excellence, was as of the moment O-U-T out of *Boccaccio*, and the word spread like wildfire.

Primo took the brunt of her anger. He had raped her, ruined her career. Once again he was exiled from her bedroom to the guest room. The best he could do was try to keep out of her way in the hope that she wouldn't throw him out of the house altogether.

As for Prometheus Productions, the company was going to have to suspend operations. Serena certainly wasn't about to allow her Swiss consortium to invest in a film she herself wasn't starring in. Prometheus would have to go back to the Underworld.

Cine Citta was buzzing with speculation about who would now be cast as Fiammetta One, Two, and Four, because, of course, Astrid already had Fiammetta Three. Catalano had been quick to get to work with the scriptwriters; those unwanted flashbacks of Serena could now be eliminated from his segment.

Rumor had it that Cleo Monti would again be offered Vittorio Anastasio's segment. It seemed likely since, before Serena's putsch, Cleo had been the frontrunner for the part of Fiammetta Four. But even though Paolo was now back as investor, no longer needing to fight against the Swiss consortium, nothing had been confirmed and emergency production meetings were still taking place. It was ironic, though, that Cleo, who was wearing out Paolo's little member in an effort to get herself pregnant—which would have disqualified her for a Fiammetta role—was now at least in the running. Serena, of course, was herself apparently ousted by achieving the unwanted condition Cleo so desperately craved.

Many names were circulating for the other two roles, among them Helga Haufman and Madeline Mandell. But Madeline was beginning to lose heart. Ralph de Rossi had arrived back from Turin on the weekend, and so far he had made no effort to contact her. Her agent, Luigi Luna, had left messages round the clock, but Ralph had not returned his calls. Luigi, a man hard to put off, was spending the day at the studio hoping to get in to see de Rossi.

*Paranoia* had wrapped on a Friday evening and on the following Monday morning Madeline and Pina were in Madeline's dressing room packing up her personal effects. Franco Mariani, involved in the production meetings for *Boccaccio,* had been gone most of the weekend, and not even Pina could get to her husband for any news. Luigi Luna kept popping in and out of the dressing room, but the agent seemed to know less than anybody and was driving Madeline crazy with his constant goings and comings and nervous chatter.

At about 11:00 A.M. the door to Madeline's dressing room was flung open and Helga burst in carrying a bottle of champagne. She literally threw herself—no mean achievement—on the couch and bounced up and down. "To Serena Pregnant, not to mention the one whodunit and the rabbit who died for the cause. The skinny bitch is out, all hail mother nature!"

"Isn't it wonderful," Pina cried. "I'll get some glasses, they're in the bathroom."

Madeline surveyed the contents of the box she'd been packing. "Isn't it amazing how much junk you can collect in such a short time?"

"Jesus, Madeline," Helga said, watching her in amazement, "is that all you can say? Primo has done us the world's greatest favor and you're fussing over half-empty makeup jars and stained throw pillows."

Madeline sank onto the vanity stool, her voice strained when she finally spoke. "How do you know the baby is Primo's?"

Helga mussed her hair affectionately. "Because I know."

"How? How do you know?"

"Because, darling, I've made it my business to have a long talk with my friend Primo. I was so thrilled when I heard the rumor that Serena was pregnant that I went right to a principal player in order to confirm it."

"But how does *he* know he's the father?" Pina asked, returning just then with the glasses.

"Don't ever doubt the thoroughness of a Haufman interrogation," Helga said. "Especially when Haufman has had special access to the source . . . as I had with Primo. He says Serena knows about him and me, but he wasn't anxious to have it spread far and wide. Serena wouldn't like it. So he cooperated in my investigation. I know when, where, and how Primo got it into Serena. It was the first time in over a year. The little nerd actually raped his wife. Her Serena Highness had no time to get her diaphragm. She *blew* it!" Helga slapped her thigh in appreciation of her double entendre.

Madeline was about to press for more confirmation but Helga held up her hand. "Wait, wait! I even know the exact date. It checks out exactly with Serena's menstrual cycle, as established by my close interrogation not only of Primo but of her doctor . . . who has a very jealous wife . . . and the amount of time she's been pregnant. Take it easy, darling, your precious Umberto is in the clear."

"You're amazing," Pina said with admiration.

"I want you to tell *that* to your husband. And when you do, tell him also that I'm the perfect casting for his Fiammetta Two."

Helga then popped the cork and began pouring for the assembled ladies, studying Pina all the while. "Pina, sweetness, are you by any chance going after the part yourself? Tell me the truth, girl."

"No, I am not," Pina replied firmly. "Anyway, as soon as Franco got the news about Serena he told me he hoped I wouldn't get that idea into my head. He doesn't think I'm right for the part in his segment. And anyway he doesn't think it would be a good idea for us to work together. At least not right away."

"Whew," Helga said, letting her breath out, "that's a relief. And by the way, you *aren't* right for the part. I am. And I could be your mother—well, your maiden aunt—maybe your older sister."

Madeline laughed, helping herself to a glass of champagne. "Keep going, Helga, and you'll convince yourself that you could be Pina's daughter."

Pina took up a glass of the champagne too and they all raised their glasses for a toast—

Just then Luigi Luna ran in for the seventh or eighth time that morning. Seeing the raised glasses, he said breathlessly, "What are you celebrating? What's happened? Has Ralph called? I just left his waiting room—did he call while I was on my way here?"

"Calm down, Luigi," Pina said. "We haven't heard anything new yet. I told you that if we did I would come looking for you."

"Have some champagne, Luigi," Helga said, pouring some into a clean cup from the breakfast tray. "Actually we're toasting Primo Galiano."

"Who?"

"The cockerel who fertilized Serena Blaire's egg."

"Oh, oh, her husband. Yes, yes, I see." He accepted the cup from Helga, raised it to the girls, drained the contents, then asked Pina if she had left a message for Franco to call her in Madeline's dressing room. "As his wife you should let him know where you are."

Pina shrugged. They had had this same conversation numerous times that morning. She wasn't going to make a pest of herself—that was that. Franco would find her when he was ready. And Luigi and the rest of them could just wait to hear what had been decided.

Luigi began pacing the floor. "Don't leave the dressing room today, we need a base on the lot."

Helga snapped her fingers. "He's right. We'll go for lunch but, Madeline, don't give up your dressing room today. Don't turn in the key. It gives us a place to operate from."

"That's a smart girl. I should represent you. I have all the most important clients—"

"Yes, yes, we've had this conversation before, Luigi. You handle Umberto and Astrid and . . . Astrid—let's get Astrid out to the studio, she can pump Catalano for information. We can't be covered on too many fronts."

Two hours later in the restaurant at Cine Citta Astrid was telling Helga and Madeline that she couldn't possibly interrupt Angelo while he was in script conferences and production meetings. If she nagged at him it would be very unpleasant for her later at home, and as she said it Madeline now knew what she meant . . .

At a table on the other side of the restaurant Angelo was lunching with the other directors of *Boccaccio.* Ralph and Franco and Angelo seemed to be in deep conversation, but Vittorio appeared to be daydreaming. No doubt, Helga thought, he would have preferred to be with his dogs and horses.

Pina now entered the restaurant, closely followed by the countess. When they got to the directors' table Pina went by without disturbing them, but the countess stopped to speak to Vittorio. It was a curious thing: Pina inviting the countess to lunch at Cine

Citta. They hadn't ever met before the wedding, and couldn't have gotten to know one another very well on the day of the festivities. So what, Helga speculated, did Pina want from the countess? A social life for herself and Franco? Franco hardly seemed the sort to get along with the horsey set. The countess did have influence over Vittorio. Vittorio was one of the directors of *Boccaccio* . . .

Well, the hell with it for now. Helga signaled the waiter to order champagne, but Astrid shook her head. "I don't think we should seem to be celebrating," she said. "Serena's pregnancy is pretty much old news. Cine Citta is speculating about the future of *Boccaccio.* The directors, my Angelo included, are concentrating on pulling the film back together and I can tell you they're all on edge. Especially if Angelo is any example. I've been staying a mile away from him. None of them is ready to confirm anything. If they see us whooping it up, celebrating, it will look like you both assume you're in the cast and it might irritate the directors—I know it would irritate Angelo."

"I'm sure Astrid is right," Madeline said. "How would anyone know we're just celebrating Serena's pregnancy and not that we figure we've got a casting victory for ourselves?"

She turned to Helga. "Just because Serena is out doesn't necessarily mean that you and I are in, does it? Shouldn't we be just hoping for the best and expecting the worst? Maybe it's the way I was raised, but I've always thought it was better to hedge one's bets."

"*Shit.* You two ladies are really getting me down. Don't you know how to risk being a winner, or at least gloat over seeing the enemy go down? Well, I *want* to gloat over the bony cunt being beaten for once. And I damn well don't care who knows it."

Astrid tried to calm her."But like Madeline says—how will you feel if it doesn't turn out the way you want?"

"Ah, screw you," Helga said good-humoredly. "At least I'll have had some pleasure, and I learned a long time ago to grab what I could when I could and not to worry about the consequences. Besides, Paolo Piccolo is back investing, as I hear it, half the money. I ought to be in pretty good shape. All I need to do is whistle and I'll have him tied to my bedposts begging for mercy. He better throw his weight behind me"—she laughed her best wicked laugh—"or else."

Madeline shook her head, no longer at all shocked by Helga but still startled by her outbursts of lusty good humor. "Does Paolo say anything about me?" she asked.

"Darling, not to be mean, but when we're together you're not exactly in the picture. Especially since the other night when you walked out on our little party." Helga pinched Madeline's cheek and laughed. "Don't look so glum, darling, you're probably in a better position than I am. Ralph's always taken a shine to you, and he has as much say in this project, maybe more, as Paolo, even if Paolo is an investor."

Astrid nodded. "I think it's just a question of being patient for a while longer—"

Helga turned on her. "That's fine for you to say, you Norwegian whore. You already *have* one of the roles. You're sitting pretty."

Astrid gifted them with one of her divine smiles. Yes, she was sitting pretty. *Boccaccio* was the film of the year. If Angelo Catalano was a stern and often cruel man, he was also a brilliant director, and certainly no one knew how to use her talent and looks to greater advantage.

* * *

After lunch, Astrid went home and Madeline and Helga went back to the dressing room. Madeline badly wanted to leave the studio. If the news was bad—and it was her nature to expect it would be—she didn't want to be in public. She didn't think she could handle that. Better to be alone . . .

A knock at the door stopped her from further indulging her gloomy thoughts. Helga went to open it.

Ralph de Rossi was standing there, and when he asked to speak to Madeline, Helga quickly excused herself and went outside, closing the door behind her.

Luigi Luna came scurrying down the street toward the dressing room, still trying to catch up with Ralph. Helga positioned herself in front of the door, blocking his way, and told him to back off, let Ralph and Madeline talk in private. They would all know the outcome soon enough. Luigi began pacing, and Helga crossed her fingers tightly.

Inside the dressing room Ralph looked closely at Madeline, took her hands.

"Well, Madeline, will you be my Fiammetta One?"

Madeline had taken a deep breath. Now she let it out with a small cry of joy and hugged him.

"I'm as pleased as you are," he said, "and I apologize for keeping you waiting like this. You were my first choice, and it annoyed me that I couldn't say so . . . until now."

Madeline laughed, shook her head, but no words came.

Ralph held her at arm's length and looked at her. "The way you are now, the way you look . . .it's precisely the quality I want for Fiammetta. Excitement, sweetness, vulnerability. They're as important to the role as your beauty, more so."

He let go of her and led her to the couch. "These last few hours must have been hell for you, but I simply couldn't get to you sooner. This job, artistic director, a fancy title with too many problems, decisions . . . Well, I have some more news. Ready?"

Madeline shook her head, still speechless.

"I wanted something important added to the script. It's meant meeting with the directors and scriptwriters to get approval. I can't work alone . . ." He looked suddenly weary. "The idea of flashbacks began as a way of structuring the film for the use of one actress as Fiammetta. Serena . . ." Now his energy and enthusiasm seemed to be returning. "But Fiammetta One is—you are—still the *true* Fiammetta. The others are imaginary creations of a jealous mind. To make that point it occurred to me that the flashback to the true Fiammetta would still be a good cinematic device, even with other actresses playing the other Fiammettas. My biggest problem has been Angelo. He'd just taken out the flashback and it wasn't easy to persuade him to put it back. It wasn't until lunch that he finally agreed and, I think, even took my point. So now you will appear from time to time throughout the film. You will be seen in all of the episodes. You will be featured, of course, in mine You, Madeline, will be the only *true* Fiammetta."

# CHAPTER TWENTY-NINE

MADELINE COULDN'T believe it. She hadn't counted on it, but now, just like Helga had said, here it was. And it was hers. Fiammetta One, the most glorious of all the Fiammettas, the true and real one, the embodiment of love, portrait of sweetness, beauty and sensuality. Since it was to be a multimillion-dollar international film it would be shot in English and dubbed into other languages. The fact that hers was the real Fiammetta would be underscored by flashbacks in which she would appear in all the other segments. Her career was going to be revived in great fashion, it seemed. Venus had turned into a Phoenix, about to be reborn.

Helga, hearing the news, hugged her. Luigi, his

percentage dancing like sugarplums in his eyes, hugged them both, then nearly flew out of the dressing room in inform the world that he was now agent to the biggest of stars. When Pina showed up, tense in anticipation of bad news, and heard the good, she let out such a squeal she almost wet her pants and had to run to the bathroom.

Madeline, wide-eyed, looked at Helga. "What do you think Umberto will say when he hears? I mean, what do you think he'll do when he sees me for the first time as Fiammetta One—?"

"I know exactly, darling. He'll throw you down on the set and fuck you right there in front of everybody." Then she added, with mock concern, "Actually, knowing Umberto, he'll probably trip and knock you and himself out before he has a chance to reach for his celebrated cock."

Madeline and Helga doubled up in laughter, and Pina returned from the bathroom to see them rolling on the couch, holding their sides. "What time is it?" she asked. But neither Madeline nor Helga could stop laughing long enough to answer her. "Listen, I have an idea, Madeline. Why don't you call Umberto, tell him the news yourself. Franco told me the hotel in Turin where the cast is staying—the Grand."

The suggestion seemed to sober them. "Helga, you call him," Madeline said. "What time is it?"

Helga looked at her watch. "It's not even three. He'll still be on location. I'll call him tonight. Anyway, I'm going to call Cleo and tell her. At least you'll be doing the film with Astrid and Cleo, if not me."

"Oh, Helga, I'm sorry . . . I've been so wrapped up in myself. What can I do to help you get the part?"

"It's all right, this girl helps herself. Or at least

does her best." She glanced at her watch. "Right about now Paolo should be sitting down to talk to Franco. He had a two-thirty appointment . . ."

Which, in fact, was the case. Earlier Helga had told them that all she had to do was whistle and Paolo would come running. She hadn't, though, quite told it like it was, not being so sure that Paolo would pay off. She was sure he'd at least do his best for her with Franco, but now with the news of Madeline she also could have some expectation that his best might be enough . . .

Last night, when she actually had seen him, having set up the date as soon as she had heard about Serena's pregnancy, Helga had reminded Paolo not only about past good times together, but also about how she had run interference for him in letting down his Cleo when it seemed she was losing her part in *Boccaccio* to Serena. Paolo had readily agreed to speak up for her with Franco, but Helga felt she needed more to seal the deal. About that he showed less enthusiasm.

"Please, Helga, I am exhausted from trying to do my duty with Cleo. I love my wife, as you know, but there is a limit. I am exhausted all the time, find myself obliged to make up excuses, invent meetings. The combination of Cleo's demands and the pressures of my business and now the renewal of my involvement in *Boccaccio* are wearing me down—"

"Paolo, I'm touched by your self-sacrifice, so I will make it all possible for you . . ." And she proceeded to undress him, to draw a hot bath for him, lave him, massage him, dry him off and lead him, eyes half closed, to the bed, where he stretched out and murmured that he was sleepy, thanking her for letting him relax.

Helga smiled, a bit wickedly. "Relax, Piccolo, because Helga is now going to make you forget everything except her . . . no more tension, no more having to make Cleo with baby." And she proceeded to massage his smallness, until it grew to proportions that surprised her and impressed its owner. And then, still murmuring to him to relax, she took it all inside her, moving easily, slowly at first, then as his whole body awoke to hers with increasing tempo, until Paolo and she managed to come nearly together, she bending over him and covering his face with kisses, and he now saying, "Helga, Helga . . ."

A while later, after they had both slept, she playfully nudged him awake. "Time to go, Paolo. Now please don't forget what you are going to do for Helga with Franco. You can't have what just happened now without what I want to happen for me later. Watch out, my boy, because if you're bad, it's back to the bedposts for you."

He laughed. "Helga, you are a genius. I thought I was forever beyond what you made happen. I thank you, and I assure you I will do my best for my Helga."

She reached out and squeezed his balls, just enough to make him wince. "I'm sure you will, my pet. I'm sure you will . . ."

A block away now, in Franco Mariani's office, Paolo wanted it to seem an informal talk, so he sat on the leather couch and Franco sat in the easy chair opposite rather than at his desk. First Paolo tried to make it clear he was not there in his capacity as backer, then said, "However, I won't beat around the bush, Franco. I've come to ask you about Helga Haufman, to ask if you've considered her for the part."

Franco leaned back, studying something on the ceiling. He appeared reluctant, ill at ease in the presence of the man who again was financing a major portion of the film.

Paolo attempted to reassure him. "Understand, Franco, I respect your judgment, *you're* the director. I'm not here to pressure you because I have an investment in the film. I'm merely asking if you've considered Helga."

Franco looked at him. "Yes, I have been thinking of her for the role."

"Seriously thinking of her?"

Franco nodded.

Paolo felt encouraged. "Franco, I don't know how important this is, but I can tell you that Helga wants *very* badly to do the part. She, at least, feels she's perfect for it. And of course I don't have to tell you that she's a fine actress and a . . . a remarkable, gorgeous woman. She's also smart, and I suspect if she believes she's right for the part, well, then there must be at least something to it."

"And she could be right," Franco said, but still hesitantly. "You say she wants very badly to do it?"

"Yes."

"Badly enough to test for the part?"

That threw Paolo off guard, he wasn't sure how to answer. "Well, I suppose it's a bit unusual to ask a star of her stature to take a test . . ." He stopped, seeing Franco bristle, then quickly added, "But of course this is no ordinary film and you are a famous director . . . perhaps she would be willing."

Franco again seemed to stare into space, finally said, "Believe me, Paolo, I wish I could be positive. I'm under pressure to cast the part immediately. My actress should already have been involved in preproduction."

Paolo, accustomed to direct dealings in business, became impatient with Franco's hedging and decided to go straight to the heart of the matter. "You can be candid with me, Franco. What exactly are your reservations about Helga?"

Franco sighed dramatically, excessively Paolo thought.

"You mentioned them yourself a few moments ago."

"I did?" Paolo was alarmed, wondered if he had inadvertently said something to hurt Helga's chances. "You mean she's too smart? You want somebody dumb?"

Franco smiled. "No, you said she was gorgeous, remarkable, and a star. She is all three. In fact, she may be too beautiful and famous for the part. I've been leaning toward casting someone who is more of a character actress even if less well known."

Paolo looked at him curiously. There was too much money riding on this film to cast some unknown ugly in the role. But he'd promised not to throw his weight around so he merely reminded Franco, "You were going to use Serena Blaire. Many people would consider her beautiful. And she's certainly a star."

"Yes . . . but she has a thin, rather unattractive body. One can shape her, as it were, into the role."

Paolo felt at a loss, searching for the right thing to say. "But what about Serena's face? She does have a beautiful face and—"

"Serena was willing to do the part without makeup. Not many actresses of her stature, or Helga's, would be willing to do that."

Paolo was confused. Wasn't it the job of makeup artists to make faces fit the character? He had no idea if Helga would object, so he left the meeting feeling things were up in the air and worrying about Helga's reaction. He would telephone her from the airport. At least in that way if she felt he'd made a mess of things there would be some distance between them. As there would continue to be, except with him tied to the bedposts, if she was angry at his performance.

Immediately after lunch Vittorio escaped what to him was the boring routine of further meetings at Cine Citta, and drove with the countess to the stables for a ride.

Later over a drink Vittorio asked her to please help him find an additional stable boy. "You see my dear," he said, swallowing the olive from his martini, "the thing is, that I shall have no time to myself once this film begins. Even now I'm expected to be spending my days in endless preproduction sessions."

The countess took a sip of her martini and placed it back on the coaster in front of her. "I took the new pups to the hospital for their injections this morning. I believe you've got a good litter this time. They must be looked after with care. Perhaps I should take them to raise while you're occupied on the film."

He reached over and patted her hand. "My dear, what would I do without you? You always come to my rescue. Shall I buy you a lovely lobster dinner tonight?"

"I have an engagement."

Vittorio kept his evenings open for her, but the countess saw other men. Vittorio wanted everything to remain as it had been when they were man and wife. The countess was willing to remain his best helper, even his part-time mistress, but no longer willing to be faithful to him sexually. A by-product for her was that she had him on a tight rope, with his need to court her now giving her considerable bargaining power. Vittorio could seldom refuse her anything.

She sucked on her olive, looking at him. "I want you to do something for me, Vittorio."

"Anything, my dear. You know that."

"Don't be too hasty. This may be an odd request. I don't want a new stallion or a diamond bracelet. I'm afraid I want to impose myself on your artistic endeavor."

She knew how to talk to him about a film. He had huge claims to being an artist. One couldn't even call one of his films a movie.

"I can't imagine what you are driving at, my dear, but please don't keep me in suspense. Out with it."

The countess sipped at her martini while looking steadily at him over the rim of her glass. Finally she lowered it. "I have the girl for Fiammetta Four. I haven't, of course, your taste or experience, but I do have a good nose for these things, and frankly I would like for once to help you cast a role, be responsible for discovering a future star."

Vittorio's last sip went down the wrong way and he began to choke. He was still red in the face when he said, "You're right, a stallion or diamond bracelet would be simpler. For example, there is the not inconsiderable matter of Cleo Monti, who just happens to be a star in her own right *and* the wife of a principal backer. Who, if I may ask, is your discovery?"

When the countess told him it was Pina, his choking commenced once again, so seriously that the countess decided she would forego her "engagement" to spend a wifely night with him.

* * *

Cleo was in her suite at the Grand, preparing to take a bubble bath. Normally she took a quick shower when she came in from location, then a long hot bath just before going to bed, but this evening was special and she was changing her routine. Paolo was flying to Turin for one night. He would be arriving any time now. She didn't want to go out. She had had a small bar set up in the living room, already placed a dinner order with room service so that by the time Paolo finished his drink the food should be on its way to their room. She would waste no time in getting them to bed. She and Paolo had work to do.

Paolo's car and chauffeur had been standing by outside Franco's office. Immediately after the meeting he had gone directly to the airport, then called Helga from a pay phone in the departure lounge. Her reaction had surprised and relieved him. He'd never be able to understand women. Far from being disappointed, she'd praised his handling of the situation, and had blown him kisses over the phone. Then she asked him to call Franco and tell him that she had no hesitation whatsoever about working without makeup. She would be delighted to test, and was available to do so immediately.

On hearing this message from Helga, Franco had quickly warmed, saying he would arrange a test for the next morning and contact her directly. She had sounded enthusiastic and thanked Paolo profusely for his help. Movie people—they were a strange lot. Paolo didn't understand movie people any better than he understood women. In the case of women, though, he decided the better part of wisdom was to lie back and enjoy them, as he had so recently with Helga and soon would with his Cleo, though with Cleo there would be no lying back.

* * *

Cleo was luxuriating in her bubble bath when Paolo arrived in their suite at the Grand Hotel Turin. She called to him as he took off his jacket, loosened his tie and made himself a large scotch and soda.

Carrying his scotch into the bathroom, he knelt down beside the tub and kissed her on the mouth. He loved that sensuous mouth. He put down his drink, rolled up one shirt sleeve and in turn fondled her mammoth breasts, slippery with soapsuds, their cherry-red nipples peeking from the foam. When she squealed with delight his little cock rose in appreciative response, and forgetting his shirt he slid his hand over the soft roll of her belly down to where he could squeeze the fleshiest part of her thighs and twist the hairs of her venus mound into little swimming curls. He tugged gently on her clitoris, and when she closed her eyes and began sucking her thumb he inserted his own thumb inside her and began rubbing it in and out, in and out . . .

She let her hand drop over the edge of the tub, opened his fly and extracted his cock, then with a generous handful of soapsuds began massaging it. As his thumb brought her to orgasm she held his cock tight, and after two or three deep breaths continued to rub until he spouted.

When Cleo brought her hands in front of her to wash them, she became serious and told him that he must take her to bed and release his sperm in the place where it would do some good . . .

Two ejaculations and three hours later, an exhausted Paolo made himself a fresh scotch and soda and drained the glass. Room service had left the table in the living room, and he could barely wheel it into the bedroom. Cleo did not wish to disturb the sperm by getting out of bed, but ate heartily from the edge of the table while resting against the pillows and smiling at Paolo, who looked thoroughly drained, which, of course, he was. He put a chair at the side of the table and picked at the meal, which he said was cold.

"Don't be cross, daddy bear," Cleo said. "This is the last time you will have to visit me on a location. I am going to stay at home from now on."

Paolo paused, holding in midair a forkful of cold spaghetti. "No, dumpling, your next film will be filmed partly outside of Rome."

"There won't be any next film," Cleo murmured. "I've made up my mind, I must not work until I conceive—which I hope I have just done. Then I must protect and care for my body at home until well after I've had baby bear."

"But what about *Boccaccio?*" he asked in astonishment. "Don't you know that Serena Blaire's contract has been canceled?"

"Yes, I know, and I'm glad she's out, but I just can't take the risk of working. I'm afraid they will just have to find someone else for Fiammetta Four."

Paolo could only shake his head. Women . . .

On Tuesday Helga tested for Franco, and on Wednesday her name was added to the cast. She was beside herself with joy, Paolo was relieved that *something* had worked out like it was supposed to, and Franco was secretly gloating because he had gotten the star he had wanted from the beginning. Actually he had considered Serena as second best and had only gone along with her because at the time it appeared to suit the project as a whole—not to mention the financial backers. But he had always seen Helga in the role and was most content now that he had her as his Fiammetta Two . . . *and* on his terms, not hers.

Ralph de Rossi was the only one to know about the psychology Franco had used. Months ago he had agreed with Franco that Helga was perfect for the part, but also agreed that she mustn't be allowed to come into the project overconfident or she would be giving directions rather than taking them. Not only was she a big name, but smart and strong-willed, *and* had the investor Paolo Monti behind her.

So with Ralph's blessing Franco had played a waiting game, keeping her as insecure as he suspected it was possible to keep someone like Helga. He had waited until the last moment, had forced her to make the first move by sending Paolo to see him. He had put on a rather good act with Paolo, even by his standards. But then he had felt less proud of himself, asking an actress of Helga's stature to submit to a screen test. When she did, though, it proved to him, and to Ralph, that she was ready to accept his directorial authority. From now on he would try to make it up to her, and look forward to working with her. Deep down he loved the ballsy dame.

Serena was beside herself when she heard Helga had been cast. It had been hard enough to swallow the news that Madeline was getting Fiammetta One, but she had a special hatred for Helga, who had fucked and tried to manipulate Primo. Besides, Haufman was the kind of determined bitch she could identify with; not as smart as herself certainly, but clever and ruthless in getting what she wanted. However, no matter how furious she was that her pregnancy had opened the way for the other women to step into the roles that had been hers and hers alone, she must not, she told herself, allow emotion to affect her good judgment. Of course not . . .

She was in London at one of the top maternity clinics in the world, having a series of tests to determine the advisability of continuing with the pregnancy. After all, being near forty, near the end of the childbearing years, presented major risks, everyone knew that. She told herself that it wasn't a choice between the film or another baby, maybe a brother for Debbie. Yes, she wanted that film, and she had earned it, in more ways than one. But abortion? She wasn't a Catholic but somehow the idea tended to upset her . . . partly because she had once seen a frighteningly graphic film of an abortion. Some people said it was edited for propaganda purposes, but it nonetheless scared her. Well, she'd better calm down about that too and make the smart decision for her regardless of anything else, including her anger at Primo for making her pregnant.

Primo, who had worried his *tesora* would never forgive him for impregnating her, especially just when her career was going so well, and being responsible for her losing her roles in *Boccaccio,* was grateful she had at least allowed him to come to London with her. He was terrified that she might shut him out of her life altogether after the physical examination that had been followed by her being cut out of the picture. A breach of contract for being blessed with a pregnancy? No wonder he'd never done well at law. Of course, if she decided on an abortion, especially if it was decided she might die in childbirth, he knew he would understand, even though it was against his religion. After all, her being pregnant was his fault, his sin in the first place. He was proud of himself for thinking so well, they should have used him more at that law office. And if she did have the abortion, well, she'd be able to go back to work, providing they let her, and maybe that's where he would come in. The last time, he didn't have anything to do with her getting the starring parts in *Boccaccio Volgare.* This time, maybe he could, and his *tesora* would forgive him.

# CHAPTER THIRTY

ON FRIDAY Umberto arrived on a day flight from Turin. He had left his car parked at Fiumicino, and after storing his luggage in the trunk of the Ferrari drove directly from Leonardo da Vinci Airport to the film studio. Madeline would be there, and his only thoughts were of seeing her again.

While he'd been gone, he'd been told by Ralph that *Boccaccio Volgare* had been recast. Now his leading ladies were Madeline, Helga, Astrid and of all people—Pina Bozzetti Mariani. It seemed she had become the countess's new pet, and Vittorio had given in to the countess, as he usually did.

Madeline would be at Cine Citta in preproduction for *Boccaccio*. She would have hours of costume fittings, makeup tests, and script consultations. So would he. But he wanted their evenings to be spent together. And today was Friday—a whole weekend was ahead. He had missed her, he was horny as a lone bull. He would show her "Latin lover" was more than a catchphrase. He would make up to her for the fiasco at that wedding.

He parked outside the directors' building and climbed the stairs to Ralph's office two at a time. Ralph's secretary told him that the production was on Stage 12 filming wardrobe tests.

At Stage 12 the red light was flashing so he waited until the filming had stopped and the light had gone out, then opened the two consecutive doors and walked onto the stage.

The first set of the film was in place, an enormous Moorish-style conservatory with pools, a waterfall, and masses of flowers that filled all of the area at the far end of the stage. Center stage was taken up by lights, camera and crew. Makeup tables and wardrobe vans were stationed almost to the entrance where he was standing. Umberto threaded his way toward the camera and Ralph, who was waiting for it to be reloaded. Ralph welcomed him back and asked the assistant to bring two chairs. "Wait until you see Madeline, my friend. You will have need of a chair. She is an absolute knockout as Fiammetta One. I'll need to talk to her for a few minutes before the lunch break but then she's all yours. She won't be needed again until Monday morning. Now don't go crazy thanking me, the schedule just happened to work out that way."

Umberto, smiling, put his arm around Ralph's shoulders. "I promise not to be grateful. Now, what is this about Pina doing Fiammetta Four?"

Ralph lowered his voice. "You know Vittorio, he

has his own way of doing things, although I suspect in this case the countess was involved. She seems to have decided Pina is her discovery or some such. Anyway, Vittorio asked to see the screen test that Pina had made for Angelo, and after seeing it he was sold on Pina. I really had no reason to veto the choice. I saw the test too and I must say that Pina seemed surprisingly competent, especially for one so inexperienced. She has a lot of energy and sense of the camera. She films very well. The child might surprise us. She seems full of surprises . . ."

When Madeline appeared a hush fell over the stage. Umberto forgot to breathe. In white chiffon that fell softly, hugging the curves of her lovely body, she moved with a transporting grace. Shimmers of platinum formed a halo but took nothing away from the delicate features of her face. She glowed with a combination of sweetness and sensuality, precisely what the role of Fiammetta One called for.

Umberto, lost in the loveliness of her, was not aware of how long Ralph had been shaking him: "Umberto, for the third time, as long as you're here would you mind getting in front of the camera beside Madeline. I would like to check your height on the set and also next to Madeline."

Without taking his eyes off her Umberto stood up and walked toward Madeline. He wasn't conscious of bright lights or people watching. He only saw Madeline. Her hand lifted in a welcoming gesture. Her warm smile was just for him. Now beside her, he looked into her pellucid blue eyes, lowered his gaze to her full parted lips. He did what came naturally, irresistibly, took her in his arms and kissed her, and felt her respond . . .

Only gradually did the cheering and applauding

of the crew force itself into his awareness, and he let her go. He would share her for now, but not for long.

While Madeline completed her wardrobe tests, Umberto arranged for a cold lunch to be set up in his dressing room—his, not hers, so that no one would come looking for her. He made sure that the table was set, the wine chilled. He checked to make certain that his phone had been disconnected at the switchboard, as he had requested. He closed the shutters, drew the curtains. Every lamp was turned on and off until he found the most effective lighting. He removed the cushions from the back and sides of the couch. When all was in readiness, he returned to Stage 12, and the moment Ralph had finished with Madeline, he put his arm around her waist and led her off the stage and out the door. He almost lifted her off her feet while helping her into the Ferrari. He drove away quickly, checking in the rearview mirror to be sure that no paparazzi were following.

Madeline, thrilled with this new aggressive approach, smiled at him, reached over to caress the side of his face, and told him how happy she was to see him. Which brought forth a surprising sound from him . . . something very close to a growl. She was delighted.

"Where are we going?" she asked.

Another growling sound, another check of his rearview mirror.

"Umberto, why are you driving around in circles?"

He swerved the car into a wide-open and deserted sound stage, parked and hurried to help Madeline out, then guided her around the corner in the direction of his dressing room, his arms raised to hide her from sight. He quickly opened the door and slipped her through it while it was still half open, paused to flip a "no disturb" sign on the handle, closed and locked it and stood fortifying it with his back. He continued to play act, though he was also dead serious. "And now, my sweet, you are completely mine."

Madeline studied his expression, shook her head. "I have always been yours, you fool. Why all this cloak-and-dagger stuff?"

He looked around the room, wanting to remember the order in which he planned to proceed. His courting battle plan.

"How lovely," she said moving toward the table. "You've arranged quite a romantic lunch for us. However, if it pleases you, my lord, I can wait for the food. Unless, of course, you want to eat—"

"I want to eat you."

Likewise, she thought, as he pulled her into his arms, kissed her lips and neck and breasts, kissed her lips again and holding that kiss lifted her off her feet and carried her over to the couch. He put her down and undressed her, kissing every part of her as the clothes came off. She was quickly ready, wanting him to enter her, hardly able to stand it as he broke off to shed his own clothes.

He paused a moment to take in the really stunning sight of her. She reached up for his cock, he froze. His erection was gone, collapsed.

Madeline sat up without a word, pulling at him to sit beside her, and hugged him against her. "It's all right, darling. It doesn't matter." Oh, but of course it did. "We'll relax for a while, then we'll try again."

Umberto pulled away from her. "This has *never* happened to me before. Never. How is it possible?" He proceeded to pound a fist on the arm of the couch. "How is it *possible?* All the faceless, silly women I have fucked, all the women I have given endless cock to . . . all wasted on women I cared nothing for beyond the moment. And now, when I have the woman I love . . . my damn cock gives out." This time he hit his forehead, as though to drive out the stupidity that had cold-cocked him.

"What did you say?" Madeline asked, taking his head in her hands and looking most seriously at him. "What did you say?"

"I said my cock—"

*"No,"* she said, and pushed him backward. "You just said you *loved* me."

She proceeded to rub herself all along his body, moved from his forehead to his toes, covering him with kisses, licking and sucking as she went. Her reward, and his, became apparent. His penis hardened. She lay down and pulled him on top of her. She spread her legs and raised her buttocks, inviting him to enter her—

A knock at the door.

Umberto swore, jumped up to grab his trousers, managed to get his legs in and moved toward the door, hiking his trousers and zipping his fly—instantly he was suspended in motion . . . head back, howling in pain. His cock was caught in the zipper.

Madeline rushed over to him and went to her knees in an effort to free him. The knocking at the door became more persistent. Umberto kept howling. She could see that the skin on the underside of his penis was squeezed firmly between the treads of the zipper, and realized she couldn't release it without causing him even more pain. They had to have help.

The knocking got louder. Ignoring her own nakedness, Madeline jerked open the door to see one of the guards from the front gate standing there. He had started to say something along the lines of "You will have to remove your car from the sound stage," now stopped and looked open-mouthed at the naked woman in front of him.

"A doctor, we need a doctor. Help . . . oh, damn it, how do you say help in Italian?"

"*Aiuto,*" Umberto said between clenched teeth.

"*Aiuto,*" Madeline repeated, stepping aside so the guard could get a clear view of Umberto's plight. "We need a *doctor.*"

Umberto muttered, "*Dottore—medico!*"

When the studio doctor arrived five agonizing minutes later he took in the remarkable tableau before him, and quickly went to work. First spraying a liquid anesthesia on Umberto's penis. The ice-cold spray set Umberto to howling again. When it, blessedly, took effect and his cock went numb, Madeline and the doctor helped Umberto to lie down on the couch, where the doctor quickly removed the trapped skin. There was only a tiny trickle of blood. The doctor wiped the area with antiseptic, applied a Band-Aid, gave the spot a gentle pat and declared that he was confident Umberto's penis had suffered no permanent damage.

Madeline had poured two large brandies, one for herself and one for Umberto, but the doctor downed hers, assuming it had been meant for him. He had, after all, extricated her friend from a most compromising situation. The glass drained, the doctor picked up his black bag and with a grin and a wink let himself out.

Madeline, who had thrown Umberto's robe around herself before the doctor's arrival, now allowed it to fall open. Her hair had come out of its clips and was covering part of her face as she stumbled, still dazed, over to the drink cabinet to refill her brandy glass.

Umberto was sitting spread-legged, holding his empty glass in one hand and his penis in the other, looking in a kind of daze, at the Band-Aid.

Madeline collapsed into a chair opposite him, sipping her brandy and staring into space, then began rocking back and forth.

Umberto put down the glass and leaned toward her. "Madelina—if you will still allow me to call you that. What can I say? I'm a man of a million blunders."

Madeline continued to rock and stare.

"Madelina, answer me."

She said nothing, and he couldn't see her expression because of the hair in her face.

"Tell me, do I dare ask you for another chance?"

She stopped rocking and sat up straight. The robe slipped from her shoulders. She brushed one side of her hair away from her mouth and took a large swallow of brandy. She still did not look at him.

"Madelina, at least put me out of my misery. Are you through with me? Are you going to stop seeing me?"

She lifted her arm, sweeping all the hair from her face, and now looked steadily at him. "Yes."

*"Yes?* Yes, you don't want to give me another chance?" He stood up and began pacing. "Please. I know, I know, I am always asking for another chance. I am always making one idiotic blunder after another. I know I have no right to ask you but—"

"But what?"

Umberto stopped pacing and looked at her. He had never seen her this way. Never heard her speak this way. It made him lose the flow of his thoughts.

"But *what?*"

"But what? What do you mean?"

Now she too stood up and went over to confront

him. "You just said you have no right to ask but—but what? *That's* what."

"But . . . but I love you—"

"Good. Maybe we're getting somewhere."

His voice softened. "Madelina—I just told you I love you. Have you nothing to say to me?"

"Good is what I have to say to you. So you're suffering, my Latin lover? Good, about time. You're not the only one, you know." She went back to her chair, still saying, "Good, *good* . . ."

"I'm *not* angry," she said, running her fingers through her hair. "I'm *frustrated. Damn* frustrated. All the months I've waited for you—wanted you because, damn it, I . . . I . . ." She cut herself off, feeling about to break into tears.

Umberto, not sure what to do, or say, leaned forward and whispered, "Forgive me for losing my hard-on. It was just that I was too excited. I wanted you too much. I wanted to make an impression on you—wanted you to think what *they* all think . . . that I really am the world's greatest Latin lover—"

"Oh, shut up," she said. "I don't care about your hard-on. Well, that's not entirely true, so long as you don't make a habit of it." She smiled at him through her tears. "I care about *you.* Yes, God knows you are a bumbler—but you are also the most endearing, loving, lovable man I've ever met. I'm relieved you aren't as perfect as your fans think. I'm not exactly Miss Perfection myself. Matter of fact, I can be quite a mess," she laughed, "as you can plainly see." She tried fixing her hair and pulling her robe together at the same time, quickly gave it up as a bad job and let everything just hang out. "I told you, Madelina is not *perfetto,* if that's the right word."

He clapped his hands. "Then you forgive me, you will give me one more chance—"

*"No,"* she said abruptly. "Not just *one* more chance . . . we both need more than that, we're entitled to more than that."

Umberto wasn't sure what she meant. He asked, "Does that mean you will go on seeing me—?"

*"No."*

*"No?* What do you mean, no? If you won't see me how can I show you—?"

Looking straight at and through him, she said, "By marrying me."

Umberto went perfectly still. He sat looking at her, saying nothing.

They stayed that way, as though observing one another. Madeline was determined not to be the one to speak first. Finally in a funereal tone Umberto said, "I don't go to church but I'm Catholic."

"Ditto."

He whispered, "I want very much to have children."

"So do I."

Again silence. Again she was determined not to be the one to break the silence.

"Madelina?"

"Yes?"

"Will you marry me, Madelina?"

"Yes."

Another long silence. Madeline was willing to wait.

"Do you want to get married as soon as the film is over?"

"No, I don't want to wait a year until *Boccaccio* is finished." And now Madeline decided it was time to take charge. No more games. "We will get married two weeks from now, before the film begins. My apartment is small but we will make do with it for the time being. We'll have to do without a big service and reception, which I always wanted. On the other hand, after Pina's wedding I'm not sure it's exactly a sacrifice. But if I leave it open and delay things, who knows what lovable craziness you might get into. We have too much trouble when we're apart. At least if we're together we'll be face to face when the troubles happen. And we'll know there's the rest of our lives to get things right."

At the conclusion of this unexpected speech he looked so solemn that she threw her arms around his neck and hugged and kissed him. "Most of all, though, I will be right there on the spot with you to enjoy the good times, which are going to be wonderful."

Umberto, pleased at that, returned her kiss as though he were ready to make up for his recent untimely detumescence right then and there. Things, he decided, were looking up, or soon would be . . . And he was more than content to let Madeline make the plans. What a remarkable woman she was. Full of surprises. Not only did he love her, at last he had found a woman who actually wanted to marry him and have his children. He didn't care about a large wedding and reception, but he was sorry for Madeline. She deserved a beautiful ceremony.

They got dressed and rushed out to look for Ralph, bursting to tell someone the news and, of course, they wanted Ralph to be a witness at the wedding.

But it was Christina de Rossi on her way to Ralph's office who they first met, and so Christina was the first to hear the news. And it was also Christina who quickly came up with a way for them to have a big celebration on short notice: "Why not make it a *Boccaccio* wedding? I've just come from the stage and you couldn't want for more space or a more beautiful setting. We'll have the ceremony in that gorgeous Moorish conservatory with its pools and flowers. Madeline and the girls can wear their costumes for the film. We'll get the restaurant to cater and hire the studio orchestra for the day. It will be a wedding beyond compare."

They agreed delightedly. When they arrived at Ralph's office, Umberto made the announcement to Ralph, who was as pleased as Christina and opened a bottle of wine to toast the joyous occasion.

Umberto, all agreed, was a lucky man—and Umberto agreed—but there were moments when a faintly sobering thought did cross his mind: his days as a Latin lover were almost over.

Ah, well . . .

# CHAPTER THIRTY-ONE

IF ON Friday all was right with the stars in *Boccaccio's* world, by Monday their universe shook and galactic war seemed imminent. Astrid was not pleased. Helga was spitting fire. Cleo was creating tantrums. Serena was conducting sneak attacks. And Madeline, although in the thick of the fray, was also battling to get her wedding launched, while Umberto was considering migration to another planet.

On Friday *Boccaccio Volgare* had looked cast and set to roll in two weeks. By Monday the production was in chaos. Two events were responsible.

The first occurred when Paolo Monti returned from a business trip to be informed that Pina, the countess's newest protégée, had been cast as Fiammetta Four. His initial reaction was to ask if everyone had gone crazy. He was told by Ralph and Vittorio that she was a natural, had tested well. He didn't give a damn. He was not going to permit his hard-earned investment to ride, even in part, on an unknown. Fiammetta Four had to be played by an international star equal in stature to Madeline, Helga and Astrid.

The producers, not surprisingly, were afraid that if Paolo pulled out his money at *this* late date the Italian banks involved would follow his lead. They spoke to Ralph, who also felt he could not risk cancellation of the film, and as artistic director he had the bad job of telling Vittorio to recast his segment.

The fallout was instantaneous. Paolo, having blown Pina out of the production, had set off a chain reaction: the countess was furious with Vittorio for allowing the firing of her star discovery, which was how she had come to see Pina, since Serena Blaire had turned ingrate and refused to see her any more. Pina in turn could not forgive either Vittorio or her new husband, feeling that Franco should have stuck up for her. Cleo was hurt and angry that Paolo, who had been cooperating so well in her campaign to conceive, had told her that she *must* go back to work—she was needed as Fiammetta Four and pregnancy could wait. Now she was refusing even to speak to him. Helga, Astrid and Madeline went to pay court and plead with her to reconsider. Actually, Cleo had never refused outright. She had simply thrown a tantrum, then pouted, none of which endeared her to her supplicant friends. She was behaving like a petulant child, Helga told her, and Cleo promptly informed her that she and "the rest of you are no longer my friends, please *leave me alone.*" Astrid then blamed Helga for having been too hard on Cleo.

Helga turned on Astrid, calling her a disloyal pervert and gutless masochist. Madeline tried to bring some sanity into the situation, saying that she could understand Cleo's problem, and both women then turned on her, calling her, among other things, a meddling *Americana.* Which led Madeline to tell them they were *all* acting like babies and could go straight to hell. And so forth.

With all poised at each other's throats, the second event occurred. And, surprisingly enough, its author was none other than Primo Galiano, who decided to make his *tesora* proud of him and show how he could put to use in her behalf his often demeaned legal expertise. The way had been cleared when, after weighing the risk of childbirth at her age as well as learning the health of the fetus was questionable, Serena had been persuaded to go ahead with the abortion. She then wanted to go back to work immediately after the unhappy decision to abort, and Primo was fired up to put his plan, which had been on hold, into action.

Now that Serena was available, able and more than willing to work, he would demand that they take her back on the big picture, *Boccaccio Volgare,* or he would sue them for millions. He would claim that since she was no longer pregnant, she had cured the original breach, if it ever was one, and so there was no reason not to honor her original contract. And if they refused, he would threaten to sue *them* for breach of contract. This was the plan he had been so excited about before Serena decided on the abortion, and only became possible now that she was no longer pregnant. Primo wasn't too sure about the legal grounds, but he at least knew from his time as a law clerk that the threat of legal action could have a real effect even without going to trial, providing there was enough at stake for the other party that they couldn't take the chance of losing not only the case, but even more important, the time and money it took to litigate.

And time was of the essence, as the lawyers liked to say around the office, for the production of *Boccaccio.* So it wasn't surprising that on the afternoon of Paolo's return and with no actress set for the fourth segment—Pina being out at Paolo's insistence and Cleo pouting in her tent—and only two weeks left before principal photography was to start, Primo's threat to sue if Serena was not immediately reinstated had a powerful effect, better than Primo had dared hope for. Maybe he wasn't a dud in this law business after all.

Paolo now called an emergency meeting of the producers, directors and bank managers. To head off Serena—they all assumed, of course, that it was she rather than her bumbling husband who was directing this campaign—what about approaching her to play Fiammetta Four? After all, the part was open, and if Serena would settle for that she'd be doing *them* a favor. There was general support for that, but it began to collapse when Paolo raised the specter of Serena inisting on being rehired to play all the roles, as she had been slated to do before. *That* would involve one pretty price, not just in terms of money, paying off the already contracted stars, but worse, would also make Catalano's life more than difficult with a deposed Astrid, and Mariani's with an ousted Helga. As for Madeline, she would be devastated, even though she did seem taken up with her coming marriage to the movie's major star, Umberto. But what would Umberto do if his intended was dumped? Ralph was the one who raised most of these questions, wondering if somehow, somewhere, this film wasn't permanently jinxed. He felt like he was on a roller coaster going nowhere . . .

Meanwhile Madeline, like all of the rest of the ladies in a near panic over the future of *Boccaccio*, was trying to get her wedding off the ground. And her dressing room had once again become headquarters for the ladies to join forces against the newest Serena Blaire onslaught. As Helga said, "Just when we thought we had the anorexic bitch pregnant and gone for good she turns up to do us all in. Jesus . . ."

Ten days later, with matters still unresolved, Madeline and the others were on the edge of perpetual tantrums, some of which were touched off by nothing more sinister than a look or a slight dig or maybe a failure to respond to an innocent question. Among them all, Helga alone was taking as much direct action as she could, going from office to office, trying to persuade the bigshots to hold firm against Serena.

On Thursday, only four days before the scheduled start of filming, the scene in Madeline's dressing room might have been itself a setup for a movie. Cleo was stretched out on Madeline's couch, attempting to chase her gloom away with a succession of bonbons. She now was much more interested in the Fiammetta role that she had seemed to reject in favor of the joys of pregnancy and motherhood—her change of heart having been provoked by the reappearance of Serena. She hadn't as yet said so, though. Astrid, staying away from Angelo Catalano as much as possible because so far he hadn't been able to assure her that her part was still secure, was sitting at the end of the couch, flipping through a movie magazine without looking at it. Madeline was at her vanity table, trying to concentrate on the catering—Sunday, the big day, was only three days away—and she had wasted most of the morning staring indecisively at the menu and chewing on her pencil. The countess and Pina were at a table in the alcove by the windows, both in mourning over Pina's loss of Fiammetta Four, both furious at their respective men, Vittorio and Franco, for giving in to Paolo's decision about that firing. They had been assigned by Madeline to open replies to the wedding invitations and check off the acceptances opposite the names on the list. They could barely stand to look at one another, and when they did they nearly broke into tears.

Helga interrupted the tableau of despair when she came through the door at high energy, stopped with hands on hips, surveyed them and gave them all a piece of her mind for acting so passive with Serena once again outmaneuvering them.

Astrid turned to her with cool deliberation. "May I remind you that it is all Cleo's fault"—and when Cleo began to rise to her own defense, hurried on—"if she had agreed to do Fiammetta Four there would be no question about Serena getting back into the picture." Which, of course, was not entirely true . . . it was Serena's decision about the abortion and Primo's surprising plan for his *tesora* that had started the whole chain of disaster. But of course they didn't know about Primo, only what had happened.

Cleo, not having much of an answer to the charge, put the box of bonbons down on the coffee table with a thump and rolled her bulk over so that her back was all they could attack.

Madeline glanced over at Cleo, sighed and said, "I really do have to concentrate on the wedding. Please, let's not fight . . ."

Helga looked with unconcealed annoyance at Madeline's reflection in the vanity mirror. "And when is your wonderful fiancé at last going to stand up for you? How can you marry a man who won't lift a finger to save your part in the most important picture of the year?"

Madeline shook her head. "The *wedding* is separate from the film. And I haven't even asked Umberto to get into the casting. We've got enough other problems to work out—"

"Well, damn it, you should," Helga said, raising her voice. "Umberto has a lot of power. After all, without him there's no picture. That ought to put some spine into the producers about the lawsuit."

"She's right, my dear," the countess said.

Pina, still remembering how Umberto had rejected her, added, "Helga is right. Umberto shouldn't stand by and let you lose the part."

Astrid agreed, and when even Cleo turned herself around to join the chorus Madeline headed toward the bathroom, on the edge of tears . . . recently she, too, had thought Umberto might have at least tried to intervene. She shouldn't need to ask him.

The countess had little sympathy for Madeline. "My poor Pina is the one who has a right to cry. A brilliant career has been cut off in the bud—"

"Pina could never have played my part," Cleo said, struggling to sit up.

Astrid turned on Cleo. "It isn't *your* part any longer. You blew it, all in the name of your famous non-pregnancy. *And* it's *you* Serena Blaire has to thank for giving her such an advantage—"

"That is *not* true. Paolo wants only for me to play the part."

"Not anymore, he doesn't," Helga said. "The part is on firm offer to Serena. It's hers if she wants it."

She hoped she was overstating the matter, trying to goad Cleo into a commitment.

Cleo was startled. "How do you know?"

"I know because I don't sit around here weeping like all of you do. I made it my business to find out. We've been trying to warn you that it would happen. Now a firm offer has been made to Serena, and Paolo couldn't go back on that offer even if you begged him."

Pina asked, "What if Serena refused to accept only Fiammetta Four? What if she wants them all?"

Helga dropped onto the vanity stool Madeline had just vacated. "If I was a man I'd touch my balls to take away the curse of that question."

"Oh, God," Astrid said, "If she doesn't accept Fiammetta Four there's a good chance they'll offer her all the parts. They're so close to production and—"

"No, *no,*" Cleo said, sufficiently exercised to stand up and pace.

"Yes, *yes,*" the countess snapped back. "And Pina should have been in the cast, Pina could have become the new Serena Blaire . . . the newest, most exciting star in the international cinema!"

"Bullshit," Helga said. "You only got it into your head to discover Pina after Serena stopped letting you sniff around her."

Whereupon the countess rose, adjusting her riding habit, marched to the front door, opened it wide and walked out.

"I says *no,*" Cleo erupted, deciding to say out loud what she had been thinking. "I say no to Serena. *I* will to do Fiammetta Four—"

"What?" Helga and Astrid said in unison.

Cleo repeated her pronouncement.

Madeline came out of the bathroom now. "Do you mean it, Cleo?"

"I mean it."

Pina threw the replies to the invitations on the floor. "But that part was mine, I should be the one playing Fiammetta Four—"

Helga turned around. "Oh, shut up. You're only nineteen, you've got plenty of time. Be happy, you've already got a famous movie director husband"—a little ripe but famous, she thought—"so don't be stupid, for heaven's sake, go home and make up with your husband."

Pina was about to answer her, thought twice about it, even smiled a bit sheepishly and headed for the front door.

Astrid was also smiling, at Cleo. "I'm glad you've changed your mind—"

"Let's just hope it isn't too late . . ." Helga looked at Madeline. "Now is the time to get Umberto involved, Madeline. Remember, Paolo is a heavy investor, and now that his precious wife wants back in . . . plus, with her there's a full cast. At least we must let Ralph and Paolo know right away that Cleo is available. Never mind, *I'll* handle that, you handle Umberto."

"I'm still not going to threaten him with breaking off our marriage, which you want me to do. I want my part as badly as the rest of you want yours, but—"

"But nothing," Helga said. "It's Umberto or nothing." She had drifted over to pick up the replies from the floor, then abruptly stopped and read one of them. "Look at *this*. Serena and Primo have been invited and have accepted. What gall. And who in hell invited them? Never mind, I'm sure I know. It was that cunt countess. She's trying to suck up again to her favorite star, now that she figures Pina's career has fizzled."

Madeline agreed she had some nerve, especially when they were threatening a lawsuit. Helga went off to spread the news about Cleo's new desire to play Fiammetta Four, and eventually, when no news came, Astrid and Cleo wandered off, leaving Madeline alone and annoyed that she had not heard a word from Umberto all day.

There was a good reason why Madeline had not heard from Umberto that day, better certainly than on some other occasions when he had either not shown up, or left too soon, or in some fashion not only did not save the day but left it in a shambles.

He had, in fact, been closeted first with Ralph, and then with the directors and Paolo Monti, and finally with Serena. It had been quite a day, but it had been coming, he now realized, for some time. When Serena had been a major financial force behind the film, Ralph and the others had been forced, they felt, to give in to her demands—which knocked Madeline and the other ladies out of their parts. He had not liked it, but he had been so accustomed over the years to separating himself from anything but his own acting involvement in films that there was little he could do about it. When Serena was out because of her pregnancy, he was delighted. After all, he was not quite the fool he sometimes acted or said he was. He realized that part of her hot pursuit of him was to get the roles she wanted in the film. Then when she no longer needed him she had quickly left. He had been relieved that she had, but he also hadn't liked the way she'd treated him—like he was some thing to be used and thrown away. So he was happy that Serena was out and the way was cleared for

Madeline and the others. Then when Pina had been put in the role of Fiammetta Four he hadn't been too happy . . . he still remembered her chasing after him, and now that she was married to one of the directors she might have more influence than was good for the film. Paolo's insistence that Pina be dropped was good news, but it was quickly offset by Cleo's sudden preoccupation with making a baby and not wanting to risk her hoped for "delicate condition" by taking Pina's place. That really left things in the air, but what *he* could do about it?

It was when Serena came back into the picture, threatening lawsuits, demanding she be in the picture again, that he seriously began to think about using some of his own influence, which everybody was always saying he had but which he'd never really given much thought to. His new relationship with Madeline also helped give him an incentive to speak up, one that he hadn't had before. A threat to her was a threat to him. When he went to Ralph right after Serena's first threat about the lawsuit, he had been told by Ralph that it was not a good situation to challenge until they knew more about Serena's real plans. If she would settle for the one role of Fiammetta Four, the backers might figure she was doing them all a favor—after all, the part was vacant on account of Cleo, and Serena was a star and so forth. He hadn't liked it, and surprised himself by asking Ralph how they could do something about Serena—he really didn't look forward to being in the picture with her. Ralph, surprised at Umberto's willingness to be involved, but pleased, told him if Serena should demand to have *all* the parts back once again, that would change things, at least for him. If that should happen the other stars, including his Madeline, would be involved . . . and the fallout would include possible lawsuits. With this latest news that Cleo definitely was willing to play Fiammetta Four—news brought by Helga, who had burst into Ralph's office to make the announcement—things had come to a head. Now it would be more difficult to give Serena back even Fiammetta Four. After all, Cleo *was* the wife of a principal backer of the picture.

At this point, Ralph asked Serena to come to his office, with Umberto there. She had assumed that the call signaled Ralph's capitulation, and when she came into the office she was all smiles and Serena charm. She felt so good, in fact, that she told Ralph that while she at one time had considered settling for only Fiammetta Four, she had now realized that she was entitled to all four parts. She was sure Ralph would be pleased with her willingness to save the picture for him. Her words were, "Darling Ralph, you know I can make or break this film. You also know, I believe, that I am very serious about pursuing my rights through the court. That would not only be curtains, so to speak, darling, for the film, but would cost you and the producers and backers a great deal of money as well . . ." She then turned to Umberto, still giving off the smile that could kill: "It's so good to see you again, I hear you're getting married. Well, I wish you happiness, as I'm sure you know. I received an invitation, which I must say was most sweet of your intended. I of course will be there. And my wedding present to you will be my being once again your leading lady in *Boccaccio*. You're really a fortunate man, twice-blessed, I might say." Followed by another dazzler that would have put the Chesire cat to shame.

It was then that Umberto for the first time in his life felt an almost uncontrollable urge to hit a woman. Ralph, sensing his condition, moved over to him quickly and took him by the arm. "Serena, I am the one who will make the decisions on the casting of this film, but Umberto's say is crucial. As difficult as it may be for you to believe this, Umberto is more central to this film than any other star, including yourself. Umberto . . . ?"

And Umberto, without missing a beat, told Serena that he would rather not work for the rest of his life than act with her. Then, turning to Ralph, he added, "Ralph, I don't want to make your life difficult, you are my friend, but I tell you that if this woman is in *Boccaccio,* Umberto Cassini is out." And he felt so good saying it that he said it again.

Serena, the radiant smile turned to a rictus, looked stunned, especially when Ralph nodded vigorously as Umberto told her that he was speaking for them both. She had, he told her, gone too far. There was no longer a role for her in his film, and she could damn well do what she liked about it, including suing him personally. At which point there was little for even the resourceful Serena to do but make one of the fastest stage exits ever, even tripping a bit as she lurched for the door . . .

It was nearly seven when Madeline came down her street, feeling increasingly annoyed over Umberto's silence. In spite of herself, she promptly forgot to remember she was mad at him when she spotted him sitting on the front steps of her building, surrounded by suitcases. When he stood up she ran over the cobblestones and into his arms, hugging him, kissing him and making the sort of public spectacle of herself that she thought she would never do. As they went up to her apartment, Umberto, toting his bags, said, "I hope I am not being too forward, but I thought it would be all right to move in with my future wife, and then take her dinner, and then—"

"And then?" she said, her voice sinking to a strange whisper, "Well, is the Band-Aid off?"

"It is, my darling. All is well, I am a whole man again. And this time I will prove it."

He took her to a trattoria on a side street off Piazza Navona, where they made the best pizza in Rome. Neither wanted to go too far or spend too long over a meal. It was an inexpensive place, noisy and popular with students. Once they had sat down to pizzas and a carafe of red wine, he proceeded to give her the big news of the day, finishing off with, "The cast is now as it should have been from the beginning—you as Fiammetta One, the real Fiammetta, and Helga, Astrid and Cleo."

Madeline was momentarily stunned, then reached out to him, pulled his face to hers and rewarded him for all to see. Then she looked at him closely. "Did you have anything to do with the decision?"

"Well, some, but once Cleo announced that she would do Fiammetta Four and Serena had refused it, demanding all the parts, it was more than Ralph or I could stomach. Besides, as Ralph explained after she left, her final demands weakened whatever grounds her threatened lawsuit might have had. You might say that Cleo and Serena, in their separate ways, really made it all possible—"

But Madeline was shaking her head, smiling. "Out with it, you're not telling me everything. I want to know exactly what you said. I want to know if I'm marrying a man or a mouse."

At which point he admitted that he had taken a stand and refused to be in the picture with Serena, and Ralph had backed him up.

"Oh, Umberto," she said quietly, "I'm so proud of

you, and grateful too. And this should shut up certain people who said I ought to be saying something to try to influence you. Obviously they didn't know my tiger . . ."

He laughed. "Tiger? I think I like that. Maybe even better than the world's greatest Latin lover."

"You've proved one, and pretty soon you're going to prove the other . . . Now all that's left is for my tiger to promise me he won't get into any brawls at *our* wedding."

He raised his hand. "I promise—unless that French boy is there, that Jean what's his name—"

Madeline blushed. "But I explained about Jean Claude."

He reached for her hand. "I know, my darling, and God knows I'm the last one to take a tone about such things. I've often behaved like a mongrel chasing any bitch in the alley. Truly, I was only joking about the French boy."

"Well, please, Umberto, no jokes. I'm nervous enough about our wedding day. Pina or the countess invited Serena and Primo, and don't bet that she won't show up looking to make trouble, especially after what happened today. And I wouldn't put it past the countess to have invited Jean Claude too. So—"

"So enough worry and enough talk, I believe we have some unfinished business." And without further words or delay, they paid their check, quickly left the restaurant and nearly ran to Madeline's apartment, where Umberto gave proof positive of his cure.

# CHAPTER THIRTY-TWO

ON SUNDAY, the day before the start of filming, Stage 12 had temporarily been converted by the crew to accommodate the wedding. The makeup tables and wardrobe vans had been stored in an adjacent hangar, and the camera and equipment had been pushed to one side and hidden behind scrims. The scenery department had borrowed a polished dance floor from one film set, a bandstand from another. Christina de Rossi had hired the tables and chairs, and when she had been unhappy about them standing on concrete, the scenic department had found a grass matting large enough to cover the reception area. The propman had then done the decorations, while Ralph and the cameraman personally supervised new lighting for the film set where the ceremony was to take place. The crew had given their time as a present to Madeline and Umberto.

Today the crew, dressed in their Sunday best, were in attendance at the wedding, and the full Cine Citta orchestra was playing light classical music. Later they too would be joining in the festivities. Predictably, many of the guests were still on edge. The casting had been settled, but raw nerves didn't heal quickly. Tensions, animosities lingered. Umberto, a properly nervous bridegroom, having his own wedding jitters to contend with, seemed oblivious to the mood on Stage 12. Madeline did sense it, but was determined that nothing should be allowed to spoil her wedding.

The last few days since Umberto had moved in with her had been almost too good to believe. He had made beautiful love to her, and she to him. Her response especially pleased her, given her earlier troubles. At times he'd been forceful and passionate, at others, gentle and tender. He was simply the loveliest man she had ever hoped to meet; kind, sensitive and loving, *and* funny. He had made her laugh until she'd had pains in her side, regaling her with some of the more notorious pratfalls in his life, not in too much contrast to his screen image. It might not always be so smooth, she realized, but half would be more than enough. All she wanted now was to be pronounced Mrs. Umberto Cassini and get on with her life.

Looking at the set where the ceremony would soon take place, she could only shake her head. It was something out of an exotic, erotic dream: the set's artificial orchids somehow looked a bit indecent, not to mention its protuberant lilies, with their suggestive shapes. The pool, by means of a gyratory motor, swirled hypnotically, its water lit from below while the cascading waterfall was spotlighted from above. Fairy lamps glowed from behind the shrubbery. Molded plaster rocks and lucite ferns gave a futuristic aura.

Madeline was wearing her white chiffon, which was perhaps too revealing for a wedding but just right for tomorrow's filming. For today, the costume department had added a hair wreath and small veil. She had asked that the justice of the peace keep the ceremony brief, and wanted no procession; Helga, Astrid and Cleo would simply come in from the wings and stand to the side of the waterfall. They were also in costume: Helga and Cleo in shades of shocking pink, Astrid in gold and yellow. It couldn't be helped. At least Umberto was in a dark suit; she couldn't have gone through with it, she thought, with him wearing a toga. Umberto would walk in from the other side of the set and stand beside Ralph, who was best man. They would position themselves upstage by the center pool, then she would enter from the same side as her bridesmaids. She would walk in quickly without music during hers or the other entrances. This was not, after all, a church wedding. It was, of necessity, a somewhat camp affair, or as everyone was calling it—a Boccaccio wedding.

The justice of the peace looked rather lost in this theatrical atmosphere and seemed to have no place to stand. Ralph came onstage to show him where there was room on a ledge behind the central pool. By gripping a giant metal lily, the justice could squeeze between the pool and an artificial boulder. Madeline cringed. Once firmly in place, he raised his hands for the ceremony to begin. Despite Madeline's instructions to the orchestra not to play during the actual wedding, the musicians could not resist and proceeded to strike up a medley of show tunes as the guests gathered just below the edge of the set. Madeline noted uneasily that Serena and Jean Claude were in the crowd, but forced herself not to think about it.

Ralph, already onstage, had the good sense to stay there as loud murmurs of appreciation sounded at the entrance of the bridesmaids. And no wonder . . . at what other wedding did one see three of the world's most beautiful screen stars in the flesh? Madeline joined the appreciation. They were, even off-screen, larger than life: Helga was a scorcher in deep pink satin that set off the flames in her auburn hair and charcoal eyes. She was a dazzler, a femme fatale, while Astrid was an enchantress, whose golden hair danced on sheer yellow chiffon, which in turn floated over a gilt mesh form. Of the three wondrously proportioned women, Cleo made the greatest impact in a pale pink slip of a dress from which mounds of shapely flesh bobbed and moved as if they had a life of their own.

Umberto's entrance had the predictable effect on the ladies. With his broad shoulders and rugged good looks, he moved in an air of faintly world-weary diffidence. An Adonis about to be devoured by Venus, the papers would say the next morning.

At her first sight of her Umberto as a bridegroom Mrs. Cassini clung tight to the professor's arm, as if her joy might unbalance her. Umberto's brothers and their wives were also on hand. His brothers were older and had left home before Umberto had become famous, so unlike his parents, his brothers had never seen Umberto on a movie set. As he made his entrance they actually applauded, and Mrs. Cassini quickly turned to shush them.

The orchestra now struck up "Here Comes the

Bride," but it was a Venus that appeared before them. Her motions were fluid, her features delicate, her hair softly glowing. She was love, sensuality, feminine grace; a work of art come to life, one man murmured, and he was quickly shushed by his wife. Actually Venus was suddenly awash in very mortal nervousness and perspiration. Umberto, however, seemed in a trance, the justice was momentarily lost for words, and Ralph had to prod them both so that the ceremony could begin.

Which it did, and it proceeded smoothly until it was time for the ring: Ralph handed it to Umberto, who held out an unsteady hand so that the ring danced in his fingers before flipping into the pool.

Silvio, the propman, knowing Umberto well from working with him on many films, had been expecting something to go wrong, and now raced to his prop box for a replacement. The conductor gave the signal for a prolonged drumroll, and as Silvio dashed onto the set with another ring there was laughter and applause.

The justice, who had gotten into the spirit of the occasion, before continuing with "Repeat after me, with this ring," looked to the gathering and announced in his best stage voice: "I believe the motto is, the show must go on." When no one laughed, he cleared his throat and proceeded.

This time Madeline held Umberto's hands to steady them while he placed the ring on her finger, then held her breath, praying that nothing else would go wrong, and sighing in relief when the justice finally said, "I now pronounce you man and wife."

Umberto took Madeline in his arms and kissed her, Ralph called "Print," and everybody laughed. Umberto would have gone right on kissing his bride but the orchestra trumpeted a fanfare, signaling that it was time to welcome the guests.

Helga, Astrid and Cleo rushed up to throw their arms around Madeline, while the elder Mrs. Cassini scurried between them to kiss Madeline and tell her how happy she and Umberto made her. Then all the guests crowded around the newlyweds. Conspicuously missing from the shower of affection was Serena. But the procession of other well-wishers seemed endless. In quick succession, Madeline was hugged, bussed and fussed over by Ralph, Professor Cassini, Umberto's brothers—whom she was meeting for the first time—and Jean Claude, who was not discreetly pecking her on the cheek but kissing her passionately. Flustered and upset, Madeline was rescued by Helga, who quickly stepped in to pull him away, hoping Umberto wouldn't notice.

Now Pina, whose frustrations over the casting had been building for some time, not to mention her annoyance at Jean Claude's obvious passion for Madeline, stepped forward and snapped, "Who invited you?" and slapped Jean Claude full in the face.

The countess answered her, "I did," so Pina fetched her a clout as well.

The countess, red-faced and livid, called Pina, her late and now deposed protégée, "an ungrateful little bitch."

Astrid, who thought Pina rather cute, shoved the countess, whose backward motion brought the heel of her left shoe onto Serena's foot.

Serena flung her arms wide for balance, in the process grazing Cleo's chin.

Cleo promptly moved to tower over Serena and lifted her hat from her head. Helga completed the exercise by grabbing it, throwing it to the floor and stepping on it, while Astrid reached down to pull at her hair.

Serena whirled about to escape the bridesmaids, and as she did so bumped into the bride, knocking her to her knees.

Madeline, furious at Serena for even being at her wedding, got to her feet and pushed her, but as she did so she tripped, throwing herself and Serena off balance, and both toppled into the pool.

From which point on it was no contest. Venus was Madeline Mandell, from the American school of hard knocks, who also knew how to swim, and in no time emerged victorious, holding Serena by the hair and threatening to push her under again if she didn't say uncle. Serena said it, having no idea what it meant, and was pulled out of the pool by Primo, who had come too late to the rescue of his *tesora.* And from the look on her face he suspected that he might be banished for life from the marriage bed. *"You . . ."* was all Serena could say, but it spoke volumes.

Astrid and Cleo then helped Madeline, now in a nearly transparent water-soaked dress, out of the pool. Helga held Madeline's arm in the air, signifying victory, and several cheers went up, including one from Umberto's mother, who had watched the pool encounter closely. Now she took off her suit jacket and quickly used it to cover her new daughter-in-law, while Madeline, out of breath but not at all displeased with herself, searched the crowd for Umberto.

She spotted him standing off at a distance, shaking his head. When she caught his eye he grinned and blew her a kiss. In moments she and Mrs. Cassini and the professor had joined him, and Umberto's mother, beaming proud as a peacock, told her son, "I tell you, Umberto, you have finally done yourself proud. But watch out, my son. This lady may be American, but somewhere there must be Italian blood!" She hugged Madeline, still soaking wet, then kissed her and reluctantly went off with the professor, leaving the newlyweds to themselves.

"I may be mistaken, Mrs. Cassini, but as I recall it was *you* who warned me against getting into a brawl." Only his quick smile and a quicker kiss saved him from a roundhouse, American-style.

Ducking and laughing, he put his arm around her and they went off, the orchestra, in tribute to Madeline, striking up "Yankee Doodle," followed by the Italian national anthem . . .

Later that night, after a wedding feast of lovemaking that was richer and more varied than any before, Madeline looked over at her sleeping husband and allowed herself to think about how miserable and scared she had been when she first came to Rome, how she had been so lucky to have made such wonderful and loyal friends like Helga, Astrid and Cleo, who'd introduced her to the movie world, and with it Umberto.

She thought too of Umberto's gentle, wise father, and his mother, who had taken to her and obviously liked her. And thinking of Umberto's mother, she thought of her own, as she usually did at the most important moments of her life. If only her mother could have been here, shared her daughter's happiness . . . it was almost too much not to share, and for a moment she felt guilty, remembering her mother's life, and death . . .

It had been years since she had said her prayers, not since her mother died, but she did now, crossing herself, thanking God for her marriage, one made in heaven, and feeling that her mother *was* there, sharing it all with her.

"Good night, darling," she whispered, and for a moment Umberto opened his eyes, thinking she had been talking to him.

"Good night, Madeline, I love you," he said, and promptly went back to sleep, not hearing her answer.

"And I love you too, my darlings. Both of you . . ."

## *About the Author*

CARROLL BAKER, author of the recent autobiography *Baby Doll,* and the just published *To Africa with Love,* has starred or been featured in numerous American and European films. She has just completed filming on *Native Son.*

A native of Greensburg, Pennsylvania, and mother of a son, Herschel Garfein, and the actress Blanche Baker van Dusen, she is married to the English actor Donald Burton, and makes her home in New York City and London.